Wasted Morning

Wasted Morning

A NOVEL

Gabriela Adameşteanu

Translated from the Romanian by Patrick Camiller

 NORTHWESTERN UNIVERSITY PRESS • EVANSTON, ILLINOIS

Northwestern University Press
www.nupress.northwestern.edu

This book is published with the support of the Romanian Cultural Institute, Bucharest.

Printed in the United States of America

10 9 8 7 6 5 4 3 2 1

This is a work of fiction. Characters, places, and events are the product of the author's
imagination or are used fictitiously and do not represent actual people, places, or
events.

Library of Congress Cataloging-in-Publication Data

Adameşteanu, Gabriela.
   [Dimineață pierdută. English]
   Wasted morning : a novel / Gabriela Adameşteanu ; translated from the
Romanian by Patrick Camiller.
      p. cm.
   "First published in Romanian under the title Dimineață pierdută by Cartea
Romaneasca, 1984."
   ISBN 978-0-8101-2637-4 (cloth : alk. paper)
   1. Romania—History—20th century—Fiction. I. Camiller, Patrick. II. Title.
PC840.1.D34D5613 2011
859'.334—dc22

                                                           2010052521

∞ The paper used in this publication meets the minimum requirements of the
American National Standard for Information Sciences—Permanence of Paper for
Printed Library Materials, ANSI Z39.48-1992.

Contents

Wasted Morning

Part One

Chapter 1

Strada Coriolan

Before, if she'd been cooped up like that for days on end, it would have seemed as if the house were falling on top of her. She always used to find a way of going out every day, now to one person, now to another, exchanging a few words, picking up the latest gossip, never returning empty-handed. To have stayed indoors with that mute of a man would have made anyone want to put an end to their days. There was never anything to talk about with him, and besides what can you talk about with a husband? "Your husband should know you from the waist down," she used to say.

Once, when she aired this view, her sister-in-law scowled at her: "Hold your tongue, Vica, the boy will hear you. You're an old woman now, but you still need to wash out your mouth."

"Puh! So what if he hears me? All the better! As if he's going to be tied to your apron strings much longer! Don't you worry: I've been in some fancy houses in my time, and I know how the ladies speak there . . . I got on well everywhere I went; they all loved and appreciated me. How we laughed at Mrs. Ioaniu's house—her, Ivona, and me!"

Her sister-in-law is another mute: you need tongs to get anything out of her. Her own poor brother, while he was still alive, always went along with her. That's what men are like: they go along with women. Only she has never managed to drag that husband of hers out of himself. When she was young, she used to listen to everything he said. How she cried, how she was sick at heart! She lost so much weight that a gust of

wind could have knocked her over. Then, one day, her godmother came
visiting, God rest her soul . . .

"What's happened, Vica? You're as thin as a rake."

"Well, there's been this and that."

"Come off it, my girl. Stop fretting like that."

That was her man, a really awkward type. Hers was a different nature,
sunny like her mother's—if only she'd hooked up with the same kind of
man, one who liked to laugh and joke. Such men do exist, but then they
have something else wrong with them. You shouldn't think one is better
than another.

So now it's getting more and more difficult for her to leave the house.
Once or twice a month, though, she takes her leather ragbag (the one
she got from Mrs. Daniel), fills it with anything in reach, dons her thick
sweaters, snaps in her false teeth, wraps a couple of scarves around her
head, uses another scarf to secure the beret she made nine years ago
from pieces of an old coat, and swings open the front door.

"What are you doing? Clearing off again?" her husband calls out from
beneath the blanket-topped duvet, his head wrapped in an old torn cardigan of hers instead of his usual faded Turkish cap that he can't find
anywhere. When he speaks, he breathes heavily between the words. Tall
and stout, he already weighs more than a hundred kilos, and the skin on
his neck hangs loose and flabby. But his cheeks are chubby, almost rosy,
with a growth of gray beard that has not been shaven for several days.

"That's one hell of a habit, to go traipsing around like that. All your
life you've been landing yourself on other people."

"Phew . . ." she utters in reply.

She doesn't even look at him. Wrapped in her protective layers, she
goes into the back room, moves some tubs around and takes a little here
and there: a jarful of gherkins, a few of the many onions she managed
to lay up for the winter, some bulbs of garlic, and some leftover plum
brandy that she's poured into a small cough-syrup bottle. She puts everything into her bag, on top of a pile of empty plastic bags. She doesn't like
to go visiting without a little something that might come in useful.

"Phew . . ." she replies.

She doesn't even hear what he says. Let him drone on to his heart's
content, let him be both the one who talks and the one who listens; men's
words should be squashed up and put under your ass, as she used to say
to Mrs. Ioaniu—how she had the old woman in fits when she said it!

She's learned what to do when he starts his whining. She comes here into the back room, mumbling fuck off back to hell where you belong, and you can take your father and all your crap with you!

Muttering to herself, she moves into the shop so he no longer has any idea what she's saying, especially as he's going deaf in one ear and only hears what suits him. She keeps it up until she gets it all off her chest. It's dark in the shop, and the only warmth is what comes from the back. She used to heat the shop with the cylindrical iron stove, but for the past twenty-five years, more than twenty-five years, there's been no point; how long is it exactly since she closed it down? The woodpile is there along two walls, and the coal bag is in a corner—why light a fire when there's no room to move? The old sideboard whose doors have fallen from their hinges, the huge jars of pickles, the sacks of potatoes, the saucepans, the bucket filled with dirty water: she somehow busies herself amid the clutter until he tires himself out. Only then does she go back into the room, bend over with a sigh to shovel coal deep into the tiled heating stove, and then open its little door to draw in air. She doesn't trust him to do anything—otherwise, the house might well be cold when she returns in the evening.

"Oh, no, I'm not going to loaf around like you, and I'm not going to goggle at you from morning to night. As if I haven't had enough these forty years!"

Her reply comes so late that he merely gawks at her and falls silent. He wonders what's suddenly come over her. I've got you figured all right—this not out loud—you've got the devil inside you. That's why she's never really cared for him, although it can't be said that he didn't take her fancy when she set eyes on him for the first time.

She had been standing behind the counter of another shop, in Strada Iancului, when a customer came in with him. She was then nineteen years old, full of life, loved by everyone; and he was a fine strapping man, with a straight nose, thin lips, and hair sleekly parted to the side—as in the photograph pinned to the wall. It's a photo from the time of their wedding, when he was still working at the Zamfirescu factory.

What a coffee shop Zamfirescu had had, near where the statue of Kogălniceanu stands today. What chocolates and candies he'd brought home to her, what fondants . . . ! What eggs and bars of chocolate Zamfirescu used to give his employees at Easter and other holidays, and, ah, what wouldn't she give to have one of them again now! Yet she gorged herself so much that eventually she could no longer stand the sight of them. Well, that's what people are like . . . And what a gentleman Zamfirescu had been: he even mixed in the queen's entourage and rubbed shoulders with the Brătianus—that family of top-notch politicians . . . Her husband stayed three years at Zamfirescu's: he didn't have much of an education, but he had neat handwriting—even today you should see the way he signs his name, with that little loop underneath.

Then she decided to open the shop, using what he'd saved from Zamfirescu's plus her father's dowry. In fact, when Daddy came to count it out, he went funny in the head and added an extra fifteen thousand lei by mistake—he who'd never give a penny if anyone asked him. And her cretin of a husband, the old creep, lost his nerve.

"What shall we do?" he said to her. "Dad's made a mistake with the money. Look, you've got to go and give it back to him."

"Give it here, and don't breathe another word about it. It's my money! At least this much I'll get out of him!"

So it turned out: Daddy left every penny he had to the children of his second marriage—oh, the hell with it all! Still, the dowry plus the money from Zamfirescu's were enough for them to open the shop on Strada Coriolan. And how the old creep started to splurge once they had it! You should have seen him seated at the back on cushions, having brought stuff home by the carriage load. Once he brought her a gold bracelet, and another time a sapphire locket and chain. But then he gave up.

"What's the point of buying you stuff if you never wear it?"

When was she supposed to wear it if she spent all her time behind the counter? The thought never crossed his mind. He went to the cinema and to football matches; he never missed one when Juventus was playing, and you'd have thought he was the Venus club manager. Now he goes out only when the weather's nice, for a stroll down to Cişmigiu Gardens, holding his merchant's belly stiffly in front of him. His old midget of a father from Oltenia, who never had one, always used to sob into his cups: What kind of a merchant am I without a potbelly? But her husband has been like that all his life: tall and paunchy. Stiff and heavy are his steps as he looks with longing at the pastry shop on the corner and the bottles of Fanta. She slips a twenty-five lei note into his pocket, but knows he won't touch it. He just likes to know he has some cash on him—that's what men are like.

"You're off and leaving me alone," he says plaintively, propped up on his pillows. He continues to watch the evening film on television, a repeat that he has seen at least once before. Then, changing his voice: "Vica, bring me a glass of water."

"What the hell, can't you lift a finger for yourself? Did your mother spoon-feed you all the time there in the country?"

But she drops her ragbag, goes into the living room and brings him the water. Muffled up though she is, ready to leave this last hour or more, she waits for him to swallow it and put the glass on the table.

"What were you saying?" he yawns, as he sinks back into bed. "What were you saying just now? You're always rambling on."

"Oh, shut up, will you!"

And she grabs her bag and leaves, rattling the windows on her way out.

She treads carefully on the uneven stones in the yard, which are still coated with morning frost. Her swollen feet are painful, even though she rubbed some kerosene on them last night and has put on thick woolen stockings. The weather seems to be turning. Dizzy from the cold air, she stops for a moment to catch her breath, takes from her pocket a right hand half-coiled inside a glove fraying at the fingertips, and supports herself against a dilapidated shutter. Rust and dust have been covering it ever since she closed the shop, more than twenty years ago, so that now it looks as if it is part of the wall. WINES FROM THE DAWN SLOPES: the sign in large letters used to be further down on the right, between the shutter and a step leading up to the shop. But she blocked up the shutter and removed the step—what was the point of keeping them if no one entered anymore? LIQUOR STORE—but what salami and sausages it used to have! What blocks of cheese! She had regulars from Strada Coriolan, Strada Sabinelor, and all the other streets in the neighborhood. They came, they saw, and they bought; exchanged a few words, perhaps drank a glass or two with a little snack. What cheeses, what sardines, what exotic delicacies she used to have!

"Really, Madam Delcă," one of them might say, "you've got an edge even on Dragomir Niculescu!"

And so she passed her youth behind a counter covered with tin plate, or running here and there among clinking glasses in response to calls from the tables.

"Vica, over here! Hey, Vica, Vicaaa . . ."

Then as now her husband lay sprawled in bed, in the room right at the back. He went into the shop only to throw out a drunk or to keep a furtive eye on whether anyone was taking liberties with her. When you were least expecting it, he would creep up behind you in a way that belied his colossal size. He came in and looked around, as he liked to do all his life, without becoming caught up in the details. The sounds of mirth were anyway so loud that no one could have heard him, but they quieted down as soon as they caught sight of him. Yes, he certainly inspired fear.

"Hey, Mr. Delcă, come and have a glass with us," a customer not yet familiar with his ways might shout.

"No, thank you," he would reply in his thin voice. "I'm not in the habit . . ."

And he loitered glumly a while longer, as if to make the drink stick in the others' throats, before going back to his room. He dolled up to go to a match or a film, or for a night on the town. She stayed behind in the general hubbub, to wait for suppliers, to receive a delivery, or what have you.

She was a solid woman, not like those broomsticks you find today, without a bum or tits for a man to get his hands on. Yes, she was a strong bosomy woman who made the floorboards creak beneath her, with a plumpish white face and curly hair tied in a loop at the neck. Had she been so minded, she could have had anything she liked—but that wasn't her style, she wasn't one of those . . . Well, there was one tall man with a black pencil moustache and an evil leer, who worked at police headquarters. She can almost see him now before her, entering the shop just to buy some caviar, sturgeon, foie gras, and expensive wine. He loaded his carriage and took it all off to one of their blowouts. How he looked at her: and it was Madam Vica this, Madam Vica that . . . His hand had a ring on every digit, and the one on his little finger was as big as this!

"Do you like it?" he asked her one day. "If you do, it's yours just as it is."

"Keep it safe," she answered. "I'm not used to things like that. I have my husband."

A good-looker, but what a scoundrel he must have been; you could see it from the way he rolled his eyes. He vanished as soon as the communists took over; left behind a wife and children and a house; no one ever heard another word. They must have really bashed him around—after all, there was something fishy about all those rings. Nor was he the only one: there were loads and loads of them. But she never gave it much thought: she wasn't like that, and anyway the work meant she was always too tired. All she heard she got from Madam Ioaniu. A clever woman, Madam Ioaniu, a woman who managed to land not one but two husbands.

"Let me tell you something, Vica," she said one day. "A woman who's ready to drop doesn't make a good wife."

She walks with a stoop, as if hunchbacked, her faded-blue coat bulging from everything she has put on underneath. Ragbag in hand, she keeps her eyes on the ground and turns them neither right nor left; it could be as much as fifteen years since she's been in the center of Bucharest, and anyway there's no reason for her to go there. She has everything she needs here: savings bank and hairdresser on the corner; pharmacy and shoemaker; a telephone next to the greengrocer, where she takes a handful of coins if her neighbor Reli is out; a grill house where she often buys sausages on her way home. She puts the paper plate on an empty stall in the market, lays her ragbag beside it, dips a sausage in some mustard and wolfs it down. Each time she debates whether to keep one for her husband—then, forget it, she says, and in a trice she's wiping her mouth with a handkerchief; forget it, he's fat enough already, and anyway he grabs a cheese pie for himself whenever he goes to Cişmigiu.

She passes, bent over, the garden square where pensioners play chess in summer. A few crows are croaking on the greenish statue of that naked woman—what the devil was her name? Vica's brother Ilie used to know, God rest his soul. How often he spoke it as they were passing by! Maybe it's the Mimph—or perhaps the Nymph. From home she can find the tram stop blindfold, telling you about every little nook and cranny on the way. Quite a few new people have moved in behind the fences, but all the older ones know her.

"Good morning, Madam Delcă, how are you? Good morning, Madam Delcă," they call out as soon as they see her.

Everyone is fond of her and thinks she's wonderful. So she stops to chat whenever she comes across someone she knows: they all have their problems, whether it's the liver, the bile, or blood pressure. If they'd all settled their unpaid bills she'd be a rich woman, but now one comes up to her and says:

"Here's twenty-five lei, Vica dear, it'll come in handy."

That's the way of the world: you're wonderful as long as you've got something to give, otherwise you're nobody; she's lived long enough to know that, she could teach others a thing or two. The school of life, life's evening classes, as she used to say to Madam Ioaniu—and how the old woman laughed. The school of life—what else did she ever know but work, work, work?

She hauls herself up the tram step, takes the coins from her pocket and fights her way through the packed bodies to the seats at the front.

Work, work, work: that was her life, from the age of eleven when her mother died and left her alone with a houseful of brothers to worry about. Her father went off to war, and the next summer her poor mother died of typhoid fever or typhus or whatever it was. The twins also kicked the bucket, and so did Sile, the youngest, because he no longer had anyone to suckle him. But she, Ilie, and Niculaie managed to stay alive; they were bigger, and God gave them a longer life. They all lived alone in the old house in Pantelimon, near the Capra church where their mother was buried; and there was no one but she to look after the whole pack of brothers; some survived, others didn't, some were lucky, others weren't. A grandmother, a Greek woman who really fancied herself as a lady, called by from time to time. She can still see her in her silver-gray Ottoman dress, fastened right up to the neck with little buttons and bordered with lace at the sleeves. And there was a fur stole around her shoulders. It's as if she's there now in person: robust, with a large chest and waist, like all the women in their family; that's why she wore such a tight corset, and had stays powerful enough to take the pressure. Only Vica can't remember her hunchback: was her grandmother really hunchbacked? In any case, she was a fancy Greek lady, who owned a newspaper kiosk near her house on Strada Sfinții Apostoli—an interconnecting house with a glass veranda. A lady, yes, but her grandchildren couldn't stand her, because she had sent their own mother away to be fostered. How could she have done that? If she'd brought her up along with her son and other daughter, ah! how different their poor mother's life would have been! She herself would have gone to a boarding school and grown up a little lady; she'd never have married a man from Oltenia or stood behind a tin-plate counter, never have tramped the mud of Pantelimon with seven little brats clinging to her. Poor Mummy! If that grandmother, the Greek woman, hadn't sent her away to be fostered, her life would have been different—perhaps she wouldn't have died at thirty-three, a solid woman in the prime of life. Those were the things neighbors used to say when the Greek lady came to Pantelimon to see her grandchildren. The neighbors couldn't bear her, nor could her grandchildren. When she told them to call her "grandma," the little devils would call out "gravema" instead. Ah, may God forgive gravema, now that she too is lying in her grave. Back home, in a cupboard, Vica still has a picture of her taken at the fashionable Fridrihbindăr studio; she's sitting with a haughty expression on her face, fur around her neck, in elegant cross-laced boots with raised heels that have been polished up with castor oil. Gravema took care of herself all her life—that's why she sent her daughter away to be fostered, so as not to have a lot of brats under her feet. She didn't worry much about her grandchildren either; when they really needed something the poor kids ran instead to Uncle Cabbage-Washer, whose house was on the other side of the church—a large high-walled house with wine cellars and fierce dogs. But he was a skinflint too, a skinflint and a curmudgeon: not for nothing did people call him Cabbage-Washer . . .

"Hey, move your basket away, woman," a short broad-shouldered man bellows just an inch from her ear. "Since you got on, it's been stopping anyone from getting to the door."

It's a rush basket holding a couple of chickens with flattened crests. A peasant woman climbed on with them a couple of stops back. Vica saw her boarding at the front exit.

"Where yer want me to put it?" she asks.

She picks up the basket and drags it in among the legs of the other passengers. The chickens flap their wings and try to wriggle their bound legs.

"That's what it's like in second class: they get on with baskets, cabbage, whatever they like. Some even bring their hound along," the man says to another standing right in front of Vica, an old puny-looking man with a cap on his head.

He merely gives a faint nod in reply, and the thick veins bulge beneath the soft skin of his neck.

"Put it down here," she offers, and pushes the basket under her seat.

"People get on with whatever they have," she says to the man in a loud voice. "They're not going to walk just because someone's a bit put out. You get on, you pay for your ticket—what's wrong with that?"

So there! Let everyone hear, especially those who screw up their face and only like to travel first class, because it smells in second class. She's never traveled any other way since she closed the shop, and she hasn't croaked yet. Coughs up her twenty-five cents and that's all there is to it;

people are still people whichever class you ride in. And she wouldn't last a week if she wasn't a bit thrifty—certainly her husband's no help at all.

She picks up her ragbag and carefully steps down from the tram.

The air smells damp. It is the end of winter, although people carrying bags still drag children sideways in sleds on the thin crust of darkened snow. Among the cranes loom buildings still without a plaster finish, heaps of rubble covered with pieces of tar, and wooden shacks that have long been boarded up. Breathing with difficulty, afraid of stumbling in the mess of wires that some good-for-nothings dumped there last autumn, she walks at slower than her normal pace. She can hardly wait to reach her destination; for some time even such a short distance has been enough to exhaust her . . . It's no fun being old. She's also feeling hungry, even though, before setting out, she had a large mug of tea and dipped a chunk of bread into it. She never does anything these days on an empty stomach—if she did, she'd get dizzy and faint and be wiped out for the rest of the day. She could bet anything that her sister-in-law hasn't got around to cooking yet . . . She's been a slowpoke all her life; you're put through the mill before she finally does what she has to do, and she never stops grousing about one thing or another. Before she moved here it was because they were too cramped; now it's because they're too far from the action and she has to spend hours on the bus . . . What would she say if she'd lived like her these forty years, in that dump of a place, surrounded by coal, worrying about the gas canisters? . . . Going to their place now is like a trip to heaven: she told them as much. But it's three years since they moved, and her sister-in-law still keeps griping: either the windows don't shut properly or the door isn't a tight fit or they're too far from the center . . .

"Keep quiet!" she shouted at her. "Stop going on like that or you'll make the Lord himself see red. What you've got here is heaven on earth, I'm telling you."

It was as if she'd been telling the future, because less than a year later poor Ilie was killed in an accident . . . Only then did her sister-in-law find out how difficult life can be, how hard it is to manage on your own. Poor old Ilie: he never once spoke up against her; she even kept an eye on all the money, so that he had to slip his sister a twenty-five lei note on the quiet:

"Here, Vica," he would whisper on the doorstep, "it's for the tram when you come to visit us next."

Her sister-in-law can't get away with that with her son Gelu . . . He takes after her—a mean type who snaps at you out of the blue. She spends all day pestering him: Gelu, sweetie, Gelu this, Gelu that, if it's not one thing it's another. Gelu couldn't give a monkey's toss, just gets on with it, keeps his head buried in his papers; the table's laid for him, then cleared, what a cushy number! . . . If she'd had children she'd have given them hell. Just as well she never had any: who knows how it would have turned out? Kids today aren't afraid of anything; they have no shame at all.

Chapter 2

Berceni District

"What you've got here is heaven on earth," she says as she drops onto the kitchen chair.

Her face is flushed from the heat, and her joints have gone so soft that she can hardly move. She looks at the unwashed teacups in the sink, at the crumbs on the oilcloth-covered table, and at a plate of cheese gone yellow on the outside.

"But where's your mother?"

"At work," Gelu lazily replies, leaning sideways against the door. "She's doing mornings this week, didn't you know?"

He's tall and thin, with unset features that seem swollen by an inner ferment he's at pains to conceal. He stares hard at her, a smile pulling his thick lips apart. Indoor trousers hang beltless on his slender frame, while a faded green shirt covers his upper half.

"If I'd known I wouldn't have struggled here for nothing."

But she stands up, removes her beret, leans over the ragbag and takes out the jar of pickles, the little bottle, the garlic, and the onions. She's upset not to have found her sister-in-law in. If you leave it up to them people never come to see you, but it's not right that for years and years she's been the one knocking on other people's doors. Her man's right about that . . . Ah, if only Mummy had lived, how different life would have been! She'd finished fourth grade and was preparing to start at the *liceu;* she already had her school uniform and beret, she can still see them now; it was July, and in August the general mobilization was declared . . . Daddy left for the front, then Mummy went and died: the full-grown woman lay down in bed and started raving, her poor lips split from the fever . . . And what was she to know, a kid of eleven? She was out playing on a vacant lot, couldn't bear staying at home . . .

Later she went through hell, looking after her brothers, lining up for that half-baked black bread full of husks. She was always the one who stood in line, because she was the eldest. How she got fed up standing there with the ration card in her hand! Even today she remembers what was written on it: either *880 grams of Bread,* or *440 grams of Bread,* or *300 grams of Bread. To be issued only on presentation of this card. Infringements will be punished with up to six months in prison or a fine up to 3000 lei or both.*

Ah, she'd been second in her class, devoured one book after another! She stood and read the bread card, so that now she remembers it as if it was the Lord's Prayer . . .

"You've no idea what it's like to lose your mother when you're eleven," she says, chewing a piece of bread. "What a terrible blow it was for us when she died!"

Even now, after so many years have passed, she still feels a helpless orphan.

"That's why you should love your mother."

She carefully returns the clean cups to the shelf and, with her back to the boy, cuts a slice of cheese and puts it in her mouth. She covers the rest with some plastic and puts the plate outside on the window ledge. Look how well it sits there on the ledge—though when her sister-in-law hears this she complains:

"If poor Ilie were still alive, we'd have got a fridge this year."

"To hell with a fridge," Vica tells her, "it's money down the drain. Just reheat the food every day and you'll see how long it keeps . . ."

"That's why you should love and respect your mother, because she's all you've got . . . Love her and look after each other," she says aloud.

So that the boy hears and gets it into his head.

Gelu keeps standing in the door, shifting his weight from one foot to the other. He yawns. He is thinking how to make himself scarce. If he starts chatting, the whole day will go. As it is, he's done nothing but mope around since waking up. His books, his drawing board, every-thing is scattered around his bedroom, and now . . .

Just look at that kid, she says to herself, as she spreads a blanket on the table and plugs the iron into the socket; she has found some unironed clothes in the bath, how her sister-in-law will be thrilled when she gets home. Just look at that kid, what a misery he is all the time! His father, Ilie, God rest his soul, had a different character; he was the youngest of them, just a toddler when Mummy died. She brought him up on her own, she was like a mother to him, and what fights there were with Daddy about sending him to school . . .

"Listen, I haven't got any money," the old man used to say. "What can I do if I'm broke?"

The greedy Oltenian used to come carrying a yoke from his home in Cărbuneşti or wherever it was. Hanging from the two arms of the yoke were baskets of vegetables, fish and chickens and vinegar and coal and whole or quartered lambs wrapped in cloth. Daddy used to sell a little of everything, gradually putting the money aside; he even built some mud houses to rent in Pantelimon district, and eventually picked up Mummy's dowry. That way he could open a shop, where he sold cheap cotton fabrics, gas canisters, cakes of soap, that sort of thing. Things went well: he grew a forked moustache, learned to dress up in city gear, and carried a watch with a thick gold chain. Then in August came the mobilization; the bells rang all night long. And by the time Daddy returned from the front everything had gone up in smoke . . . But that Oltenian with his head well screwed on, who at eighty still had all his teeth and could crack nuts between them, he simply started all over again trading with people in the country. Mummy was dead, so Daddy lost no time building up trade with the villages. Later he dug up Old Miss Clodhopper from somewhere, moved in with her and had another batch of kids.

"Come too if you like," he told them when he shacked up with Clodhopper.

But they stayed in the old house in Pantelimon, near the Capra church where Mummy was buried . . .

She unplugs the iron for a moment, as it has become too hot. She opens the pantry door, but all she finds there are some dried biscuits; she takes one, dips it in a glass of water, and starts to chew it.

"I'm off, Auntie. I'm really up against it with work . . ."

He lazily drags his slippers, falls onto a chair and rests his face on the palm of one hand. He runs the fingers up and down his cheek: shall he shave today, or not? The old woman's chatter has dazed him: just when she's finished those old stories of hers, just when you think you're free, she starts all over again. She seems to be talking more and more these days, and she certainly eats as much as ever.

But he too is feeling restless today. He leafs through the sheets of paper with calculations, writes something here and there in the margins, lets out a yawn, stands up and looks out of the window. There's nothing to see: the same street with blocks on one side, and opposite, right in front of his window, the wasteland enclosed in barbed wire. A ramshackle tin house, a tram shelter from the days when this was the end of the line. Through the thin walls of the apartment he can hear a radio and some quarreling voices. He lifts his shirt sleeve and with two fingers mechanically squeezes the pimples on his arm. There are days like today when he can't bring himself to do anything. The whitish sky, the mud heaps in front of the block, fear mixed with impotent rage at the thought of life ahead, his mother's irritability, his awkwardness with girls, his lack of money: everything together makes him sit there sullenly hunched up squeezing each of the pimples in turn. What is life? As he sees it now or as it seems when he's in a good mood and can forget all the problems? He throws himself onto the bed, screwing up his eyes and gritting his teeth as he waits to chase away the unbearable memory. But when it returns it works him up into a fever: an early odor of cool spring quivering with life; water streaming from the piles of blackened snow on the edge of the pavement; and he, youthful and alive, running out into the unexpected sunbeams, dashing across the road against the red light, afraid of arriving late.

The girl had narrow delicate shoulders, and arms covered with soft dusky hair. One of her stockings, laddered above the knee, had been hurriedly mended with white thread. He caught a glimpse of it as he was clumsily trying to unfasten her zip. He felt her rigid and heavy in his arms, without her usual volubility, but haste and fear pushed him on. He kept fumbling over buttons, glancing from time to time at the alarm clock ticking on the table beside them. He had wasted nearly all the time with senseless phrases, and now the friend who had lent him the room would be back in an hour at the latest. Something, perhaps the memory of the laddered stocking, perhaps her awkwardness, suddenly moved him and made him want to postpone the fever. He let his hand slide down her shiny head of hair, which was tied at the nape with a black lace, but she pulled away and furtively glanced at him, hostile and mistrustful: no, there was no point trying to fool her any more. Furtively—that was how she had looked at him on the way there, as she ran her soft damp fingers along the dusty fences and the yellowish wall, as they climbed the stairs to the flaking door where, with mounting unease, he fumbled to get the key to turn in the grimy lock. The sofa bed creaked continually, and he kept his head away from the wood paneling. Though more and more affected by the stiffness of her body, he pressed on and grew almost frightened, watching his movements from outside, as if it was all something he had to complete at any price, a duty from which there was no other escape. Doubtless she could sense this as she lay staring at each little irregularity on the pale ceiling, her lips pressed tight over small sharp teeth. Blinking often in short bursts, she emitted flashes of hostility between her half-open lids—a scowl of contentment at the visible signs of his failure.

"Stop poking like that," Vica says to him. "Just look at what you've done to yourself." Her thick wrinkled finger is pointing at the bluish marks on his arm, while he, eyes shut, continues to probe for more pimples.

She has quietly pushed open the door and is standing there half-bent, holding a plate with some slices of bread and cheese.

"Leave me alone," Gelu angrily shouts. "Leave me alone," he repeats more softly.

He went to the window and looked out, one hand on the frame.

"I'm sorry," he whispered to the girl, moving to a corner of the room, until the cold sharp-edged wood cut into his flesh. "Forgive me," he mumbled, so downcast, so overcome with despair that he no longer noticed the clock or tried to cover himself. Now anything could happen. He recognized in himself all the fear of those hours, as if he had known before that that was how it would work out. Now he could even say that word, the one he had least thought he would ever utter to someone. And late, very late, he felt her thin arm trying to slip beneath his tensed shoulder, and her soft hair fluttering over his cheek.

"Just look at yourself—you're nothing but skin and bones. That's why you've got no energy and feel sleepy all the time. I've always looked after myself properly, and so has my husband. I watch how he fills a plate, dips in some bread and turns it into a sludge; then he eats it like that, with a spoon. You're getting to be like Mealache, I tell him, that old man who mixes the soup and main course he gets from his daughter-in-law; why should I open my mouth twice, he used to say, if it all goes down the same place? But my man answers back: Well, I'm really getting on, aren't I? D'you think I'm not an oldie? I'll be seventy-nine this summer."

"He's an old man all right!" the boy snaps over his shoulder. "If he's not old then tell me who is."

What a happy little soul! Just like her husband, just as surly and evil-tongued; whose life is he going to ruin next? You're one hell of a misery! I'd have knocked some sense into you if you'd been mine. I'd have made a man of you . . . At his age you'd think he'd have a bit of sense. It's his mother's fault: she screwed him up. And now she's the one who complains: "I don't know what to do with Gelu, I don't know how to go about it. He sits all day in his room ignoring me, and if I say something to him he flies off the handle. When his poor father was alive things were different in the house. You know what a cheerful, good-natured man Ilie was."

"What can you do?" Vica replies sympathetically. "Just let him get on with it." But she is thinking: Why are you surprised? He takes after you. You used to be just the same. What were you like with me and anyone else who dropped in on you?

She ought to say that to her face, but she can't be bothered. Her sister-in-law was really lucky to find Ilie, God rest his soul. He had a gentle nature, the poor man, so she just did what she liked with him. The sister-in-law's face never lit up when she opened the door for Vica; she never gave her a friendly look. And she must have taken a dim view of those twenty-five lei that Ilie slipped to his sister on the doorstep . . .

"Here, Vica," he had said, "it's for the tram when you come to visit us next."

It's true: her sister-in-law changed when she saw she was alone in the world. Now she says: "Come again, Vica, let's have a chat together, just the two of us. The house is so quiet it really gets on top of me."

And so she goes to see her again, like today. She gets down to some sewing and ironing, but no longer has the old strength in her arms. God forbid that you'll ever need anything from your relatives or anyone else, Madam Ioaniu used to say to her, because they'll leave you to the wolves. She was an educated woman, Madam Ioaniu, educated and refined. She had two husbands and saw each of them to his grave.

"Never grow old, Vica, that's all I say. And never land yourself on other people . . ."

How many times she said those words to her!

⌒⌢

"You take it, I'm not hungry. My papers are all over the table, and it'll just get in my way."

Gelu holds the plate with bread and cheese, leaning against the frame of the kitchen door as he tries to decide whether to go in or out.

"You have it. Anyway, there's not much else to eat: Mom doesn't get paid till tomorrow."

"Me have it? I'm not thinking about food."

But she takes the plate and puts it on a corner of the cupboard. Then she starts to clean the gas stove, removing the rings and putting them in the sink. If she turned around, the boy would see her laughing with her toothless mouth; she has just now taken out her false teeth, which are too tight to wear for long. What a misery you are, she laughs. Now he's sorry he snapped at her like that, as if to bite her head off. It's not her fault: she was bringing him something to eat . . . Maybe he's not so bad after all, but he's been badly brought up: it's his mother's fault, she screwed him up when he was little . . . It was Gelu this and Gelu that, just do this for me, sweetie . . . The truth is, he was a pretty child, plump but pretty, with curls like little rings . . . She used to bathe him, rub oil into his joints, spit over her shoulder to shoo away the devil, kiss him on the bottom, take him to the shop. His place was under the counter, where he used to crouch on all fours looking at the scales. Then, after the currency reform, her husband gave him a sack of money to play with . . .

"Come on, eat it," he snorts. "What are you waiting for?"

He alone knows what's come over him. He's already turned and left the room. It suddenly comes over him—just like that . . . She stretches out her hand, takes the piece of bread, takes the cheese, stuffs it into her mouth. It's not worth putting her teeth in, because they're too tight. She gave the guy five hundred lei to make them for her but he still couldn't get them right, goddamn it . . . Maybe Gelu's not a bad kid, but something comes over him sometimes; well, he's a big boy now, he needs a woman too.

She stretches her hand out again, grabs a bit of cheese, and stuffs it in her mouth. What was he on about that time a year and a half ago, not even that long, when his father passed away? Poor Ilie lay dead on the table and people kept dropping in—colleagues from work, neighbors from the block and from where they'd lived before, each with a flower or a candle, as is the custom . . . How sad she was then, she didn't know whether she was coming or going . . . At the crack of dawn she came back with five kilos of meat, nice lean meat, that she'd bought with money borrowed from her neighbor Reli. At five o'clock she'd been standing in the meat line; she alone knew with how heavy a heart . . . Lining up to buy meat for the funeral repast . . . But there wasn't a fridge—poor Ilie hadn't got around to that—and anyway who could give a damn then about meat? Two women had to hold up her sister-in-law, who wailed in disbelief that her turn had come to suffer the pains of living . . . Who'd given a moment's thought to meat? But she wasn't going to let good meat go off, so she went and put it in the frying pan . . . She turned the pieces with a fork; maybe she put one in her mouth to see if it was done, and then wiped her face with her hand. It was hot in the kitchen: she remembers tears and sweat running down her face. Suddenly she saw him there looking crazy. Gelu had taken leave of his senses:

"Is that what you're in the mood for?" he screamed.

And he ran to the stove and turned all the knobs.

"Is that what you're in the mood for? At least you might have thought that there'll be a lot of people here. Do you want them all to see you frying meat?"

And she stood by and let him turn off all the gas rings. She noticed that the meat was already cooked . . . All she said was:

"Why are you rushing around like a lunatic? And why did you turn the gas off? Have you gone crazy? What's it to you if people see me? Do you want good meat to go off, after I stood in line at five o'clock? Only I know how sad I was, lining up to buy meat for my brother's funeral . . . It would be better if I'd died instead of him. It was me who brought him up, me who was a mother to him, but meat goes off in a couple of hours in this heat unless you fry it. And what will you give that crowd this evening when they come back from the cemetery? 'Cuz they'll all come back, and what will your poor mother give them to eat? When good meat goes off it's money down the drain. You've got to learn to respect it, like you should respect older people who know what's what . . ."

Swallowing what she said, he muttered something and left. Ever since then he's looked at her distrustfully, but you've got to know how to handle these teenagers. You can't give them an inch, or they'll get completely out of control. Just as well she never had children of her own! Kids today aren't afraid of anything; they have no shame at all . . . And as for bringing them up, she knows how hard that is . . . After all, who brought Ilie up? Wasn't it her who washed and fed him? She was only eleven, with

Ilie in her arms. It was around then that one of them zep'lins flew over
Bucharest and everyone went out to look at it; she was there too, with Ilie
in her arms. But Mummy was still alive then. Everyone was standing at
street doors, some even on rooftops; people came in from the outskirts to
gawk at it—did they know it was bringing bombs and death in its wake?
They all came out to greet the monster, some holding a candle, others a
lamp. It was all so beautiful! Light and lots of people, like at Easter, with
beams of light in the sky as well. But our people were trying to get it, to
catch and shoot it! When the guns started booming, it was like all hell let
loose. And she had to rock and comfort poor Ilie: hush now, there, there,
sssh . . . The poor thing turned blue from so much crying, and he was as
heavy as a stone. They got used to it in the end, of course, and as soon as
she heard the church bells, the big one at the Patriarchal Cathedral and
the others at Capra church, as soon as the policemen started to blow their
whistles, Mummy grabbed Vasile and, with the twins hanging to her
skirts, put out the fire double quick and took everyone off to Cabbage-
Washer's cellars. He had cellars like no one else's in that part of town! But
the day when the bombs fell on Piața Obor was like the end of the world;
look, Maria, said Cabbage-Washer, your kids are so scared they've done
it in their pants. They were all clinging to each other, screaming all the
time, but in fact it was old granny Anghelina who'd done it, not them;
what a stench there was! how the earth was shaking! Well, kids are kids,
poor Mummy replied to Cabbage-Washer, but granny Anghelina didn't
say a word, she just walked with her legs apart and tried to stop her teeth
from chattering . . . Old she may have been, but she was still scared of
dying . . . The planes had dropped bombs on Obor, just down the road
from where they lived, in broad daylight. Lots of poor people died, as
well as women who'd gone there to collect wood. But, God knows how,
they'd managed to take shelter in Cabbage-Washer's cellar.

"Well, I'm off too," she says.

No point wasting any more time here: there's no one to talk to and
nothing to eat. Her sister-in-law is completely potty, with that big boy in
the house; a big boy and nothing to feed him with. She should have made
a big pot of food, with meat and sauce, so he'd have something to dip his
bread in. And then she wonders why he's so irritable and mopes around
all the time!

Gelu looks puzzled as he gets up from his table. He was sure she'd
spend the whole day bugging him, and now, when he sees her shuffling

to the door bag in hand, he tries to say something but nothing comes into his head. He just traipses along behind her, digging his fingers into the palms of his hand; he never likes to make up with people, and anyway he hasn't got any time for her today . . . If she wants to stay, she can stay; if she wants to go, she can go . . .

"You look like Napoleon in Russia, Auntie," he says, staring at her stiff beret padded with quilting material. She has wrapped her scarf around it to cover her ears, and tied it in a knot under her chin.

"Napoleyon in Russia—you can say what you like, but it keeps me warm. Anyway, who's going to chase after me at my age? Only Old Nick, only the prince of devils," she laughs.

Gelu too gives out a little laugh, still with some spite in it. He looks at her gray eyebrows; only now does he realize that she's stopped dyeing them—since when, he doesn't know. Her hair is also white at the roots, though still reddish as it thins out further up. He suddenly remembers when she used to comb her hair in front of the mirror that stood on the large heavy table; he sees on the washstand a white china pitcher that he liked as much as the oval photographs on the wall, where the young bride and groom—Vica and Uncle Delcă—looked at each other with shiny garlands on their heads. Their bedroom is visible in some of the pictures—the room in which he never sets foot, because he can't stand the smell of damp and kerosene that has got into their furniture and clothes.

How strange are his memories of the shop: it used to be so huge, with ceiling-high shelves. How he liked to play under the counter and watch with fascination the almost imperceptible movement of the scales! And that evening when they gave him a sack of green banknotes as tall as he was . . .

"Since the currency reform you can use them for anything—tear them up if you like."

But the men stayed whispering in a corner, while Auntie Vica combed the hair hanging behind her over a chair; long hair, black and curly, which she hadn't yet started to dye.

"I've taken my teeth out—that's why I probably sound funny. I can't stand wearing them for long. I really hate them and only put them in when I'm in the street. Otherwise, people would see me and say: Look at that toothless old woman . . ."

"If you stay another hour Mom may be back."

"No, I'll come again another time—as soon as the weather gets better. Now that I'm out and about, maybe I'll drop by and see Ivona for a bit."

Now she'll start the stories about her fancy ladies . . . He almost feels like laughing: his earlier irritability has gone. But she says nothing more, just carefully makes her way down holding on to the stair rail.

"Look after yourselves," she shouts back up the stairs. "Make sure you eat properly and stop moping around like that. That's why you're so tired and irritable."

Chapter 3

Domenii Park

She walks slowly, eyes down, taking care not to slip on one of the pieces of wire that some no-good builders left lying around in the autumn. She is bent forward as she walks along, leather ragbag in one hand: there had been no point in waiting any longer, she'd left them the gherkins, as well as a little of that *țuică* firewater, some onion and garlic—the kind of little things that always come in handy.

"You shouldn't have gone to the trouble," her sister-in-law always says. "Really there was no need. Besides, you know I never touch a drop of liquor. And I never use onions."

That's what she says, but quick as a flash she squirrels it all away in a cupboard. She's like that: turns up her nose, but would eat the last crumb from your plate. Yes, she'd left what she had in her ragbag, but she hadn't got anything out of it. She could have waited all day for her sister-in-law to come home, and there was nothing to eat in the house. Besides, Gelu said there was some time to go to payday. A year ago her sister-in-law had promised:

"Look, I'll give you twenty-five lei a month from Ilie's pension: he said before he died that that was what he wanted. I can't manage it this month, but I'll give it to you next time you come."

"Forget it," Vica had said. "You haven't got enough for yourselves."

Always the same exchange.

She had no faith in her sister-in-law's promises—which was just as well, because what could she expect from her? She was a spendthrift: her money went as soon as she got it; she'd never be able to live as they did, two people on six hundred and fifty lei a month. What with the rent, the electricity, the television . . .

She walks slowly and carefully as she passes the telephone booths. There are two of them, at the end of the tram line, both out of order, both with broken windows and ripped cables. There are more and more vagabonds in Bucharest: the city's filled up with hobos and country bumpkins. Fortunately she has almost nothing left in her ragbag—just a few pieces of dried bread. Her sister-in-law, wasteful as she is, always buys too much bread and wants to throw it out as soon as it gets a bit hard.

"Why are you doing that? Give it to me! I'm the garbage bin around here."

How Gelu cracks up when he hears that! She takes it home with her, to make breadcrumbs, or to dip it in tea and eat with a spoon. That's all she gets from her sister-in-law; she used to spend and spend in the same way when poor Ilie was alive.

"You should come around when it's our paydays, Vica. Don't wait, or it'll all be gone," poor Ilie used to say.

Yes, they were always broke a week before payday and had to go around borrowing from people. Two salaries but still they couldn't manage! So how was it that she made ends meet? Only because she had an iron will.

"I admire you, Madam Delcă," Ivona said. "I really admire how you run your home."

When Ivona says something she means it. And if she sends a post-card—*Dear Madam Delcă, you haven't been to see us for ages; we'll be expecting you on such-and-such a day*—you can be sure she'll be waiting for you, not wandering the streets.

"Muti was so fond of you," Ivona would tell her.

And she would suddenly pull out a handkerchief and begin to cry. Even when the mourning period was over, Ivona kept shedding tears for her mother. She had good reason: "Muti" had kept house for her and brought up the boy, as long as she'd had the strength.

On the day after Muti died, Ivona had said: "Oh, Vica dear, I don't know how to make a funeral cake."

"Don't worry about it," Vica had replied. "As if that was any use to the dead—may God forgive me! What is of use is if you eat and live well when you're alive."

"Muti never liked those get-togethers every few months in memory of the dead. So, what I'm going to do is give you fifty lei every two months, for you to remember her by. I'll send a postcard for you to come and pick it up—so we can also have a chat. Or I could send you a mail order, if that's more convenient."

In a week it'll be two months since she coughed up last. She's not a bad sort, Ivona, a kind enough girl. Vica has known her all her life: thin as a rake, a bit manic, long nose, short hair dyed blonde, just like when she was twenty. She's been going to see her for years now, whenever she gets one of those cards in the mail. Her face positively glows as she opens the door for Vica.

"How wonderful to see you, Madam Delcă! I've got so much darning to do that I don't know where to put it. I don't even have anything to wear—that's why I'm half-dressed like this."

Ivona hangs on her neck and kisses her on both cheeks. She kisses her back. She's very fond of Ivona.

"You've golden fingers, Madam Delcă, really you do! I only wish I could have been like Muti or you, but I'm so awkward—completely hopeless in fact. My husband even composed a little couplet about me: *Needle, thimble, and thread / Fill her with such infernal dread.*"

And does he also think up poems for his floozies when he goes out whoring? He should have his balls cut off, she felt like saying. But she kept silent, not wanting to upset Ivona. She knows what things you can and cannot say to people.

She stops and begins to wait patiently for the tram. It is drizzling. The fine droplets tingle on her face, but they don't bother her. She has thick clothes underneath and an overcoat on top—a good solid coat from the old times, turned inside out nine years ago and stuffed with a couple of layers of wadding. She even used the trimmings to make herself a beret, which she wears pulled well over her forehead to protect her from the rain. A scarf keeps her warm around the ears. She could even say she's doing fine now. If you've got your head screwed on and know how to look after yourself, you don't need to worry about the cold or the rain.

An old woman wearing woolen mitts passes alongside her, dragging a gas canister on a trolley. I wonder how old she is. Good God, and to think that I'll be like her one day! Couldn't she find anyone to lug her gas canister home for a few lei?

The tram arrives. Wrapped up well, she makes for it with small hurried steps.

"After you, dear, hop on!" an old gentleman says to her, in a kind voice. A real gentleman, like in the old days.

"*Merci*," she replies.

But she brushes straight past him. He looks taken aback and pauses for a moment by the step before climbing on board himself. She walks further along to the second-class car; she's always used it since she closed down the shop, and it hasn't killed her yet.

"Big deal! So you save five bani . . ." her sister-in-law mocks.

Five bani are five bani. You put them all together and they soon add up. If she hadn't made those little savings, they wouldn't have managed for a week on what her husband brought home.

She doesn't have time to get to the rear door before it closes. Normally, she wouldn't use the other one for anything in the world: she's not so old as to get on where you're supposed to get off; everyone in Bucharest knows that the exit's at the front.

She certainly knows. She remembers the yellow horse-drawn trams that used to have little curtains in summer, when the horses were fitted with cloth hats and blinkers. What fine sturdy nags they were! The tram used to pass through Piața Sfântu Gheorghe, where there was a statue of the she-wolf, then down Dorobanți to Colțea hospital, and on to Clopotarii Vechii and the depot in Bonaparte district. The whole line for just twenty bani. That young devil Nicolae used to lie in wait on the sidewalk with his mates, and when the tram turned the corner they'd jump on the buffers trying not to be noticed, because the driver would confiscate their caps and give them a good hiding if he caught them. Later they used to do the same with the electric tram, Number 14. He was really crazy, that Nicolae, but also as smart as they come! It's a pity he never made it in life, when you think that he was always first in class, ahead of the director's son, who shared the same bench but was always in second place. He understood everything in class, without having to make an effort, but afterward he'd skate off down some back alley to play knucklebones. Clever, but not right in the head. His father gave him a daily hiding, either because he'd lost all his clothes betting at five stones and come home naked—she can still see him carefully covering his set of stones—or because the tram driver had caught him and taken his cap away. She also remembers other trams: for example, the one that went

past Ienei church, down Strada Regală and Strada Câmpineanu, stopping at the official stops but also elsewhere if you waved a hand, a stick,
or an umbrella. And then there were the omnibuses, which didn't move
on tracks and were best avoided, because they passed over many holes in
the road and shook the living daylights out of you. Yes, she's a real native
of Bucharest and knows all there is to know about trams—unlike those
newcomers who are flooding in from the country. The city is filling up
with peasants, so there's no room for people born and bred here. They
live one on top of the other in a concrete block, saving up money to buy
a car—peasants like Delcă's second cousin, Oița. Such are the times we
live in!

She makes her way forward with difficulty, swaying between the rows
of benches. The rubber floor mat is saturated with grime; she must take
care not to slip and break something, God forbid. Look, there's an empty
seat by the window.

She hurries over and sits down.

She's got off to a bad start today. At least if Ivona is in! She can hardly
be anywhere else at this time: she's a pensioner now, like her husband.
Together they must have four thousand a month to spend, maybe more—
just for the two of them. It's two or three years since their Tudor took
off for the West, a little before his grandmother, Madam Ioaniu, passed
away. Ivona still keeps his room as he left it: she hasn't rented it out, and
no one ever sleeps there. A big empty house and Ivona keeps her son's
room like a burial vault, decorated with color pictures from his travels.
So what if he gets to see all those countries? Is that so exciting for them?
Ivona saw him a year ago, when she was given a visa to visit him, and
this summer it was her husband's turn. That's all the contact they've had.
Tudor isn't allowed to come to Romania, so God help Ivona if she needs
anything in her old age. She's all alone in that big house, while her husband spends the day off with his floozy. You only ever catch a glimpse of
him as he snatches his jacket and heads for the front door. The Lord have
mercy on Ivona: there'd be no one to get her a glass of water if she ever
had a funny turn! That's what kids are like nowadays: you give and give,
and when their turn comes they're nowhere to be seen! Ivona herself,
though, isn't the kind to worry much about others; she's only ever really
thought about Ivona.

"That's how I am, Madam Delcă," she said once. "I'm a rational being,
and that's helped me a lot in life."

Oh, yeah? If my man spent the day chasing ass, like yours does, he'd soon lose his little pecker. I'd make sure of that! But that doormat Ivona has just gotten on with her work at the office, her women friends, her cigarettes drooping from her mouth, her little cups of coffee. She has no idea what her Niki-Wiki gets up to.

"That's the sort of person she is," her mother, Madam Ioaniu, once said. "She taught herself not to show what's going on inside her."

Madam Ioaniu liked to spell things out.

"I don't have any secrets from you, Vica ... Sit and work here in my room, so we can chat about one thing and another," she used to say. "I've just been thinking: why hasn't Vica been to see me? And I told Ivona to send you a postcard."

From time to time she received a card: *Dear Vica, you haven't been to see us lately: we're waiting for you. Phone first. Muti's always at home in the morning.*

Often she set off at once, especially if it was summer and the streets were not icy. She took the nine o'clock tram and would be ringing at the back door by a quarter to ten. Sometimes their cleaner, Leana, would open for her. Madam Ioaniu would be upstairs, in a leather armchair that had split open and been repaired a number of times; it had gradually turned black over the years, so they had put a rug over it, and it was on this rug that Mrs. Ioaniu would be seated. There were many more rugs in her room—on the divan and on the walls—as well as several paintings and a large mirror that stretched up to the ceiling. It was a Venetian mirror, whose dark wooden frame was inlaid with mother-of-pearl. It had collected dust and yellowed with age, but how it had shone thirty or more years ago! There were so many things in Madam Ioaniu's room: leather-backed chairs with golden studs; hatboxes from years gone by, trunks full of old dresses, piles of French books with yellowed pages that released dust and a sharp odor when you touched them ...

Madam Ioaniu was to be found in her armchair, book in hand. Quite a life she'd had—always resourceful and cultivated! And now she sat there reading, glasses on nose, face crisscrossed with little red veins. As a blonde, she had spent her youth fighting off spots and blemishes with special creams ordered from Paris, but they had cleared up only as she approached old age. Then brown marks started to appear on her hands. Now she is heavy and big-breasted, but in her younger years she was tall and slim, as you can see from the photos in all those albums. She spends the whole day in that armchair, even taking her afternoon nap there. On the wall above her head, a large dark picture shows an old man peeling an apple. How many times Vica has seen it!

"Why do you keep that ugly old thing here? I'd be scared to set eyes on it at night."

"Oh, Vica, it's worth a lot, that picture—it's by a painter from the old days. I used to meet him every summer at the Black Sea, at Balcic, and he gave me the picture as a present when he saw that I liked it."

And she went on with her stories! It bored her to spend hours alone in that armchair, while her daughter and son-in-law were at the office and Tudor was off at school. How happy she was to hear him climbing the staircase!

"Stay and work here in my room," she used to say, "so that we can have a bit of a chat together."

Suddenly she'd rummage through her trunks and pull out an armful of rags: old velvets, natural silk, fine cambric sheets, lawn and batiste underwear, so rotten that it fell to pieces if you tried to put it on. And there were blouses and dresses, moiré and rep, shiny satin and lace veil, costumes in fine material from prewar English dressmakers, camel-hair overcoats, various kinds of lace—heaps and heaps of the stuff. Vica turned it all this way and that: and what marvels she extracted from it! Made-to-measure clothes for Tudor, nightdresses, kitchen aprons, bathing costumes—once even a pair of "fisherman's trousers" for Ivona, at a time when they were in fashion. The sewing machine never seemed to stop—unless the scissors were needed for some operation. She didn't use patterns or anything like that. If Ivona brought her a fashion magazine, she didn't even glance at it.

"I don't need that. I know what needs to be done."

She worked away, while Madam Ioaniu helped her with the overcasting. Then suddenly she'd see her get up, sneak into the kitchen, and return with a pot of fresh coffee and two cups: oh, yes, that was the life! Madam Ioaniu lit a cigarette and held it between her fingers, curved and tipped with red like the claws of a bird. Ever since she'd known Madam Ioaniu, as a young woman, she'd had that bright red on her nails. "A real devil of a woman!" she thought, whenever she looked at them.

Madam Ioaniu had gnarled fingers, yes, just look at those knots at the joints; and she claimed that that was why she put on that red varnish, so that you wouldn't see how ugly her hands were. Is that also why you paint your cheeks? Vica almost blurted out more than once.

How she piled on the rouge when she went to the cinema or to visit friends! They used to take it in turns to play the host for their Thursday games of poker.

When her own turn came, once a month, she would say to Vica: "Don't come tomorrow: the girls are coming!"

"Of course, Thursday is when Muti has her girls around!" that wretch of a son-in-law would say, laughing at how they still called themselves girls at their age. But it didn't bother them in the least: they'd played poker all their lives, even after the communists came to power, confiscated their wealth and stuck their men in jail; some were killed, others survived, it was a lottery. Still they went on playing poker—except that they no longer had a cent and used dried beans as stakes.

Later, though, they started to play for money again, with five bani as the opening bet. And Mrs. Ioaniu would always make an apple pie when the girls came to her place.

All her life Madam Ioaniu was amazing: everything she put her hand to turned out great. Once, Vica was working round the clock to finish a dress for Ivona, and she asked Madam Ioaniu, just like that, to help her with the overcasting. And well, no sooner had she picked up the needle than she was sewing away as neatly and skillfully as any dressmaker— and from then on she'd always take on the task, while sitting in her armchair and telling the story of her life. There was certainly a lot to tell. She'd had two husbands and seen them both to the grave. The first, a big shot professor, was arrested by the Germans as soon as they waltzed in during the First World War. They stuck him in the can, only they knew where; they didn't hold him long, but he was wiped out by the time he got home. Anyway he was old, and maybe he'd been ill, 'cuz he was soon pushing up daisies.

"You must be hungry, Vica," she said, suddenly interrupting her stories. "Wouldn't you like a bite to eat?"

"Will a cow eat clover?"

The pangs of hunger had been gripping her for some time, but what can you say in someone else's house?

Taking a key from her dress pocket—she was the one in charge and kept everything locked up—Madam Ioaniu opened the sideboard and took out a plate of cakes. At that time, when she still had her strength, you could always find something to eat in her house. And she always slipped something into Vica's ragbag before she left: a jar of paste, a tin of fish, a few dried cakes, a piece of cheese.

"Take it, it'll come in useful."

"All right, I will—seeing as I'm the garbage bin around here."

How Madam Ioaniu laughed at that!

Why should she turn up her nose at the offer? No reason at all. She wasn't that stupid. Besides, they were so happy with the work she did for them.

"You've golden fingers, Madam Delcă," Ivona used to flatter her, while trying on a dress and admiring herself in front of the mirror. "What would we ever do without you?"

And Madam Ioaniu would nod from her chair and laugh. She liked to hear the compliments, because she was the one who got Vica to come in the first place.

"I've known Vica for such a long time. Since you were at my sister's fashion house, isn't that right, Vica? How old were you then?"

"What, when I was at Mrs. Geblescu's? Sixteen, or maybe it was eighteen."

At the time Daddy had moved in with Old Clodhopper and had some more children with her, so he'd farmed his first batch out here and there as apprentices. She'd gone to the dressmaker, Nicolae to some craftsman or other—only that blockhead ran away every evening, until Father gave him a real thrashing and took him to someone else the next day. Anyway, she found herself at the House of Fashion, on the corner of Bulevardul Pache, with Madam Ioaniu's sister, Margo Geblescu—the Mistress, as the girls called her among themselves. She stayed a year there, poring over pieces of fabric, sewing away all day. And all those years later, it was as if she could still smell the odor of the charcoal iron—how she used to shake it to light the brazier! What dresses they used to have, what overcoats! And those wax models! She also saw plenty of real ladies, the gentlewomen of Bucharest, each more scented and elegant than the other, each part of the Mistress's clientele. Some of them took a liking to her: she was neat and fair-complexioned, with a head of dark curly hair, like that of her grandmother, the Greek:

"Let me have Vica on trial," they would say; "she's a charming girl."

Yes, she saw plenty of women from high society. That's why she could tell her sister-in-law, who always puffed herself up with airs and graces:

"I've seen some fine ladies, not like you. Real ladies. I know what life's like at the top."

She didn't like spending all her time sorting old clothes of one kind or another, but at least she escaped the mud streets of the Pantelimon district. Ah, if only Mummy hadn't died, her life would have been different! But in August 1916 the bells tolled one night, a bugle sounded at the town hall, and Daddy left for the front. Then the zeppelins started coming at night and the airplanes during the day; bread disappeared, then meat, corn, and beans; winter arrived and people didn't have any firewood . . . They still had what Daddy had put by before he went off. The sound of artillery got closer and closer, and the streets were filled with carts carrying refugees, carts carrying barrels of water, carts carrying wounded men on straw. But they soon stopped running to look; they were crawling with lice, and Mummy used to search them for their eggs. She can't remember which month she died in, only that she was playing with Nicolae on some wasteland and her aunt, old Cabbage-Washer's wife, came to take her home. So she found herself an orphan, at eleven years of age, with a troop of younger brothers to worry about.

Later, the Germans were always pestering them for things: sugar-loaves, kerosene, copper frying pans, and saucepans; they even took the bell from the Capra church. In some houses there was still someone left to stand up to them, but what could a bunch of poor orphans do? Sometimes a neighbor would protest on their behalf, or take them in and protect them. Then the twins died, one after the other. They were buried in Holy Week, when people who die go straight to heaven. But they were just toddlers who hadn't started sinning and all the rest of it— where did they have to go? The neighbors took charge then, making the funeral cake, fetching the water, sharing what little they had. Afterward the Germans came for their church bell, like they did for all the others in Bucharest; they'd break them into pieces and use them to make bullets. All over the city you could hear the sound of bells being smashed up. People looked at each other without saying anything, just made the sign of the cross, unable to believe that this was happening in their lifetime. But it was also said that there were some miracles. Once, the Germans came to take away the relics of Saint Dumitru, but although there were a lot of them they simply couldn't lift the coffin, however much they huffed and puffed; the saint had become too heavy. This really got them worked up: they put dynamite under the chest and set light to it, so that the smoke wafted up to heaven, but the chest and the relics survived intact, as if nothing had happened, while all the Germans croaked on the spot. They lay around like dead flies, with no hands, no head, no feet. The Good Lord couldn't allow such infamy—just after the Easter celebrations! Those were the times she had to live through, she and the poor kiddies. Some pulled through, others didn't: it was potluck. No one knew what fate held in store.

She's been looking out the window for a long time, without seeing the houses or the streets and trams. She sits hunched on her chair, hands together over the leather ragbag on her lap—the one she got from Mrs. Daniel. Her husband, Mr. Daniel, was a big shot in those days, a top communist and a buddy of Zaharescu's; the two of them went abroad all the time, while their wives stayed at home. You should have seen the things they brought back: the leather jackets, the boots, the scent bottles, the cosmetics, more than they could possibly use! Mrs. Zaharescu still gave her some mending work, but the other, Mrs. Daniel, just threw things out. It was from her that she got that plaited leather bag.

"Take it, Madam Delcă. Keep it as a souvenir."

She also gave her a worn Persian carpet, which she put in her living room, and old shirts from her husband, a large man but not a giant like Mr. Delcă. She would stitch and repair them, but you couldn't say he got much use out of them; they were old and frayed, after all. Mrs. Daniel couldn't bring herself to give away anything really good. She lives in Israel now, together with her husband.

Hunched on her chair, hands together over her leather ragbag, she looks out the window. All of a sudden her eyes focus on the houses that the tram runs alongside. She jumps up, grabs the bag and hurries toward the door, quickly, quickly, though taking care not to trip over—God forbid that she should break a leg. That linoleum's like a skating rink, as if you're walking on a thin layer of mud. The times are rotten, people are rotten, everything's rotten—there aren't even proper winters anymore!

"Hold on a second, please," she begs the tram driver.

She grips the rail tightly and puts one foot on the tarmac. What if the idiot starts off now?

The driver spits to one side, holding the handle but not turning it.

"Why don't you stay home?" he asks.

Maybe she heard, maybe not—anyway she doesn't answer. She brings her other foot down gently, still holding on to the rail.

"Why don't you go home and wait to croak, instead of loafing around town?"

The swarthy young driver doesn't even turn as he says it. His curly black hair falls long and greasy down to his shoulders. He's wearing a loud striped shirt and a little sheepskin.

"Drop dead, Gypsy boy! Go on, go fuck yourself!" she shouts back at him.

Too late. He's already closed the doors and moved off.

"Get out of here, you motherfuckers! You're all over the place."

She stands there cursing, but the tram is already at the next corner.

The road seems wider than before, and the cars keep flashing by, one after another. How can you squeeze across? She takes a few timid steps, but the cars keep coming, one after another. The drivers smile at any girls they see, eyeing them up.

"Are those skinny kids what you call girls? As if you can find any real girls these days!" she mutters, watching the layer of ice that still lies frozen beside the tram lines.

One step, then another, eyes on the layer of ice. Suddenly she feels a strange sensation all over, a kind of itching or prickling. Her fear of the truck that has turned the corner and is advancing from nowhere spreads through her like a tickle. The fear is so strong, in her heavy old body, that her clothes feel too tight on her. Relying on gut instinct, she scrambles toward the other side of the road, still such a long way off. She hears the roar of the engine close by, as deafening as the heartbeats in her breast. The truck screeches to a halt, and the driver climbs out whistling. He walks past her without so much as a glance, whistling all the time.

"Why you fucking little . . ." she mumbles.

Thick weary blood beats in her temples against her skull. Legs trembling, she continues slowly forward, her eyes on the layer of ice beside the tram lines. She hears the truck driver return, still whistling as he climbs into the cockpit and slams the door. She stops and stares, hunched over, as if she has suddenly remembered something, The driver is behind the steering wheel; she can see him clearly through the glass.

"Well, I'll be damned!" she says.

Pieces of ice have remained in the gutter, mixed up with scraps of wet newspaper that peep out here and there. But otherwise the ground is clear: Domenii used to be an aristocratic neighborhood; she can walk to Ivona's without having to worry. She takes one hand from her pocket and rests it against a wall; the crooked fingers stick out through holes in her gloves. She's still wobbly on her legs.

Well, I never! I was wondering where I know him from. He seemed so familiar. He's Reli's brother-in-law—the Reli who works at Pipera. What could he be doing around here?

"Like I said, another inch and that would have been the end of me. The halfwit would have run me over."

"Oh, my poor Madam Delcă! You must be more careful in future. When we reach a certain age, we have to take more care of ourselves—as Muti used to say. Ah, how fond she was of you!"

Ivona went to look for a handkerchief, already on the point of tears. It must be said that she had good reason, since Muti had kept house for her. Ivona's never liked that, never been good at it. She's more one for the office, for the world of coffee and cigarettes. Unfortunately she hasn't taken after her mother, who pulled off anything she tried her hand at. She certainly had her wits about her.

She walks hunched over, eyes on the ground, legs still wobbly. She'll pass out if she doesn't nibble something really soon—what has she eaten since this morning? Zilch. A crust dipped in a big mug of tea, then a bit of bread and cheese at her sister-in-law's—not enough to keep any-one going. If she goes out on an empty stomach, she's good for nothing the rest of the day. Luckily it's Saturday, so maybe Ivona will get her to stay for lunch. Tomorrow's Sunday, and Ivona may be cooking for some guests; she always does that the day before. Maybe she'll offer her some. Otherwise, though, since her son Tudor left home, the fridge is always empty. You wonder why they keep it.

"Niki and I don't need a lot of food," she says. "Meat and sweets espe-cially are real poison at our age."

"Maybe," she replies, rather dryly. "If you say so . . ."

But in her head: give me meat every day, and sweets, I don't need any-thing else. That's how it is. She and her husband have always liked to eat and drink. The things he used to bring home when they were young, in the first few years after they married! How he'd take her out as soon as he heard of a good new place to eat! They tried everything: the fattened chicken soup, the tripe stew, the blanquette with wild mushrooms . . . There was no end to his curiosity; after all, he'd come up from the coun-try as a child. She liked it best of all in October, on Saint Dumitru's Day, when the two of them would sit at a shaded table and feast on sweet-breads, *mititei* sausages, ram's testicles, mutton *ghiudem* salami, and goat pastrami, washed down with a carafe or two of new wine. And when it grew dark, the kerosene lamps would go on, a fiddler would strike up a tune, and her man would give himself airs as he came over and played right up close, just for him. Later, they'd have a sour giblet soup and set off home in the best of moods, in a horse-drawn carriage. How many times did they do that around the time of the wine harvest! She remembers it even now, as if it was yesterday. They've grown old, of course, but they still like to fry meat and sausages, to eat them with gherkins and a nice glass of *ţuică,* and to wipe up the sauce with a piece of bread. People who don't eat properly are weak and irritable, catch everything going around, suffer all the ills of the world. What Ivona says about this is just words—the chatter of a woman who doesn't like housework and therefore sticks to fruit and a strict diet. But who can live on that kind of stuff? If she were to buy only fruit and fancy meat, her money wouldn't last more than a couple of days. Two people, six hundred and fifty lei, with the rent and electricity and television . . . So what Ivona says is idle chatter, because when Leana comes to do the housework or laundry for her, she runs off in a flash to the place that sells ready-made meals—though even then she comes back with only three or four portions.

But at least Ivona is the kind of woman who keeps her word. She said she'd give her fifty lei every two months, and she hasn't forgotten once. In a week it will be two months since the last time, so maybe if she sees her today she'll give her the next fifty in advance. Why shouldn't she, in fact? She's loaded, and what difference does it make whether she coughs up today or next week?

"I was on my way here from my sister-in-law's, and do you know what I thought? I'll go and see how you're getting on. I'll go and see how Madam Ivona and Mr. Niki are getting on." Yes, that's what she'll say.

Ivona is always pleased to see her. She's very fond of Vica and thinks highly of her. Besides, she gets fed up alone at home, especially now that she no longer goes to the office. That scumbag of a husband's no use: if she ever needs him, he's off playing with his floozy. Yes, maybe Ivona will give her that fifty today—what's fifty lei to them, after all? Ivona's a nice girl, with a heart of gold; it's just that she's been unlucky in life. And maybe a bit loony. Pity she didn't turn out like her mother. Now that woman was certainly all together: she knew where her interests lay. If something suited her, fine. If not, she didn't waste her time.

Poor Ivona wasn't lucky enough to take after her mother, to attract men to her with that come-hither look. Muti could wrap them around her little finger—like this! Ah, how she bossed that first husband of hers! He was a professor and knew all kinds of big shots; he was thick as thieves with lawyers and ministers, and even hung around in the queen's circle. But what good did that do him? At home she was the general: she snapped her fingers, and he did what he was told. Anything to keep her happy! She'd had a lover before they got married—and the poor guy knew nothing about it! The door was always open at their house: anyone who wanted to could just wander in, so that's what her lover used to do too. Anyway, it was Mrs. Cristide who told her all that—but can you rely on someone like her, who prances about looking like a cheap whore? Maybe Madam Ioaniu had a lover before she married, maybe she did, but then things changed. She turned over a new leaf. Madam Ioaniu wasn't one of those! She had plenty of brains. It was she who told her to put her seven thousand lei in the savings bank:

"However little you've got, Vica, you should put some of it away. Then you'll know you've got a reserve, so you won't have to go begging in your old age. Mark my words: even if it's family or friends, you should never be at anyone's mercy."

Yes, that was one good thing Madam Ioaniu did in her life!

Three more houses to go, now that she's turned off the boulevard and can see the iron fence and the black lamps on either side of the gate. They haven't worked for the past thirty years, since they gave up bothering about them. There were two others by the front door, but the tenants went off with them. Madam Ioaniu was forced to rent it out to some tenants when her husband was in prison, so that she was left cooped up with Ivona and little Tudor in a cubbyhole under the roof. And that was the moment when that jerk Niki skipped out to his little whore. At first Madam Ioaniu said she'd replace the lamps at the gate when they got rid of the tenants, but then old age caught up with her and Tudor grew up and left. Now Ivona and her husband are alone in that big house, so what's the point of doing repairs? The walls outside are crumbling, but no one does anything about it. Maybe you notice it especially because of the new block next door. For a long time it was wasteland, after that fourth of April when a bomb fell on it. Madam Ioaniu's house escaped more or less, apart from a few cracks and some broken windows; it was lucky they weren't in the shelter at the time, because it took a direct hit—a hundred were killed, perhaps more, who knows? Yes, Madam Ioaniu was certainly lucky: her husband had made her leave Bucharest, along with Ivona and that scumbag Niki. He was a colonel, a general, and he knew the bombers would be coming because he worked in tele-communications. That's why the communists went for him and locked him up: he'd seen too much, knew too much.

And now look at the block they've built there. What a load of money the guys who moved in must have—real big shots, communist boss men like the Daniels or the Zaharescus! New masters, old masters: some have kicked the bucket by now, or seen their star wane; others have cleared off abroad, or are getting ready to. And their houses are as old as them, on the way out . . .

Madam Ioaniu's is flaking all over. She's passed away, of course, like her sister, the Mistress, and their husbands. Now you can see that the house has grown old too. Madam Ioaniu had it from her first husband, Mironescu: he didn't live long, but he left her the house, the silverware, the crystal, and all the rest. He was Ioaniu's best friend, and when he was on his deathbed he asked him to marry her. So Ioaniu, who'd been secretly in love with her for a long time, without any real hope, went ahead and married her.

Madam Ioaniu herself told her all the details—and not just once. But Mrs. Cristide says it wasn't like that at all: everyone in Bucharest knew that Mrs. Mironescu—that is, Madam Ioaniu—had been sleeping with Ioaniu for ages. Mrs. Cristide found this out from her husband's mother, her mother-in-law, because everyone gets to know everything around here. Anyway, you can't exactly gag people. But when you see Mrs. Cristide, with all that paint smeared over her, how can you believe a word she says? One thing's for sure: you didn't hear Madam Ioaniu speak much of her first husband. She hardly ever mentioned him. Only once did she blurt out:

"I didn't enjoy being with him, Vica. You know what I mean?"

They were drinking a cup of coffee at the time.

"Of course I do," she replied. "It was no fun for me either, in bed with my husband. I felt like running a mile when I saw he wanted to start pawing me. He didn't know how to go about it. He must have known what the problem was. Anyway, I said thank God when he left off me."

How this women's talk made them laugh! How silly it got sometimes! Madam Ioaniu would tiptoe in with a steaming pot of Turkish coffee and two little cups, along with a bottle of țuică to tipple. It was a good brandy, and Madam Ioaniu liked to eat and drink. She was in her cups that time when she told Vica about her first husband.

"I didn't enjoy being with him. I should say that he was older than me, twenty years older. He was nice and thoughtful, but how I used to cry at the beginning. After a while I got used to it. I didn't go out much, but I had a few loyal friends who would drop in whenever they felt like it. If I'd spent all my life with Ștefan, I'd never have known what pleasure was. That's what happens to some women. Or, who knows? maybe I'd have had something on the side, like so many do."

Since she mentioned it, maybe that's what she did. You see, maybe her thoughts led her astray sometimes: who can ever know? She took any secrets with her to the grave. As for her poor husband, he looks tall and thin in all his photos, with a long nose: the spitting image of Ivona. Madam Ioaniu hardly ever referred to him. Maybe the subject bored her stiff, or maybe he was only a dim memory after sixty years. Anyway, she only spoke about the other one, her Ioaniu. She went on and on about him, until you couldn't take any more.

Vica pushes on the tall iron gate, which is never locked. There used to be a summer pavilion at the back of the yard, covered with ivy and resurrection plants. In fact the whole house was covered with ivy and wisteria and resurrection plants. There also used to be flowers that looked like morning glory, only larger, like cartwheels: Madam Ioaniu planted them herself and knew exactly what they were called. All summer there was a fragrance of mock orange and rose of Jericho, as well as ordinary roses and lime blossom; even in the street it was so strong that it made you sleepy and gave you a headache. It felt as if you were on a different planet. The whole yard was filled with big yellow rosebushes, and the fence with red dwarf ones. Madam Ioaniu looked after the flowers, but once, a long time ago, she had had a gardener, and later a young soldier, her husband's orderly, had helped with everything around the house. The rosebushes started to blossom in June, each type taking its turn for a while, and they kept this up until late autumn, in November. Madam Ioaniu looked after them. It's as if she can see her now with the pruning shears and basket; she used to give her some roses when they said good-bye. She didn't cut them at random, though, but chose the ones she thought were about to wither.

"Why don't you stop for a bit?" Vica would say to her. "Take a break: you've been at it nonstop since this morning."

As if she didn't spend all her time standing behind the counter in those days! But she knew what to say to people like Madam Ioaniu, to get in their good books. She knew what you can and cannot say in such circles, and that's why they all liked and appreciated her.

Anyway, that had been enough to get Madam Ioaniu started.

"Ah, Vica, I've always had such a lot of energy, never needed more than four or five hours sleep. I used to enjoy traveling and dancing, and I was crazy about shows. I went with Lulu to every ball at the Officers' Club and danced all through the night, but I was still fresh as a daisy when the carriage brought me home in the morning. And do you think I went straight to bed, like the society ladies did? Certainly not! I'd always get the orderly to light the fire in the bathroom. And, after taking a shower, I'd call the maid and tell her what to cook and what needed to be done around the house. Then I'd take the carriage back into town, call in at Dinischiotu's or Dragomir Niculescu's to order the week's supplies, and finally make some more visits or go to a show. A few times, when there was some really big problem, I thought my life was over. But I also had my share of happiness and of things I enjoyed. I've always loved flowers and scents . . ."

As she talked and talked, Madam Ioaniu sat in her armchair on the dingy fabric covered with a few cushions and a rug. Once she got going it wasn't easy to stop her. Sometimes she would repeat a story she'd told before, but Vica let her continue, despite the rumbling pangs of hunger in her stomach. You don't have much choice when you're in someone else's house.

She's hungry now too, so hungry that she feels faint. Her legs barely carry her across the uneven slabs in the yard to the back door. That was the entrance she used when they all lived at the top, under the roof; the stairs seemed to go on forever. Madam Ioaniu climbed them with her in silence: what could she have said? She felt grateful even for that little hole, since the other ladies were in prison, and the real princesses were living in cellars or garden sheds. At least she and hers were still in their own place, even if they had to squeeze into an attic while the rest of the house filled up with tenants.

In the end they got rid of the tenants, but that was not the end of the story. Since Tudor had left the country, the state would take over the house after Ivona and her husband died. Ivona already explained this on the day when she first told her that Tudor would not be coming back. As for Madam Ioaniu, it was a long time before she mentioned it. That's what she was like: if she didn't have an interest in telling you something, there was no way of getting it out of her; she'd be silent as the grave.

She rings the bell. Rings a long time, stops, then rings again. She presses on the yellowed button and listens to the tinkling in the upstairs rooms; it seems to travel down to her on the wooden staircase that has a metal support fitted to each step. She waits a moment and tries again. A rustling sound inside, like footsteps. It's an old house, with old furniture. Everything creaks—the floorboards included, even if no one's moving about, even if no one's walking on them.

She can't believe she's been so unlucky. She waits, rings, waits, then steps back and looks at the door. Ivona must have gone out. But what if she comes back in a moment?

Chapter 4

Madam Ioaniu

She covers the steps with a newspaper she has brought with her, then puts a couple of plastic bags on top of it and sits down. It's winter and she's not going to catch a chill sitting on cold stone. But she feels she'll collapse if she doesn't take the weight off her feet for a minute. She has shooting pains in her legs, and a wave of faintness rises from the pit of her stomach. It's past midday, and she's been wandering around without a bite to eat.

Maybe that Ivona will stop gadding about and come home! Her mother brought a real fucking nomad into the world! What kind of woman is that who doesn't like to stay in and do the housework like everyone else? It's not surprising her son took off for Germany, America, or wherever, only he knows where; or that her husband spends the day with that floozy, no one leaves home if things are right, everyone knows the woman's to blame if her husband starts wandering. Why should he stay, after all? To look at that skinny bundle of nerves and her horse teeth and droopy nose? To listen to her jabber away to her friends on the phone, all the time puffing on a cigarette? Any man in his right mind would want to get the hell out.

She sits on the newspaper, on the empty plastic bags, and tries to gnaw the dry chunk of bread she got at her sister-in-law's. It's not easy with her dentures in the ragbag. That swine of a technician robbed her of five hundred lei, and they're so tight that her mouth's one big wound. Nothing but thieves in Bucharest nowadays: wherever you go they're waiting with their hand stretched out. What can they expect if you only get six hundred and fifty between the two of you and have to pay for the electricity, the rent, the television license?

She sits there, but it won't be for long. She can't let night catch her on someone's doorstep. No one ever comes knocking on their door—her husband's right about that. Why's that? Have they got the plague or something? Why doesn't her sister-in-law or Gelu drop by—or Nicolae and his floozies? Poor Ilie, God rest his soul, was the only one who used to visit them, and even he was always in a hurry. Let them all come and watch some television; they can have a bite to eat, because she's always got something in the house. And when they leave they can slip her a note or two:

"Here's twenty-five lei, Vica. It'll come in handy."

When she still had the shop she couldn't get rid of them, and no one ever left disappointed; she would lay the table and spread out the best she had. Those who came brought along their whole tribe. Now none of them even remembers. That's how things are in this world: you give and people think you're great, otherwise you're not worth a fig. But maybe Ivona will show up after all, maybe she's just around the corner buying some food. Just so long as she isn't at one of those hen parties they have at each other's places when their husbands are out; she's seen them at Ivona's and knows how they spend the whole week preparing all kinds of dainties to show off to the others. How they jabber away over the sweets and coffee, not keeping their trap shut for a minute! Old dears who've never done a stroke of work. The communists did a good job on you! They took my shop away, but they took a lot more from you! There they are, though, still enjoying the *dolce vita* like before. When things went sour on them, they had enough carpets and crystals and jewelry to sell. Just look at Madam Ioaniu: her house is still full of the stuff.

She always fell on her feet, like a cat. Two husbands and saw both of them to the grave—no flies on her! At eighty, she still used to doll herself up with rouge and eyebrow pencil to go to the Palace Hall movie house with her daughter; her son-in law would pay for them once a week and go off to his floozy. A real devil she was, Madam Ioaniu! She'd get up very early, make herself some coffee, and sniff around the kitchen, deciding which dishes and how much of each needed to be prepared. She waddled from here to there, big-bottomed and bosomy, a cigarette dangling from her mouth. If Ivona smokes, it's because she's taken after her—and the same goes for her miserly streak. What a cheapskate Madam Ioaniu was!

She'd even count the potatoes for an Oriental salad—two each, she'd calculate, taking control of the kitchen like a general. If an extra person
showed up for the meal, someone's plate would obviously remain empty.
And she got worse as she got older. On the other hand—though that was
in the good times—she'd never let Vica leave without slipping something
into her ragbag: a tin of liver pâté or something, cookies, or a piece of
cheese. One day, she remembers, she gave her three eggs and one of them
broke on her way home. Anyway, Vica wasn't stuck up like her sister-in-
law: she didn't turn her nose up at anything. Why should she? She'd have
been the loser. What good would that have done anyone?

"Here, Vica, take this: it'll come in handy."

"Okay, I will—seeing as I'm the garbage bin around here!"

How that made the old woman laugh! She laughed, drank cups of coffee, and had a tipple from time to time. She also liked to eat. What a
guzzler she was, greedier and greedier the older she got!

She gets up from the cold stone. She feels stiff, and the shooting pains
are worse than they were in the morning. She also needs to take one, she
can scarcely hold it back. The bladder gets weaker with age, everyone
knows that. That's why she can't bring herself to leave. If that madwoman
shows up, she'll be able to do it inside. She takes a few steps and looks at
the gate. Maybe Ivona will stop gallivanting and come home. That's why
her mother had so much trouble finding her a husband—before she got
Niki in her clutches. Yes, she searched high and wide to make sure Ivona
wasn't left on the shelf. Vica remembers what she was like before she got
married. Like she is now, in fact: flat as an ironing board, with a long
drooping nose, horse teeth, enough to make any man run for his life. The
suitors weren't exactly fighting over her!

That's why her mother couldn't stand the sight of her, even when she
was a little girl. Yes, Madam Ioaniu was a crafty one all right: you never
got much out of her, at least while she still had her wits about her. She
was as sly as a fox and as silent as the grave. One day, though, she did
blurt something out.

Vica was bent over her sewing machine, while Madam Ioaniu, perched
on her cushions like Lady Muck, was jabbering on and on; she got worse
and worse as she got older. And it was always about her second husband,
Ioaniu. For years she hadn't even mentioned his name, but now that she
had her widow's pension she even answered the phone with "Hello, this
is Sofia Ioaniu, the late general's wife . . ."

"Oh, yeah, kiss my ass . . ." Vica muttered.

"What was that you said, Vica?"

"Oh, nothing really. I was just cursing this bobbin."

"Well, if it was nothing . . ."

And she went on with her stories: how Ioaniu had been Marshal Averescu's blue-eyed boy; how he was wounded at Predeal, Mărăşti, or God knows where; what medals he was awarded; how they met for the first time, when she'd been thin as a rake and still in mourning for her first husband. And how he fell for her all over again—because he had done once before but hadn't plucked up the courage to tell her. Hadn't plucked up the courage—oh, yeah, pull the other leg! Plenty did pluck it up, and the old woman had it off with one man after another before she got too old. There's no smoke without fire—otherwise why would that Cristide shoot her mouth off, having heard it from her mother-in-law? But Madam Ioaniu didn't like to speak about all the dicks she'd stuffed inside her. Instead, it was always the same old song: how Ioaniu bought her bouquets of flowers, and perfume, and French powders, and fur coats, and toiletries from Paris; and how he was jealous when he took her dancing at the Officers' Club. Lulu this and Lulu that—in fact, he was called Gheorghe: Lulu was the old woman's way of sucking up to him. Lulu this, Lulu that, on and on she went.

"Ah, yes, they were the happiest years of my life. I always liked having fun, but I didn't have much chance when I was young—I don't know why. I had Ivona soon after I got married, when I was little more than a child myself, and it was such a difficult birth that I never really got over it. Ştefan wanted so much for me to have another child—but he never managed to persuade me. It was thirty hours of agony with Ivona. I could no longer tell whether it was day or night. I gave birth at home, where the midwife had set up a kind of harness above the bed. I pulled and pulled on it, screaming and shouting all the time. And everyone in the house crept around on tiptoe! I was too young: it scared the life out of me, and I never wanted to hear of having another child."

"Maybe you weren't so wrong. When I was young, I was glad that I couldn't get pregnant—glad to be free of the burden. What did I need kids for? Didn't I have my brothers to look after? And then came the nephews and nieces."

But Madam Ioaniu wasn't listening. Once she got going she paid no attention to anything else. That's how it was the day she blurted it out:

"I liked to go out and to have people around, and I was crazy about dancing. But poor Ştefan was more reserved: he couldn't dance properly and spent a lot of time working at the library. So you know what I did? Some mornings I'd shut myself in my room, put on a record, and dance alone in front of the mirror. I thought: what would it have been like if I'd had a different husband, one I saw eye to eye with? You know the kind of things young wives sometimes think about. But I wouldn't say I was depressed: I was a jolly sort of person, laughing all the time. And Lulu got to like that in the end. 'Your bells peal all around the house,' he used to say. But I was almost afraid to touch Ivona. I was so weak after giving birth that I didn't suckle her, and the poor thing fell ill. She was a good child, but a sickly one. She stayed like that all through her childhood."

She never really liked her daughter: she was too much like her husband—a good man, but delicate and a lot older, and with a long nose. No, she hadn't liked her daughter, but all her life she'd had her on her back. She'd never let on, though, the old slyboots; she knew which side her bread was buttered on. But now the she-devil was telling Vica, because she told her everything. She was the only person she'd ever told that she felt no real affection for Ivona.

"The maid used to bring her to me, but what is there to see in a newborn baby? A bundle of white lace, and inside . . . I didn't even know how to change a nappy: it seemed so complicated, and I never did learn. It's true, I was afraid of touching her—afraid that I'd break something; she had a long, bald, misshapen head and cried all the time, and there were all these blobs on her face. Poor Ştefan was so happy that he always found her beautiful. Okay, she may be nice enough, interesting and intelligent, but she's certainly never been beautiful. When she was little, she already had an adult's maturity and way of being. Maybe that's why I don't think of her as ever having been a child. I loved her, of course—how couldn't I? Maternal instinct and all that . . . Animals also love their little ones. But as a kid Ivona was too serious, a bit weird . . . And, before I knew what was happening, she'd grown up."

So that's how it was. She wasn't any keener on looking after her daughter than I am on becoming a bishop. She had her whims and fancies, that's for sure, like all women who never do a stroke of work. And she was never completely right in the head—otherwise why would she have kept all those bottles and boxes? Okay, she liked to hoard things, like all misers do, but what use could they possibly have been to her? Why couldn't she bring herself to throw them out?

"I used to like flowers, Vica. Yes, I liked having them all around the house. But I liked perfumes even more."

Sometimes she'd watch her get up from the armchair and shuffle across the room; the older she became, the more she stooped. Then she'd suddenly reappear clutching a load of scent bottles that she'd dug out of some drawers or God knows where, some no bigger than her little finger, others the size of a kitchen jug—bottles with wonderful golden or silver-threaded stoppers, and such glittering labels. And that smoky green or blue glass: she couldn't throw them out even when she was eighty! She'd shuffle back, arched over with her big bottom and bulging bosom. Her back had got more bent with age, and her nose longer and more hooked. She put the bottles on the table and studied them.

"That one was when . . ."

She remembered everything about all of them. Like an elephant!

"And that one was from . . ."

She knew all their names, repeated them over and over again. So difficult you couldn't possibly remember them.

"Lulu gave me that one shortly before our wedding. Every day he sent a courier with some flowers—or a bottle of perfume. I saw the courier's red helmet from the window. He also sent things for Ivona: cardboard boxes crammed with cakes or candied fruit or chocolates from Capşa's. Both her father and Lulu used to spoil Ivona . . ."

"He gave me that one after an abortion. How attentive poor Lulu was when he came to fetch me! He made me stay in bed for a whole week. It was the first abortion I'd had since we'd been together—that's why he was so anxious. But it was a good doctor, and I'd had quite a few in the past. My other marriage had lasted a long time, after all. There was no need for him to know, though. Why should your husband know everything about you? Don't you agree, Vica?"

"Your husband should only know you from the waist down," she replied.

How Madam Ioaniu laughed at that! She laughed and looked at the bottles on the table.

"Money down the drain!" Vica said, making a wry face. "Why did he get you all that stuff? He'd have done better to buy some land to build a house."

"Yes and no. Land seemed the safest thing to buy in Romania, but you see it hasn't been worth anything since the communists took over. Anyway, Lulu sure liked to spoil me!"

Then the old woman collected the bottles together and went to put them back in their drawers. You'd have thought they were gold coins or something! What was the point of keeping them? The fact is that her mind was going as she got older—and she became more and more of a miser. She wouldn't come back and sit down until she'd put them all nicely in place.

"Poor Lulu! When we got married, he was in the prime of life but had always been a bachelor. He was a professional soldier, very stern and very correct, but with me he changed completely. God, how he loved to spoil me, to indulge all my whims! We'd go out every evening, to the Continental or Mon Jardin, or else to a dinner and dance at the Officers' Club. We had a group of friends that we'd go with. He had a heart of gold, although you had to know how to behave with him. He could fly off the handle if you weren't careful . . ."

Ha, ha, what a devil you were! she thought to herself. And what a materialist—always putting yourself first. You certainly knew how to land on your feet. How lucky some women are in life!

Vica suddenly hears something move behind her. She swings around, her heart racing in her chest.

"Psst! Go on, clear off, you mangy little devil! Psst! Psst!"

A skinny, wretched-looking tomcat is climbing down a pear tree in the yard. How that tree used to be in the old days, what big juicy pears it used to have! Now it's dry and stunted, and last summer the caterpillars got stuck into it. Of course, everything withers when there's no one to look after it. There haven't been any flowers or rosebushes in the yard since Tudor left and Madam Ioaniu passed away—or, even earlier, since she started going senile. As long as she was all there, she used to take care of the flowers, the house, and the outhouse in the backyard. It was she who laid down the law: no one else would have dared to cross her. Loony Ivona and her creep of a husband knew that the house, the carpets, the silverware, and what was left of the jewelry were in the old woman's name; and on top of everything she was drawing her husband's pension each month. Wherever it was he died in jail—Sighet, Jilava, or Pitești—the fact that he'd been a politico didn't stop her picking up Lulu's pension. After all, he'd fought in the Great War too, been wounded several times, and received a fistful of medals. And during the German occupation Madam Ioaniu—or Madam Mironescu, as she was then—had agreed with her husband, the professor and an old chum of his, to hide him for months on end. Later, the Germans carted her husband off to a prisoner-of-war camp, but they didn't get their hands on Ioaniu. Dressed as a civilian, he somehow or other managed to cross into Moldavia. He fought at the Battle of Mărăști in 1917, being wounded yet again, and it was then that the king, the queen, and Marshal Averescu showered him with decorations. As for the Second World War, it was lucky for him that he didn't hit it off with Antonescu—because that meant he wasn't sent to fight the Russians on the eastern front. But then his luck ran out, and he still ended his days in the can. The old bag did have some luck, though. She gritted her teeth and put up with things; she let out rooms, and traveled all over the city giving private lessons in French and German. But the fact is she got left everything: the house from her first husband, along with the carpets and crystal ware, plus the pension her second husband had stored up. She managed to get through it all in the end.

That's why, after years without mentioning him, she started to answer the phone with "Hello, this is Sofia Ioaniu, the late general's wife . . ."

"Oh, yeah, kiss my ass . . ." Vica muttered.

But the old slyboots, who could jabber away till the cows came home, didn't like to talk about what had happened to her husband and where he'd kicked the bucket. The communists managed to scare her all right! But one day she did blurt something out about the money she got from cooking meals at home for people.

"Do you remember how slim I was in my younger days, Vica?"

It was true: she'd been slim and tall, with big tits. Her Ivona wasn't lucky enough to take after her in that way—or to have any of her sex appeal.

"My waist was as slim as that, like a wasp's. After I gave birth, I used to tie a girdle around me as tight as I could. It was the midwife who taught me that. No one could believe I'd had a child: I was as slim as a teenage girl. I filled out later, but when I turned forty I started to be a lot more careful: just an apple now and again, or sometimes no bread at all. You know yourself what my figure was like before they arrested Lulu. But when all that trouble hit us, I no longer had time to look after myself."

"Why be slim anyway?" Vica chipped in. "The bigger you are, the better you look—that's what I think. It's the skinny ones who get ill all the time. You must have noticed how irritable they always are, and how little energy they have!"

It was then that the old woman said it, without thinking.

"You know, I started to put on weight when I started to cook all those meals for people. I'd taste every dish to see how it was coming along, or adjust the size of the portions. What other pleasure was there in those days? Mark my words, Vica, it's not good to have no joy in your life; you're sulky and bad-tempered all the time, poisoning yourself as well as others. It's best not to deny yourself some little pleasures: they don't do anyone any harm. So, anyway, when I took in lodgers I stopped being so careful about my food. Some people eat because they're nervous, others because they're bored, but the ones who find it hardest to control themselves are those who eat for the pleasure of it. And food is the last pleasure left to us in this life."

That was the only time Madam Ioaniu talked about her lodgers. As for what happened to her husband, she never breathed a word. No mention that Antonescu put him in the reserves; or that he was later called up by the communists and sent to fight further west, even as far as Czechoslovakia. Everything Vica knew was from Ivona, or from Mrs. Zaharescu, whose husband was a big shot after the war. After a while, though, someone stuck the knife into Zaharescu and he was no longer such a big shot. Or maybe it was just that his turn came to be changed— that's how the communists do things, changing people around from time to time, changing their line about things. Not that she ever worried about the big shots: the ones who got the chop always seemed to end up okay. She's worried about her own husband: the poor guy's old now, nearly seventy-nine, and since he retired they haven't been able to put a cent by for a rainy day. All they've got are those seven thousand lei, and God help them if anything really bad happens. No, she's not worried about the big shots: they're doing well enough even now. That goes for Mrs. Zaharescu too, even if she complains so much that you'd think she's suffered at the hands of the regime. In fact, her place is chocka-block with fancy stuff from abroad, and her elder daughter has gone off to England for good. Some say she left to do a bit of spying, others that it was because she could get everything there, or because her father is no longer as high up as he used to be.

To hell with them all! Some people are born to land on their feet. She's not going to bother about them; she's worried about herself and her husband, that they have only six hundred and fifty lei between them for the electricity, the rent, the television license . . . And she's been catching her death of cold waiting for that loopy woman to come back—waiting for fifty lei, she hopes Ivona chokes on them. And she's so hungry her head is beginning to swim. Some people seem to have had no problems all their life. Or else they don't make a song and dance about them: they're like water off a duck's back. That's what Zaharescu's like. And that strumpet Mrs. Daniel. Or flaky Ivona. Anyone else would throw a fit if she saw her husband out with his floozy all day. But no, it's as if she doesn't give two hoots! Like mother like daughter, that's what I say. Madam Ioaniu had two husbands and buried them both, but that didn't stop her getting on with her life—dolling herself up, playing poker, ambling off to the latest film at the Palace Hall.

You might say her husband, the Ioaniu, struck it lucky: he was demoted to the reserves and avoided being packed off to the Russian front. How many left their bones in some field out there! Yes, you could say he was lucky: he didn't do anything that got up the commies' noses. It was they who called him up, and it was for them that he went to fight in the Tatras. But a fat lot of good it did him; he still ended up croaking in a prison cell—in fifty or fifty-two, who knows when, because the old woman kept mum about it. Kept mum, but everything comes out in the end. She even got to hear about Mrs. Cristide's husband, who also died in prison. She told her how people used to die there like flies: former ministers and lawyers, fat cats and their relatives, as well as ordinary people who just got unlucky. Brătianu was one of those who never came out: they threw him in a cellar and let the rats eat him alive. Apparently they told him to beat it out of the country—either Brătianu himself or a nephew or brother, I'm not really sure—but he said: "A Brătianu doesn't run away!" So he stayed put and went through hell. Maniu also kicked the bucket, and many more of them politicians. Out of the thousands there, only a couple escaped with their lives.

Neither Mrs. Ioaniu nor her daughter heard when Ioaniu died soon after being thrown into prison. They got an official letter only the next summer, and they went to the cemetery to tidy up the grave. They even wanted to have some ceremony, but what did the old woman know about such things? Anyway, they couldn't find where he was buried, among the acres and acres of wooden crosses from the past year. But they did find out he'd died in the infirmary—that he'd fallen ill and refused to eat

anything, because no one gave a damn about him. They'd have looked
after a dog better. He was stubborn and thought that if he starved himself they'd take him to the infirmary, but they just said fine, so he's not
eating, and took him to the infirmary only a few hours before he died.
Someone heard his last words and passed them on to Madam Ioaniu.
He still had his wits about him and knew that he was on his last legs. He
kept pleading with them not to bury him in striped clothes, because he
wasn't a common thief but an honest man, a soldier and general with
any number of medals, who hadn't done anyone any harm. The funny
thing is that someone decided to grant his wish. And that's how Madam
Ioaniu managed to find out where he was buried: a gravedigger remembered one of the dead men being buried in his pajamas; he'd been quite
surprised, especially as it was midwinter and a snowstorm was raging.

So that's how Madam Ioaniu found her husband. She held a com-
memorative feast for him and put a marble cross on his grave, and after
the usual seven years had his remains moved to their family vault at Belu
cemetery. She looked at his teeth and could see it really was him.

Tough as nails she was, that woman, you never saw her shed a tear.
She didn't cry once amid all the horrors: her husband six feet under, her
sister locked up in the can, her daughter out of work, her son-in-law off
with his floozy, the Securitate on their back, and she herself without a
pension or anything else coming in. And, on top of it all, her grandson
Tudor in danger of being kicked out of school.

"You have to know what you want in life, Vica, and to keep at it
through thick and thin. That way you end up achieving something."

God knows what the old woman was thinking when she came out
with that stuff. But, well, in the end things did work out for her. She got
her widow's pension, Tudor passed his final exams at school, and that
jerk of a son-in-law got tired of his floozy and returned to the fold. He's
got another one now, and although he's like a cat on a hot tin roof he
does come home some of the time. One minute he's there, the next he's
got his jacket on and is heading out the door.

"Niki's playing tennis," dumbo Ivona says.

Everyone knows where he is, but everyone pretends to believe him.

"Oh, yeah, tennis balls, eh? They should cut his off rather," Vica said
in a low voice.

How that made the old woman laugh! She didn't like her son-in-law,
but she was too refined ever to say anything. Besides, she'd gone to so

much trouble to find a hubby for her ugly duckling. Where is she off gallivanting right now? What can she have got up to, the stupid bitch? A nice house, all kinds of lovely stuff in it, a pension of four thousand between the two of you, and you're out traipsing the streets. The sly little devil: she wouldn't give you a cent if she could help it. Why does she save it all up—it won't be any use to her in the grave. Sly and miserly, that's why hubby cheats on her like he does. She gets more and more tightfisted as the years go by.

"Go fuck yourself with your fifty lei!"

She stamps her feet to keep warm, then groans as she bends down: what's this, she can't even bend now! In the old days how she'd scrub the floorboards, and lift and carry really heavy things! As for her husband, it's ages since he could tie his laces by himself. It's because of his belly. All he can do is put his shoe on, stick it on a chair, and shout for her:

"Vica! Viiicaaaa! Come and do my laces up!"

"Is that how your mother brought you up, out there in the sticks? Why do you put your shoes on the table like that? Anyone would think you're the village idiot?"

But she comes. He's been a cocky little bugger all these forty years, and she's not going to change him now. With a bad sort like that, you can bang your head against the wall as much as you like, you're never going to change him. And he must weigh more than a hundred kilos! All he has to do is bend over, and a blood vessel might go pop in his brain; he could end up a vegetable or drop dead there and then. That really would be tough.

So, after letting off a bit of steam, she comes over to help him.

She bends over, picks up the plastic bags, folds them, and puts them away in her bag. All in slow motion. She's slowed down a lot since she got older. Still she can't bring herself to leave. To think she's come all that way for nothing. What a fool, she mutters to herself, what a crazy stupid fool! She follows the waste pipe from beneath the staircase, turns into the front yard, and moves in short steps toward the gate. The yard is empty: he's off with his whore, and she's fuck knows where. Never at home, always dashing from place to place! You'd think someone had stuck a red hot pepper up her ass.

No sign of life in the yard—as if everyone has moved. That's how it's looked ever since Tudor fucked off abroad and the old woman started to lose it. She'd been all right until then—over eighty, though people gave her sixty-five—but then the kid didn't come back and she got fluid on the lungs or whatever it was. Vica was doing a lot of work there in those days, and she used to see the old woman lying in bed while her son-in-law was in the dining room rubbing his hands.

"She's going," he would say. "Poor Muti is slipping away."

How he rubbed his hands, how his eyes shone with glee! He'd say the same thing to everyone who came into the house. He said it to her as well, even though they'd hardly spoken to each other before.

"She's going," he said. "Another day or two, or maybe a week, although I doubt it'll be that long. Poor Muti!"

He couldn't contain himself once he saw that his mother-in-law was on her way out. What was going through his head? That Ivona would kick the bucket too and he and his floozy would be left with the house, the jewelry, and all the old woman's savings? That must have been what he was thinking as he walked back and forth rubbing his hands.

"Do you realize? Poor Muti will be gone in two or three days at the most."

But the old woman wasn't having any of it. Whatever it was, fluid on the lungs or some other crap, it didn't manage to polish her off. Her son-in-law rubbed his hands for nothing in the dining room. She stayed in bed and kept going till the end of March, which, as everyone knows, is a bad month—the one when you die if your number's up. Once she'd reached the end of March, the weather got warmer, and she was able to get up. Right away she was shuffling around the house again. Shuffle, shuffle—and the quack came and said she was out of danger. Only she was no longer the Madam Ioaniu she'd been before. She looked her age now: skin and bones, staring eyes, face drooping down. And her voice had such a twang that you couldn't understand what she said. Was it the illness, or because her grandson Tudor had run off like that? She'd brought him up all along, and spoiled him like nobody's business. From when he was tiny until the day he left, she'd been the only one who looked after him.

"That's it, Vica: I won't see him again in this life, and I don't believe there's another. I envy people who can believe in God, in the immortality of the soul, and all that. I was never able to . . ."

She said that one morning when she was sitting in her armchair and they were alone together. She'd given her something to overcast, but she wasn't in the mood and soon gave up. It's a good thing she did, because Vica had to undo everything and start again.

The old woman was sitting and talking about the boy. Tears rolled down her cheeks.

"You know, Vica, when Niki brought Ivona back from the hospital and I saw it was a boy, it was as if I was seeing a baby for the first time. I felt so sorry for him, the little helpless thing! And just then he sneezed, I don't know why—maybe because of the light or a sudden draft. And he made a little movement with his hands, like this—like a grown person. It surprised me so much, I'm not sure why. He had the face of a little old man, like most babies do in their first month, but I thought he was beautiful as I watched him wake up and open his eyes. If I'd believed in God, I'd have said he was a miracle. I couldn't understand how he'd suddenly appeared among us. I felt kind of intimidated by the way he looked around him and seemed to take everything in. Ivona was taking quite a long time to recover from the cesarean, so I was the one who fed him, bathed him, and learned to change his nappies. I wouldn't let anyone else do it instead. And when Ivona was back to normal and started to hover around him, I saw that she didn't have a clue what to do. The poor girl's completely hopeless around the house—clumsier than a man! So, when I saw how she held the baby, and how she didn't have the patience to feed him with a spoon and one day nearly scalded him in the bath, well, God forgive me, but I got really upset with her. It made me angry to think that she was his mother, that she'd brought him into the world."

She sat there motionless, on the soiled slipcover, cushions, and rug, talking for hours about the boy. It was then that she blurted something out about her husband's arrest, and she cried at the memory. Thick tears rolled down her cheeks as she talked and talked . . .

"The times were hard. 'My turn will come soon, very soon,' Lulu told me one evening. He knew the precise moment when they'd come to get him. He'd worked it out logically, from the sequence of arrests in the army, and he wanted to prepare me. We spent days emptying drawers, burning papers, letters, and books, so the Securitate didn't find anything. They took the sofa apart, tore up the floorboards, leafed through books, but they didn't find a thing that could be used against him. Of course, they didn't mind finding you guilty without any evidence, but he wasn't in one of the first batches they arrested. As far as I could make out, they played a waiting game and kept wearing him down with interrogations.

Pretty soon he fell ill. He was never actually tried and sentenced, so it was easy enough to 'rehabilitate' him in the sixties along with all the others . . ."

Ah hah, so that's how you got to draw his pension, Vica thought. And now the old woman was coming out with it: she no longer had any reason to keep it quiet. She only kept her mouth shut for her grandson's sake, so that he might be promoted in his job and allowed to join the Party. After all, Tudor certainly had a brain in his head—and he was ambitious as well. Always with his head in a book. Yes, they hoped things would work out well for him. The first time he went abroad, he just looked around Germany, Holland, or wherever. Mrs. Cristide, their neighbor, said she was sure he'd stay there, but he came back. The next time, though, he left for good, so why should his grandmother have held her tongue any longer?

"If we heard a car stop in the street after dark, we'd sit still and look at each other, white as a sheet. I'll never forget that year as long as I live. How long the seconds seemed as we waited for a knock on the door or the sound of footsteps on the stairs. We didn't dare look out the window to see whether it was that dreaded black van. You know Mr. Romanescu, don't you, Vica? Well, even after ten years in prison, he was still as sharp and humorous as ever. And do you know what he told me? 'At least in prison I didn't have to worry that they'd come and arrest me. Of course, when I heard their steps in the corridor, I'd be worried stiff that it was my turn to be taken for interrogation, or sent to Jilava or one of the camps on the Danube–Black Sea canal. It's ten years now since they let me out, but even today there are some evenings at home when I think I can hear their steps on the stairs. You remember how they used to come up, gun in hand. Nowadays all kinds of young people ask me what it was like—some straight out, others beating around the bush. But I always say I won't tell them anything. I have many reasons for that, and one is that they simply wouldn't understand what it was like . . . ' But Mr. Romanescu did tell me, the poor man. He knew what we'd been through, so he told me how afraid he'd been before his arrest. Some people were so scared they didn't sleep at home: they'd wander the streets, move from pillar to post, bury themselves somewhere in the provinces. I remember one old man who'd start lining up at five every morning: he knew they were hardly likely to arrest you in a line, so he'd spent whole days like that. When he saw one of them sniffing around, he'd go off and join another line. The poor man!

They picked him up in the end, of course . . . A few months after they came for Lulu, just a few months, Margo was denounced and put on trial as well. They kicked Ivona out of college; the Italian School, where she taught a few hours a week, was closed down, and she couldn't find work anywhere. She'd traipse all over Bucharest to give private lessons at three lei an hour—hardly enough to pay for her shoes to be resoled. I also gave some lessons—German and French—as well as looking after Tudor. If it hadn't been for him, I don't think I'd have lived through all the ordeals."

Ah, well, everyone meets their match! She was always a fiery, passionate woman. You could tell that from the way she laughed. And how her eyes would light up at the sight of some food, or when she drew on a cigarette!

"Then I understood how you can tremble with fear that something might happen to a child, how you can suffer with him all the diseases he catches. Something gave me strength, Vica: I felt it every morning. If I'd been a believer I'd have said it was God. Something gave me strength all those years: I don't think I even cried once, so that Ivona wouldn't see me. I had to be healthy and to avoid brooding on everything that had happened. I couldn't moan and groan, or think about all I'd lost, because without me Ivona and her innocent child would be all alone in the world."

She certainly loved the boy—perhaps more than anything else on earth. And, after he'd gone, there was no longer any point in holding her tongue. It wouldn't be of any use to him, because there was no way he was ever going to come home. So the old woman sat there talking and talking. She reckoned that she didn't have long to go and would never set eyes on him again. His mother and that creep of a father would see him—in Germany, Austria, America, wherever he landed up, only he knows where.

But she would never set eyes on him again.

"I'd like to think that I will, but I can't bring myself to believe it. If I had the gift of faith I'd be sure we'll meet again one day. But as it is I feel that it will never happen." And she never did set eyes on him again.

She treads slowly and carefully, her legs weak from hunger, and she has more and more difficulty holding it back. Maybe she should go into a yard or a passage. But how can you do that in broad daylight? At least the streets are no longer a skating rink, and she doesn't have to worry as much as she did in the morning. Even the patches of black ice have melted. All around are luxury villas, detached houses with gardens, sidewalks filled with lime trees—a rich neighborhood, that's for sure, like it always has been. Only now it belongs to the new masters, since the old ones have died or fallen on hard times or cleared off abroad, as they are still doing today. Old masters, new masters—that's the least of her troubles. She's worried she might fall over and break a leg. Yes, over there in the gutter, there are still some patches of ice and some heaps of soot-blackened snow.

She reaches the stop, but there's no sign of a tram. She might as well get her twenty-five bani ready for the second-class fare. She fumbles for her purse in the ragbag, but those goddamn plastic bags get in her way. To hell with them! Why did she saddle herself with them in the first place? It's the purse she wants. Where the hell can it have got to?

Her legs are even more wobbly, and she has an icy feeling in her chest and back ... Where's that purse: she has twenty lei in it, plus some small change ... Thick blood pounds in her temples and forces her to lean against a wall, her bent hand wrapped in a black woolen glove that is holed at the fingertips. The purse—ah, fuck that Ivona and everything to do with her ... She hasn't been through the ragbag since she left Gelu's. Where the hell can that purse have gone? The earth must have swallowed it.

The blood beats like little hammer blows in her temples, and she sees red and black by turns. God help her: she can't be struck down just like that, dead or left a cripple.

The doctor at the clinic checked her blood pressure after poor Ilie kicked the bucket, and ever since she's been carrying Hiposerpil, Carbaxin, and diazepam around with her. If she hadn't looked after herself, she'd have long been resting next to Mummy in the Capra churchyard. She stands by the wall trying to remember, and suddenly it comes to her in a flash. She couldn't have lost it anywhere else than at creepy Ivona's, because only there did she rummage in her ragbag. She must have dropped it when she took out the plastic bags and put them on the steps.

She starts off again, very slowly, then turns the corner again at the boulevard. What a fucking awful day—it's been one thing after another! She soon stops, searches her bag again, and opens out the piece of paper where she keeps her tablets. She takes out one, just one, and swallows it. It's hard without water, like when you stuff grains of wheat down a goose's throat. She folds the piece of paper again and puts it back in her bag, then sets off once more. At least she feels calmer now.

The doctor at the clinic told her:

"Try to avoid getting upset or emotional, Mrs. Delcă."

That's what they told her, and she took it in. Now she's always got some Hiposerpil, Carbaxin, and diazepam on her: she pops one whenever something happens to excite her. It calms her down, and she stops worrying. You've got to look after yourself as much as you can, not do anything that puts a strain on your arteries. If you don't look after yourself, you can be sure no one else will.

When she gets back to the house, the gate is still unlocked, and the mangy tomcat, its fur pulled and twisted by others younger than itself, is still at the foot of the withered pear tree.

"Psst! Clear off, you little devil!" she hisses.

But the skinny creature isn't afraid: it sits there and trains its beady yellow eyes on her. For God's sake, that's no tomcat—it's been sent by the Prince of Darkness, sent to fuck her over good and proper.

At the end of the house wall, she turns into the yard and walks beside the waste pipe toward the steps. Her heart is fluttering wildly, like an anthill, and she has a hollow feeling in her chest. Will she find the purse or not? She had twenty lei in it, plus some loose change. The blood beats like little hammer blows in her temples. God help her, so she doesn't collapse there and lie paralyzed! Her poor old man always tells her:

"You've got to stay alive and look after me—because I'm eight years older and I'm going to die before you."

"Come off it, you old creep!" she replies. "You'll end up burying me, you'll see. You've screwed up my life anyhow, always doing things your way, never giving an inch."

She walks bent over, in tiny steps. No point looking yet—she wouldn't see anything from that distance. Is it there or not? She stops and leans a crooked hand on the wall as she rummages in her bag for the piece of paper with the Carbaxin. She opens it out, takes a tablet, and swallows it. It seems to go down more easily: it's just a question of habit. Carbaxin isn't so strong: poor Ilie, who used to drink coffee after coffee and smoke one cigarette after another, used to take a fistful of Carbaxin at night. He couldn't get to sleep otherwise. Poor Ilie, she can't believe he's bought it; she dreams of him every night.

"Well, that's life: we all go sooner or later," she tells her sister-in-law when she sees her on the brink of tears. As if it helps to cry and hit your head against the wall! Does that solve anything? No, we'll all go sooner or later; not one of us will be left.

Carbaxin is good: it calms her down—except that her heart is still pounding away like a hammer. There are the steps. Nothing on them. No purse. She can't believe her eyes: there goes twenty lei, without counting the loose change, without counting the purse. She sees red, then black, stretches out her arm, and leans against the wall. Good God, so long as something doesn't burst in her brain!

She can't believe it. She keeps circling the empty steps, keeps bending down and feeling under them with her fingers. The devil took it. He must have—otherwise how could it have vanished into thin air? Or else one of those thieves who just come up and steal from you—Bucharest is full of them nowadays. What a fucking awful day! Nothing's gone right, and that loopy Ivona's off walking the streets. What a day! No point circling round and round: the purse isn't there, she can see that, but she can't bring herself to leave. She keeps walking round the steps, looking underneath, bending down, groping with her fingers, as if she can't see well. No, it's not there—that's all there is to it!

Her eyes wander along the waste pipe, and all of a sudden she bursts into peals of laughter—like sobs.

The purse.

What devil could have put it there! Only Old Nick himself could have found a place like that. She'd removed her dentures at her sister-in-law's, because they were too tight, so now she was toothless. But it didn't matter: she could laugh as much as she liked, there wasn't a soul to see her. Her mouth opened from ear to ear as she carefully put the purse at the bottom of her ragbag, under the empty plastic bags. The Good Lord must have taken pity when he saw her suffering! And, although she hardly ever set foot in a church, she'd go and light a candle this Sunday. Once upon a time she used to read the Bible in the evening—you just have to open it and you can find whatever you want: stories, life counseling, you name it. But then her husband bought a television, so now she watches all the movies, whether she likes them or not. The only ones she really enjoys are the love films, in which the lovers get separated and one of them dies, or they find each other again after twenty years, when it's too late. And she lies in bed, crying over their sorrow. She lies there and watches everything, until her husband finally switches off after the popular anthem that closes the programs.

Ah, how the Good Lord looks after her—and she feels a joy she hasn't known for a long time. It's been years and years since she felt so happy and peaceful. Except that she still needs to piss. She could go at the back of the house, but there are paving stones everywhere and they'd get stained. And who knows who might come along . . .

But there's not a soul in the yard.

And it's so quiet. Only up by the attic window some bluish pigeons are flapping their wings. That's where the old woman used to live, with Ivona and her kid, when Ioaniu was arrested and that scumbag Niki left them in the lurch to be with his floozy. It was around that time that she was forced to close her shop and started doing sewing work in people's homes. What else could she have done? She could have joined a dressmaking cooperative, but she didn't like the idea of someone bossing her around. She preferred to have clients of her own, changing from day to day; she never came home empty-handed, and she always had a chat and picked up the latest gossip. They would fight it out with each other over her! They'd once been grand ladies, but now they'd grown old and had to pinch and scrape, driven from their mansions into cellars or attics. One of her clients, a former princess, was reduced to washing bags of dirty clothes for someone or other, in the garage of the house where she'd lived earlier. She had three kids, who were always clinging to her skirt as she worked, and she'd speak to them in French or German. Then she started looking after other people's children, for two lei an hour, all the while boiling, scrubbing, and starching linen, as well as jabbering away in some foreign language. And you'd be surprised how well it worked. The little good-for-nothings were soon yapping in French or English or German . . .

All this too, Vica knew from Madam Ioaniu, who with her own eyes had seen the high-born Madam Cantacuzino slaving over the laundry. She'd been a fine and decent woman, a real princess, even when she was reduced to scrubbing the grime left by all those unwashed bodies. At first the communists had wanted to shoot her husband, the prince, but he escaped with his life and came out of prison twenty years later—there too it was a lottery! It took Ioaniu less than two years to conk out: they didn't even have time to put him on trial. But if it was written that you'd go on living, you could spend twenty years slurping chloride of lime from the slop bucket and still make it through to the end. That's how it was, you see, at Jilava or Sighet or other prisons where there was dysentery: those who slurped chloride of lime managed to stop the runs and come out of it alive. Whether that's true or not, she can't say—she's just repeating what she was told.

At one point you could read about it in the papers, but now you've no way of knowing. People still talk, of course, that's what people are like, but one says this, another something different. Only those who were inside keep their trap shut; they don't want to go back in a hurry.

People died by the hundred or thousand in there, does anyone really know how many? Was anyone even counting? If you were lucky you pulled through, if you weren't you bought it—it was as simple as that. What can she do about it? Doesn't she have enough worries of her own? Does she need to know about anyone else's? The real question now is whether she should go behind the house, or try to hold herself back a little longer.

Some little brats are shouting and yelling nearby. She'd better wait until they're gone. It's enough to split your eardrums: they'd soon shut up if she gave them a few slaps. Their parents are to blame for not bringing them up properly: they only bother about themselves and let them run wild all day with the house key around their neck. The youth of today! They've no sense of shame. Not afraid of anything.

"The world's gone to pot," Madam Ioaniu used to say. "And the longer it lasts, the more it goes to pot. Sure, I used to like having fun when I was young. But nowadays you see them kissing and pawing each other on every street corner. In our time kids never answered their parents back—isn't that right, Vica? I've never had any time for prophets of doom and all that stuff. But do you know what I think? I think mankind is on its way back to barbarism. The barbarians will be upon us. In fact they're already at the gates, and we're all going to become savages again."

Ah, the old woman sure was educated, thank God! She'd read loads of books in her life and remembered every single one. Educated, but with her feet on the ground; everything she did, she did well. That sister of hers, Margo, was more crazy—that's who Ivona must take after. In those days no fair lady would dream of going out to work, instead of being kept by her husband. Only Margo Geblescu would get the itch to go to Paris looking for dress designs and God knows what monkey business on the side. Twice a year she'd waltz off there with her hubby—a good-looking man, but with plenty of screws loose. In Bucharest they lived in Strada Bonaparte, off Kiseleff Gardens if you please; a right old mansion they had there, and the money went through their fingers like water. It was real bedlam. Geblescu was a fast liver, who'd go off to parties and spend all night playing cards and chasing women; one of them must have got her claws into him, because one day he vanished into thin air. That was the last Madam Ioaniu ever said about him. Then the war came, and after that the communists. Did they lock him up? Did he buy it inside? Or is he still alive today? Only he knows.

It was about that time that Vica started going to Madam Ioaniu's and Ivona's. They were completely broke and cut off from the rest of the world, so she worked for them more or less on credit; there was certainly not much in it for her. She had other clients, such as Madam Zaharescu, whose husband was a big director, and Madam Daniel. But she also went to Madam Ioaniu's, having met her as an apprentice at the fashion house of her sister, Margo Geblescu.

Her sister, Margo, no longer had a husband, nor the fashion house on Bulevardul Pache, nor the mansion in Strada Bonaparte. All she had left was an old house and a little vineyard, in Otopeni on the outskirts of Bucharest. That was where she went to live.

"Why don't you go and see my sister?" Mrs. Ioaniu said one day to Vica. "She lives in Otopeni, and she'll give you a nice demijohn of wine."

When she got there she rang the bell. It rang and rang, but no one came to the door. It seemed strange, because she'd heard Madam Ioaniu phone ahead to say that she was coming and would bring a couple of demijohns to fill up.

"Who's there?" She heard the voice just as she was about to say fuck it and leave.

"It's me—Vica."

But in her head: why the fuck are you keeping me here at the door?

"Just a moment."

But it took ages, perhaps half an hour, before Margo finally opened up and gave her the wine. In the bus on the way back, she kept wondering why she had kept her hanging around for so long.

Only years later, after Tudor had grown up and left home, did Madam Ioaniu tell her all about it. Or was it Mrs. Cristide? Anyway, the fact was that Margo, left without a husband, had found herself a boyfriend and was keeping him there hidden from the communists. She'd been a beautiful woman and could still turn a head in the street: not as tall as her sister, but elegant and good-looking, with tiny, size-four shoes. Somehow or other, she managed to keep that man there for years and years: he'd come out only when Riri, the daughter she'd had with her husband, went to school—or at night, when he was allowed out to water the vines. Otherwise he stayed put in his hideout: he didn't cough and didn't fart, except at night, when he wandered around the vineyard and the garden.

The communists found him in the end, though, and carted him off to prison. It was his wife who told them, out of spite that he was hiding at Margo Geblescu's. At the trial, Margo got five years herself for harboring a criminal—and she served every last day. She used to say that she'd got off lightly, but she died not long after she was released. Her daughter Riri then lived for a while with Madam Ioaniu in that crowded attic. She was expelled from school and went to work in a factory, but in the end, well, she got married and settled down in France, where her children are now grown up. Madam Ioaniu once showed her some photos of Riri.

But it was only after Tudor left home that she told all this to Vica. Or was it Mrs. Cristide who told her? Thank God, she'd been completely in the dark when she went to the vineyard with the demijohns—otherwise she'd have been a bundle of nerves. There had been no need for her to be informed about such things. Her own problems were enough. No need for her to know what Margo was up to: it was her business; no one had forced her to get mixed up with a married man, and to keep him hidden in her house! It must have been a funny life for him. What could he have felt when he crept out at night to water the garden and vineyard with a hose, or to stroll alone among the four-o'clocks? It was their business. As you make your bed, so you must lie on it! In any case, the old woman was lying like the devil when she said she'd had no idea what her sister had been hiding. She'd known all right, but kept her trap shut.

She shifts about again, feeling numb from the long wait. Those devils aren't going anywhere in a hurry. She climbs up onto a step, moves back off it—then suddenly all the bluish pigeons fly off with a swishing sound above her head. To hell with the little buggers, what a nerve they've got! They're capable of sitting on your head and leaving their droppings. They even brush against her shoulders, almost touching her face with their wings. Now their flap, flap, flapping deafens her—enough to fill the whole yard. How many of them are there? A lot, so many they make you dizzy. Like clothes on a washing line when the wind's blowing. You little buggers, just wait till that mangy tomcat gets his claws into you! No one leaves any food out for them, so they go around nibbling wherever they can. In the old days Madam Ioaniu used to put some grains on the window ledge—or perhaps some breadcrumbs. And Ivona would mewl at her with that phony voice of hers:

"Oh, Muti, people will think you're Saint Vineri if you keep giving to animals like that."

Phony, but also stingy. Not a soul would ever get anything out of her. Mean and stingy, and always with ants in her pants. Where is she traipsing around at this time of the day? Her mother wasn't like that: she was a woman with brains, who thought things through properly; she knew how to look after herself. If something was in her interest, fine, she'd go for it. If it wasn't in her interest, she wouldn't give it another thought.

She looks all around: not a living soul; yard empty, street deserted; if Ivona shows up, she'll ask her to let her in for five minutes, so she can at least have a pee. Those little devils are climbing all over the fence and look set to stay. If someone stuffed those sticks up their you-know-whats, they'd soon quiet down a bit! Ah, well, she'd better be off then; she's already wasted enough time. At least she's found the purse!

She shuffles down the street. When she gets off the tram, at the market, she'll buy three *mititei* from the stall: two to eat there and then, the other for the old creep, who sometimes feels like having one, the poor thing. He's a poor creep all right, mute and grumpy, but they've been together forty-nine years. So she'll take a sausage back from the market for him.

Okay, not much further now. She'll turn the corner and then it'll just be a couple of steps to the tram. A short ride from there and she'll be home.

Suddenly she stops in amazement.

"What the hell!" she says, standing stock still. Just two meters away, at the front door, no, the midday sun hasn't blinded her, but she can hardly believe her eyes. She doesn't understand it. And the pigeons are off with a whoosh toward the attic.

No, she hasn't come back from town: the fucking bitch is only now going out. Ivona—with her little gray hat, green overcoat, and fox around her neck, that little silvery fox with half its fur missing, which she said they wouldn't take off her hands at the secondhand shop. Only she really knows why she couldn't sell it, 'cuz you can't believe a word she says; she's a born liar, what with that long nozzle and foxy mouth of hers. There she is locking up: two turns of the key, a little sniff, then a quick look left and right! Just like a little vixen! But suddenly her eyes wander toward the back door, and now she too is frozen to the spot.

Frozen, because she's been seen.

Huh, am I going to get even with you! But before she can open her mouth, the vixen is scurrying toward her:

"Oh, it's you, Madam Delcă! Have you been standing there in the yard, without ringing or shouting, without saying a word? Or maybe the bell doesn't work. But I don't understand: this isn't the first time you've been here. Of course I was in, doing all kinds of things. You know what it's like—no end of things to do. There seems to be less time than ever since I retired. I should have gone out long ago, but I just couldn't get away."

I'll make you pay for this, she thinks, but her face gives nothing away. She says nothing, doesn't even glare, acts as if she believes her. She knows what a girl like Ivona deserves: give her a smile, then pocket her dough! It's just a pity she took out her false teeth at Gelu's, so this kid here will see she isn't wearing them if she opens her mouth. But what does it matter? No one's going to run after her at her age—except maybe Old Nick. So she breaks into a broad smile:

"Oh, don't worry about it! I was just passing, on my way from my sister-in-law's, and I thought I'd see what Madam Ivona and Mr. Niki are up to. So what if we hadn't actually bumped into each other? It wasn't a life-or-death kind of thing. Don't give it another thought."

Chapter 5

Ivona

She kept her coat on, just removing the fox fur and putting it on an arm-chair next to her gray felt hat.

She kept her coat on so that Vica would realize she was in a hurry. They'd come in for five minutes, just five minutes, because she'd asked her. It was the umpteenth time she'd pulled this stunt: she doesn't show up when you're expecting her, but she just comes and rings the bell when you're up to your eyes in work. And she rings and rings, doesn't go away! She's so sly, the way simple people are; they know which side their bread is buttered on. And what a nerve they have! What insolence! They've got it into their heads that their turn has come. Wherever you go, the streets are full of country bumpkins, while people of quality are harder and harder to find. Every day you hear of someone falling ill or dying, not to mention all those who've packed up and gone abroad.

It's true that it was worse twenty years ago, when you were afraid the police would come knocking on your door, or some ruffian would shout "bourgeois scum" after you in the street. They didn't need to hear you speaking French with a friend; there were any number of things they could go on to work out that you were refined and cultivated. Nowadays they leave you alone, but you just have to look at their faces in the street, or hear the way they speak among themselves. They've swept away a whole world that knew the meaning of good manners. Young people have been brought up badly, with results that are there for everyone to see. Even the few who knew their place and had an inkling of good sense are getting more and more like the rest every day. Take this shameless old woman Vica, for example, who worms her way into a little corner and won't come out again. To land yourself on someone like that, ringing their bell nonstop for an hour, then pretend to go away only to sneak back and spy on them from around the corner: no well-bred person would ever engage in that kind of farce!

Moving nervously, she knocks her elbow against a photo album left carelessly on the edge of the coffee table. The day before yesterday she dusted it down and spent some time examining its dark-red leather cover. What fine solid objects they produced a hundred years ago! People had the time and patience to do everything with such care. Who was it who telephoned her as she was leafing through the album and made her leave it lying there? No doubt that pest Mrs. Cristide. Anyway, her careless movement now sends it flying: she tries to catch it, but she is too nervous and it slips through her trembling hands. Ugh, the photos will come unstuck and scatter all over the place! It's all Vica's fault: she's to blame for everything that's gone wrong today.

None of the photos has come loose, thank God; they were stuck down well. Thank God . . . She bends down, picks up the album, and puts it back in its place. Only a small card remains on the carpet, scarcely larger than a visiting card. An off-white, yellowed card. She bends down again and picks it up:

> *With best wishes for the New Year, 1914*
> *Sophie and . . .*

The second signature is illegible. It's written in black ink, with sharply pointed letters—a man's handwriting. And just as she is wondering whose it could be, she recognizes the second signature. It's so familiar to her, and it produces the same reaction in her: a brief spasm in her chest, a painful astonishment, a glimmer of hope. It's his signature, yes, his writing—which means he might come again, might be coming back. But, at that very moment, she feels sad and surprised that she could have such a thought.

Only the sense of astonishment lingers as she walks impatiently up and down the living room. How can it happen that nothing remains of a man? She sees the little white bag stained with wine and dark slime, and her own long dry fingers placing it in the funeral box. How is it possible that nothing remains of a man, yet here are the traces of his hand before your eyes, as if he wrote them an hour or two ago? As if he could still come back . . .

So she had hoped then, at eleven years of age, as she lit a large candle and prayed for an hour at a time to the Sainte-Vierge, the patron of the Notre Dame *lycée* that she attended. So much time had passed since then, but she still dreamed of him night after night—of that huge bedroom filled with solid walnut, where he lay between the tall bedposts amid bulging embroidered pillows. He was gasping for breath. Sometimes he had an open wound at his neck, or else there were suspicious greenish stains on his cheeks. They probably came from the burial vault where he'd been kept for so long. At least that's what went through her head. She never actually said it to him.

"You're not dead," she said each time in her dream.

And she stood on tiptoe so that he could kiss her on the forehead.

"You're not dead," she whispered encouragingly. "We were all mistaken: Muti, you, me. But now everything's right again, and you're going to get better."

He was half-raised between the pillows, so that he could breathe more easily. Close up, she recognized the whistling sound of his respiration.

Her frail dry fingers, the nails less shiny than in her youth but still perfectly oval, pressed on the yellowed business card:

JULIETTA. *Photographer by appointment to the Royal Court.*
Negatives retained for future prints and enlargements.

How she loved poor Papa. Now she can only just make out his long pointed handwriting and no longer remembers his normal way of speaking; all she can still hear is his hoarse, whistling, muffled voice as he said to her:

"Have a good trip!"

She was standing at his bedroom door, about to leave for a stay in the country, near Sinaia, with Tante Margot and Oncle Alexandre. That summer, they told her, Muti would stay with Papa in Bucharest—which was why they hadn't covered the windows with that blue paper that used to turn yellow from the sun by the time they returned.

The luggage chests were waiting downstairs, and she, Ivona—or rather, "Yvonne"—was dressed and ready: little hat on her head, coat buttoned from top to bottom, *sac à main* strung around her delicate wrist. Dressed and ready, leaning awkwardly against the tall white half-open door of his bedroom.

"Yvonne!" Muti called up, probably from the foot of the stairs.

"Yvoonne! Come down at once! Here, Maria, take the hatboxes before you forget, and go and put them in the motorcar. Make sure you keep them straight, so the feathers don't get crumpled. Then go upstairs and find out what's keeping Yvonne."

There was no need to send anyone upstairs. She was dressed and ready: she'd heard the automobile engine under the window, heard the voice of Tante Margot in reply to Muti.

"There's no point, *ma chère*, we'll be late anyway. You know Alexandru's habits . . ."

She heard everything, but she wasn't going to shout back: "Okay, coming . . . ," wasn't going to race away downstairs from her sick father's bedroom. Leaning against the half-open door, she watched as he struggled to raise himself up on the pillows, trying to smile but managing no more than a grimace with his unnaturally yellow face; as he swung his trembling legs off the bed—long weak legs, white and hairless—and fumbled with his feet for his slippers, so that he wouldn't have to use up his little remaining strength by bending down; as he came slowly toward her, his back bent under a dressing gown draped over his shoulders, dragging his feet and catching them in the overlong tails of his nightshirt; as he held onto the furniture, short of breath, and tried to put a smile on his unnaturally yellow face, while his sparse, flimsy gray hair became moist with the effort and stuck to his scalp. It was her father, but she didn't feel like rushing to embrace him. She stood glued to the door, gripping tightly the ornate golden handle; she didn't feel like kissing him. In fact Muti had forbidden it for some months, and now she felt a strange tightness in her chest as he drew closer. A strange tightness in her chest, a slight fear, but also a shameful, improper repulsion at the thought that he might touch her.

"Have a good trip," he said hoarsely, without advancing further.

It was as if he suddenly realized that he didn't have the strength to reach the door.

"*Au revoir, papa,*" she said, in a whisper that seemed to her shrill, hurried, and unnaturally loud.

She turned on her heels, relieved that she was about to go down the wooden staircase, and felt her tartan traveling skirt swirl beneath her coat. But she was still gripping the door handle, warm beneath her touch, when she heard his hoarse whistling:

"A safe journey . . . in life . . ."

Yes, of course, just when she turned away and was on the point of leaving, he plucked up the courage to utter that emotional phrase of which he felt ashamed, but which she still remembered fifty years later. It was perhaps the only note of pathos ever sounded by that distant, meticulous, and fearful man—a father she loved so much, though later no one spoke of him except in conventional phrases and gestures. He had kept hoping that he would never have to utter that phrase. How often he had turned it over in his mind during long nights of croaking for breath, when he would struggle to sit up and spit into a white bowl that was never placed at the right distance, or during days when his tired hand would stretch out for the cord and no one would be there at the moment when he felt bad and needed them most—either Sophie was out visiting with Margo, or Maria was chattering with the coachman in the kitchen, or the soldier sent by his friend Colonel Ioaniu was out strolling with their Hungarian maid, or the nurse had gone to evening mass. At such moments he found himself alone in a house normally filled with people, where they no longer locked the front door because the doctor might be needed any time or the priest might come once again to administer Communion.

How he must have turned that pathetic phrase over in his mind as the night nurse (or Maria, or the soldier) helped him to sit on the edge of the bed with his legs dangling—the only position in which his breathing came a little more easily. He would spend hour after hour like that, his dressing gown wrapped around his shoulders over a long nightshirt, his body soaked with a sticky sweat, his temples thundering with blood—waiting for the gray streak of dawn that came earlier and earlier as summer approached, waiting for the sound of horses' hooves on the paving, the swish of carriage wheels, the clang of milk crates. That was always the hour at which he felt a little better, when the blood-red aurora turned rosy-pink and the chirping of the birds in the garden became deafening. He slipped gently back into bed with a sigh and stretched out a trembling hand to ring for Maria to come; she would draw the heavy curtains and open the windows wide, and he would breathe in little mouthfuls of fresh June air.

How much she must have loved him, if still today, fifty years later, she has an absurd, confused hope that he might come back—that the world might return to exactly how it was then!

Exactly as it was then: the same day, just before the feast of Saint Constantine and Saint Elena, when Muti, holding a slightly faded parasol, moved along the flower beds in the garden and bent down here and there to straighten a bud with her gloved hand after the previous night's rain; while she, Ivona, went on with her piano exercises, unable to stop herself casting impatient little glances out of the window: where has she got to? has she reached the line of shadow that divides the yard into two? And she hit a wrong note, *da capo* again, and at that very moment an organ grinder, an old man who'd somehow wandered off Kiseleff Avenue, passed beneath the window and drowned out her piano with the notes of "And who in days of old . . ." *Da capo,* again *da capo*! "When my love and I were alone in the world . . ."

Then came the sound of a carriage: *Papa!*

"*Mais voyons, Yvonne . . . Soyez attentive!*"

It was cool and shady indoors, and there was a vague odor of peonies. The day before, Papa had attached rings of cherry to her ears.

"*Ça lui donne un drôle d'air,*" Muti said disapprovingly.

In fact she meant something else, something that little Yvonne understood well enough: that she would stain her organdy dress, and that she should go to the fence and take a look at Ionica, the schoolmaster's daughter, who also had cherry rings on her ears. Yes, if Muti goes to visit someone, if Mademoiselle Lisette has an appointment at the milliner's, and if Madam Ana falls asleep over her knitting, then Yvonne will be able to take up position at the fence and watch all the other children in the neighborhood, who are allowed to put cherry rings on their ears and to play knucklebones on the wasteland.

"*Mais, voyons,*" Mademoiselle Lisette said, "*soyez attentive!*"

The rubber-wheeled carriage glides off from the front gate. The same world: Muti in the garden pavilion covered with ivy and honeysuckle; flowers whose clever white fingers stick shyly to one another and whose speckled tongue is coated with a pollen fleece.

"What's that flower called?" she asks.

"*Chèvrefeuille . . . ,*" Muti replies absent-mindedly, pulling her cardigan tightly around her shoulders. Then: "The romance began during a holiday in the mountains, at Govora."

Muti looks around somewhat uneasily. Is it the look of a mother worried because she's lost sight of her child, or of a woman afraid that she has been overheard?

Yvonne isn't listening. She understands everything, but she's bored by the stories that Muti and Tante Margot keep telling. She runs toward the house, her arms spread wide like a bird's wings. She flies toward the house and feels the scent of roses and four-o'clocks in her nostrils; it will soon be dark, but Papa still isn't home. She stops breathless in the hallway, her image reflected in fragments in the little squares of the gilded mirror: a ghastly strip of sticking plaster on her head, a grazed knee, a pallid half-face, the distorted collar of her little navy-blue dress ... As she hovers there waiting for Papa, she glances uneasily at the blue enamel frame of the clock. She looks more closely: she still has to make an effort to read the roman numerals between which the clock's golden hands appear stuck. On the blue enamel of the frame, surrounded by gilded floral wreaths, a shepherd and shepherdess—she wearing a blonde wig and a pink balloon-shaped dress, he with tight-fitting white stockings—face each other self-consciously in an elegant ceremonial posture, one on either side of the frame.

Again the swish of wheels on paving stone, the snorting of horses, and the sound of footsteps ...

Papa's lacquered shoes and glazed leather gloves. He gives his hat and ivory-handled cane to Grigore, while Yvonne rises on tiptoe for him to kiss her on the cheek.

"Back so soon?" Muti says, surprised.

She comes up the path with Margot, leaning over from time to time to whisper something that makes them both burst into laughter.

"You look like two girls in a boarding school telling each other secrets," Papa observes in a paternal tone.

"You exaggerate," Muti retorts.

"You exaggerate": that's one of her pet expressions. Restrain yourself, stop exaggerating, why do you get so excited? she tells Papa.

"You exaggerate. That little neurasthenia of yours always makes you exaggerate."

She smiles as she says it, but her severe look is urging Papa to be more tactful. The engine of Jean's automobile can be heard: he's such a devoted friend, so cultivated and distinguished, and he's made such a fine political career for himself. Papa turns his ivory-white cigarette holder in his long bony fingers. He looks unhappy as he listens to Muti in silence, until someone—who can it be?—sneaks alongside him unnoticed. A head with a strip of sticking plaster on it rests against his elbow; he takes fright and wonders what is going on, whose head it could be.

How many years had to pass before she understood—*hélas*—that the clock can never be turned back; that Papa would never return from the distant voyage about which Muti spoke to her when she appeared out of the blue in Sinaia to take her back from holiday.

"What's that funny smell?" she asked as she stepped into the hall.

There was indeed an unusual smell, all over the house: a smell of flowers, but of too many kinds, mixed together with candle wax and incense like in an Orthodox church. And there was something else too, which made her feel a little sick. She took deep breaths, as if making a point, her nostrils flaring more and more. Like a little horse, she thought, that's what Papa would have said to her:

"Why are you snorting like a little horse?" he would have said, stroking her on the head.

Her loud breathing and jerky movements, jerkier than usual, must have been quite a success, because all eyes were on her. Mademoiselle Lisette, Muti, Tante Margot, Maria . . . And her success made her breathe even louder, in her desire to be the center of attention. The furniture, the staircase, and all the woodwork creaked; it was cold and damp in the house, and all the mirrors were covered up.

How well she remembers that long rainy Sunday, the rushing sound in the gutters, the ticking of the blue enamel clock with its frozen shepherd and shepherdess, and the curious, admiring way in which everyone looked at her: yes, on that day she, not Muti, was the most important person in the house! She heard the rain beating against the windows, thudding against the paving stones, as she climbed the stairs to her room. She pushed on the ornate door handle, went in, and sat on a stool in front of the mirror. She'd been hoping to see someone else there. Each time she sat in front of the mirror she had a vague, absurd hope that she would see herself looking differently from how she knew she looked. She'd always hated her face—either since she first saw it in a mirror, or since she first understood what was being said about her in French.

"*Dommage! Elle n'a rien de Sophie . . . Dommage qu'elle ressemble tant à son père . . . Mais elle fait de son mieux . . . elle est bien gentille.*"

She sat on the stool and looked at herself in the mirror. It had once been Tante Margot's boudoir, before she married, and Muti had changed nothing since then: the old silver jewelry box, lying on the studiously untidy dressing table inlaid with mother-of-pearl, still didn't close properly and revealed the same coral and amber necklaces. After all, Yvonne was a dutiful child, and you could be sure that she wouldn't touch anything if it wasn't allowed. She looked in the black ebony-framed mirror, which went right up to the ceiling; the mother-of-pearl beamed pink streaks, *bleu-vert* streaks, into the half-shadow of the room, while a dim yellow light came in through the windows. Yvonne had always been a dutiful child, who never pulled the eyes or the hair from her dolls, and now too she just sat there and looked at herself in the mirror. No, the strange event that had happened while she was away had not brought about any change in her face.

A pity, a real pity—she was the same as always.

As Muti said, her new black velvet dress did not do her justice: it made her complexion even more sallow, and her horribly thin and brittle hair, which sprouted like down on her forehead, hung more sparse and lusterless than ever. She stared at herself long and hard, then took a silver-framed hand mirror and turned it this way and that to catch herself in profile, eventually holding it at an oblique angle. But she looked even worse like that. The drizzle had turned into thundering rain outside, and a damp mist clouded over the windows and hid from view the ivy and honeysuckle on the pavilion at the bottom of the garden. It was cold, very cold. Oncle Alexandre had left with the car and was due back soon to take Muti and Tante Margot on a visit somewhere. The sleeves of her black dress accentuated her thin hands and flimsy fingers, and she clasped them together in despair. How much longer would she have to wait until Papa returned from his journey? Tears began to flow freely. She cried in spite of herself, with no sighs and no sobs. She cried delicately, as young ladies do, without twisting her face and having first gently closed her bedroom door.

"Just a few little alterations, that's all," Tante Margot said. "And a little adjustment at the waist. I'll send you someone or other . . ."

"No, not someone or other!" Muti protested. "Remember what happened to me last time!"

"What I meant was I'll send whoever you like. Tell me who."

"How should I know?" Muti muttered. "Of course I don't expect your top seamstress for such a trifle—I think Vica should be able to manage it. She's nimble enough and knows her place. And she's also neat and tidy . . ."

She always flew down the stairs to greet Papa, arms outstretched, frisking like a little horse. Why was she so light-footed, even when her eyes were filled with tears? Now they were rolling down her face, warm and copious, while others misted her eyes as the rain misted the windows outside. It upset her so much, and she looked so awful in the mirror . . . She felt that her nose must be swelling and turning red, but then suddenly she no longer cared. It would have been so nice to find Papa at home: he'd be going right now into his oak-paneled study on the first floor, where Muti had put some recently purchased armchairs and a leather club sofa. She would have entered on tiptoe and put her hands over his eyes, or slipped her head under his arm. He would then have fidgeted with all the objects on his desk: his papers, the blotting pad, the paper knife, the huge bronze inkwell, as if he was startled and taking a long time to work out who she was.

"What's all this, young lady?" he would exclaim, giving her a sharp look.

But she knew that it was all in jest.

"How is it possible that a cultivated and intelligent young lady cannot find a pleasant way to use her time without getting bored? Maybe we should go for a little carriage ride to the racetrack. Or we could get off somewhere and make our way on foot to a patisserie. Which one would you prefer: Nestor's, Angelescu's? What are you in the mood for today: Indianas or Carolinas?

She went downstairs so softly that neither Muti nor Tante Margot heard her. As she turned onto the last flight, she crouched down to make herself invisible, her head resting on her bony, boyish knees, her eyes fixed on the golden stuccoed walls. Her tears dried up as suddenly as they had appeared. She greedily inhaled the new odor of her body—a strong, slightly acidic odor, which rose from between her thighs. She tried to breathe more slowly and gently, pricking up her ears to catch what they said.

"I knew she was attached to him in a way that wasn't quite normal. You saw the jealous scenes she put on for me when she was little . . . I remember once when she sneaked in like a puny little cur and I felt a terrible pain in my finger where she'd bitten me till the blood came. That's why I've tried to protect her, that's why I've been careful to avoid bringing her along these days. The rest of the family blame me for it, but I'm convinced I'm doing the right thing."

"The comments about the funeral were very favorable, you were wrong to be worried . . . ," Tante Margot broke in. She spoke hurriedly but in a friendly tone, as she did when she wanted to change the subject.

"Exactly as it should have been—a mixture of ceremony and sobriety. The same was true of the speeches, although I wasn't too keen on the one by the students' representative. In fact, the students made a very bad impression by going off to the Hippodrome for their ritual Battle of Flowers. Alexandru showed me a short item in the paper: *Romanian students earned a black mark for themselves by the way they behaved.* Poor Ștefan was right when he said that the custom in this country is to be ungrateful toward anyone working for the public good. 'From an ungrateful nation . . . ': do you remember?"

"I always scolded Ștefan for not drawing a line between family and strangers! How can you expect anything of strangers when your first obligation as a man is to your family, not to the people in general? I mean . . . So, when your own daughter . . ."

"But Sophie, poor Yvonne is just a kid."

"A kid, maybe, but *terriblement égoïste.* Believe me, I don't like to talk about it—and in front of anyone else I wouldn't say a word. But at least if she'd asked me something about him! She knew what state he was in when she left, but no, not a single question. She's not interested in anything but herself. After all, there are some things that children can sense, things they can figure out, even if adults keep silent to spare them the pain. I see you're not coming back at me: that must mean you disagree. Well, do you know what your pet is doing right now? For the last hour she's been in her room dolling herself up and admiring herself in the mirror? I glanced in to see what she was up to, because that kind of silence worries me—I was afraid she might be in shock, that she'd made some connection between Ștefan's illness, her holiday, her dresses . . . But no, the apple of his eye is sitting there lost in admiration! It would have been a cruel blow for him to see her, and at least the Almighty spared him that. You've no idea how painful it is for me to be telling you all this!"

"Well, if she was looking at herself in the mirror, that is a little . . ."

Tante Margot conceded it *à contre-coeur,* sitting cross-legged in an armchair with a cigarette holder in her right hand. Meanwhile her left hand toyed with a pearl necklace as long as a rosary—one of those double necklaces that women were then beginning to wear with fashionably short, low-waisted dresses.

"Still, as a mother, you shouldn't worry and fret like that. When you have a child you have to think of her, not of yourself. *Tant mieux* if she doesn't get worked up easily. *Tant mieux*—she won't suffer so much in life."

Poor Tante Margot: she spoke as if she already knew what it was to suffer. But she did it with that vamp-like air she had developed a few years after she married: hair cut short, parting at the side, fringe hanging down to her eyebrows, silk scarf tied coquettishly at the back, short skirt showing little knees tightly wrapped in smoky silk stockings.

She spoke as if she already knew what suffering was. No, it was still too soon, even for her: Alexandru's escapades, his fame as a skirt-chaser, were trivial matters. A good fifteen years would pass before she knew the meaning of fear and loneliness, of poverty, prison, and humiliation.

"I wonder," Muti half-whispered. It was her usual reply when she was thinking of something else.

She had her hat on and was pulling a long black veil over her face, quite unlike the little picot-edged veil she was in the habit of wearing.

"Yvonne!" she shouted suddenly in a different voice. "Yvonne!"

She crawled back up into the shadow of the banister. Inexplicable streaks of dust remained on her black velvet dress. Why—the question flashed through her mind—hasn't the house been swept for days? The dull pounding of her heart shook her frame as she continued on all fours up the staircase. So long as a door doesn't open now! So long as Maria or Madame Ana or Mademoiselle Lisette or God knows who doesn't suddenly appear.

She slowly tiptoed back into her room, threw herself on the bed and stopped up her ears. For a long time she let Muti go on calling her.

She keeps her back to the clock to avoid panicking, but she can't stop herself counting its chimes as she nervously presses her thin lips together and crushes the visiting card between her fingers. The weak puffs of her rushed breathing become entangled in the unbearably even striking of the clock.

And then, silence—such silence that it was possible to hear the woodwork creak, or the piddling sound made by that impudent Vica in the bathroom. Midday: if she isn't gone in ten minutes, she may never go.

By the time she gets to the center all the shops will be shut . . . Maybe she should go and knock on the bathroom door: something might have happened to the old bag; it's not at all out of the question. In fact, given her age and her weight, it's a real miracle she's got away with it all this time. How often she and Muti have warned her.

"Be more careful with your diet, Madam Delcă. After a certain age, you must cut right down on fat and sugar. Think of your blood pressure and your cholesterol. You can't have pork chops every day, however fond your husband is of them."

"Don't make me laugh! When do you think was the last time I had pork chops? It's months and months since I last had more than a tiny scrap of meat."

That was always how she shut them up.

She tries to suppress the shiver of disgust that comes over her when she imagines what might be happening in the bathroom. The day after tomorrow, when Leana comes, she'll get her to clean more carefully than usual—with disinfectant. It would have been better if she'd opened the door right away! Given her the money and got rid of her! Like this, she'll still be forced to cough up, and she'll have wasted her morning as well. Forced? Is that really how it is? You want to help someone out, someone you've known all your life, and you end up under their thumb. You end up giving them a fortune, just to get them off your back. As Niki says, that's always what happens to generous people. "You have to understand that that's what charity means," he teases her. "*Tu te fais avoir!*"

Niki with his practical sense, Niki who knows the way of the world so well . . . It's from him that she's learned to look at things more lucidly—with difficulty and late in life, to be sure, but learn it she did in the end. She no longer has any illusions about this old woman, for example, as she used to have in the past. It's not affection or gratitude that makes her always come ahead of the day they agreed on for handing over the money. No, she's made it part of her schedule to come a week or ten days early, so that she can get twice as much. A hundred lei instead of fifty. She hasn't any scruples, as any decent, well-brought-up person would have. Simple people are incredibly crafty—crafty and impudent! And they certainly know when something's in their interest. They're not like us, not like cultivated people: they don't get caught up in the web of feelings or ideals; no one ever brought them up that way when they were children. No, they know which side their bread is buttered on: they never lose sight of their interests, and follow them at every turn. Of course, they can sometimes put on a show of devotion or gratitude, but only to cheat you more in the future.

That's what Niki often explains to her.

"I could write a whole novel...What am I saying? I could write twenty novels about all I've seen in my lifetime! Ten, twenty novels!"

And he would have written them if things had not taken such a turn for the worse. Niki has read so much history and philosophy, and seen so much in his professional work as a lawyer. She, emotional and idealistic as she is, would have been incapable of making the most banal speech in court. But Niki explained to her that to be a lawyer is to know people as they are in reality, not as they claim to be. It's a profession that has disappeared now, like so many others. What did it mean to be a lawyer after 1946, when the verdict was known before you set foot in court and all the witnesses were acting on instructions? What was the point once trials were held behind closed doors? Niki would have written novels if they had been normal times, because he's seen a lot of things and is so, so talented! Talented both as a writer and as an actor: always au fait with the latest funny stories, able to adapt them to any situation and to interpret them . . . With his sense of humor, he can go anywhere and hold the fort. And he always knows the latest gossip, because he has a wide circle of contacts. Sometimes he still springs a surprise on her, like when he took her on a social visit somewhere near the Armenian Church. Who was he chatting with there? One of those up-and-coming writers in the communists' good books: she's seen him many times since then on television, noticed his Party line articles in *Scînteia*—what the devil's his name, it's on the tip of her tongue? Anyway, that time he was talking about his various trips abroad.

Niki also liked the company of painters and enjoyed going to their studios. Doesn't he have some Mirea canvases carefully rolled up in his office?

"Wait and see the price they'll fetch one day," he tells her from time to time.

She is the soul of discretion, and wouldn't dream of moving a needle or opening a drawer in his office—not only because it would be unseemly, but because she isn't curious by nature. She's interested in her dear little Tudor, in Niki, in Muti when she was alive, in a few friends—and that's all. The rest of the world doesn't really matter for her. But she finds it flattering that Niki has so many acquaintances—all the people he's met playing tennis or in his work as a lawyer. Muti had some prejudices against Niki, especially after they arrested *pauvre* Tante Margot.

She was the only one who thought there was something suspicious about his curiosity and his numerous acquaintances. But, of course, she was wrong to be apprehensive. That's what they've reduced people to—they no longer trust their own family!

"It's not normal that an honest man should go chasing after all those guttersnipes. He doesn't just put up with them: he can't wait to be off socializing with them. Forgive me for saying this, Yvonne!"

How unjust Muti was when she said such things! After all, how can people live if they don't trust one another? The communists are at their most Machiavellian when they make everyone suspect everyone else: that's the basis of their power in the end! Who taught her this? Well, none other than Niki! When she sees him take such an interest in others, and form such correct judgments about them, she can't understand how anyone could imagine he was playing the Securitate's game. Poor Niki, with his intuition, he must have sensed Muti's suspicions—especially in the last years of her life, when her mind wandered more and more and she dropped hints left, right, and center. God, how embarrassing it was! It wouldn't be surprising if she said the same stuff to that old woman in there, who shows no signs of ever coming out. Ah, these simple people: if we weren't so easygoing with them, maybe they wouldn't be so impudent. Poor Muti really went out of control toward the end. And Niki, so sensitive and with such insight, must have been aware. Maybe something actually reached his ears. He never gave any sign of it, though. No one could say that his behavior changed for the worse in any way; Muti never heard him say an unkind word about her. Nor did he ever try to explain himself—as if Niki ever explains anything! That's his temperament: discreet, not secretive. But is there anyone alive more willing to accept the blame?

"It's my fault, dear, all my fault," he whispers.

He's not capable of saying any more. But, being a woman, she's learned to guess it. Despite all the many things that have happened, she continues to have complete confidence in Niki. Muti, for example, couldn't grasp how someone can be curious by nature, without having a special reason; how someone can enjoy being well informed. No doubt that was a pleasure Niki developed through his profession. As for his little flirtations, Muti proved to be the most intolerant person imaginable. She couldn't accept that not everyone's made the same, that men in particular sometimes need a bit of a change, that this doesn't necessarily affect how they feel, that it's a little diversion from which they usually come back more relaxed and more attentive, because in the end they do feel a sense of guilt. But no, Muti insisted that it wasn't at all pleasant for everyone to know that your husband is a *coureur.* However youthful in spirit Muti may have been, appearances were the important thing in life for her.

"If you put all your energy into keeping up appearances," she used to say, "you'll succeed in living in a way that's right and proper."

Yes, but not everyone's the same. You can't judge all men by the standards of Uncle Georges, who used up all his energy at work, had the correctness of an army officer, and for the rest remained like a child even late in life. Of course, a man like that is much easier to handle than one who's as active and sociable as Niki is. It's probably because of that temperament that Niki was never able to get down to writing. When you're lively and dynamic by nature, it's hard to be satisfied with such a sedentary existence. Writing isn't the right hobby for Niki—she's convinced of that, even if she doesn't tell him so in as many words. Besides, if you know you haven't a hope in hell of getting published, what's the point of wasting your time? She never contradicted him, though. On the contrary, she let him dream on.

"When I retire," Niki promised, "I'll sit down and write. Sure, I won't find anyone to publish it. If the censor doesn't like what you write, if it isn't all about the Party and the working class, you can go whistle for a publisher. But I'll write for my own pleasure. All my life I've had to keep putting it off, but when I retire I'll finally have the time."

Of course she encouraged him. "Naturally you should get down to writing something, with your talent and your knowledge of people." People's character often changes after they retire: men in particular sink into depression, start to have dark thoughts. But you shouldn't let yourself go, when you can finally breathe more easily after a lifetime of worries. You have to learn to look on the bright side of things. Look how difficult it is without Tudor—God alone knows how difficult—but we have to remember that it's turned out well for him. He's managed to achieve a lot on his own: to find a job in the West, where it's not as easy as some people think. At least no one will blame him there except for things he does himself. At least he knows that he's free. At least he can travel. At least he has what he'd never have got here in a whole lifetime. At least . . .

She suddenly throws the visiting card into the ashtray, having crumpled it in her hand like a fool. She turns around to look at the clock, almost sure that she'll no longer have time to go out today. Not that she has such a lot to do: the only thing on her agenda is Tsutsu's religious wedding in the evening, but it annoys her to let time go by aimlessly like this.

Isn't something moving there in the bathroom? As if . . .

She turns and picks up the ashtray from the little coffee table, which has remained in that dark corner of the lounge. The table is still intact, with its little wheels, its serving tray, and its old gold inlay that makes it look like a chessboard. The poor little table! All it needs is a coat of varnish and a few missing screws and it would be as good as new. A proper joiner, who knew what he was doing, wouldn't take long to fix it. But where can you find people today who really know their trade?

"As soon as Petruța leaves," Muti dreamed, "the very next day, I'll ask my joiner to come and see to the lounge: the little coffee table, the *secrétaire,* the chipped sideboard—and then, only then, the furniture in the dining room. I'll do it as soon as they move out."

How many years lost waiting to come back down from the attic into their own home! Niki too went to so much trouble, approached one acquaintance after another. Only someone as mistrustful as Muti could have doubted him! Only she could have thought that, when he went to ask a contact at the ministry to put in a word for them, all he did was bluff his way into the building, bluff his way past security, leaving you to wait outside, then climb the stairs, go to the toilet, prance about a bit in the corridors, and finally come back down, full of himself, and tell you he'd seen someone important whose name he unfortunately couldn't reveal. That was Muti's theory—another example of how unjust she was toward Niki. So what if none of their applications ever received an answer? Wasn't the same true for everyone during those years? After Uncle Georges went the way of all flesh, they continued to make submissions and to wait up there in the cramped attic; they'd bump into the tenants on their way down to wash in the servants' washroom, or as they cleaned the staircase of the filth that others had left behind, always walking timidly on tiptoe and speaking in a low voice . . .

"Switch off the radio," Muti would say, breathless from the climb. "Petruța's prowling around again. Switch it off, I tell you. I don't understand how anyone in possession of their faculties can be so careless.

Anyway, what's the point of listening to Voice of America? Sandu Geblescu was right: the Americans sold us down the river long ago."

Muti, like everyone, thought for a time that things would get better. But then she stopped hoping for anything, except that Tudor would finish school, that the tenants who'd been forced on them would move out, and that she'd be able to get the joiner, whom she'd known all her life, to come and repair the old furniture.

"They'll move soon," she said, "and then I'll get my joiner to come." They'd move soon because they were raising their sights all the time as he went up the hierarchy.

With him it wasn't so outrageous, but his wife left you speechless. Wasn't she the same peasant woman who had appeared at their door one day with a wooden trunk in one hand, her thin braids tied together in a bun on her head? The woman who went about the house barefoot, her heels cracked, blowing her nose with her fingers in the yard? And now here she was a factory manager, always rushed off her feet, with no time to remember that it was Muti who taught her to use a handkerchief and toothbrush and persuaded her to stop treating her scalp with kerosene.

"Since it was you who educated her, you could teach her to say *cuvette* instead of *guivetă* for a washbasin," Niki once chipped in.

Childish irony on Niki's part . . . But he was right to think that Muti was being naive for once. How could she think you can change the psychology of such people by treating them as equals—or by humiliating yourself and confiding in them? It was naive to imagine you can win their trust, or even their good will. No, they're more cunning than we are, and in any case they won't believe us. That's precisely how they've got where they are now, by believing less than anyone else. They're convinced that everything is a lie, that everyone is a liar. They're the ones who have no illusions about anything.

"I don't expect anything good from them," Muti said sometimes, "but I hope they won't do us any harm at least. If they were given our place to live in, I'm sure it was so they would spy on us. Don't forget they landed on us just at the time when poor Margot was arrested."

"That was a long time ago, at the beginning! But why spy on us now?" Niki said with a tone of disgust. "What more harm can they do to us?"

"The times are not so different," Muti said. "However innocent you think you are, you can't help feeling afraid. So, all we can do is wait patiently."

Muti tried to establish some kind of relations with Petruţa, because her husband was rarely to be seen. People like him spend morning till night in meetings: God knows how they can take it! In fact, he didn't change so much after they took him out of factory work to join the Securitate, then gave him a job in the Party, made him take a crash course for a diploma, and finally parachuted him into a manager's office. He changed much less than his wife, simply swapping his beret for a hat and wearing a suit and tie all the time. But his clothes became crumpled very quickly—perhaps because he kept putting on weight. At first it was only his jaws that swelled up, but then his neck rolled down over his collar, his movements became heavy, and he groaned as he climbed a flight of steps. Of course, for them one of the proofs of success was an ability to survive their guzzling and fressing bouts. And there was no way he was going to get any exercise, since a chauffeur picked him up in the morning and dropped him off at night.

Muti probably had these things in mind when she said that it wouldn't be long before they moved out.

The crunch issue turned out to be the wood-burning stoves, which got on their nerves more and more. First, they were offered a new apartment in the Floreasca district, but Petruţa turned this down because it was on the first floor and would have been difficult for their dog. Eventually, though, they settled on a place in Strada Roma, and lo and behold! the magical day arrived. Peace and quiet reigned in the house, which now seemed so huge that the sound of creaking woodwork was enough to terrify anybody.

But, however patiently you wait for something, it often happens that you no longer enjoy it when it arrives. They hadn't even finished the cleaning and decorating when Muti began to insist on getting the joiner to come. How could she have done that, with the place still in such a pitiful state? Niki took the opportunity to remind them that, in the difficult times, he had often suggested selling off some of the more valuable furniture. But, to be fair, he hadn't been right. We didn't have much of real value, and in those days they'd been offering ridiculous prices at the pawnshop or in flea markets. It was therefore probably just as well that Muti held on to things so stubbornly.

Anyway, one fine afternoon she went with her to look for the joiner in a popular district somewhere near Piaţa Mare; Muti didn't remember the exact address, so the two of them wandered around arm in arm for quite a long time. Some louts yelled at them: "Hey, hat ladies! Here come the hat ladies!" It was getting dark and they'd almost given up hope when they finally stumbled across the street. They went into a wretched-looking building that stank to high heaven and knocked on a number of doors, only to discover eventually that the joiner had died a week earlier. Muti was so taken aback—as if there was no one on earth who could replace him! She'd been thinking of him all those years, and besides she had that old-timer's mistrust of newcomers whose skill hasn't been tested. Later, whenever anyone suggested another joiner to her, she would either vacillate or refuse point blank. She lost all her enthusiasm, the poor woman.

Yvonne takes off her coat, crosses the room and hangs it on a hook in the hall. The annoyance is making the muscles twitch on the left side of her face. She takes her felt hat and fox fur, goes up the stairs, enters her bedroom, then opens the wardrobe and puts them carefully on the top shelf. She sighs. Obviously she'll end up giving the money to that old witch!

"Well, fifty lei isn't such a big deal! You gave fifty lei and spent the rest of the day enjoying yourself. Almost cheap at the price, if you think about it!"

That, more or less, is what Niki will say when he hears the whole story.

"That Madam Delcă of yours is certainly a character. I've known lots of others like her. Ah, if I were to describe them . . ."

The smile on his healthily tanned face will be conciliatory but anxious; his eyes will look to one side and avoid meeting hers. There will be no special reason for this, nor for his way of talking fast as if he fears the questions she might ask him but never actually does. After so many years of living together, you can detect so much in a false smile. And yet *pauvre* Niki has no need to feel anxious. Knowing as he does her thoughts and habits, he should know there is no danger of her saying anything unpleasant to him. A good upbringing forces you to control your impulses—and to appear not to notice things that, if pointed out, might make people living beside you feel humiliated. If you have been brought up like that, you will be the first to suffer from an intemperate outburst on your part, the first to feel that it is both degrading and mortifying.

In his letter before last, dear Tudor suggested to his father that he should stop going out so often and spend more time at home. Niki felt hurt for a few weeks, naturally thinking that she had been complaining of his behavior. It was a real source of pain to her: that the person you've spent your whole life with should be unsure what they can expect from you! Since then he's seemed even more anxious in her presence, even more unsure of himself. That's doubtless how he'll be when he comes home later today. With a seemingly indulgent smile—in fact, reassured by the knowledge that she isn't planning a scene—he will carefully place his empty coffee cup on the arm of his chair and, acting out of long habit, immediately rise to his feet. But he'll also try to give the impression that he isn't in a hurry, that his movement toward the door is purely accidental.

It will be a contradictory movement—to leave or not to leave?—about which she will naturally make no comment. She'll even pretend that she hasn't noticed it.

"I'm not surprised at what happened," he will continue, now striding up and down, hands behind his back. "I should even be pleased, because that kind of reality shock is the only way you'll understand what world you're living in—what world *we're* living in. But I can't be sure about that. You've certainly seen a lot in your life, working all those years at the office, but you always seemed to have your head in the clouds. If you haven't understood by now, there's not much chance you ever will. Why don't you just look around you? Can you see anyone willing to give anyone a helping hand? Can't you see how the times have changed, and how people have changed with them?"

It will be the afternoon hour when he usually takes his racket off the hook and disappears. But he's already been out this morning, so maybe he'll decide to stay in. Not yet daring to believe it, she will smile and feel flattered at the attention he is giving her. After all these years, in which he has vanished and returned so many times, here they are chatting away as they used to do at the beginning. In the shadows of the lounge, Niki's sun-tanned face will appear almost youthful to her. His body too will appear almost youthful, benefiting from well-chosen clothing and long practice in warding off a potbelly. Only his eyes worry her a little, since they have begun to water for no reason in fairly ordinary light.

". . . because, unlike me, you still feel obliged after thirty years of communism to behave in a way that fits your social rank. You can laugh as much as you like, but that's precisely what it's about. Your father-in-law ended his days in prison, your Aunt Margot was on her last legs when they let her out, and none of the others you admired so much as a young woman did much better—but you didn't even notice that something had changed. You know as well as I do what happened to creatures that didn't adapt to a radical change in the climate. Well, don't you think you're the same? Why do you feel obliged to support your domestics, to give them clothes all the time, to empty the kitty for Madam Ana, instead of putting her in an old people's home? It was when we were living upstairs that you and Muti—Muti especially—got it into your heads to become so sensitive! I watched you in the street too, opening your purse for every beggar you came across. How often did I tell you that most of them are swindlers, fitter than the rest of us! You didn't listen. You never learned a thing."

His tone is bittersweet, but who can expect a honeyed tongue after so many years of living together? Besides, it makes her feel good to hear him talk so much about her. Behind his mocking words—and when isn't Niki mocking?—she senses the whole little complex he's had since she first met him. However much the world around him changes, *pauvre* Niki will never forget, deep down inside, that he is the son of a vendor from the Obor street market, and that it was his marriage to her that opened the doors to a higher world.

She is the only one to have grasped this secret, and she finds it touching.

Pauvre Niki! This little wound of his—which only she is aware of—has made her turn a blind eye to so many things. She has been easygoing toward him, for a number of reasons, but it is only recently that she has succeeded in understanding him. She has a vivid memory of the last Christmas Eve when Muti still had her wits about her and darling Tudor was still in Romania. In fact, darling Tudor was off skiing in the mountains with his usual gang, but she insisted that they celebrate Christmas at home in the usual way. It was certainly a lively occasion: they'd even managed to find a Christmas tree—actually a spruce—and there was one of those discussions with Niki that only he knows how to have, in which he argued that it was better not to have a tree at all than a miserable spruce. But everything went well, and in the end he admitted he'd been wrong. A perfect Christmas Eve. Everyone was there: Lilly and Victor, Ortansa and Radu Priboianu, and General Petrescu's grandson with his wife, both a young forty-something, although she was nothing to write home about.

"*Est-ce qu'elle est bien née?*" Muti was wont to ask about such people.

How the poor general had suffered at the wedding! Everyone could detect her lowly origins from the way she looked and behaved: she still hadn't learned what to do with her hands, and however much effort you made there was no way of having a normal conversation with her. At least she didn't have ideas above her station, though.

They played some carols on the gramophone, listened to "Silent Night" in German, sang the Romanian *Florile dalbe* together, then took it in turns to put on a little performance to earn a present from Santa Claus. She had bought something suitable for everyone, and they all agreed that it was the most enjoyable part of the evening. The most successful, of course, was Niki! Afterward they brought Muti in, sat her in a rocking chair, and turned off the lights . . . She can still see the bright greenish-orange afterglow of the lamp globes in the darkness, immediately followed by the electric candles, whose reddish ends looked exactly like lighted fuses. And then came the sparklers, which made Niki rather nervous: "Watch out, it's not a real fir tree. It's a spruce, and they catch fire like tinder."

But there was no accident, and when she looked out the window she felt a childlike joy at the sight of the huge thick snowflakes that would soon cover the houses and cars. She stood there for a while. The house was filled with a rare mirth: everyone laughed and cracked jokes, feeling no need for her to act as hostess, and so she was able to take a breather and stare out into the street. Moments of life when you felt happy, inexplicably happy, remain in your memory. Later you realize that such moments of peace and happiness were dogged by great misfortunes to come, and yet they still make you feel good as you look back on them. So it was for those moments when she watched the snow falling outside, even though she saw nothing out of the ordinary there: just a few couples hurrying back early from a party, and a small group of children singing carols. None of them even knew the old ones, and all they could come up with was a hideous song about a rabbit and Prince Ştefan or Mihai that had been tormenting everyone in the streetcars since November. Yet she was as happy at that moment, switching her eyes between the street and the lounge, as she had been in the past when Papa was still alive and Tante Margot and Oncle Alexandre had come to spend Christmas with them as usual.

The guests left at a reasonable hour. Muti was slightly agitated—who knows what memories had stirred in her confused mind?—and had some

trouble falling asleep. This got on Niki's nerves . . . He must be suffering
from stress, because sometimes he gets upset over nothing. Of course,
his education has taught him not to let it show, but her intuition tells her
when he's upset . . . Niki, having drunk a glass or two more than he was
used to, came back to the lounge as excited as a little boy. He hung all the
sparklers on the spruce branches, and set them alight as soon as he saw
her enter the room.

"I've never felt at ease with you," he told her, once the last of the white
light had burned itself out.

She was so shocked that she lost her voice. Then, all of a sudden,
the anger stored up in her over the years as a result of his bad behavior
melted away. What remained in its place was a strange feeling that she
found almost flattering, something very much like pity. It's difficult for
a man to accept his wife's superior status: that seemed to be what was
emerging from his disconnected sentences. He went on drinking and
spoke more and more incoherently.

"It's all my fault—you're not to blame," he kept repeating.

For the first time he tried to face up to his countless affairs, his
absences from home, even his coldness toward Tudor. He even admitted
that he hadn't always carried out his duties as a parent.

At first she thought that that Christmas Eve might put their marriage
on an even keel again, but the sad truth is that nothing much changed as
a result. You might even say the opposite, given that he stayed away or
came home late more and more often.

"Where can you still find anyone willing to help their neighbor for
free?" Niki will continue, sitting down again in an armchair. "Mutual
favors, okay, one piece of information for another, a little present in
return for help with something: that's the only law that everyone obeys.
But no one will lift a finger unless they can be sure of getting something
back. You'll say it's always been like that in this country: Balkan corruption, the legacy of Phanariot rulers, customs and habits going back two
thousand years. Sure, I don't dispute it. That's the world around us, and
we're not going to change it—not you, not me, not anyone. All I'm saying
is that *you* need to change, or else you're in for a rude awakening."

That, more or less, will be his conclusion . . . She can hear his mocking
voice, with an old, very old, trace of tenderness. Yes, tenderness, despite
everything. However slippery he may be, she's not wrong about that.
Tenderness is the only name for it.

As always, she will listen to him with a sense of triumph, having managed to shift him onto familiar ground that is theirs alone. Here, she can be sure of not sharing him with any of the other women who have poisoned her life. He will open her eyes to the world, and she will listen with rapt attention—much as they did thirty years ago. Sometimes she is thinking of something else, but at regular intervals she flashes him a look of agreement or throws in a supplementary question—much as Tudor's puppy used to run and fetch the ball that he threw repeatedly for him to bring back, racing up and stopping motionless half a meter away, sniffing the asphalt, and jumping up on him at the least pat of affection.

"Yes, you've already done your good deed for the day. And the Lord on high will reward you with good health and happiness in your marriage. He's a fine handsome man you have."

Jesus, what a fright she got suddenly finding the old woman behind her! Whatever next? To see her straddling a broomstick? She obviously has no intention of leaving. That's what it means to be uneducated and impudent. Look at her laughing with her mouth wide open, showing her false teeth. So that's what she was doing in there all this time: putting her teeth in to show them off! Half an hour ago, in the yard, you could hardly understand what she was mumbling between her bare gums. What a laugh Niki will have when she tells him!

"It doesn't surprise me," he will say. "But I can already predict you won't learn anything from it. You'll go on in your own sweet way."

He's right, absolutely right. Her delicate, indecisive nature, her inability to come right out with what she's thinking, lands her in one tight corner after another. But this is really the last straw! This time she'll simply kick the impudent old woman out of the house! As for the fifty lei, forget it! She'd better be gone when Niki gets back for lunch: he can't stand having her around.

"Come now, Madam Delcă, why all these thank-yous? Don't mention it any more. I'm glad too that we met in the end. I'd have felt bad if I'd heard you made the journey here for nothing—because I know how hard it would be for you to do it again. I know how hard these things are at our age."

She's so mean that she spends all day at home in the dark. That's not what her mother was like: she'd always leave them on. But this one doesn't even switch them on when she goes scurrying to answer the phone! Nor does she say: "Take a seat, Madam Delcă, you must be tired. Sit down. I'll be back in a minute, and we'll have a chat together."

No, nothing like that! Off like a flash to the phone, showing me her ass instead of looking at me. If it hadn't rung, she'd have shown me the door right away. So here I am, stuck in the dark. I almost broke my leg trying to find the armchair. The leather's cracked, so they've put a rug and cushions on it to cover it up. It's the big one Mrs. Ioaniu used to sit in. I'm a bit on the heavy side myself, but I always feel small sitting there.

She stretches her swollen legs—a shooting pain that nearly creases her up. Then she lets out a sigh and rests her neck against the back of the chair.

Mrs. Ioaniu didn't just loll there for the fun of it. After her illness, she found it more difficult to move around and had to struggle even to stand up. As soon as you went into her room, you were hit by the smell of old books, mildew, and aging flesh. She became thin, her eyes were glassy, and sometimes she had the shakes. Her white hair, once so thick, kept falling out until you could see her scalp. But that didn't stop her twisting her pathetic little curls, no thicker than a finger, which tapered off like a mouse's tail. You always found her in the armchair, ears pricked up. She must have been bored alone all those hours, and she perked up whenever she heard steps on the staircase.

"Who's that? Who's there?" she would ask, in that gasping voice of hers.

"It's me," I said. And then from the landing: "Can't you tell it's me?"

It was that foxy Ivona who got me to ask her that—to make sure she wasn't off with the fairies, after spending all day staring at the wall in silence. What a hypocrite! She wanted to know if she could draw the old woman's money out of the savings bank and put it in her and Niki's names. They're a match for each other all right. She's a greedy little skinflint: that's why she got me to ask her mother. That's why I said "Can't you tell it's me?" when I reached the armchair. And Madam Ioaniu stared at me with her glassy eyes—those eyes that had once been such a deep deep blue. It's possible she couldn't see much with them any longer, because she used to complain of white rings, and that's something you never get rid of. She must have had plenty of other things wrong with her. Anyway, she had her fair share of life—she was pushing a hundred by the end.

"I recognize you," she said after a moment, in her quivering voice. "You're Vica."

She shrank and shrank, and developed one of those hunchbacks. Her face was all wrinkled—nothing but folds and creases. And the day came when she really didn't know who was coming in and out: she'd sit there staring at the wall, hardly able to drag her feet across the floor. She'd been tightfisted all her life, but now, for some reason, she got into the habit of collecting all kinds of junk: rags, bread crusts, corks, pieces of paper, old tram tickets—things you'd never dream of keeping. She used to put them in a kind of purse she made for herself and kept hidden away so that no one else could find it. So some of her mind must still have been there, if she could remember where she'd put the purse.

"Muti worries me," that moronic Ivona would say. "I'm afraid she's got hardening of the arteries. God, what a terrible year it's been—one of those that begin badly and lurch from one rough patch to another."

She said she was sad that Tudor had run away. Like hell she was! As if it didn't suit her down to the ground that he'd stayed in the West!

"Muti worries me, and I'm afraid that in her state she might do something foolish. Like forget to turn off the tap, or set the house on fire, or go wandering off somewhere."

When she complained like that to me, it was usually because she'd stumbled across Muti's purse in some corner or other.

Then one day it actually happened: Madam Ioaniu vanished into thin air. They came home and found the front door wide open. Fortunately Mrs. Cristide, nosy as ever, saw something was wrong when she left to go shopping, so she phoned that vixen Ivona at her office.

The vixen and her skirt-chasing husband combed the neighborhood, told the police, and asked at all the hospitals. They left no stone unturned, and that scumbag Niki even went to the city morgue. Chasing as usual he was: not because he adored his mother-in-law, but because of what people might say.

People would have said that, with Tudor no longer there, Niki had been making life such hell for his mother-in-law that she'd taken to her heels. Gone just as she was, in that velveteen housedress I made for her that buttons up at the front. Gone without her handbag, without any ID—without anything.

They were lucky it was already warm and summery. Was it May? Or perhaps June? And Madam Ioaniu was even luckier that she came across a man who knew her—a gentleman well on in life, a real gentleman, like in the old days. They knew each other by sight, and after a "please, would you mind?" and a "but of course, madam" he had her back safely within a few hours.

After that, the vixen never let her mother out of her sight. When she went out, she double-locked the door and put the key in a hiding place. But, just in case, she also attached a sheet of paper to Muti's breast pocket with a safety pin: *My name is Sofia-Denisa Ioaniu . . .* , followed by her address and telephone number.

It's as if I can see Madam Ioaniu now, seated in her armchair on those covers and rug. You'd have thought her the Gypsy Queen of folk legend, with that paper on her chest informing the world who she was. Smaller and frailer, hunched up and wearing a mouse's tail of hair at the back, Madam Ioaniu sat staring at the wall without saying a word. She had no idea when others came in and out. It could have been a thief come to empty the house.

The old woman no longer had a clue about anything. That's why her daughter put that paper on her pocket. And it was just as well, because she vanished again from time to time—only the devil knows how, God forgive me! Either she was much smarter than they were; it's well known that old gagas can be incredibly cunning. Or else that scum of a son-in-law quietly opened the door for her, so she could skip out for good; with a bit of luck she might get run over by a tram, or freeze to death without any outdoor clothes. He'd certainly had enough of her there in the armchair, staring straight ahead without a word, hunched up and shriveled like a mummy. At some point Ivona added an oilcloth to all the other stuff on the chair, no doubt because Mrs. Ioaniu was wetting herself like a little child. So maybe he just opened the door for her on the quiet. You can only expect the worst from a man like that.

Madam Ioaniu could see through him all right—which is why she'd never been able to stand him. She'd added Tudor's name to all her bank accounts when she thought she might be dying, so that her money would go to him alone. And, after Tudor left and she recovered from the fluid on her lungs, Niki began to suck up to her: blah blah blah, think carefully, Muti dear, now it's the State that would pocket all your money if the worst were to happen, blah blah blah. The sly old woman played dumb: what's he driving at? He knew what he was driving at, though: he wanted her to remove Tudor's name and add theirs to her bank account—his and that flaky Ivona's.

He knew what he wanted, but he never came straight out with it. In fact, he'd never dared to speak his mind to Madam Ioaniu, since that time when he'd skipped out while her sister Margo and her husband, the general, were in prison. He'd left the vixen holding their baby and gone off to his floozy. A few years later he came back with his tail between his legs, either because they wouldn't give him a divorce or because he and the floozy got fed up with each other: only he knows. Madam Ioaniu didn't let fly at him, didn't say a thing, but she made sure he never forgot that she'd kept the house together in his absence, selling off her rugs and jewelry and taking in lodgers. That's why he couldn't speak his mind to her, still less ask her straight out to put her money in their name because she was going to croak one day soon. So the cunning old woman pretended not to understand what he was driving at. But she still had her wits about her: I know, 'cuz she once blurted out that she'd like to add Ivona's name to her account so that she'd know she would be all right in her old age. She said that in confidence, when we were alone together. But unfortunately she knew that her daughter couldn't be relied on, that the dumbo would go and blab to her hubby everything you said to her. His wish was her command. And she'd have immediately told him that her mother had added her name to the account. She couldn't keep anything secret from him, so it didn't make any difference whose name the money was in: his or hers. No difference at all.

So, when Madam Ioaniu's grandson left home, one reason why her brain started to go was that she was at the mercy of her son-in-law. Otherwise, why would she have stashed away all that stuff in the house: the rags, the old tickets, the corks, the meat bones? She did it so she could take them with her into the big wide world. However gaga she became, she knew she was at her son-in-law's mercy and that you can only expect the worst from a man like him.

She'd had too much time to see through him. Only that airhead daughter of hers could be taken in: she's always believed every word that scumbag Niki feeds to her. If he told her to eat fire, she'd do it without thinking twice, just to keep him happy. There she is now, whining to him over the phone. He makes fun of her all the time, and she soaks it up like a doormat.

"Is there really no way you can come home sooner, Niki? Okay, I won't go on: I just wanted to know whether I should expect you. No, of course not, you know that for me a meal is only a formality. Really. Yes, okay, then I'll nibble at something or other. It's just that you said you'd be home early this afternoon. What? Yes, you said it this morning, on your way out."

Ha, ha, serves you right! You're less snooty than you were a few minutes ago, when you stood like a cop at the bathroom door, rigged out in that jacket and fancy hat, ready to take to your heels as soon as I came out. Yeah, run for it without giving me my fifty lei! You cunning little vixen, you're so sly and stingy no one can hold a candle to you. But with him it's a different matter. You dance to his tune, like a bear on hot coals! Look at her whining over there, when she ought to be smashing the phone into his thick skull. Go play with your whores, go on, fuck off to them! You can come back when your mother rises from her grave. If she was woman enough to tell him that, and to smash the telephone into his skull, he'd soon come running back with his tail between his legs.

But a man like that, who you can't trust further than you can throw him, might end up clearing off for good. Well, he can just get lost! That tart isn't going to shack up with an old dodderer like him just for a share of his pension. She's not that dumb. If she's been luring him into her web these past ten or fifteen years, it's not for some measly pittance. She's after the old woman's house, her silver, her rugs, and her money in the savings bank. Ten years, fifteen—or however many it is she's been rolling over like a kitten for him. Once those devils sink their claws into you . . . After all, Ivona isn't going to live till kingdom come. Madam Ioaniu had nine lives like a cat, but even she couldn't keep spinning it out. And Ivona, who poisons herself with coffee and cigarettes and never had a brain in her head, won't last nearly that long. God, what a half-wit she is: to hide behind the curtain for hours and then come rushing out like crazy, with that hat on her head and that moth-eaten fox fur! And, oh, yes, sorry, she absolutely must go to the center. I'll tell her where she can go! And then she nearly had a breakdown when she saw the time. What do I care? As far as I'm concerned, she can rub her ass on the ground if she can't control her demons. It must be ages since that scumbag Niki was a husband to her in more than name! And some shameless hussies, like mares, can't do without a male to cover them. None of that mattered to me, and I said thank God when I escaped from it. A few years ago my husband still tried to get at me, but I said "Aren't you ashamed, at your age?" and I thanked my lucky stars when he left me alone. But as for Ivona's Niki-Wiki, let the devil kick him in the balls: all he's good for is twiddling his thumbs, screwing whores, and burning hundred lei notes. If you give him a pile, he'll blow the lot on poker, drinking sprees, and fancy women. And that half-wit can't stop licking his ass—there she is whining to him again on the phone. You can whine as much as you like, that son of a bitch takes his orders from his harlot-in-chief. She's the boss: all she has to do is snap her fingers and Niki jumps to attention. She may be a cheap whore up from the country, but she sure knows how to handle him.

"But, whatever you do, don't forget Țuțu's wedding at seven o'clock . . . Of course not—but we mustn't arrive at the last minute, with the church already full. Clemenţa has the eyes of a hawk . . . No, dear, of course I don't think you'll show up just as it's beginning. Am I the kind of woman who nags for no reason? . . . If you quibble over every word, I suppose it's better for me to say nothing . . . No, I'm just waiting for you to say something. Why should I be angry? So you'll call me again? As you like . . . Whatever you think best . . . But there's no need to call me if you're going to be back early . . . No, Niki, really, I promise. I'm not worried at all now that you've phoned."

What a motherfucker! Can't you see it's no use sucking up to him? He'll only listen if he's scared shitless of you!

My husband's right after all. "You just keep going on at me all the time," he complains. "But I'd like to see what you'd say if you had other men to deal with."

My poor hubby: he may be sulky, mute, and bad-tempered, but we've been together forty-nine years! Yes, sulky, mute, and bad-tempered, but didn't he get a job at the factory after I closed the shop, so we'd have a pension in our old age? He used to come home after work in filthy blue overalls, with an itchy skin rash from those fucking chemicals; and he couldn't get rid of it for years, however much milk and other stuff he swallowed. I can't describe how I felt when I saw him at the end of the street, pitter-pattering along like a bear! I don't know what came over me, but I felt like bursting into tears. He may be sulky, mute, and bad-tempered, but on payday he pulled a wad of notes out of his pocket and handed over every last cent. I counted it and did some sums: this for the rent, that for the television, the coal, and the wood. He didn't keep a thing, just took the twenty-five lei that I slipped into his pocket from time to time. Not that I was worried about that: I knew he wouldn't touch it, but, well, a man likes to know he has some money on him. That's a real man—a man you can rely on. If I was in Ivona's place, knowing Niki-Wiki could draw whatever he liked out of our savings account, I wouldn't be able to sleep at night. I'd be afraid he'd scurry to the bank and then run off to his floozy with the money between his teeth. But that doesn't occur to Ivona, crafty as she is. You just have to see the way she licks his ass. That's why he runs rings around you, dumbo. You're an old bird now, and you still don't know how to talk to your husband. She just whines away, without even thinking there's a stranger in the house—without thinking that I'm faint from hunger and have cold sweats. Ugh, what an awful day: one fucking thing after another! I must've been nuts to leave home, where I've got everything I need, and traipse the streets working myself up into a state. When I think of all that way home, I just feel like staying put in this armchair. But I'll have to get up soon. At least if I could have a crust of bread! That half-wit's so fucking selfish she won't think of it, so I'll have to look after myself. I'll just take a quick peek in the kitchen and stuff something in my mouth. And if the vixen catches me, I'll tell her I went to get a glass of water. Easy when you've got your head screwed on.

What a kitchen! You'd think they were as poor as church mice! Two rolls as hard as rock and a bit of rotting cheese: otherwise zilch. So why should that motherfucker of a husband hurry home? To crack his false teeth? If only there was a pot of stew—even some mixed vegetables would do. Ah, fresh bread and stewed vegetables—and a little glass of ţuică.

That's the door creaking: I'd better not turn around with this cheese in my mouth. It's no bigger than a nut—but all I could find to keep the wolf from the door. Turn I do, though, 'cuz I can hear footsteps on the tiles next to me. What a sight she is: that phone call's really knocked the stuffing out of her! She looks so thin and pale, you can almost see the bones sticking out. Nearly all her hair's fallen out. And those horsy teeth! It's scary just to look at her.

Yes, God doesn't mess around: there's justice in the world after all! He saw her keep me waiting in the yard, with my stomach empty, after that long trek across town. She kept me waiting even though I rang the bell enough to blow her brains. My legs were trembling I was so famished—like they still are now.

"Do you need anything, Madam Delcă? Just tell me if you do."

What a pain in the ass she is! And so snooty . . . Does she think she picked me up from the gutter or something? I wish she'd stop looking at me as if I was her servant. Go to hell with your moth-eaten fur. I didn't ask you to hide behind the curtain for hours. Don't take it out on me 'cuz your hubby's off whoring! Don't you snap at me—I've had enough already for one day. You could go down on bended knees and I wouldn't stay here another minute—not one minute! I'm a nice polite girl, but there's a limit to everything. If you keep playing with fire, it's your own fault if your fingers get burned. What have I done to deserve it? I go from house to house, and this one growls like a bear, that one doesn't open the door or won't even give me a glass of water. Aren't I human too? Didn't I have a shop on Strada Coriolan, with customers who came from all over the place—even from Strada Sabinelor, even from the other side of the railway. And not one of them left without buying something. I gave them credit, no problem—so much that if they'd all paid me I'd be rolling in it by now! I used to buy furniture for my brothers and send them parcel after parcel with blocks of cheese, fine charcuterie, and wines from Dealul Zorilor. But now not a soul comes to see us. Has one of us got the plague or something?

"But . . . what are you doing there at the hall stand, Madam Delcă?"

What am I doing? I'm ending your little game, that's what I'm doing. What a nerve she's got! A minute ago she wouldn't even look at me, and now she's struggling to understand me! Anyone who sets foot in this house can go to hell. Fuck you, you little vixen—leaving me starving at your door. I hope you get struck down tomorrow, and you can't get better till I give the word. I hope you end up being fed with a spoon, like your mother.

"Come now, put your coat back on the stand. You can't leave so soon: we haven't said two words to each other. I hope you're not upset with me. We've known each other for so long. Come on, put your hat and coat back. By the way, would you like me to give you one of Muti's hats to do up for yourself? You're so clever at that sort of thing."

"Yes, Madam Delcă, the funeral service for General Pantazi's wife was on Wednesday at the White Church. You must have heard of him, from the days when we were young. How quickly youth flies! I don't know, you feel the same as before inside, no? But when you look in the mirror it's another story. He died a long time ago, of course. She was a fine fine woman—as good as they get. There must have been a hundred people there, maybe more. The church was full, and when I looked around I saw what it means to be well educated. No one was even a minute late, and we all stood without moving for an hour because the priests hadn't arrived yet. You know what, no one moved an inch—to walk around the church, to kiss the icons, to eye one another up. Not an inch! We just stood there until the priests and the archimandrite showed up . . . Help yourself to some cheese and sour cream, Madam Delcă. Florica brought it for me. I don't know how much longer she's going to keep coming; she's getting on herself and, well, it doesn't get any easier as the years go by . . . Anyway, the archimandrite performed the long service, as if for princes, and everyone went on standing still. I really liked that, believe me. After all the horrors they've been through, a hundred people were still behaving as people should. In the end a colonel from the reserves who'd once been the general's comrade gave a speech—a man who was, let's say, a little simple. But he spoke from the heart. They were a family of boyars, he said, who had lived like boyars and endured poverty and the increasing vulgarity of life like boyars. Left alone to suffer her lot, the general's wife had devotedly brought up their daughters as daughters should be brought up . . . One of them, who's been living abroad for a long time, attended the funeral, though without her children—both because they're too little and because there's no point in bringing children to such ceremonies . . . The younger daughter, whose husband managed to get her out to the West just a year ago, can't return to Romania yet, especially as she hasn't been given citizenship over there. As for the general's wife, I guess they'd probably have got her out too, but she was a woman of great dignity and wouldn't have easily agreed to being a burden for her children. However close parents and children are, you have to remember that it's not easy for those who start a new life from scratch in the West. And instead of helping your children, as any parent should, you end up doing the opposite. You land yourself on them without a pension, without anything. It's hard being a burden for your children, don't you think?"

"Yes, you've got to have money of your own when you're old; you can't go around begging from others. Whether it's family or friends, you can't be at anyone else's mercy. Madam Ioaniu used to say the same, God rest her soul . . ."

A yellow curtain, stained with oil and frayed at the edges, hangs over the kitchen window and its dirty iron bars. Madam Ioaniu sewed the curtain together, while the general himself put in the bars, after the umpteenth burglar had climbed over the roof of the shed and through the window. They no longer had an orderly by then, and the general was arrested three months later. A layer of dust and soot has covered the out-side of the window. Leana will wipe it away, as usual, if they can get her to do the spring cleaning.

That's assuming they will have the usual guests for Easter.

A yellowish-gray light slants in through the window. The morning is already over, and the invisible sun will soon begin to go down in the ivory sky. Ivona stands up and walks over to the food safe. She glances outside but can only see the corrugated roof of the shed, shriveled over time, and further away the dark, damp pavilion on which leftover patches of snow glisten like bird droppings beneath a hard sugar-glazing.

"Hum, I thought I still had a little vegetable stew . . . My God, what disorder in there. I don't understand how people can be short of time when they no longer have to go to work. No doubt their strength starts to fail . . . Do you like vegetables stewed in oil? Tell me honestly, Madam Delcă. You're not a vegetarian, so I think it's only normal to ask. I wouldn't be at all surprised if you told me you don't."

On the wall above the stove, the yellowing tiles are splashed with glossy solidified oil. They were white when Mrs. Ioaniu put them up after the tenants left—the same white as the repainted sink and water pipes. The paint has peeled away since then, allowing dark metal to show through like ladders in a pair of stockings. A dark-green damp stain looks down like an aqueous lens from the top of the wall, and beneath it beads of crystalline water form on the surface. In the shadowy corner opposite, high above the food safe, long strands of spiderweb hang trem-bling from the smoke-blackened ceiling.

"What did I want to ask you, Madam Delcă? Huh, the things age does to your memory! You end up birdbrained, as the common people say. It'll come to me in a minute. But finish it up. It's a long time since break-fast, and you must be hungry."

Well now, we've stopped being so snooty, have we? I must have given her a fright just now. She saw she couldn't get away with it and dropped all that bullshit. So now it's all lovey-dovey, just us two, such good friends: nothing but sweet talk. You must be hungry, Madam Delcă, blah blah blah, you're not going to walk out on me like that, Madam Delcă . . . And crocodile tears. "What would I do without you? I'd fall flat on my face." If I'd taken what she did to heart, I'd have been out of here long ago. Anyone else wouldn't have let her forget it. But I know how to behave in society; that's why everyone likes and appreciates me wherever

I go. That's why this crackpot Ivona has suddenly seen reason. She's changing her tune now.

"What do you say, Madam Delcă, shall I fry you a couple of eggs?"

Has she got ants in her pants or something? There she goes again, fidgeting around in the food safe. Well, I suppose she's not really evil, just not quite right in the head. Take all that jabbering about the stiffs in the church. So what if they just stood there—big deal! Who wouldn't if they knew their work was being done for them?

"Just you sit there, Madam Delcă. I'll take care of the eggs."

No, she's not really evil, but look at her: all thumbs! Can't even fry a couple of eggs. Waving that fork around as if she's going to stick it up her ass next. And if you take your eyes off her, she could quite easily burn them to a cinder. She may read books and all that, but she's completely lost in a kitchen and doesn't have a clue how to behave with people. What she did today, her mother wouldn't have done in a million years. Madam Ioaniu certainly had her head screwed on right. Sure, she had plenty of faults, but which of us is without sin?—as the priest says in church. And she lived longer than most: she was nearly a hundred when she finally croaked. Not that it was such a good thing to hang on like that: she hardly knew she was still alive, hunched up on that oilcloth in the armchair. In the end there was no point asking her if she recognized you. She'd just stare at me with her beady eyes. All she remembered was where her little cloth purse was. But she still kept watching in case the door was left open. Then she'd be off like a shot, and Ivona would be phoning like crazy and wandering the streets looking for her. And just when she'd given up and was kissing her good-bye, some stranger would call from the other side of Bucharest and ask them to go pick her up.

How Ivona would soft-soap her in those days—even more than she's doing now.

"Please come and see us more often, Madam Delcă," she'd say. "I'm so worried about Muti! It's as if I had a little child in the house. I daren't leave her alone for a minute."

But I can only be pushed so far! They could have paid me in gold, and I still wouldn't have gone more often. I don't have patience with little children, or old people either, especially if someone's standing over my shoulder and telling me what to do. I didn't fancy spending hours and hours in that empty house, where the shutters were kept drawn and the only light was from the candle burning in Madam Ioaniu's room like in a cellar, and where you heard creaking sounds all the time. What a life: to sit beside that stuffed mummy in the armchair, who didn't move and didn't breathe, just stared blankly at the walls! And you had to change her each time she let herself go. And again the floor or God knows what would creak, and you'd expect a ghost to spring out from somewhere. It was enough to scare the wits out of you, to give you a really funny turn.

So Ivona didn't get her claws into me, or anyone else for that matter. And Madam Ioaniu kept doing a vanishing act—only she knew what she got up to. Last time she did it, they took two days to find her.

They never found out where she'd been. She was in quite a state when they brought her back: her slippers were covered in mud, and she'd lost the cardigan she was wearing when she skipped out. The weather was like it is today, late winter, and they didn't understand how she could have gone two days without freezing to death. They questioned her, dropped it, then questioned her again—but nothing! She must have remembered something, because she kept muttering: "It was dark, dark, dark . . . and a big white bird . . ."

"Muti must have slept in a dovecot," that scumbag Niki laughed.

Where could she have spent those two days? And what happened to her cardigan? They never did find out. As long as Madam Ioaniu was alive, she kept muttering without being asked: "Dark, dark, dark . . . and a big white bird." That's all they ever got out of her.

One day it finally got through to Ivona that the only thing to do was give up her job. She retired on what they saw fit to give her and started looking after her mother full time. She didn't like losing out by taking her pension early, but she never groused about it. Anyway, it wasn't long before Madam Ioaniu passed away. It all happened very quickly.

Ivona couldn't go back to work then, and she'd never liked to stay home cooking and cleaning. The years she'd enjoyed were when she taught at the Italian School, but that was a long time ago and they kicked her out when her father, the general, was arrested. Or maybe they closed the school down. Yes, she was always unlucky, Ivona.

The one thing I regret, she told me at Madam Ioaniu's funeral, is that, if I had to retire anyway, I didn't do it earlier. Then Muti wouldn't have got into that state and suffered the way she did, sitting in that armchair without anyone to change her. She developed lots of sores and didn't even have the strength to complain any more. When I think of what must have gone through her mind as she sat there alone and immobile! In the end she could hardly even move her hands.

Well, that's life, I told her. When you get to that point, your body and mind just pack up. Like it or not, the time will come for all of us to get our marching orders. Not one of us is going to be left hanging around.

"You're very quiet, Madam Delcă. What are you thinking about?"

"About Madam Ioaniu, God rest her soul, nothing else."

How many years it is since the three of us used to eat here together: Madam Ioaniu, the boy, and me! Ah, what a load of macaroni we had to eat in those days! That's what I brought Tudor up on, she said to me once. And when I sit on this chair it's as if I'm sitting at home. I can almost see the boy wolfing his food down, in a hurry to get to school or to go out and play. You must chew more carefully, I told him, otherwise it'll go down the wrong way. But the poor thing wolfed it all the same, with one eye on the clock—just so they wouldn't find an excuse to kick him out of school.

What's she doing now, wringing her hands and fiddle-assing around in the food safe? They don't like anyone to know their secrets, but nowadays everything gets found out in the end. Even Madam Ioaniu blurted out once that the school had wanted to give Tudor the boot but she'd demanded an interview and saved him. She and Tudor stayed on edge for years, though, in case they tried to get rid of him again. Anyway, he was a right old bookworm and had tons of ambition: he'd cry to himself in bed at night if he got a bad mark, till Ivona and Madam Ioaniu wondered what was up and what they could do to calm him. It was obvious he didn't take after his whoring father; he was more like Ivona's father, who'd been somebody in his time. A fat lot of good it did Tudor, though. He had to carry the can for everyone: for his real grandfather, for his step-grandfather, the general, for the whole family. At least that's how it was until the general died in prison. They used to drop like flies there: anyone who'd been anyone in the past—ministers, generals, people who'd been close to them, people who'd been nothing at all, just struck it unlucky and found themselves behind bars . . . In fact, Ioaniu had already been dead for some time, but no one had wanted to go to Madam Ioaniu's house and tell her; it was no fun being a bird of ill omen. So it was only after two years that they got around to telling her in writing that he'd died like a dog in prison. But, you see, that meant there was one less that Tudor had to pay for: it meant he could go on studying and finish school.

"What do you put on your face, Madam Delcă, to keep it looking so nice and wrinkle free? It's not so easy at our age. What do you wash with? What cream do you use? Or is it a secret? You don't have to tell me if it is . . ."

"A secret? Oh yeah, you mean like beeswax floor polish? No, all my life I've washed my face with anything around—laundry soap, dish soap, you name it. And I've never used any creams or powders: they've got poisons inside them that ruin your skin."

Yes, incredible what a fresh complexion she has. You wouldn't give her a day over fifty, if that. That's one of the advantages of being fat. Over time, your muscles become flabby, and only fat can still keep your skin taut. It's well known that obese people have a good complexion. Unfortunately you can't have both: good skin and a good figure. One or the other has to go. That's life.

"Leave the dishes, Madam Delcă. Please don't wash up. Come on, let's go through to the lounge."

As if Vica's the kind of person who'd just drop everything and follow me! If I'd got her to wash dishes, she'd have pulled a horrible face. But, well, let her scrub and scrub if that will calm her. It's dark in the lounge, but that doesn't bother me. The world is so ugly in broad daylight—especially here in Bucharest, where the shop windows are so dull, the streets are so dirty, and people dress with such bad taste. No one looks after the parks and green spaces. And if a tree gets planted somewhere, the passersby trample all over it like a herd of cattle. Even old trees, which could clean the air a little, are pulled down for no reason. People you see in the daylight look ugly but couldn't care less. Long ago—when I was still at school, I think—I read a short story in a magazine; the action took place on the beach, at Balcic, but there wasn't much of it, and the story was really about the states of mind of one character. In fact, I don't remember what he was like, only that he looked with a very critical eye at everything around him. He was particularly merciless about the women he saw there. Well, the character or the author—anyway, the one doing the descriptions—suggested that only girls up to the age of twenty should be allowed to take their clothes off on the beach. Motherhood, he wrote, makes women look ugly; only a fresh young body is beautiful. I was

shocked by this rather original author. But that's the thing about art: it's
what shocks you that stays in your mind.

Ivona goes slowly up the stairs, opens the first door, and enters the
room, running her dry fingertips along the wall. She switches on the
ceiling lamp—it's the darkest room in the house—goes up to the dressing table and turns on the wall lights. She stares at herself in the mirror
too intently, greedy and impatient in case the old woman finishes the
dishes quickly and catches her unawares. It drives her to despair that she
looks worse and worse as the years go by. She studies the white locks,
white for the length of two fingers from the roots up, and clumsily ruffles
her thin dry curls. Her long nose is too wide at the tip and pockmarked
with large pores, and her colorless lips have grown thinner and receded.
Little burst blood vessels stand out in the yellowish white of her eyes.

Screwing up her thin drooping eyebrows, Ivona tears her face away
from the mirror. Out of the corner of her eye, she sees her silhouette
moving in a misty haze. At the end of the dressing table stand two silver
candelabras, blackened and covered with dust.

When Leana comes, she must get her to clean and polish them.

After Ivona switches off the wall lights and the ceiling lamp, only a
thin strip of light percolates in through the closed shutters. It is a soft,
calming darkness. She turns to the dressing table and feverishly hunts
among the objects there, pushing aside a silver casket so that its pearl
and amber necklaces spill out with studied carelessness, pushing aside
too a powder case and atomizer, until she finds her tube of lipstick and
vigorously draws a cross on each cheek. A dark-red cross on the right, a
dark-red cross on the left. Then she takes a few steps back. How funny
she looks! She closes her eyes, to blot everything out, and mechanically
smears the lipstick along her cheekbones.

She moves back a little more.

Ah, yes, that's better. Just a dash of lipstick and everything looks different. It's true that the darkness helps. A woman must be appearance
conscious for the sake of her own morale . . . Again she ruffles her thin
dry curls. How quickly they've sprouted this time!

She turns on the heels of her flat shoes and is delighted with the
youthfulness of her movement in the soft shadow. The bracing scent of
lavender has long seeped into the rosewood of the wardrobe. A sunbeam
suddenly produces a dazzling sparkle in the encrusted mother-of-pearl
of the dark mirror frame, then just as suddenly moves on and loses its

brilliance. A single worry still haunts Ivona. She leaves her bedroom and searches for the lounge clock with her eyes. It was about now that Niki said he would be home. Assuming he'll be half an hour late, that means the old woman should be going. Rightly or wrongly, Niki can't get on with her at all, so it's best if she goes. Anyway, she has no reason to stay longer: she's used the toilet, she's eaten something. What about her fifty lei? Ivona could give them to her, as she'd otherwise have to mail them to her in a week's time. But she'll only draw her pension tomorrow and doesn't have enough cash. Maybe she should take it out of Niki's money, or from what she's set aside to pay for the hot water. If she gives the old woman her fifty lei, she won't have anything to hold against her. Ah, how little details like that can throw a touchy, emotional soul! Look at how the old woman shuffled without a word to the coat stand and made ready to leave—she who is usually so impertinent. And that ridiculous beret she's had for thirty years, which Tudor, the dear boy, mentions in all his letters: *How is Madam Delcă? Does she still call on you in that fantastic beret of hers?* How her hands were trembling when she stretched them out to take her coat! No, there's no doubt about it, she'll never become the practical woman that Niki would like to have around the house. When she saw her there in the hall, she said to herself that it's not right to behave badly with someone who's been coming to your house for so many years. And at her age, can you know how much longer she'll last?

In the end she's just a poor old woman, whose property was confiscated by the regime, and for whom the future can bring nothing but troubles. If she'd let her leave and then heard, God forbid, that something had happened to her on the way home, how she would have blamed herself in the future! The poor woman felt so ashamed at being put in her place that she didn't want to say another word. So she'd just tried to gratify her in every way possible.

"I've been in this room so many times, but I don't know that picture there. I thought there was nothing in the house I don't know."

"There's no way you could have seen it, Madam Delcă, because it's an old photograph I came across by chance a few months ago. I was so happy to find it! All our family is there. My God, look how young they are! Tante Margot was a pupil at the Central School. I think Muti avoided displaying the picture out of respect for Uncle Georges, because, you see . . . here is Papa. He's her first husband! Papa and Uncles Georges knew each other, thought highly of each other, but nevertheless, you understand, it wouldn't have been a good idea to hang it on the wall. Yes, Papa is the man reading at the pedestal table; of course I look like him. And the other, younger man, with the blond moustache and boater, is Titi Ialomițeanu, a good family friend, also from Muti's hometown of Buzău, where my grandparents and his parents used to see a lot of each other. Both my grandparents died in a terrible accident: first their train's brakes failed and it crashed into another one carrying petroleum, then it went off the rails and a number of wagons caught fire. What a horror! The doors wouldn't open. That was how Muti and Tante Margot became orphans. Muti married Papa, and Margot started boarding at the Central School and spending her Sundays and holidays with us. Afterward, as you will remember (not I), the war broke out."

Glossy new walnut paneling. Two doors on the right, and between them a little table with tall legs and a heart-shaped panel. Above, on a marble base, an ordinary table clock with a large white face, whose roman numerals can be read from across the room.

A quarter past five, in the afternoon.

Along the left wall, beneath the mirror, a mahogany sofa. Its back, in the form of three semi-ovals, is rounded off by a garlanded frame. A young girl—fringe on her forehead, curls covering her ears—sits back against the cushions on the sofa, in a posture of rigidity and indolence. Her slightly raised skirt reveals delicate ankles and patent-leather boots with low heels and silver buckles.

A young man, who a moment ago was keeping her company, sits cross-legged on a chair drawn up beside the sofa, his arms draped awkwardly over its rounded back. His fresh face is frozen into a dreamy look. He has gently slanting eyes, or perhaps they only appear to be so because of his prominent cheekbones. His slicked-back hair, with a parting right down the middle, does nothing to conceal his rather large ears. He is formally dressed for a visit: beige suit, stiff shirt collar.

Another tall little table, also with three legs, to the right of the sofa. On it a photo of a young couple in a wide frame. Thin and short, in a Prussian officer's uniform, the man rests his elbow on a pedestal table.

King Carol and Queen Elisabeta.

A bronze Apollo plays a lyre on the mantelpiece behind the sofa, under a mirror that reflects the bust of a young woman on the other side of the lounge. A huge bun, two large waves of hair, a slightly fixed stare. An impression of hauteur and inner calm, intensified (or actually created) by the haziness of the mirror. It is enough to look at each detail with a magnifying glass: for example, her forehead is quite low, her thin lips are tightly pursed, her nose . . . and so on. But, as soon as the glass is set aside, her gaze again becomes dreamily detached. The high black collar of her lace blouse is visible beneath a sprawling white silk shawl.

In the middle of the room, a pedestal table and *gris-vert* velvet cover layered with lotuses or water lilies. Its twilled silk border has large bows and fluffy white or golden tassels that stretch down to the carpet.

A single person at the table: a middle-aged man, his forehead and temples extended by baldness.

He is absorbed in a magazine, although, judging by the way he holds it between his skinny fingers, he would seem to have originally intended only to leaf through it. His face is emaciated, with dark circles around sunken eyes. His cheeks are closely shaven, while his moustache, its tips twirled in the old style, is surprisingly thick in comparison with the sparse covering of blond or grizzled hair on his head. His watch chain runs from one waistcoat pocket to the other, where it is attached to the end of a mechanical pencil. His frock coat has been put on properly, but he is not wearing a collar or tie.

On the pedestal table, a cigarette case, an ivory cigarette holder, and a finely carved ivory paper knife. Next to it, a wastepaper basket and a potbellied bronze vase with little twisted loops, full of papers, envelopes, cuttings, and magazines. The hour for correspondence.

Above the table, the long stem and translucent pendants of the Dutch chandelier, the only patch of light. Solemn shadow everywhere else: dark-sheened paneling, heavy furniture, a slight tension on the faces. It is a special moment, a pose of people caught up in ordinary conversation that the camera begins to capture, and whose solemnity their faces try to retain.

Part Two

Chapter 6

Teatime

"... a difficult moment ... I remember you saying it at the time, professor: We're passing through a difficult moment, and it's not at all impossible that we're heading for a catastrophe."

As usual, when he has to speak at a gathering of any kind, the guest has a purple face, and his thin white girlish neck is studded with red patches. He addresses the host with his habitual overpoliteness, turning his shoulders deferentially and directing his innocently blue, quizzical eyes toward him. But Professor Mironescu does not need to look up from the offprint he has been reading: he knows the respectful affection that the young man has toward him, as well as his lack of self-confidence. He is sure that what is stimulating his wiry eloquence is not a lady's beautiful eyes but the master's severe yet appreciative attention.

"... Your words struck me forcibly, because they departed from the received opinion of the time."

A shake of the head censures his unseemly note of praise. Where does that leave him? It leaves him with a rather embarrassed sense of homage, as if he has contracted a debt—an unpleasant feeling that the other has stripped him of his clothes and is reveling in the indecency of it.

The professor takes another envelope from the vase. A cigarette is burning away on the rim of the ashtray, sending a coil of grayish-blue smoke up above the table.

"I don't find it surprising that the Romanian public was unconcerned at first ... Not everyone has the gift of political foresight. That cannot be expected of public opinion—only of politicians. It's they who should always be a few steps ahead, instead of allowing themselves to be carried, or dragged, along by events. They must guide the public, even if it's not in the direction it would like."

"Really? You want them to lead the public in a direction opposed to its wishes?"

The host peers at him over the golden rim of his spectacles. It is the ironical gaze of a professor who has spotted your weak point, a pedagogic gaze, though, encouraging you to answer because the whole thing is an exercise in oratory. Does the young man understand everything that the watery-green eyes and the modified wrinkling on the bony face are trying to convey?

Without words, a partial misunderstanding is possible even between two people who are in sympathy with each other. "Well, no, . . . in my view not at all. I can't say I've ever had any taste for autocrats, nor for ambitious or power-hungry politicians."

Turning even redder, the baffled guest glances toward the pedestal table. That's usually how he looks when a little secret of his has been discovered. Our whole secret life is watched over by the eyes of strangers, but his is even more secret than that of others, because that is how he wanted it to be. At awkward moments, when a deed or thought he has been hiding somehow becomes known, he puts on that bewildered look of a man rudely awoken and plays for time to strengthen his defenses and make a few quick calculations. What secrets have come out? How far did the enemy advance after breaking through?

This is what his baffled glance toward the table is really asking.

Professor Mironescu smiles encouragingly to his former student, trying to help him control his emotions, as he did at the exams that he always passed magna cum laude or summa cum laude. He's a deeply touching figure, this modest ministerial functionary who is silent about his own merits and brushes aside praise with a cursory wave of the hand. He has only one human weakness: teatime seems to arouse in him an appetite for chatting about politics.

"Actually I didn't mean to contradict you . . . ," he hastens to assure the young man.

He puts the sheet of paper he has been holding onto the table. Then he carefully removes his gold-rimmed spectacles, places them beside it, and begins to rub the sore indentation on his nose with dry fingertips.

"We all know that Romanian public opinion is rather malleable in the hands of an authoritarian politician," he continues. "He could quite easily take it in a different direction from the one the public would like to see. We also know very well the reason for this: the masses in our country lack any real experience of democracy, and a tradition cannot be created in the space of one or two generations. They therefore don't know how to stand up for their demands. They're prepared to call off any action at the drop of a hat, and after so many troubles they are thankful for small mercies. Above all, they don't feel any solidarity with one another—a fault you can find in every layer of society. So, I hope you understand that I wasn't contradicting you. I do believe that the masses in Romania can be taken in a direction contrary to their wishes."

"Maybe that's already beginning to happen?"

And, as he says it, a sweet, ingratiating smile lights up the face of the young Ialomiţeanu. The professor laughs, putting his glasses back on.

"Now wait a minute! I wasn't referring to Brătianu. Believe me, I wasn't making any allusion to the present day, nor prophesying anything about the next fifty years. It was a theoretical point, *in abstracto*. That is, the Romanian people could easily be taken in a calamitous direction, becoming more and more mired in corruption and poverty—our age-old afflictions . . ."

With a bony-handed gesture of displeasure, the professor picks up the sheet of paper from the pedestal table, briefly skims it, and drops it back into the vase. Such banal observations to be making! He opens another envelope and starts to read its contents, while his knee jerks mechanically and his left eye opens and shuts at an even faster rate. It is a tic he has developed recently at moments of nervous tension, when something other than his will seems to press half his face into a grimace. The ivory paper knife in his clammy hand produces a scream from the silk paper. The watery-green iris darts from one corner of his eye to the other, across a sclera stained with yellow patches and red streaks.

A wart, off-white like a blighted plum, interferes with his vision in one eye and causes the professor to make a vain unthinking adjustment of his spectacles. His other hand meanwhile fumbles on the table for his old cigarette case, which has a little lighter attached to it.

An unconfident movement—furtive and guilty.

"Do as you please! But the first puff will make you cough again . . ."

Sophie's cold words give voice to his own anxiety, so he doesn't look toward the end of the room where she sits in the Italian armchair, her white silk shawl draped over her shoulders. His hand hovers over the velvet table cover, and he seems to be playing for time as he scratches the edge of an embroidered water lily with a yellow fingernail.

The silence torments Titi Ialomiţeanu because of an old but unjustified guilt complex: he feels that his lack of social graces has driven the professor back to his correspondence. Holding his hands behind his back, he studies a piece of chinaware on the mantelpiece: a dreamy shepherdess with neat blonde curls clutches her temple, wearing a very low-cut dress and small Louis XV–style shoes; there is the obligatory dog and the obligatory rock, and a shepherd is moving gracefully toward her with a little basket of flowers in his hand.

A sharp rustling sound—the professor has rolled the sheet of paper he was reading into a ball and is holding it in his clenched fist. A stranger who observed the scene would blame the hosts for being negligent toward their guests and at most allow some attenuating circumstances: Sophie's peculiar state at that moment, or the professor's eccentric character and casual manners; he no longer wears a stiff collar, for example, arguing that it chokes him and makes him cough—which makes Titi Ialomiţeanu wonder whether he should take this familiarity as a mark of affection or mild disdain.

The sensitive young man nevertheless blames himself for the vexing silence. For better or worse, however, he has become used to the ways of the world, so that, when he has finished examining the Frankenthal figurine, he feels able to straighten things out. It is many years since he began to mix in high society, here in this very salon, to which he has remained loyal in accordance with his conservative nature. But how different it seems now, how peaceful and bourgeois! He remembers when he first presented his visiting card in a bunch of flowers to remind Sophie Mironescu of their childhood years together in the patriarchal world of Buzău, and when he was kindly invited in to join them as it happened to be their *jour de réception*. At that time his dress and manners left much to be desired, and the thought of dancing or even speaking on the telephone would torture him for weeks in advance. It was no surprise, then, that he found this rather ordinary salon so daunting. It's true that in those days the people who attended it in considerable numbers were not the kind to be seen at ordinary occasions. The newlywed

Mironescus, not long back from a honeymoon in Italy, were themselves much more enthusiastic and open-hearted in sketching out future intentions and projects, exchanging addresses, and cultivating influential friends, relatives, or contacts. What a marvel the Mironescu salon was for the young Ialomițeanu! After so many solitary walks to the Flora café or Rondul Doi, in shoes with holes in them, frayed trousers, and his elder brother's oversize coat, after so often eyeing elegant carriages or automobiles bedecked with roses or carnations for the festive Battle of Flowers, here he was suddenly in the same room with the august objects of his admiration—even if there was no chance that they would notice him!

The young Ialomițeanu starts to walk around the salon in his tightly buttoned new suit, clasping his hands behind his back. But after a few paces he stops again—this time in front of the photo of King Carol and Queen Elisabeta. The monarchy was a lively issue of the day. If he wanted, he might pillory the man who, after ruling happily for forty years, had shown at the first test that he was the same as when he arrived from Sigmaringen to sit on the throne of the Voievods: an obedient, mediocre Prussian officer. Or, on the contrary, he might commiserate with the poor monarch who, at a venerable age, when he might have been allowed to find spiritual peace, had suddenly been forced to choose between spilling the blood of his ancestors or the blood of his subjects, over whom he had reigned more or less justly for nearly half a century. This new King Lear, as some newspapers called him, found himself from one day to the next in a strange and hostile country, in a family prone to discord, abandoned and betrayed by those he had trusted and showered with honors, even asked without further ado to renounce his throne and adoptive country.

But no, the young man is not going to address this issue, about which so many speeches have been made, so many solemn words pronounced. He is not capable of such an irreparable blunder. He could not be so unwise, in a house where the host makes so much of his long-standing friendship with the minister Athanasiu. On the other hand, the same factors mean that he could pick up quite a lot of inside information here. The professor enjoys talking more and more as his health declines, and it is clear that any question will elicit another long theoretical argument to the effect that a scholar should remain above the political fray, which usually spatters with mud anyone who gets too close to it.

So? So, when considering which theme to address, an experienced man of the world would rather meet his host halfway and put him in a genial frame of mind to answer specific questions later on.

He stops abruptly—his movements always seem abrupt, as if dictated by reason rather than any natural impulse—and sits down crosswise on a chair, his arms over its back.

So, first he will ask a pretty anodyne question: "Does the professor really think it is possible to escape from the politics of the age, from the pressures of the surrounding society?"

He has lowered his shoulders deferentially, and only the merest hint of teasing glimmers in his innocent eyes.

The professor looks up, surprised. He was a million miles away and has a sense of being rudely awoken. But only for an instant. The questioner's good manners, and the fellow feeling he inspires, quickly get the better of any irritation.

Fellow feeling—perhaps much more than that. Perhaps an affection that has developed without being noticed, in response to the young man's attentions. Constant praise from someone gradually makes you accustomed to it, so that you would miss it if it were to be withdrawn one day. But loyalty is one of the qualities of youth: the professor may be volatile in his moods, and Sophie has her feminine caprices, but the young man is ever considerate, ever eager to offer his services. He is undoubtedly one of that rare species for whom the greatest happiness in the world is to make themselves useful to people they love. How can you fail to value such generosity? And how can you not feel more and more well-disposed to the person who offers it to you?

Seeing him every day as you do, you inevitably grow fond of him and begin to notice the little affinities with yourself more than the trivial defects, even if your affection is still slightly disdainful. But then you suddenly realize that you have adopted Titi Ialomițeanu—something you would never have dreamed possible when he appeared for the first time, at one of Sophie's *five o'clocks*. He stood at the door, like any provincial kid, so timid that the valet had to wrench his hat and gloves away from him. His shirt collar had a gray line around it, his jacket sleeves were worn, and his trousers were splashed with mud—not to speak of their old-fashioned style. And when he insisted on presenting Sophie with that bunch of ordinary garden flowers, you had to plead hard for her to conquer her repulsion toward the young greenhorn. Such an aversion for the poor and unsuccessful comes naturally to women: it has a lot in common with canine snobbism. And, however superior Sophie is to other women, she cannot defy the laws of her sex and social position, which mean that little sartorial slip-ups are seen as veritable crimes. She may overlook them, after much prompting on your part, but she will never actually forgive them . . . Although the young man's native intelligence led him to correct such faults, Sophie will never forget how he looked when he was received in their house for the first time. You, on the other hand, remember your own youth only too well: how you preferred to give the first balls a miss, on the pretext that either your jacket or your trousers didn't suit you; or how, if the ball was in your own house, you locked yourself up in your study and came down only after your poor sisters repeatedly implored you, pointing out that there was no one else to make up a quadrille. You, being more tolerant and open-minded, can avoid taking such things too seriously!

Indeed, as the object of his sustained admiration, you will eventually include the poor young man in a family portrait.

Ah, how solid and mediocre are our family feelings, born of habit and trust, spiritual comfort and mutual toleration! It is they that give the necessary stability to life and, by protecting the mind, free it for the service of higher ends.

Keeping his glasses on his nose, the professor relaxes his lean frame on the chair and allows his soft gaze to glide out of the large clear window toward the clematis plants on the terrace. The sky is perfectly clear, too intensely blue for an autumn day, and from time to time the golden coronas of the trees in the garden sparkle metallically in the soft, honeyed light. For a week now, the perverse late-summer heat has been weighing on everyone and making them look haggard and dreamy-eyed. This morning, however, a cold mist enveloped the garden—thick and compact like the steam that pours from a defective ship's boiler. Toward midday the warmth and golden light returned, but the professor saw a group of inoffensive white clouds in the implausibly blue sky. A sign of a change in the weather?

Looking gently at the young man, his face concedes that, in so far as you are a creature of habit devoid of idealism, you may believe in a life of isolation so long as politics and the activity of society are proceeding normally, but that those who work for the cultural improvement of a nation rarely fall victim to such an illusion. For the first result of culture is to strengthen relations of solidarity in your society—both horizontally, with people living today, and vertically, with previous generations. So, even if they think of themselves as autonomous individuals, perhaps even as the center of the universe, those who sincerely work in the service of culture must feel, at least some of the time, that they are part of a single organism. At difficult times like the present, when collective interests are beginning to take first place, you will find it impossible in good faith to keep your fate separate from that of others. And if, despite everything, you persist in trying to do it by honest means, the inevitable egoism that comes simply from protecting your own corner will make you bend in one way or another to the atmosphere of the times. Of course, it will depend on you whether you make minimal adjustments or go all the way and grovel in the dust. But, even if you mobilize all your reserves of dignity—not an easy feat to keep up, especially in the long term—the results may still be unsatisfactory, as in a badly lit room where flowers grow at a strange angle, neither rising nor creeping, but keeping a precarious balance shored up by sap and cellulose.

He is almost panting by the end of this long bout of oratory. The emotion is unjustified, as at the national festivities on the Tenth of May, when the first fanfares bring disgraceful tears to his eyes—only this time the lump in his throat is due to nervous fatigue. His bony hand now reaches out more decisively to the table, no longer mindful of the need for Sophie's approval, and his gestures are swift and sure as he raises a cigarette to his mouth and flicks the lighter. It is at such moments that his original ascendancy over Sophie reasserts itself, over that white shape listening motionless in its silk-tasseled shawl. She is doubtless aware that something has dispelled her power, but she waits patiently, confident that it will be restored to her in the natural course of things.

The professor continues to smoke quietly, his pale balding head thrown back. His mind is no longer on the afternoon rush of excitement, and he is filled with a petty, childish sense of victory.

Victory over whom? Over what?

On the sofa, Margot yawns unobtrusively and examines her boots. She still considers them new, even though it is three months since her *beau-frère* Ştefan brought them for her from Vienna. On the same occasion, he gave her a blue-eyed porcelain doll that had real hair and said "mama, mama" when you tilted it.

"A doll! What will she do with a doll at her age?" Sophie asked indelicately.

"What do you mean?" Ştefan retorted. "She's still a child, isn't she?"

As usual, he was influenced by Sophie's opinion. He turned his head from one to the other, then back again. He wanted to stroke Margot paternally on the head, but as usual he only managed to touch her ear with his fingertips.

"Soon there'll be another one to play with it," Ana hinted.

Try as she might to be discreet, she could hardly wait for an opportunity to open her mouth.

And they had a funny look in their eyes, Sophie, Ştefan, and Ana.

Really, how could they imagine she didn't understand such allusions? Look at that time Uncle Georges took them in his car to the Filipescu mansion. They were just taking off their drill costumes, their goggles, and helmets, when Miza and Radu Filipescu ran up to them, followed by a droopy spinster type: she was twenty-nine, and had one of those noses! In fact, nothing about her was right. She was wearing a splendid necklace—two intertwined snakes, with ruby eyes—but at that hour of the day . . . A traveling suit or a peasant costume would have been more suitable—anything but that!

Even Sophie commented on it.

"But who is she, in fact?" she asked Georges Ioaniu, who also happened to be around that day.

"C'est la seule amie de Miza avec qui Radu n'a pas couché."

And Sophie couldn't help interjecting:

"Dommage!"

Ştefan made discreet gestures: the child! Margot is here! And Sophie added some reassuring ones of her own: it's all right, the child doesn't understand.

"Ah, Margot darling, it's a miracle when the Good Lord opens a woman's tummy and lets a baby out . . . The way the bones open is a real miracle," Ana had answered shortly before.

(Sophie to Miza, at a *jour de reception:* just imagine, *ma chère,* she wasn't embarrassed to ask Madam Ana how babies came out, and where.)

Come on, she knows perfectly well where the opening is. There's many a time—now, for example, in the salon—when she looks at them and is sure she understands more than they do. They, on the other hand, like her classmates, don't know her at all. How terrible it is to be alone and misunderstood! Yesterday evening she played the piano for hours and wept bitter tears, convinced that she will die young, soon after her first ball and her first kiss. They will dress her in white and hold a Catholic mass, because that will be her last wish.

It will be a rainy afternoon: shiny black saloons, solemn organ music beneath somber colonnades, the dizzying scent of lilies and tuberoses, Sophie with a thick veil so that people can't see if she's really crying, *pauvre* Ştefan crying for real but glancing at Sophie to see if she approves, Madam Ana half-faint at the sadness of it all ... The gloomy cathedral, the funeral music from Donizetti's *Parisiana,* the Allegro con fuoco from Senna's *Dolore.* And, before a month is over, they'll all be going to see *The Spider,* which was out of bounds for her, and Sophie, excited by the acting of Tony Bulandra, will suggest dinner at the Café de Paris and dance the tango there with Titi Ialomiţeanu ... Hard to imagine a ghastlier oblivion.

Margot has a lump in her throat. How terrible to be given such a short life and to be *seule et incomprise*! It's better to die young, though, before you develop wrinkles and your hair falls out—perhaps a virgin, or anyway before becoming pregnant. She hates the idea of having a big belly; people can always tell, even if you wrap yourself up in a white shawl. Who might bring tuberoses to her funeral? Ştefan will follow Sophie's lead, and so will Titi, and Miti Popazu is off in Vienna. So, no flowers. A neglected tomb. What a pity: so young and charming and graceful! If she'd wanted, she could have kept house instead of Sophie and Madam Ana ... Who checks up on lazybones Nela every evening, to make sure she's dusted her shoes and polished them with the prescribed castor oil? She could also serve tea and keep the conversation going—even right now, for example. After all, she can talk politics and knows which are the burning questions. "What will our little kingdom do in the present situation? Shall we side with France and Russia so that we can liberate our fellow Romanians across the Carpathians before they're mowed down at the front line? Or shall we side with the Triple Entente, to liberate our Bessarabian lands that we lost to Russia at the end of our victorious war over the Turks? That is the dilemma facing the little Romanian state."

These are the issues of the day in every salon—even in her dormitory at the Central School. If she was the hostess, she'd introduce them and liven things up.

"In other respects," the professor continues, in a voice that reaches Margot from afar, "this country ravaged by history may offer more scope than any other to a man of enterprise. If your ambition is noble, if you want your work rather than your person to prosper, you will be happy to subordinate your individuality to the collective. As I was saying, you will understand that you are not the center of the universe but only one little point, neither its heart nor its brains but simply one cell in a vast organism. But you will not be a full-grown man unless . . ."

Teatime was really boring yesterday, when those three women from the Orthodox Society came and Sophie sent her to chat with them while she got all dressed up. All three of them sat bolt upright, like black ravens at a funeral, never saying more than a yes or a no or an oh-dear-me. But in the end she did make them more relaxed, and then Sophie came down and started playing the hostess. Ştefan also put in an appearance, but he quickly withdrew to his study when he saw how things were shaping up. After a while, Titi Ialomiţeanu arrived with a carriage and driver and wanted to take her and Sophie out for a ride in the Kiseleff Avenue district, but in the end she went with him alone and they didn't even stop off to play tennis.

"*Mais qui sont ces dames?*" Titi asked, once they were seated in the carriage.

"They're oh-dear-me ladies," she explained, using an expression the queen was known to use.

What, what? Titi was at a loss to understand. So she had to explain in detail how such ladies thought it good manners to preface every sentence with an "oh-dear."

"Oh, dear, what rainy weather we've been having!"

"Oh, dear, what a funny setting that ring has! May I have a look?"

"Oh, dear, well, all right. Oh, dear, is that possible?"

". . . because, for each one of us, it is the proof that we have reached maturity. I mean spiritual maturity, of course, not biological. And for each one of us it will have consequences as profound as . . ."

The professor gets up from his chair, keeping a slight grimace on his face.

There he is on his feet.

The frock coat corrects his posture, lifting up his shoulders and enveloping his newly emaciated body. He looks at the others over the gold rim of his spectacles—an affectionate green look. He wouldn't dream of leaving the salon at this hour, with his correspondence and people dear to him still here; he just wants to draw his chair closer to the pedestal table.

"Please, don't let me disturb you . . ."

His right hand conducts an uncertain pianissimo, while his left, weak and clumsy, pulls the chair up behind him. Its legs drag along the thick Persian carpet, distorting its pattern and colors.

Inside his trousers, which have become too large for him, his flabby buttocks seem no more than an extension of his wasted thighs. He is seated once more, but now only half-perched on the edge of the chair, as if about to get up again at any moment. But there is no question of that. His posture merely reflects the moment of feverish excitement that followed a period of doubt and skepticism. His is a cyclothymic personality structure, as he readily admits.

He looks out the window again, where it has grown suddenly darker and a spell of colder weather is looming. Deceptive straw-yellow corollas, their scentless petals hardened by autumn mists, open here and there on the paths of golden gravel running alongside Sophie's impeccably laid clumps of roses. Eye-catching bright-red leaves hang on a branch from the dense vault of ground ivy, wisteria, and clematis.

"I hope the professor will forgive me a lack of modesty just this once," the young man begins hesitantly, "because until now I have hardly ever committed the sin of vanity. But, without wishing to set myself up as a judge of political events, I would like to say in all modesty that I have been disappointed. Do you not agree that our politicians were singularly lacking in foresight? It was to be expected that the public would let us down. But is it normal that even the most clairvoyant should prove so disappointing? Or perhaps they knew what was coming and—I hardly dare say it—had already been bought off."

"I know the feeling," the professor smiled. "I too sometimes find them disappointing and give them a wide berth. At such times I keep telling myself that all we see before us has come about in just fifty years. And, above all, I repeat that wonderfully perceptive quotation from Beaumarchais: *Calomniez, calomniez, il en restera toujours quelque chose.* Unfortunately, it is only in fifty or seventy years' time that we will know the stuff our politicians are made of—and what they have succeeded in doing in a historical situation that is, as always, unfavorable to them. As you know, I am a fervent supporter of universal suffrage, which is in line with my whole way of thinking, yet I sometimes wonder what will become of our politicians when the gates open wide and the views of a Carp or Brătianu about the fate of the nation carry as much weight as their coachman's. Qualities soon turn into defects if they are pushed beyond the limit, and a world in which we were all compulsorily equal in every respect would be a heavy, airless prison. But I think I may have misrepresented what you had in mind."

"No, no, but I can't forget how quietly the king went off to his castle in Sinaia, and how the government itself started preparing to go on vacation. We were all here together, in this salon, when Uncle rang and you picked up the phone. You do remember, don't you?" he asks Sophie.

Titi Ialomiţeanu's blue gaze drifts timorously to the other end of the room, where Sophie, more absent and more scornful than usual, is pulling her white shawl over her full body. Does the young man's excessive politeness conceal a hint of malice, mixing together admiration with distrust, fear, and, above all, curiosity? Such is the combination of feelings that Sophie has always aroused in him, ever since their first encounter as children, when he tore himself away from his mother and raced down the wooden staircase, causing general consternation that he might break every bone in his body. What had caused his panicky flight? He couldn't quite put his finger on it, even today. But he well remembers the fear that overcame him when he first set eyes on her: such a beautiful little girl, with long blonde curls under a huge flowery hat. So blindingly beautiful, all diaphanous frills and rustling ribbons. Admiration and fear, distrust and curiosity—that is the oldest of their memories, but until now he hasn't had a chance to remind her of it.

"You do remember, Madam Mironescu, don't you? It was when that uncle tried to persuade you to go on holiday that summer, despite everything. Unless I'm mistaken, he suggested a trip to Măldăreşti, but you said that for the time being you couldn't bear the thought of a car journey."

"You mistaken? No, there's no danger of your ever forgetting anything. You convinced us all of that long ago!"

"Whereas your memory, my dear, is unfortunately . . ."

Ştefan Mironescu's prompt, smiling intervention was designed to cushion the effect of his wife's cutting repartee. You have to understand her: the state she is in at the moment inclines young women to whims and morbid humors, especially if they are sensitive and idealistic. It would be a pity if the young guest were to read what she said as a sign of disregard or even contempt. There were other moments when she displayed impatience with Titi Ialomiţeanu, and each time he was forced to step in to ensure that the young man was not hurt.

An attentive host, the professor would beam conciliatorily at one and then the other, his fleshy, slightly chapped, lips parting to reveal yellow but strong teeth, in a smile so benevolent it seemed almost forced. Then things would seem to sort themselves out. A blushing Titi Ialomiţeanu assured the lady that he wouldn't dare lay claim to any other quality, but when it came to his memory . . . It never played tricks, and the more something or someone interested him, the more reliable it was . . . That is why he might be forgiven, because what happened in the Mironescu house was of the greatest interest to him; it was almost as close to him as his parental home.

"They are *my* memories—my private memories," the young man concludes with a smile, reviving from his humiliation like a phoenix from the ashes.

Passing rapidly over the incident—which he takes to have been trivial enough—the professor nevertheless chokes back a trace of displeasure. Why displeasure? Is it because the young man is already pressing ahead with the conversation, not showing the slightest touch of ill will—indeed, displaying great friendliness toward the hostess? As if he had been the aggressor, and she the victim! A true role reversal, which somewhat devalues the spouse's tactful intervention and makes it appear pointless and absurd to a critical eye. Ah, what trifles! what petty nonsense to be worrying about! Fortunately the professor makes up for his oversensitive nature by a healthy urge to simplify situations.

To treat his neighbor with generous indulgence.

All the better, then, if bashful Titi takes advantage of the older man's protection to send a playful gleam toward the eyes of a still sullen Sophie at the other end of the room. Let's all be friends again!

All the better—especially as she doesn't seem to notice.

Deep in thought, she shivers under her white silk shawl. Despite her protruding eyes, rather thin lips, and many other imperfections, and despite her advanced state of pregnancy, she hasn't ceased to be attractive. And feeling, like any woman, that she is being looked at, she turns her head and looks back at the young man. Yes, she does have rather protruding eyes, but her long straight lashes shroud them and make her mysterious. Not even then does Titi know what is in that look: scorn? friendliness? complicity? indifference? boredom?

An ivory-white sky hangs brooding over the shadowy garden: night will soon fall. Usually, tea would be served at that hour, but how unbearably people behave when they don't feel they are being watched! Sophie seems about to stand up from the sofa, but today she feels even heavier and for the last few days she has been dragging her left leg.

"Patience, my dear!" her godmother, Fănica Filipescu, has been saying to her. "Just a few more days and it will be over. Then you'll be able to walk like you used to."

Life goes its sweet logical way for so long. So why does it imperceptibly lead you to a point of no return, even when you would like to turn back and hide like a child in your mother's skirts, after you have taken a few steps alone in the dark? And why does an act like giving birth, natural enough because it renews life, have to be so painful and disgusting? And what's the matter with Madam Ana? Why hasn't she shown up today?

Usually at this hour the door opens and Madam Ana appears pushing a little tea trolley. What a nuisance! You've got to keep your eyes on them all the time and remind each one of their duties—even if your left foot is dragging and your belly starts to hurt out of the blue. Sometimes it's a really bad pain, like the cramp you have with colitis; you'd go and lock yourself in your room if tea had been served already. You'd leave the men to go on with their idle chatter, which you tolerate with an indulgent smile, as you will the games your child plays.

"For example, Take Ionescu is in favor of entering the war at once, although not long ago he was thoroughly demoralized and saw nothing but disaster ahead. *Finis Romaniae* . . . How do you explain his change of position?"

"Oh, Take Ionescu!" the professor says, with a dismissive wave of his hand. "Look, leave aside his electoral blocs—and there are too many of them, surprisingly many—and just concentrate on the man himself . . . It's well known how he shifts from one opinion to another and can put together a fine speech about anything under the sun—Goldmouth Take, as people call him . . . But I don't want to discuss his 'versatility,' shall we say. Rightly or wrongly, he's been taxed with that many times before . . . What I do think is beyond doubt is that he's driven by a certain kind of personality structure . . . Let me make myself clearer: the fact that he heatedly adopts one attitude in a circle of close friends, only to keep silent or let himself be drawn into the opposite attitude in the official world of protracted policy discussion, suggests to me that he is powerless to resist external influences. It's a kind of weakness of character."

He has strayed from the subject. And he knows he is no longer talking about the leader of the Democratic Conservatives, but about things he has reproached himself for all his life. His indomitable sincerity would push him to recognize in public that he is the first to suffer from such faults, were it not for the fact that Sophie would disapprove of it. Her good sense instinctively shies away from that dubious mixture of humility and arrogance, which seems to her a piece of cheap bluster worthy of a ham actor. Of course, the well-known conventionality of women leads Sophie to think in that way, but her peculiar lack of humor also plays a part. Still, he never forgets that, as so often before, she may be right and he may be wrong. She may be a child in comparison with him, but her big blue eyes, so wise and omniscient, never stop following him. A child, maybe, but one who knows life by sheer instinct and has no need to understand it. That is the wily female intuition that governs the world, so that a man like him has no option but to bow his high bald forehead to her in submission.

Titi Ialomiţeanu doesn't give up:

"But don't you think . . . Doesn't it seem to you . . ."

"Yes, my dear man, it's very clear to me. I understand."

The professor waves his two bony hands in the air. A little patience is called for: just another minute and he will find a formulation to cut through the last hour's meandering. With the acumen of a good teacher, he knows better than anyone what has been agitating the young man.

"I understand your point. You mean to ask whether we are hopelessly in thrall to our times, whether we are completely lost and powerless, whether our will—even supposing it is single and indivisible, not as fragmented as it appears to be—counts for more than a grain of sand . . ."

The ringing of their newly installed telephone can be heard somewhere in the house. Sophie can't be far away: she's just left the salon to deal with tea. The professor expresses in clear and precise language what the young Titi can only fish up from the depths of his troubled soul in the form of conventional questions.

". . . or whether, despite everything, the people who fight to rule us have the necessary qualities, taking it in turns with one another, in response to the king's conciliatory offers, and therefore whether there is any way of guessing what the permanent mixture of calculation and chance that is the stuff of history and politics will bring. So, does an inexorable law of progress protect us, or are we just spinning round and round in a circle? Do we really have any chance of drawing closer to the civilized nations of the West—which has been our dream for the past century? Or is that just a mirage, a pointless effort, given that they have been advancing much faster and the gap between us remains as large as ever—or rather, grows immeasurably with each obstacle that we hit our heads against? Is it possible, by concentrating your mind and making lucid calculations, to know which way the war will go, and to join in at the most advantageous moment? Or are all such efforts in vain, since the future course of history cannot be foreseen, any more than you can see further than your nose in a winter snowstorm?"

The young man's vociferous approval gives him the satisfaction of knowing that he has been understood. The door finally opens, letting the distant noise of the house into the salon: Sophie's prattling on the telephone, an exclamation of surprise . . . But Titi Ialomițeanu pays it no attention—not out of excessive politeness, but because sounds closer to his ears gladden him much more. The familiar squeaking of the tea trolley, the tinkle of teaspoons and sugar tongs—and the glacé fruits, pastries, and chocolates that Madame Ana gracelessly drops onto plates. The young man is hungry, and for that very reason he avoids turning his head like the plague.

"Don't you think neutrality all through the war is a solution?" he heroically stammers out.

"Ștefan!" Sophie calls in a metallic voice.

She probably wants to check from the door whether tea is being served properly, much as a general conducts operations from a hillock through his field glasses. But her hair is disarranged, her shawl hangs carelessly over one shoulder, and her slightly swollen face has lost its gracefulness . . . Breaking with habit, she stands and waits at the door in front of the clock, instead of sending Nela to fetch her husband. Titi Ialomițeanu feels a certain pleasure—why?—that she is departing from convention. Something unusual must have happened to disconcert her and revive the modest customs of her parental home in Buzău, in rather the same way that Transylvanians, after many years of living in Bucharest and conforming to the pronunciation of a literary language, revert to their dialect in moments of high emotion, as if they had never spoken in any other way.

Nevertheless, a lifetime of orderly work has made the professor reluctant to leave anything unfinished. He continues to speak as he slowly raises himself from his chair.

"Er, yes, my dear . . . Yes, *chérie* . . . I thought I heard the telephone earlier. Please, just one moment and I'll be with you.—So, if we consider that the creation of a tradition and an institutional continuity should be this country's fondest wish . . . after all this time when it has known no peace . . . Yes, *mon petit* . . . I'm just coming . . . So, I know what you mean to ask: you want to know whether I'd have confidence in Prime Minister Brătianu, given that I'm an independent and that my views are sincere, even if a little naive . . . Or else the whole issue is beside the point and only chance will ever result in a Greater Romania, or . . . Yes, my dear . . . Who did you say has died?"

He listens for a moment, then turns around.

"Gentlemen," he says in a grave voice, which sounds so strange and solemn, "King Carol is dead."

And the clocks begins to strike, like a slowly sounding gong.

"*Voilà*," the professor says, rather taken aback, and a wave of his bony hand suggests very clearly that Fate itself is flooding the salon with those round, metallic, evenly spaced sounds. "*Voilà*."

Then, disregarding the young man's urgent questions and Madam Ana's expressions of woe, he thoughtfully approaches the one who, with a gentle submissiveness that was thoroughly feminine, insisted on giving the gloomy news to her husband first. No doubt she has another migraine and will have to press aromatic vinegar compresses to her head. But his smile evaporates as he makes out the other thing she is whispering to him; here again is that inexplicable emotion he felt on the Tenth of May, when the festive fanfares produced a lump in the throat of this grown man. Someone weeps inside him as the gong rings out purposelessly, announcing nothing more than the afternoon hour of six o'clock.

With a ceremonious bow, the professor asks the assembled company to excuse his wife and himself, as they will be gone for a little while.

There is no need for such apologies. Nibbling a pastry and breathing in the aroma from the cup of tea in his hand, Titi Ialomițeanu draws his chair closer to the sofa to keep the young lady of the house company—as good manners require of him. Soon, however, he is reaching again for the plate with the pastries. Social obligations sometimes force him to skip lunch, and often he has to struggle with his youthful voracity at tea-time in this familiar salon.

But today, owing to the unexpected events, he will be able to eat his fill without keeping an eye on himself. So he looks with pleasure at his young companion, who for her part is savoring a slice of chocolate cake. At that moment he is more relaxed than ever before, in the calm bliss of a schoolboy who hears the bell ring for recreation. He is no longer forced to keep up the conversation, and he can wait patiently until the professor has sorted things out with his wife.

"You heard what Sophie said, didn't you?" the girl whispers to him. "She didn't only say that the king is dead."

She knows what Sophie said: her fine ear picked it up, or her sharp eye understood without her needing to hear it. Titi Ialomiţeanu will be her confidant, her knight in shining armor, and with a little patience she will steal him away from Sophie's influence. But as for what Sophie said, it would be unseemly for a young girl to repeat it; it would not be nice to speak with Titi about what has started to happen upstairs, even though muffled voices and the scurrying of footsteps can be heard on the other side of the door, and even though horses' hooves and carriage wheels can be heard in the street taking Ştefan to Colţea hospital, from where he will return soon with the obstetrician.

No, it would not be proper to tell him something like that. But, since they will spend some time *tête à tête* in the salon, she will find a way of insinuating it to him.

Chapter 7

Afternoon in the Rose Garden

Margot

"Now come on, Margot dear, a well-bred young lady doesn't show herself stark naked at the window. Hurry up, we've got a lot to do today. There's no point your looking every couple of minutes: the guests won't arrive until this evening. Come here, young lady, let's see what we can do with your hair."

First of all, she isn't naked at all, just wearing a bra and trousers. And second, she isn't standing at the window, but practicing how to do a Boston waltz in front of the mirror. Ah, how she loves that dance—so modern, so emotional and sensual! She just adores it. What is Madam Ana on about? *Savez-vous planter les choux, à la mode, à la mode?* She's fed up to the back teeth with the same old tune, fed up traipsing around the school yard arm in arm with Coralie and Sévastie, in a gray dress and percale blouse; only at exams is she allowed to wear something different, and then it's a white muslin dress and a ribbon-like scarf with the class colors—such has been the rule at the Central School for the past thirty years. Does Madam Ana know what other horrid regulations they have there? After ten o'clock no one—not even the headmistress—can enter the place. No one! They're all shut up in a besieged fortress—a convent! Does she understand what it means to be allowed out only once a fortnight? And what if your own sister, either off her own bat or conniving with the headmistress, forgets all about you on one of the two Sundays a month, claiming to have got the days confused? Does Madam Ana understand how bitter an orphan's fate is?

Of course, there are a lot of things that Madam Ana doesn't understand, or pretends not to understand, but if you remind her of a orphan's bitter fate she immediately puts her curling iron down somewhere and clutches you to a breast that smells of the kitchen and laundry. Then you're her little darling. "You're not all alone in the world," she whispers in her cracked voice. "Didn't I suckle both you and Spiridon? You'll never be alone as long as I'm alive. Besides, you have a sister who loves you, as well as Mister Ştefan, a good and learned man if ever there was one! And one of these days you'll find a good match and have a fine wedding.

"Look at little Miss Sophie: what a wonderful match she found! Your godmother Fănica Filipescu was right: get married, get married, she kept telling her, and we can see how well it turned out. It was the will of the Almighty to put your parents in that blasted train, in one of the seven wagons that caught fire and went blazing through the fields as if it was hell itself. Everyone was screaming, and those who managed to jump clear were on fire as they kept rolling on the ground. The others went on screaming in the train, squashed up there like sardines, screaming for help—but what good did that do? Was anyone mad enough to jump into the inferno? Even the fields were alight, and those seven wagons burned like candles at Easter. I heard that one fat merchant in a fur coat kept calling for help and offering sacks of gold, so that a few bold men managed to get close enough and grab his gold and his coat, but then left him inside to roast. Ah, young lady, it was the end of the world! This is the end of the world, I said to myself, God is punishing me for my sins! So how come that he decided to forgive me? I don't know. How was it that I found myself lying on the ground, with my skirt and petticoat pulled up, and just one of my ankles twisted? It was a miracle. Only the sweet Lord knows. He must have said to himself: she's committed so many sins, she can start by paying for them on earth. Or maybe he took pity on my poor little Spiridon, knowing there was no one else to take care of him. Anyway, his will was done. Mine was the only third-class wagon that escaped, and I thought: Great is the power of the Lord; I am his servant, not worthy to kiss his feet, yet he has pulled me from the flames and saved me! Afterward, I even wondered how I didn't die of fear . . . Keep still, young lady, stop turning your head—there's nothing to see out the window! I keep telling you: the guests will all arrive this evening."

The guests will all arrive this evening, but there's already a carriage at the end of the street, jolting along and avoiding the grayish-green paving stones put there for the repair work. Why did Sophie tell Titi Ialomițeanu to *come early* today? Why is she so nervous and troubled, and taking it out on her little sister?

"How can you sit shut up in this foul air, when outside . . . especially at your age? And why is your room in such a state? Is there a Maria at school to keep tidying up after you?"

All right, just leave her alone, she knows the score. She knows it even with her fingers in her ears: well-bred-young-ladies-like-to-rise-early-when-the-air-is-fresh-and-like-to-sit-in-a-well-aired-room-doing-their-Greek-translations-their piano-exercises-their-painting-and-embroidery.

"*J'en ai assez!*" she shouts angrily, reddening to the roots of her hair. She snatches the dark-stained silk panties that Sophie has been waving in front of her nose. "*J'en ai assez! J'en ai assez!*"

She has turned her back, so that she doesn't have the satisfaction of seeing her cry. No, she'll never become an unbearable neurotic like Sophie! She won't shout at everyone over the slightest little thing. She's not afraid of a little blood and doesn't faint all the time, as modern girls do. She doesn't need jars of salts or sugared water, and if there's a war she'll become a Red Cross nurse and help to ease people's sufferings.

"May God have mercy on us, young lady. Hard times are coming, there'll soon be war: that's what Mistress Sophie told me yesterday. And I told her that poor Spiridon should be given some more leave, so he can come and see me and relax a bit at home. Mister Titi was mobilized at the same place, and he's been out for three months now. But Mistress Sophie said it wasn't easy to arrange, though she promised to do what she could. How many times must I tell you to stop wriggling, young lady? The iron's gone cold, but if it had been hot I might have burned you, God forbid!"

Phew, thank God she's gone off to heat the iron! Quick, to the window: there's the carriage, there's the carriage, except that it's driving past without stopping. It can't be Titi, then. So why did Sophie tell him to *come early* today? Anyway, it's super being on holiday; no more Miss Bastien to watch for any slacking or any contact with the school servants! So, with this straight back and narrow boy's shoulders, she could pass herself off as a red hussar or a mountain chasseur; she could enlist and no one would be the wiser—except later, after she has laid down her life for king and country, with a kick in the air like when she does the cancan in the dormitory at night before Miss Bastien has appeared. Who is the best dancer by far? Who knows how to wave her billowing bed sheet best? Why, Margot, of course! All the other girls agree. So what if home leave is canceled for seven Sundays? Besides, who would snitch on her? So, another kick in the air! Coralie showed her the new knickerbockers she got from Paris, with flaps that close over each other and dispense with the need for buttons. Stingy though she is, Sophie promised to order some for her—who knows who she'll get to do it, and how? When something suits her, she'll pull out all the stops—like last week, when they all went out after lunch to have a coffee at a kiosk, *et soudain Sophie m'a fixée dans le blanc des yeux et nous nous sommes entendues du regard.*

"Please, Ştefan, just this summer," Margot began. "Let's go on holiday this summer, because we don't know what next year has in store for us."

But she found it very hard to keep a straight face, because he'd forgotten to remove the napkin from around his neck. She didn't point it out to him: it was so funny to see it. Chivalrous as always, he offered her his arm, and they walked together to the kiosk. Hah, hah, hah, what a fine couple they make! He tall and thin, with long legs and a napkin around his neck; and she . . . She left him with the napkin because she thought it funny. But Sophie, why didn't she call it to his attention? Why did she wait and only later suddenly burst out:

"Take that off for God's sake! You look like some weird animal. The servants think we're a laughing stock."

The truth is that Sophie doesn't know how to joke.

As for Margot, she went on simpering: "Please, Ştefan, just to Sinaia, just one week."

"I've already said there's no question of a holiday this summer," he snapped.

And he began to remove the napkin.

"Oh, pleeease, Ştefan," she went on.

Sophie said nothing, fanning herself and playing the martyr. She wasn't going to take sides.

"You won't let up, will you? If anyone needs a holiday in the fresh air to restore him, then that person's certainly me. I'm also the first to regret that the frontiers are closed. But where do you want to go, now that there are all these supply problems and we can't be sure what will happen from

one day to the next? Where do you want to risk going with all our suitcases and hats, linen and pots, not to mention the wet nurse?"

"You know that Jean could lend us his car any time . . ."

It was the first time that Sophie said anything.

"Maybe. But don't you know that, if there's a general mobilization, all
the means of transport in a danger area are requisitioned—everything,
from carts to motorcars?"

"You're exaggerating, as usual."

And they could get nothing out of him, except the promise of this
party like in the old days. So, quickly to the window, before Madam Ana
reappears! How strange: another carriage is coming, only from the other
end of the street. Theirs is usually the only house that carriages come
to, so what can all this coming and going mean? It's coming from the
other end: look, there's someone with a panama hat sitting inside. Why
did Sophie tell dear Titi to *come early* today? Quick, back to the mirror: comb her eyelashes again, deal with that spot on her chin, then a
few steps back and a chaste kiss to herself, followed by a more passionate
one. She searches feverishly in the silver jewelry box, but no, one doesn't
wear pearls at her age and at this time of day. Maybe the coral necklace?
Or the amber one? She searches feverishly in the silver box, fingering
necklaces and chains, a locket—yes, that will do nicely, a locket contain-
ing a dear face and a lock of blonde hair. Why is the lock in them always
blonde? Sophie has blonde hair too, but what bulging eyes! And how
creased her stomach is since she gave birth: two rolls of fat appear when
she removes her corset, so big you can fill your hand with them. You can
see she never takes her blouse off and never lets her hair down . . . The
locket, ah, the locket: she looks dreamily at the silver-plated object, closing her eyes and sighing, *les rêveries d'une jeune fille*, there's another spot
under her nostril, careful, her face reddens from the strain, her fingers
press hard, and she hears the skin pop. A drop of a thick, milky substance—the remedy for blackheads. First you squeeze them dry, then
bathe your face in boiling steam and brush on a solution of five grams
of sulfur, twenty grams of camphorated alcohol, five grams of glycerin,
a little rosewater . . . Then you massage your face. On the first evening
you leave the solution to work for half an hour—then apply it again at
two o'clock, three o'clock, four o'clock, all night if you don't notice any
irritation. Careful! Steps on the stairs! *Les belles se rendent dans le jardin,
pour cueillir des roses soir et matin.* What a heavenly waltz the Boston is:

and a one-two-three, a one-two-three, dance with me, Madam Ana, ha, ha, ha, how peculiar she is, heavy and peculiar, and how she tries to pull herself away . . .

"Come on, Mărguță, that's enough. I haven't the time to play, and I'm not in the mood either. Take a deep breath and calm down: you keep running to the window, then back to dolling yourself up again; what is it you hope to see? There's nothing there, I tell you. Come on, let's get this over with. Mistress Sophie will be back any minute from the attic. She's been there to give that good-for-nothing Grigore his medicine: she said that if he still won't take it, I should go and lance the swellings and rub them with salt. Come away from the window, young lady; there's only the bangs on your forehead left to do. We'll be in real trouble if Mistress Sophie comes back and finds your underwear lying all over the place— and all those papers, letters, and envelopes, whatever they are, and your pile of books. Do you think you can get away with that, young lady? One of these days you'll be getting married, and you won't find it easy then. Who will let you carry on as you do? Look at Mr. Ştefan: he's a decent man, the salt of the earth, but even he has some habits you can't get him to give up. Yes, young lady, the good times will be over then. Turn your head a little, like that. And don't say you'll never get married: God forbid, that would be a big tragedy. How can you say that? What kind of girl says she isn't going to marry? Well, some might say it, but it doesn't mean they don't want to. They're not stupid: they know what happiness it will bring them. Just look at Mistress Sophie. She's found a wonderful match, and you can see how happy she is in her own home."

Les belles se rendent dans le jardin, pour cueillir des roses soir et matin, but she's not happy at all, not at all, *et mon beau-frère cloué au lit, et il pâlit. Et elle se rend dans le jardin, pour cueillir des roses soir et matin, voilà les roses blanches, jaunes, grenat,* and a hat, a panama hat!

Yes, Madam Ana can let the young lady's curls flow loose at the back, like a Valkyrie. Does Madam Ana know what a Valkyrie is? Oh, get a move on! . . . She looks good in profile holding that silver-handled mirror. Very good, even. Nothing interesting yet in the street: chestnut trees with parched leaves full of dust; a tar brazier on the corner, a gentleman fanning himself with a panama hat and walking fast without a glance to left or right. No, the last thing she wants is for her hair to be tightly pressed together. She doesn't want it twisted over her neck, like in the far-off days of Pazvante—not that she learns about Pazvante and his rebel warriors at school, where all the heroes and references are classical and French.

"Where do you get all these expressions from?" Ştefan asked her. "How do you know what 'horny as a goat' means?"

"How do you think?" Sophie interrupted sourly. "From the kitchen and the servants' room."

And Ştefan, however much under her influence, laughed out loud when he heard that "being horny as a goat" meant the same as "blowing your own horn."

"You're right, *mon choux*," he immediately backtracked, when Sophie complained that such talk was out of place with a *jeune fille*, and that he seemed to throw reason overboard when foul language unworthy of decent people came to his ears. Did he perhaps think that such shameful expressions should be included in his dictionary?

"There are many ways of checking how good a dictionary is, and besides . . ."—but the rest was lost in a fit of coughing.

He must have been choking with laughter, because he clamped his handkerchief to his mouth.

"Poor Mister Ştefan is wasting away, and the doctors haven't a clue what's wrong with him. One minute it's consumption, the next it's not consumption, and then he must do all in his power to go abroad for treatment. So Mistress Sophie says let's go, but he's stubborn, like sick people are, and he says it's not possible at the moment, maybe a bit later. No, no, she says, let's go now. How is it that other people can move around and we can't? But he won't budge: it's no as far as he's concerned. You see, Margot sweetie, he's as decent as they come, but he's still a man. You can't get him to change his mind. Look at all the trouble Mistress Sophie has with him."

What's that noise at the garden door—as if someone's pushing on it? Someone in a beige flannel suit and panama hat seems to be twirling his stick, in the way that Titi usually does. Ah, it would be best if Madam Ana went to the attic to see how Grigore is doing—right now, so that she can make him better. Otherwise who will let the guests in this evening? No, no, she doesn't need anything else: she can tidy up by herself. But Madam Ana must go now, as she was told to do some time ago.

"I'll go in a minute, young lady. But Mistress Sophie told me not to trouble myself: she'll take care of Grigore. So I wouldn't like to make her cross, today of all days. She said she'd have a word today with Mister Titi about my poor Spiridon: it's not easy, you see, because war will break out soon. But perhaps she'll get him a little bit of leave. Mister Titi has all kinds of connections, after all."

Phew, finally!

She is tiptoeing down the stairs when she hears a faint ring on the bell. Why did Sophie tell him to *come early* today? And if she's still in the attic who's going to open the door for him?

She hurries across the living room, still on tiptoe, her eyes darting watchfully. Golden strips of torrid light filter through the ancient glass of the roof window and cut into the thick air of the room, where particles of dust are whirling around in constant motion. But there seems to be no one outside. She doesn't need to open the front door, because she can see clearly from the hallway: no one is standing there, beneath the wrought-iron lamps.

No one on the other side of the door.

Has she been hallucinating, in broad daylight?

She struggles back up the wooden stairs and listlessly opens the door to her room. Its emptiness is deafening, and it smells of staleness, singed hair, perfume, and congealed blood. What an ugly room! And how long there is to go until evening, when the dinner guests are due to arrive. It's so early, she says to herself, looking disconsolately at the clock face on its black and red-veined marble base. On either side of the dial, a cameo is mounted in a blue enamel medallion: an Apollo with lyre on the left, a Neptune with trident on the right.

She doesn't feel like doing anything until evening. She drags her feet toward the garden window. But what does she expect to see? The ivy-covered pavilion, the wicker chairs beneath the walnut tree . . . Why isn't Sophie in the attic looking after Grigore's swellings? How did she get out there? Surely she isn't inspecting her rose beds in the full heat of the day? And isn't what she is wearing a bit exaggerated? That deliberately stunning garden costume, with an old straw hat and a slightly hitched-up skirt! Maybe even a pair of clogs. You'd think she's there to water the flowers, but a kid of five knows you don't do that with the sun high in the sky. She's obviously lost her head: the hose is flooding the paths with useless water; no gardener creates that kind of swamp. When did she come from the attic, and by which way? Down the service staircase? And how did that panama hat get in the middle of the garden? What an ill-matched couple: old straw hat, brand new panama. How absurd!

She laughs until the tears come. Ah, she's had enough of these school holidays. She'd like to go back soon, to stroll under the trees in the yard with Sévastie and Coralie, to make cakes in the domestic sciences classroom, to daydream beneath the arcades lined with little orange and bluish-green tiles, to mess around with test tubes in the science laboratory: she would do all of that, because she's good at everything. *Mais tu serais une brillante couturière,* Miss Rancoeur told her, I've never met anyone with such taste in my shops at Reuniunea. So she could open a high-class fashion house, and escape that way from this damp, sunless prison.

In future she'll stay at school during the holidays, putting up in one of the little rooms used by governesses. And if war breaks out, she'll care for the wounded and help to relieve their suffering. One day the patient in her care will be a prince! Or a French officer.

"*Est-elle bien née?*" the prince's mother will ask, when she finds her standing so dedicated at the head of his bed.

"*Madame!*" she will reply with dignity—and a Valkyrie lock will come loose from her nurse's headgear.

But as she won't utter another word, they'll think she's just a poor waif, abandoned as an infant in a pink basket, mewling like a kitten, with a priceless locket around her neck. She and the prince will suffer and flee into the wide world; they will be inseparable, and in the end it will be accepted that they are married. But Sophie will never have an opportunity to set foot in the palace of her sister and *beau-frère.*

If, on the other hand, war does not break out, and she isn't given the chance to become a nurse or governess, then she will behave in an openly frivolous manner: she'll cycle everywhere *toute seule*—not just at the velodrome, where loads of boring ladies ride round and round in circles, but in the streets of Bucharest.

She will go out alone, like that famous woman Miţa the Cyclist.

She's doesn't want to know about the Pallade brothers, with whom she flirted at Sévastie's engagement party, nor about anyone else. She will drown her sorrows in the notes of her Bechstein piano. In fact, she could play right now—or else go downstairs to see if Uncle Ştefan is busy with his correspondence.

She goes down again, this time clutching her album to her chest. She knocks on the door, pushes gently on the handle and . . . well, well, well. What a strange day! Surprise makes her muff her curtsey.

"Do you know how Brătianu would have answered Czernin, the Austrian ambassador, about the rumors of our entering the war?" Titi Ialomiţeanu is asking.

How modern he looks with his blond moustache and copper highlights! It suits him so well: so elegant, such a presence! But she greets him coldly, even when he calls out to her:

"Aha, here's our young supporter of the Entente!"

In vain does he look at her as he did on that evening when they went for a drive to the Kiseleff Gardens, with Mişa the coachman. In vain, in vain. Things happen in life from which there is no going back, even when they leave behind broken hearts and inconsolable memories.

Margot inches forward to her usual place on the sofa, so slowly that she can feel her upper thighs grow sticky at the top. It is a warm, viscous moistness—rather unpleasant, like all reminders that you have a body, even if you live only for the mind.

"Oh, really? I must confess I didn't know."

Pauvre Ştefan! It's obvious that he's only replying out of politeness. Titi has disturbed him by coming at the hour that everyone knows he spends on his "hobby": his correspondence. *Pauvre* Ştefan! He's so amiable and sensitive that he'd do anything not to embarrass his guests. And Titi too is so sensitive and amiable: he tries to make up for his intrusion by firing off questions at random, one after another, as if uninterested in the answers. Everyone in a difficult situation, no way of putting things right, and it's all because of *her*. Sophie alone is to blame, because only she lured Titi into the pavilion at the bottom of the garden, in among the flooded paths.

Of course, she lured him there only to compromise him—and now she's waltzing in as if nothing happened. She's changed her clothes, though, swapping the tucked-up skirt and summer blouse for that *vieil or* afternoon dress; she doesn't realize how bad she looks in it. There she is, pretending to be surprised at the sight of Titi Ialomiţeanu, the poor thing. He turns red, but she—of course!—laughs, fans herself, and goes to sit at her place on the sofa. All that's missing is for her to take her sewing out of the basket. But no, she throws herself into the conversation, such a know-it-all nowadays when it comes to politics. To think of the affront she has suffered at the hands of Titi, who burst in on Ştefan like that just to get away from her! Guilty and compromised: she should go to the bathroom and open the veins in her right arm—with a lancet, no less! Or, if she can't lay hands on one, she should fill the bedroom with lilies, especially as Ştefan has been sleeping in a separate room recently. Or, if she can't find enough lilies, she can always take the veil and become Christ's betrothed; not at Pasărea convent, though (where Sophie went one Sunday when she forgot to pick her up from school). So many sins weigh on her soul that she'd have to go to an isolated hermitage in the desert . . .

But the most terrible, the most exciting, thing of all is that the door to the clematis terrace is open.

"The heat was unbearable today, wasn't it?" Titi Ialomiţeanu asked. "Don't you think that people are more restless than usual?"

Titi Ialomiţeanu

The heat has been unbearable—which is another reason why people are so restless. The general situation is more critical than ever: everyone says that we've signed up and war is knocking at our door. In these days of confusion, honesty is no longer a coin in circulation. That's Professor Mironescu's view: he's so vain that he thinks he's the last honest man in Romania! Everyone's predicting how the war will go—badly, most of them think. So it's a question of trying to manage the best way you can. So much the better if you make a fortune out of it all—food and catering, speculation, export permits, whatever . . . It's certainly a good time for making money!

Is there still a politician whom ten people would swear is honest and thinks only of the nation, instead of being out to line his pockets? If you ask ten people about any particular politician, you'll get ten unfavorable, or outright hostile, answers—even if you take the ten from the same party, or the same faction, as the politician in question. They'll tell you he's a British agent, or in the pay of the German ambassador, or that it wasn't for nothing that he went to St. Petersburg with Filipescu. The view is that Take Ionescu is a spokesman for Russia and his enemies for Germany—not because they believe in either cause but because they're paid for it. Everyone curses the government ministers without exception. How can any man of quality escape this brouhaha with his reputation intact? *Calomniez, calomniez, il en restera toujours quelque chose,* as the professor likes to say. So who is left to guarantee anyone else's honesty?

Professor Mironescu, with his academic ideas! To speak of honesty, as he does, is sheer utopianism—a blindness arising out of personal vanity. He doesn't even realize that a lot of people think he's just sucking up to the government. You needn't suspect him of misappropriating public funds, only that he feels flattered and sees some benefits for the phonetics center he dreams of setting up. So it probably won't be long before we hear him praising Ionel Brătianu to the skies. And, lacking a feel for politics and the real world, he'll find a way to go over lock, stock, and barrel to the Liberals just as they're about to end their time in government! You were the first to predict all this, and now your prophetic powers are being confirmed. Look at the disaster looming ahead: not a stone will be left standing. At times like these, it's not just that honesty has dropped out of circulation: its very existence is becoming an impossibility. In a world where everyone cheats, you have to keep your eyes peeled, especially if you don't have an ace or two up your own sleeve. It's senseless, or ridiculous, to devote yourself to some grand research.

To an absolutely definitive work?

When everything's going up in flames, who needs your pretentious scribbling? Only Professor Mironescu can still believe in something, not realizing that the age of the scholar in his ivory tower is well and truly over. It was always a Romantic fantasy, now it's just plain obsolete. This being so, the only goal can be to keep your head above water. That's the only success we can hope to have, including in these crucial days when everything is so confused—not to speak of the heat and the feverish agitation.

The cab jerked along over bumps and potholes, throwing up a cloud of dust as it zigzagged from sidewalk to sidewalk in an attempt to avoid, first, an asphalt mixer, then piles of cube-shaped dark-green stone connected with the road works. He was stifling beneath the hood, and greasy beads of sweat trickled from his slicked-back hair over a reddish moustache to his collar. He never stopped wiping his face with a monogrammed handkerchief.

When the handkerchief was soaked, he tried using the back of his hand, like yokels do, wiping it afterward on the plush seat. But the material was so dusty that he gave up. Oh, what a feverish and loathsome day! Scorching heat, general irritability, newspapers spewing invective and wild accusations left and right—hardly surprising that people have become so suspicious, or that, much to your dislike, they regularly identify you with one particular camp. For example, at the ministry you keep having to deny that you take orders from one head of department or another. It's all most unpleasant, especially as you are not eloquent enough to make your denials convincing. Besides, let's not have any illusions that people believe what you tell them. The more you repeat it, the more leery is the look in their eye as they nod agreement. Think of the friendly chat you had today with Bădescu. I just try to remain on good terms with everyone, you explained, but I'm always suspected of being so-and-so's man. If I have excellent relations with the new undersecretary, Vasiliu, that doesn't mean I've gone beyond the norms of professional behavior. And, if I've had a raise, if I make inspections by motorcar and am asked for my views more often than others, that doesn't mean anything either. So what if I had the same post under Vasiliu's rival and predecessor, Grigore Zlătescu? They make the absurd claim that I pursued conservative policies under Zlătescu because he was linked through the Racota family with the Conservative government of the day, whereas now I'm preparing to switch over to the Liberals, as my frequent association with the Mironescus is supposed to prove.

(*N.B. Zlătescu today, laughing: Mironescu would be surprised to learn that he's now placed unhesitatingly in the Liberal camp; he thinks he's independent but doesn't realize that he's the only one who thinks it; he buries his head in the sand, instead of looking reality in the face.*)

Of course, when you had that friendly chat with Bădescu, you might have explained that you still had links with Grigore Zlătescu, who's been moved to another department, but not completely sidelined, as people in our ministry seem to think. You might have told him the truth: you meet Zlătescu once a month, as you did today, for a regular exchange of information, and from time to time, when it's appropriate, you do him a little favor. That's sufficient proof of your loyalty. But you preferred not to mention such things, since the principles of your internal policy require total discretion.

(*N.B. Today Zlătescu confirmed the rumor about Ionel Brătianu's resignation. He got it from the Racotas, who expect their cousin Maiorescu to be appointed prime minister at any moment. Promised Zlătescu to sound out pro-Liberal circles about this, via Professor Mironescu.*)

All the above is further evidence of how uncivilized this country is, as Professor Mironescu rightly points out. In more civilized European countries, officials may serve in the same position for decades, so that their name eventually becomes associated with their respective institution. That kind of stability doesn't exist here, as you can testify from the reactions you have seen at the ministry. During these eight years that you've been head of this department, with hopes of further promotion ahead, undersecretaries have been walking in and out the door with each change of minister. But that doesn't mean at all that you're a new Fouché, settling in like Napoleon's police chief, as someone said an old friend has been suggesting.

Who can speak more ill of you than former friends and mistresses? Both have more than the usual share of vanity, envy, and jealousy.

Given your placid nature, all you can do is keep a smile on your face and try to shrug it off. The usual response is to meet an attack with an attack, so there aren't many who have the nerve to strike the other cheek if you turn it to them. Just act as if nothing has happened, perhaps throwing a touch of humor in for good measure, and your attacker will be at a loss what to do next.

The result can only be favorable, especially in the eyes of the gentle sex, who always tend to sympathize with the victim. So, even if you're forced to take part in meetings of rival Conservative factions, that doesn't mean you're anything other than a man who does his duty wherever he's put—and, what is more, a bachelor, with sufficient time on his hands.

Don't forget, though, that you haven't yet risen high enough to join the Jockey Club. Of course you'd feel flattered, as anyone would, especially as you know how much you've suffered for your awkwardness in high society. But no one can claim to have seen you in a dishonorable situation—in a crowd shouting "Down with the government!" for example, or smashing the windows of *Steagul* on the grounds that it's a pro-German paper. Nothing has been able to make you deviate from your guiding principle: to be on good terms with everyone.

Thoughts kept crowding into his head, each with the same intensity, but at some point that was hard to identify they no longer followed immediately one after another. They felt as logical as before, only each one lingered more in his mind. If he'd had to describe it, he would have said that they opened little by little, petal by petal, like a blossoming flower.

It would have been just a poetic flourish, of course, because he'd never actually seen a flower open up. One morning you wake up to find that the bud of the night before has turned into a full corolla, with at most one or two petals wet and crumpled. That's one of the mysteries of nature, like the parental embrace that one day results in a new little brother or sister peeking out at you from a lace-covered basket.

His thoughts and images were becoming slower and more confused, while the carriage, jolting along dusty side streets, took him closer and closer to his friends' house. A profound unease took hold of him: why did Sophie tell him to *come early tomorrow*?

He stopped fanning himself with his panama hat and jotting down brief, secret thoughts in the notebook that he took with him everywhere. He looked out and saw that it was beginning to rain.

A few moments later he seemed drowsy beneath the raised carriage hood, which protected him from neither the dust nor the heat.

Or maybe he'd actually dozed off?

For now his ear heard quite differently the familiar silence of the torpid, deserted street, the pounding of the horse's hooves and the rattling of the carriage on the broken paving; the creaking of iron shutters as a store owner hurried to open up, and the sprinkling of water on the hot sidewalk beneath its striped tarpaulin cover; even the bursting of warm ripe mulberries as they fell onto the asphalt and spread their sweet, sticky juice amid the buzzing of wasps.

But why did she ask him to *come early* today?

His character inclined him to obey the request, but he did it without pleasure—indeed with a certain displeasure. Another jolt, another sour taste left from a cheap restaurant lunch—and now he has to make a special journey, on a day when there has been so much to do and the air is filled with rumors of war. A jolt, a sinking feeling in his stomach: just think, this might be your last week on earth, no exaggeration! In a week you might be running blindly, rifle in hand: will you be the one the bullets spare? If not, the wounds don't bear thinking about . . . You can already see the terrifying sight: there you'll be, still running a few steps after the shell has ripped open your abdomen, already trying to patch yourself up; a mist will form over your eyes as you squat down, not yet registering what has happened, not yet feeling the pain; your cold, blood-soaked hands will try to pack your entrails mixed with earth and grass back inside you, but they keep slipping out again, time after time. Ah, those goddamn discussions in the officers' mess!

He makes an effort to reopen his eyes, then carefully shuts the notebook on his lap. In the morning he noted down the things he had to do during the day, using many abbreviations and initials. The first urgent matter: to find a way of avoiding the call-up.

1. Make a list of contacts, however unlikely to deliver.
2. If possible, start visits with the most influential. Don't forget Dumitru, from the interior ministry,

Then:

1. Get new suit from tailor.
2. Order a basket of Capşa's candied fruit for the party at the Mirxxxs. "*Voulez-vous nous faire l'honneur de venir dîner chez nous après-midi Vendredi, 12 août, à sept heures? Après dîner on fera un peu de musique, en petit Comité. Votre bien-dévouée, Sophie Mironesco.*"

And all that trouble at the office! In the end he locked the files under consideration in a drawer, where they risk remaining *sine die*. Order and disorder mixed up in a way he hadn't expected at all.

He was the last to leave the office—as everyone expects by now—and at Strada Sărindar he ran into his friend Bădescu, who insisted that they have a drink together at Mircea's Bar.

(*N.B. Bădescu on Prime Minister Brătianu: he's not a popular man, but that doesn't matter to him. He lets the press drag him through the mud without defending himself in any way; he loathes the newspapers—the brains of the modern world—and apparently never looks at them. So, Bădescu—pro-Liberal attitude. Generally well informed. Might openly declare himself a Liberal at the next elections.*)

Bădescu didn't deny what you've heard from Marghiloman: that General Prezan gave officers a list of papers to be forbidden in the army, *Steagul* being the first. As for Mrs. Prezan, two men at the very top are competing for her: his lips were sealed about their names, and so were yours, although there is evidence that King Ferdinand is involved. Curiously, he knew nothing about the explosion in the Dudeşti neighborhood, unless he didn't want to talk about it.

It was late when you said good-bye to each other, so you took a cab to get to the tailor as fast as possible. While he was making a final adjustment to a sleeve, you had lunch in a diner. It was packed with all kinds of people, many of whom had probably hurried back from their holidays. Again you wondered why Sophie told you to *come early* today. Some imprudence on her part is to be expected—an unhealthy, even embarrassing, overexcitement that you wouldn't have thought possible a few years ago, when you saw her as the embodiment of inaccessibility.

What it is to see a man—or woman—at close quarters! A French maxim, perhaps by La Rochefoucauld, says that no one is a great man for his valet, who sees him in unflattering positions. The proverb (or maxim) just expresses the idea: it doesn't stoop to giving vulgar examples.

The fish was good, the prawn risotto superb, the stuffed cabbage unwise in this heat. You made a pig of yourself, knowing full well that it would lie heavy on your stomach. Then you went briefly to a café, still not sure whether to arrive early at the Mironescus.

One of your principles (from which you have rarely deviated) is to be prudent with women in all situations, even with those you know well. It turns out that well is never well enough, since you can never be sure what they might get up to when their interests and their vanity are at stake. It's become second nature to you to be on the lookout for their traps. Their guile is recognized by everyone, but so too is the blindness with which men are carried along not only by their desires—as they claim—but also by all the bluster associated with them. So, given that prudence is *ta qualité maîtresse,* should you go early or not?

You still hadn't made up your mind when you returned to the tailor. The sleeve now fitted perfectly. You put the new suit on and left your old one to be cleaned and ironed. There was no longer time to go home first. On your way in the carriage, you kept asking yourself why she had asked you to come.

However much you are guided by reason, you can't claim to understand people if you keep being surprised by them. Sophie herself has caught you unawares with caprices that you could imagine on the part of a woman, but not coming from her and directed at yourself. Take that surprise visit she paid on your birthday, having doubtless remembered your address from the time when you were ill and the professor, in a fit of generosity, sent his manservant to inquire about you. This time, more spectacularly still, she came herself—and, by a stroke of luck, your room was clean and tidy. Suddenly here was the young Mrs. Mironescu visiting you on the quiet, in a hired cab, her face thickly veiled. How wonderful that the neighbors would think an elegant lady was going up to your room for a secret rendezvous—although, to set against this, you had to fear an argument with your landlady, since she had made it clear you were not supposed to bring ladies to your room (at least, not for the rent you were paying).

It was hard for you to imagine that, as Sophie opened the doors of the carriage entrance, crept along the dark corridor ignoring its various odors, and climbed the creaking staircase, she experienced it all as an exciting adventure. It seemed to open up the prospect of a new life, as she confessed to you later. Once inside the room, throwing discretion aside and ignoring your sensible advice, she risked compromising herself by opening the round window, which she delightedly compared to a ship's porthole. Everything seemed so charming, except for a moldy smell that bothered her. "What can you expect of a rented room?" you remarked. In any case, she was in a strange state of mind, never having seen a bachelor's room before.

At least, that was what she said.

Then came her confessions, while she sat laughing on a wattle chair. She had been through some terrible times as a young girl, and once even thought of devoting her life to study and asceticism, in her little room on Strada Iosif; she'd go with fellow students to bars and places of ill repute, read a lot and travel a lot, sit in Saint Mark's Square amid the fluttering of pigeons' wings, listening to the song of gondoliers, drink absinthe in a café in Montmartre . . . Fantasies such as these, and others no less extravagant, had haunted her for some time, but then she had begun to dream of a warm hearth and the glittering pleasures of social life.

Did she make a mistake when she followed that stirring within her?

Some memories make her think of a flower cast aside on a garbage heap, but alas! there are some flowers that grow on garbage.

She sighed and tactfully refrained from developing her thought. Were those tears in her slightly bulging, greenish-blue eyes? Her long lashes always make them look moist, and she is certainly not unaware of the special charm they give her, as she often blinks for no reason at all.

You didn't know what to answer, or how to proceed, so you kept looking at her in silence. She made a pleasant impression, but you were also uneasy about the drift of what she was saying. You tried to persuade her to get up from the rickety straw chair, pointing out that you had recently had to wedge one of its legs back into place. She paid no attention. She didn't seem afraid, as she sat there nervously playing with her gloves, but reason told her that she ought to be. It was possible that she'd seen other bachelors' rooms after all. We shouldn't have any illusions about human beings, especially not about women; things are always worse than we imagine. She was rumored to have been *au mieux* with Georges

Athanasiu—otherwise, why would his wife Lisette have been so hostile to her? She herself told you that they only made it up a couple of years ago.

Sparing you the need to speak, after another long silence, she said that she'd chosen you as her confidant because you were an obliging sort of person who, unlike others, seemed to have a feeling heart. A couple of years ago, you would never have dreamed that people would relate to you in that way, but since then more have opened their souls to you than she imagined, without your having to do much to draw them out. It was your behavior, as usual *comme il faut,* that impelled her to visit you so unexpectedly—that and the mad impulse you had that day when you were left alone with her in the salon during the professor's first illness: when you kissed her!

Now you timidly caressed her, and her hair became ruffled as she brusquely stepped away. She said she should be going, but you promised to be good so that she'd stay longer and she looked around the room for a mirror—even "a tiny little one." In the end she decided to comb her hair in front of the window pane—"like maids do," she said with a laugh. Her mood would swing abruptly, from gay to melancholic and back again, although neither really suited her. Then she suddenly unfastened her hair: you'd never seen such long blonde hair on a woman, so abundant that she could have wrapped the whole of her naked body in it. You actually paid her this compliment, only on another, later occasion. For the moment you said little, both because you didn't want to frighten her and because you had lost your voice. You buried your face in her perfumed hair, as intoxicating as the rustling of her frilly dress; you took her in your arms, shakily brushing your hand against her burning underwear, while she pushed you away and, with perfect self-control, told you to let her continue doing her hair.

You were much too intimidated: things were not easy. When she left, you asked if she would come another time, without daring to fix anything definite or to indulge in vain hopes. You'd been forced to make a move because otherwise she would have despised you, but before long you were losing your head. (Interestingly, you realized this and hesitated, before telling yourself: "Well, it does no harm just this once.") While she was getting dressed again, and complaining at the lack of a bidet (she with her luxurious bathroom at home!), you thought about the disenchantment that follows a victory.

Then you remembered what you had told her at that moment of dis-traction: you struggle to overcome your defects, such as your stage fright when you have to speak in public, in the hope that you will one day suc-ceed in politics or the diplomatic service. As she was preoccupied with herself at the time, she might have immediately forgotten your words. But it would be most unpleasant if she mentioned them to her husband, since Professor Mironescu hopes that you will join him on the path of philological research—which doesn't exactly excite you, although you don't tell him so as to spare his vanity—and a report of your confession might lead him to behave differently toward you. Of course, the fact that you have your eyes on a career in politics or diplomacy shouldn't be a reason for such a rational man to be angry with you. But the professor's psychology is becoming murkier and murkier, with neurasthenia lurk-ing around the corner. You are not in possession of all the facts, but some of Sophie's silences during a conversation are eloquent enough, as are some of her looks and exclamations. You have to hand it to her for being so discreet, for knowing when she should be quiet about something! So it's likely that she hasn't passed on what you confided in her—especially not the hopes you have in Marghiloman, who supports an alliance with Germany. Don't forget that her relations with her husband are no lon-ger as close as they used to be and that they are leading fairly separate lives; his illness seems to carry some risk of contagion. Still, when you visited him last, he paid you a rather double-edged compliment about your dress: "Before long you'll be ordering all your clothes in Vienna and Berlin and having your underwear laundered there, like our famous Conservative leader . . ."

What was that supposed to mean? That he was one of Marghiloman's courtiers?

All this simply shows that it's best to listen to other people's confes-sions, while holding your own tongue. The fewer things people know about you, the less vulnerable you are. Of course, everyone conceals things about himself that would be embarrassing if they became known, but on the other hand you can't stop little bits of gossip circulating about you. That's the custom in these parts. *Bucarest, une potinière,* as the pro-fessor puts it.

Nevertheless, so long as you disclose nothing, and so long as you're in luck and there are no witnesses, you can always deny anything that's said about you. You won't be at anyone's mercy.

So, that's the practical way of looking at the question of personal disclosures. Prudence dictates you have to weigh the pros and cons of everything in life, as you are doing right now in wondering which carries the greater risk. Is it better to go early to the Mironescus, or should you turn back and only go there later?

Suddenly a breath of wind, mixed with the smells of sun-scorched brushwood, wild privet, and rotting flesh, makes him lift his handkerchief to his nose. He irritably pokes the cab driver in the back with his stick:

"Where the hell are you going, you idiot? Turn around this minute! Do you hear me?"

They had already passed the Mironescu house, and had it not been for the wasteland stench God knows where they would have ended up. Fortunately, in among the bruised soapwort leaves and the clumps of belladonna, a bare-toothed dog lay glistening dark-green in the sun, its lifeless shape plagued by a gray swarm of flies. What a bargain the elder Mironescu had picked up when he bought building land out here in the sticks! But he paid for his stinginess both in the winter, when wolves appeared in the yard, and in the summer, when he had to burn rags to drive away the mosquitoes. Nearly forty years later, the place had still not lost its wildness.

Fortunately, he woke up just in time to administer his corrective poke, and the driver pulled on the reins and turned around, with a few jolts worse than any that had gone before. Soon they were back in front of the house.

Alea iacta est! The sour taste in his mouth had become a burning in his stomach. His new suit already had quite a few creases, due to the perspiration that fell off him in the intense heat. He had one foot in and one foot out when the driver shouted:

"Hey, sir! Sir!"

The creature had finally found his voice. With the artfulness of his kind, he can sense whether you're going home, visiting friends, or calling on a lady, and he knows that you don't like to haggle in front of a house where you have been invited.

You fumbled endlessly in your pockets, but you were so nervous that you couldn't find any coins for a tip. How could you of all people be subjected to such an insult—you who are known among your peers for your generosity! In the end you took out a twenty-lei note and handed it over, just to see the back of him. Of course you'd have given him less if you hadn't been in front of the Mironescus' house; it's not your style to go around with your head in the clouds, like Professor Mironescu!

So you quickly walked away, fanning yourself with your panama and nervously swirling your stick. At each step you had to unstick the heels of your kid shoes from the molten tarmac. As if from a lump of Turkish delight.

Your fear continued to grow, catching you by the throat and choking you. You stole a few glances at the house, to make sure that no one was watching you from a window. And again you wondered how much truth there was in the images that others use to describe us with a tender or mocking irony.

We should have no illusions: people are constantly talking about us, whether in the avid conversation of friends, in the gossiping of servants, in the biased judgments of our superiors about our efficiency, or in the chatter of salons where we have never set foot . . . So, you kept asking the old obsessional question: how much truth is there in the images that others pick up here and there about us? And, knowing how little your dealings with the coachman reflected your normal self, you shot another fearful glance toward the house.

No one.

Luckily all the shutters are down for the siesta. The golden gravel paths are deserted, and so too are the pavilion and the rest of the garden, where wickerwork chairs strand strewn in the shade of an old walnut tree. The curtains are motionless over the terrace window in the drawing room where the professor deals with his correspondence. The door to the terrace is always closed, probably fastened with nails.

So, no one there. And, since you live for others to think well of you, you keep telling yourself that this unfortunate episode, which no one else knows about, can later be erased from your mind. In the end, the memory of a man or woman who has lived a little is inevitably a grave-yard of trivial, or not so trivial, acts that cannot be acknowledged.

You walk a little further, comforting yourself with these thoughts and twirling your stick a few more times. The heat and anxiety have gone to your head like an intoxicating cocktail. You come to the back door and the vault of red roses over the yard, crowned with the orb of the blazing sun. The air seems to vibrate like a sheet of water above the lilac branches—a well-known hallucination in the midsummer fields. What an untimely hour, what a suffocating day! But you force yourself to carry on regardless, and suddenly the beads of sweat no longer bother you, even giving you a pleasant feeling of relief. If only you could shake off the claw over your heart as you push on the unlocked gate. Were you supposed to ring? To ask the valet—for whom? Oh, why on earth didn't Sophie say more than just *come early tomorrow*?

So you push the gate open, the gravel making a familiar crunching sound beneath your feet. In front of you, in a plaster ovum, you see that far-off year: 1879. Your nerves are so on edge that a slight rustling makes you jump. You turn your head and breathe a sigh of relief. A cat is watching you, its eyes no more than a thin yellowish film floating in the blinding white light. The tip of its tail moves slowly from side to side among the leaves, then it jumps out of sight into the long grass.

Now the flight of three steps and the wrought-iron lamps that Sophie found to her taste when she was supervising the work on the house. They do not match the rest of the building: they are too new and too shiny, like in a *nouveau riche* household, as the professor put it.

Having driven all thoughts from your mind, you press on the button and wait. The faint ringing, lost in the menacing darkness of the house, makes your muscles tense. You mechanically draw yourself up straight, stick in one hand, hat in the other, ready to bow with a smile at the first opportunity. You do not dare to ring a second time. Why do your mother's moist eyes suddenly flash before you? How well you know her crow's-feet and those little white spots on her swollen eyelids set among sparse lashes! The look in her eyes is enough to dispense with the need for spoken reproaches. As she gets on with her work at the loom, she merely gives you the banal news that she has settled her debt with the grocer or milkman, or that on Wednesday it will be five weeks since your poor sisters were last invited to a party, which may be for the best, because they don't have any new clothes to go out in. But not a word about the prayers to the Virgin that the priest was paid to say so that they won't end up old maids in this slum district, ashamed to let gentlemen see them home. In Buzău they had once been somebody, even if it had been public knowledge that they were on the brink of ruin ... Not a word either about your salary, which she has no way of guessing except from the chocolate Easter egg you bought for her at Capșa's or the overpriced cakes you brought from Angelescu's when you wanted to make things up after a quarrel. And not a word about the Bucharest salons where you seem to be welcomed with open arms, although she believes in you as only a mother can in her eldest child. Of course she's not actually heard anything positive about you, but people have said that you were seen with so-and-so in a motorcar or a carriage . . .

You stood stiffly in the doorway, awkward and impatient, feeling the reproach in those tearful eyes and sealed lips, and in that frail wrinkled neck bent over the loom. You inched up on your toes, ready to run away from the only place in the world where you aren't constantly thinking of how to apply your life principles, but where your character and habits still don't allow you real peace. Even here, the only way you know of fighting for what you want is through anxious sidelong glances and forced smiles, through gentle pressure on the door handle that allows you to slip in quietly. And when you finally have one foot in the dark lobby, you dare to think fleetingly of the antique jewelry and gold coins and silverware locked away in the cellar: can one be sure (you ask your mother) that burglars won't whisk them away one day, especially in times of war? Wouldn't it be wiser—as you have suggested to her more than once—to convert everything into assets that bring in some return? Wouldn't a portfolio of stocks and annuities be a more secure investment nowadays? Why does she stubbornly refuse even to consider the possibility? It will be her decision, of course, but let's at least spend a minute or two discussing it: gold in a cellar doesn't beget little ones, but cash does bring in more cash. And if one of the girls also manages to find a good match . . .

She suddenly looks up at you, in a way that suggests she isn't listening. You can read hostility in those faded blue eyes, yes, without a shadow of a doubt; if you weren't so frightened of the word, you'd even think it was *hatred*. But then she looks down again at the loom, and her gnarled fingers, tips hard and full of dark hollows, go on with their toil. This evening, when she has finished the housework, she will clean them with a lemon and carefully rub in some ointment, then apply the obligatory compress to her lined face. Even in this poor district, amid all the troubles of life, you have to remain what you are, preserving your appearance and your little routines.

You cough in annoyance at her old woman's obstinacy. But you're reluctant to leave her in pain like that: you'd like to take your leave of her again. Silence. A creaking door. What a bad moment your quarrelsome little sister finds to snap at you! What has got into her to speak to you like this, as if you were no longer her elder brother, a brilliant student and now a model civil servant, the pride of the family?

"... as if good matches just stroll around waiting to be had, as if we don't need to be introduced into high society by a brother who, as a matter of fact, would never dream of ..."

A bad moment—as bad as the feelings behind it. You're on your way out and you're still fuming: no, you shout, you won't slap her for being insolent, as you would have every right to do as her elder brother, but nor will you forget her behavior; you'll be wary of taking her sisters anywhere in future, that's only normal, given the bad taste they show in the way they dress and the ridiculous way they behave; they don't need new trinkets all the time, just the natural grace not to show you up in society ...

And you run into the badly paved street, as if the Furies in person are behind you. Long fast strides, quick movements meant to express energy but also the pain in your kind, delicate heart. What you said to Lelia was the truth, nothing but the truth; you've always felt humiliated by their cheap trinkets, their way of chuckling in the middle of a conversation, their stubby fingers and thick ankles, their jagged yellow teeth. These and so many other details have made you feel all too ashamed.

Humiliated and ashamed, in greater measure than the poor things deserve ...

The whistling of a bird relieves you of this painful memory, erasing it as suddenly and as gratuitously as it appeared. You've half-turned and looked with amusement at a yellow-throated, black-tailed bird hopping in the grass at the foot of the pear tree. Did it make the whistling sound? Or was it the tomcat whose arched body can be seen behind a hawthorn bush, its tabby fur dissolved in a patch of dazzling sunlight that makes it seem precious and alive like a dark sandy shore? Ah, how nice it would be to relax now on a shady bench on the Avenue, listening to the birdsong and playfully peering through the window of a passing carriage, with plenty of time on your hands to arrive at the same moment as the other guests! *Voulez-vous nous faire l'honneur?* What could be simpler than to escape now, at the last minute? Isn't that what man was given the gift of reason for? There's obviously no point ringing again. Just do it! Back down those three steps ...

Here we go. The bird is still hopping about in the grass like a clockwork toy, and the cat's head is moving in time with it behind the hawthorn.

Every bird dies by its own tongue, as the proverb says. The gravel, the familiar gravel, crunches beneath your feet: how little you care now why she asked you to *come early . . .*

After just a few steps, however, a troublesome idea occurs to you: what if the valet finally came to the door and saw you making off? If that is the case what will you say later, when you arrive with the other guests? Will you mention your earlier call—or will it be wiser to say nothing? What a crazy idea it was to ask you to come early! It's part of your nature to feel guilty without knowing why, to feel you are being pursued for something you can't put your finger on. You'd better look around again to make sure no one's there, in the doorway, at a window or in the garden . . .

"Vous voilà enfin! Mais c'était à prévoir, que vous seriez en retard . . ."

You turned around to make sure. If you hadn't turned your head, you wouldn't now be bowing, sullenly but politely, as the graceful Mrs. Mironescu comes toward you holding a basket of roses under her arm. An old straw hat hangs casually on her back, held by a cotton velvet ribbon that digs into her full white neck, while her bare shoulders rise above the low neckline of her gardening dress. Good Lord, she thinks she's at a *bal pare* again! And what a conspiratorial smile! Nothing annoys you more in life than foolish things done for no reason: after all, there's a rational solution to everything . . . Instead of inviting you in to say hello to her husband, she's asked you to follow her into the garden—supposedly to show you a special variety of rose . . . If you hadn't turned your head, she'd have seen you almost at the gate and noted that you had complied with her request, but you'd have had time to make your getaway and would have spoken with her only a few hours later, in the presence of all the guests. Now you are forced to follow behind her, stepping from one stone to another to avoid the wet ground—God knows how it got like that!

There is even mud on the path.

How this trek annoys you! The "let me show you some new roses" line is as old as the hills—and especially out of place with someone like you, who is not exactly known as a nature lover.

"Couldn't we stop here, dear Madam Mironescu? It's not very nice underfoot—for you I mean, with all this mud."

You didn't speak as clearly as the situation demands. Still dissatisfied, you take out your handkerchief to wipe your forehead, but hesitate when you see it isn't very clean. She laughs, as if it is funny, and continues to lead you forward. You feverishly try to work out which windows you are passing, and how great the risk is that someone there might see you by chance.

How great? Infinite! Ah, how fleeting are things on this earth! Less than three years have passed since that endless dinner where you felt so unhappy. She was wearing a lace dress, and her wonderful hair was done up in an intricate hairdo; the certainty that she was irresistible made her assume an especially languid, especially alluring, posture. At first the mere sight of her intoxicated you, but as the evening drew on all you did was drink more and more.

Professor Mironescu looked at you reproachfully when you reached out for your glass, but there were moments when even that didn't bother you. You even wanted to propose a toast, but your tongue was so furred and sluggish that everyone could see how difficult it was for you to pronounce the words. After a couple of ironical claps, you therefore gave a wave of disgust and went to the smaller salon, and from there onto the little balcony. It was snowing gently, and you could hear the tinkling of sleigh bells; the night had something strange and oppressive. You were soon freezing there, but she didn't come after you or send someone to bring you inside; you were so unhappy and so much in love. A blinding flash lit up your mind. You suddenly felt completely alert and wondered what it would be like to press a pistol to your head and pull the trigger. Those were the kind of thoughts you had that night! But you weren't so clear-headed after all, because as soon as you went back inside the heat of the room made you feel ill—the heat, plus the fact that some-one, probably Georges Ioaniu, was keeping her company. Scarcely able to control yourself, you said good night to the professor alone and beat a hasty retreat. No sooner were you in the carriage than you felt like throwing up.

And you certainly brought a lot up, as you bent over a garden fence, dejected and humiliated.

But that was nearly three years ago. Now you suddenly realize why the path is wet: it is because Sophie has inexcusably left the hose on. There she is, just ahead of you, but no longer as supple as she used to be. She obviously isn't aware of it herself, since she still acts as if she is irresistible. But how could she be, now that she's engaging in these maneuvers that can only put you and her at risk of being compromised?

That's why you make a last desperate attempt to open her eyes.

"Do you remember Pasărea monastery, my dear Madam Mironescu? Do you remember those guest rooms that more often than not are used for clandestine liaisons? I've heard from reliable sources that anyone who sets foot in that most terrestrial paradise has their name recorded by the Mother Superior . . . No, madam, why do you say I'm slandering the servants of the church. I've been told that her list is made available to government officials, so they can buy people's consciences more easily, and that the secret police even make it easy for unmarried couples so they can get various important figures in their power . . . What do you think of that? Do you remember how you kept insisting that the two of us should go on a little trip there together? Don't you think we were taking an unnecessary risk? In fact, there's no place on earth where you're safe from dangers and prying eyes."

To counter her rude giggling, you suddenly halt, a little off balance, on a patch of solid ground more and more cut off by the water that has been sweeping up petals, leaves, twigs, and blades of grass. You stop and wait. She should tell you what she has to say and be done with it, since the situation is becoming intolerable for everyone. Then she should take you in through the front door so that you can greet the professor and excuse yourself for coming early—after which you and he will be able to chat for a while in peace until the other guests arrive.

You've become more and more impatient, a little off balance on that little patch of dry ground. But she presses ahead, swaying her hips ever so slightly and leaning over for a second to raise the tip of her dress from the muddy path. Her ankles are visible now, but she walks on regardless, while you continue to wait and offer her that nervous smile of yours— the smile of a faint-hearted aristocrat trying to remain dignified as he approaches the scaffold on a chill June morning. But it is a smile she doesn't see, as she has her back to you. Meanwhile your legs are developing pins and needles in that unnatural position. You try to recollect the layout of the upper rooms facing the garden: the bedrooms, Margot's boudoir, the bathrooms, the study opposite them . . . But what about the servants' quarters on the attic floor? So many rooms, so many windows glistening in the hot afternoon sun, so many voracious openings aimed down at you. You rest your weary shoulder against the old cherry tree. All those eyes looking out the windows, all those arrows shot at your beautiful young body, as at the virginal Saint Sebastian . . . Eventually she sees fit to call something out, in a shrill voice that goes straight through your eardrums. It hasn't helped you to stay on that patch of dry ground: she has no intention of stopping, or even of turning around to see where you are! So you might as well follow her some more—otherwise you'll end up playing hide-and-seek and racing noisily around the garden.

You try to catch her up, panting a little, to make her stop one way or another. Ah, if only you hadn't turned around to make sure that no one had noticed your early arrival, you wouldn't now be sliding in the mud and dirtying your beige trousers, goddamn it! If you go on chasing her like this, you'll end up wanting nothing else than to leave her here in the lurch with her roses and her air of mystery. Why don't you take your courage in both hands? Just go ring the doorbell, make some excuse for arriving early, and drop in unexpectedly on Professor Mironescu. You've landed yourself in such a pickle that you can't see any other way out.

You are seething with rage, determined to put a stop to it somehow or other. Best do it right now, here where the two paths meet: one leading straight back to the house, the other to the wickerwork chairs beneath the walnut tree . . . Maybe she's harebrained enough to endanger her name for nothing, but it's not acceptable that she should also put your hard-earned reputation at risk. So, hurry up, plant yourself in front of her and, however choking with emotion, pour out the words you've been turning over in your mind:

"I really don't see why we're doing this tour of the garden, dear Madam Mironescu . . . There are times when one is less fit for conversation—and that's why I'd suggest another day for . . . Or in a few hours perhaps, when the paths have dried out . . . No, I'm not as difficult to get hold of as you think . . . Only these days, with all the turmoil and the business to attend to . . . Do you remember the prediction I made? Well, it's not impossible that, after all the turmoil and confusion, we'll end up wiped off the map of Europe . . . No, I don't feel good about what's likely to happen! It's just that, like any other man with a little sense, I'm glad that I could see where we were heading—toward the disaster that I so often allowed myself to predict to you . . . No, no, I'm not trying to change the subject, but surely you'll agree that this isn't the time or place for us to have a proper talk. But, if you wish, in a few hours—or in a few days, at a calmer moment . . ."

You are at the end of your tether. Your darting eyes survey the clematis terrace outside the never-opened windows of the professor's drawing room. You keep looking on all sides—only not at her, so you can't see her move coming! God, how tactless! She takes your hand and tries to pull you to her. That really is the last straw.

You are red as a beet, your ears burning as the blood thunders inside them. You wonder whether what you hear is her stubbornness talking:

"We can't go back until I've talked to you . . ."

Talked to you about what? What commitments does she want to worm out of you after a few amorous encounters? In a flash you're halfway back to the front entrance, taking long quick strides that mimic energy, no longer caring whether your trousers get dirty—clothes don't matter to you, any more than anything else.

Now the three steps.

The bell.

Out of the corner of your eye, without having to turn around, you see her finally go up to the tap and switch off the water that has been flooding the garden, then bend down and disconnect the hosepipe.

Ştefan Mironescu

After a tickling sensation that has for some time been constricting my breathing, I at first simply shrug off the new cough. I absent-mindedly raise my handkerchief to my mouth and persist in trying to reread the line I have just written, even though it is swimming before my eyes. *Nous sommes très peu connus* . . . I would find it hard to say exactly when my pencil flew out of my hand; the explosive force and the terror that spread through my body have blotted out the other details. It is a desperate, choking cough; my eyes bulge out of their sockets, while tears and saliva trickle onto my chin and shirt. For the umpteenth time I curse myself for my unaccustomed negligence: if I had been more careful, I could have avoided this fit that has doubled me up in my chair. I open my shirt with trembling fingers: my throat is a raw wound deep down, and I hold my arms across my chest in a vain attempt to gain some relief from the cough. An aural hallucination, the sound of a horse and carriage, floats in the air above me.

At last! In a daze, I rest my neck against the back of the mahogany chair. *Nous sommes très peu connus et avons, par conséquence, besoin de publicité occidentale:* I mechanically read again the stained sheet of paper. I then check my damp handkerchief and breathe a little sigh: no, there is no patch of red; I open it out and bury my lined temples and

cheeks in it—or, anyway, the sharp edges that remain after all the weight
I've lost. Or maybe I haven't lost so much, I say to encourage myself. The
tears and saliva have made the ink run on the paper, so I irritably screw
it up and throw it into the wastepaper basket.

I breath cautiously, so as not to revive the dreaded cough, and pull
the cord of my glasses over my ears. Not a thought about the terrifying
symptoms. A break in Italy would soon put me back on my feet, although
a trip abroad seems more impossible every day and I'll just have to wait
in stoical resignation. In any case, not a word to Sophie!

How would *pauvre* Sophie react if she suddenly learned the truth
about my condition? I would keep my manly dignity, maintain a discreet
distance from her to avoid the risk of contagion, and not breathe a word
about the terrible future that might continue to separate us. Repressing
any thought of my more and more ineffectual love, of the increasingly
fierce desires aroused by my illness, I would stop myself from making any move toward her, even if indifference and unjustified irritation
would be poor disguises for the voracity of my attention. Unfortunately,
these would be all she saw—not the religious ecstasy that each of her gestures, though so well known by now, regularly induces in me: the smile
in her eager, credulous eyes, her artful way of whispering something, the
graceful embarrassment with which she hides her face behind her fan,
and that dreamy way she has of staring into space. (Only a vulgar misog-
ynist could imagine that at such moments she is thinking of a new corset
or something even more mundane.)

A strange vibration, a groundless exaltation, which has come over me
more and more often. I breathe cautiously, so as not to awaken the cough
hidden inside me, and I feel exhilarated thinking that Sophie has no idea
how I feel in the fibers of my being, which become all the more sensitive
as they wear themselves out. She doesn't know how I live, internally and
externally, or how, despite everything, she eludes my avid attention and
remains as opaquely translucent as ever.

As hard to understand as ever—though predictable in each of her
reactions.

Raison de plus que je sois très honoré d'écrire dans votre revue: how
much sincerity there can be in the most conventional of phrases! For the
truth is that I can't hold anyone in higher esteem than this unknown colleague who, doggedly and intelligently, busies himself with his famous
philological journal while the world around us is going up in flames.

I carefully round off each letter, forcing myself to disregard the burning in my eyelids, the feverish dryness of my hands, and the disinclination for work that I have felt for some time. The pedestal table is much too low and makes me crouch over it in an unhealthy position, yet nothing can induce me to change this room that I have used these last ten years for my correspondence; it is the closest one to the front door, so I can go and open it myself if I hear a timid ring on the bell.

The same table, the same bronze vase. Sometimes, while waiting for the bell to ring, I relaxed and went over to the fireplace for a while, the ornamental handle of the poker tight in my fist. In a superstitious gesture, obviously calculated to make myself more interesting in my own eyes, I kept only some letters of no importance. A ruthless executioner, I stood ready to intervene if the fire showed signs of spluttering out beneath the pile of burned paper. As I watched the tireless flicker, I relived a childish temptation to grab the silky-soft flame with its bluish-white core, as if fueled by spirit.

Maria would enter around that time with a tray of coffee and sweets, in keeping with the Oriental tradition that was still observed in the house. My only modernizing gesture had been to have electric lighting installed, and therefore an electric doorbell in place of the old tinkling device . . . And now, at last, here was the timid ring. Maria, taking jealous offense, went back to the peeling plaster and creaking doors of the dimly lit servants' quarters, while I hurried to the front door to rescue the shy girl, a literature and fine arts student, from any prying eyes. I knew that Sophie wouldn't dare to ring twice, that she might even run away and leave me wondering whether I had been prey to an aural hallucination.

Never consenting to remove her dark cape—which testified to the old-fashioned but touching romanticism of a young woman from the provinces—Sophie sank noiselessly into the armchair across the room from the pedestal table, and her furtive but eager looks betrayed the longing for adventure in her serious young heart. Nothing could have stopped her from shyly reappearing at the door at the same hour as before. It was best to leave the little wild beast well alone if you didn't want to scare her. And that's precisely what I did. Driven by a rigid honesty, I continued to pore over my subscription journals and to answer correspondence, while she sat drowsily waiting on the sofa—perhaps for a chaste embrace. Once or twice, when she yawned, I heard a slight creaking of her jaw or the clicking of her tongue on the roof of her mouth; at other times it was the rustling of pages as she leafed through, more than read, a novel or book of poems.

So, I came to feel protected not only by the gods of hearth and home, but also by a breathing sound as gentle as a sigh.

Later, Sophie kept coming at the same hour (only now down the stairs) to the drawing room with the tiled fireplace, while I continued to work through my correspondence. Already thinking back nostalgically to the clumsy start of our romance. Clumsy and also fortuitous—in the same way that a young state chooses almost by chance one ordinary day in the year as the hallowed national day.

Whatever the reasons, unknown to both of us, Sophie appeared at the door after her afternoon toilet, wrapped in a perfumed haze, and sank coquettishly onto the sofa, with no other concern than her husband's comfort and the serving of tea.

Why didn't I, like Faust, call out *Verweile doch*! But would I have suffered the moment to tarry, when I had only just come back from the dead and life's lottery was holding out the prospect of unexpected joys?

Sadly, whether you call out or not, time does not stand still, any more than the law of progress has been confirmed in a century that began with such hopes in it, or any more than the best can replace the good, or any more than women, however sensible, can live without company . . . And yet, the same drawing room with its tiled fireplace, the same time of day, the same bronze dish loaded with letters and offprints, the same full wastepaper basket . . .

And the deceptive feeling that the world's pulse is regular, that time is on our side so long as we stick to our habits. Our routines . . .

But isn't that the sound of a horse and carriage?

Unfortunately, the carriages that enter our street—apart from the odd stray with a drunken driver, or the odd coupé harboring an amorous couple—can be coming nowhere other than here, since there are no other entrance steps to pull up at. And I'm not in the mood to receive a surprise visitor, nor am I suitably dressed.

I go to the middle of the room and prick up my ears. All my senses are concentrated in one: I am no more than a huge listening machine. No, it wasn't a hallucination: that really is the jolting of a carriage. It's an unmistakable sound, especially now, with half the street dug up for repairs. Just think: I had to shorten my siesta and, after a quick wash, creep sluggishly down the wooden staircase while the rest of the house went on resting—and all just to preserve my routine, to wrest a few solitary hours and extract enough spiritual strength to see me through the evening reception. Like an Antaeus who has touched down on earth . . .

What a disappointment!

At least if it wasn't someone too irritating—Marie-Liliane, for example. But if it was her, Sophie would know and be waiting. "My friend? It's only because of you that she shows me any attention." That's probably the only time she has reproached me for something out of jealousy, and it wasn't as absurd as all that. Not as unjustified as the other times! After that, she felt too sure of her ground—my confession that once, a long time ago, I had considered marrying Marie-Liliane made her even surer—and she no longer thought it necessary to keep up the pretense of seeing her as a rival.

Behind the window that looks onto the terrace covered with ivy and clematis, I feel suddenly invigorated by the thought that it might be Marie-Liliane after all . . . Why not indeed, even if Sophie doesn't seem to know? Marie-Liliane certainly won't be coming to our party, where too many different kinds of people have been invited, but she might take it upon herself to call around unannounced. It wouldn't be the first time—perhaps just to leave a little present with her card . . . If I knew for sure it was her carriage, I'd ask her in for a while. I'd gladly trade the charms of solitude for the pleasure of her sparkling and witty conversation, whether the subject is her mystical crisis, or the school where she was the only girl in a crowd of boys, or embroidery or the Koran or the ten operations she's had, which gave her the chance to learn Arabic in the hospital. You never know what you'll end up talking about with Marie-Liliane. She's such a delightful girl that she can make you forget she wasn't born beautiful. Sometimes—especially if I'm eaten up with worries—I find myself idly wondering what my life would have been like if an unjust fate hadn't decided in advance that Marie-Liliane was to remain a spinster. It is precisely this line of thought that spares me any feelings of remorse . . . Now, the more I think about it, the more I'm sure that she's the surprise visitor. That's why I hover around the window with my eyes peeled, not seeing anyone outside.

When was it that I decided to open the terrace door?

A few strenuous attempts leave my palms and forehead bathed in sweat. If I'd thought a little, I'd have remembered that it's a long time since I've seen the door open, and I'd have called someone to help me. Did Sophie have it blocked up? I don't remember anything like that.

Anyway, it's becoming ridiculous. I ought to give up, especially as the carriage wheels seem to be fading into the distance.

I suddenly feel disgusted and a growing exhaustion comes over me. What's the point of wrestling with this door anyway? Meanwhile I remember an old scene: *maman* between two maids one Saturday evening, inspecting the fresh laundry for things that she'll have to mend herself. And another scene, perhaps older: *maman* red-cheeked under her starched headgear, stirring a huge pot of jam and complaining—to whom?—that no one attends to it properly . . .

Have I really become so helpless that I can't free a blocked door?

No, there we are, it's open!

A hot dry puff of wind strikes me in the face like a feverish breath. I feel the white light burning my eyes and blink rapidly behind my thick lenses. No, the carriage wasn't a hallucination.

Look . . .

An ordinary carriage, its hood lowered, is weaving its way toward the end of the street, past holes and bumps, asphalt machine and grayish-green paving stones. I have the impression that someone is poking the driver in the back and giving him orders. I'm not sure whether the details I see are really there. Maybe they are due to my faulty vision, or maybe I'm just imagining them. As usual, I can't rely on my senses and I do well to doubt them. It's well known that they can trick you.

Like reason can trick you.

The key thing is that there's no one on the entrance steps: no Marie-Liliane, but also (I say by way of consolation) no unwelcome visitor to bother me.

From the steps, I naturally look out into the garden and can scarcely believe my eyes. I pull a sour face as Sophie, an unrecognizable Sophie, appears there disguised as a gardener. Her showy carnival gear really isn't to my taste! To think that in the early years she used to insist on knowing what I disliked in one of her hats or dresses, or even in the way she talked! Nowadays she says with a kind of hurt smile that men don't understand a thing about fashion, that they're only interested in *certain things*.

No need to underline that in the old days I was I, and now I'm "men." Such a cheap remark, said so naturally, simply because she's at a different time of life!

What upsets me more than her dress is that she's out there struggling with the garden tools. Why does she tire herself with such things, when we've hired a gardener to do them on my modest professor's pay? Of course I should go and stop her, but her bad mood today makes me think twice. She could quite possibly inform me, with that special female logic, that I'm to blame for her getting involved in something that's usually done by the servants. For some time now she's taken offense at every little thing. Of course she finds it hard to put up with my illness, and looking after the house seems to get her down. That's probably why she sees her husband as the source of all kinds of difficulties.

Well, I'll let her get on with her watering and her roses, as if I haven't even noticed. I'll withdraw my eyes from the walnut tree and the wicker table and chairs, back across the layers of rose beds. The still blinding light of day is forming a rainbow above a jet of water. I see that Sophie has left a tap running and that the path is filling with water. But it doesn't seem to bother her: she's still happily picking roses and putting them in her basket.

Come, I tell myself, make a discreet exit. If we observe strict rules of conduct, our good upbringing should protect others from our aggression and ourselves from our own inner demons. Take refuge in those rules, since you're an adult now and are beginning to see things a little more clearly; it's easier for you to impose such civilized egoistical reasoning.

So, just leave the door slightly ajar. Draw the heavy green drapery and the translucent beige curtain that reaches down to the glossy, mirror-like floor.

Forget all that and get back to your correspondence . . .

Veuillez agréer, Monsieur, l'assurance de ma haute considération: no, I really should stop worrying about the boredom that awaits me a couple of hours from now, when the carriages start pulling up and the guests who aren't away on holiday, or who've hurried back because of alarmist rumors or their own native caution, take it in turns to present themselves. It's no longer just a question of rising prices, food shortages, and other abnormal signs: we all know now that things have got worse, and that's why before dinner we'll all talk incessantly about *joining it.*

Do we really want to join the war, or are we threatened with invasion if we stay out?

But who's going to invade us? Why, the Russians of course!

Brătianu has certainly been asked to join, in the form of ultimatums not only from the Russians but also from the Allies, who we hoped would defend us.

Defend us against whom?

How can anyone still ask a question like that? As if we didn't know.

We don't know anything, because Brătianu's language is getting more and more cryptic.

Brătianu's Sphinx-like silence has protected Romania until now!

Brătianu is holding his tongue more than ever, and whenever he gets a chance he clears off to his estate in Florica . . .

You're right—to loll around on his fancy sofas and hatch some disastrous plot or other. He'll only leave off when he sees Romania wiped off the map of Europe!

Brătianu won't give up trying, because he hasn't forgotten that the British left us in the lurch once before, at the Congress of Berlin.

Don't people realize how petty-minded Brătianu is, even after all this time? He's still haggling like at a bazaar. He wants to enter the war at the best moment and refuses to scale down any of his ambitions.

Brătianu is afraid the Allies will do a deal with the Russians behind his back.

Well, gentlemen, all I can say is that it's a disaster for a small country like ours to be drawn into a general conflagration . . .

And who do you think will do a deal above his head? Who will sell us down the river?

Come now, sir, you know as well as I do.

You mean the British? Those who are standing up for principles . . . ?

Perfidious Albion!

Roars of laughter.

General unease, explosions of mirth, racy remarks, alarming news, coarse male laughter, the tinkling of women's voices, a threatening future, unprecedented high spirits, a lot of people milling around minister Athanasiu (to no avail, because government circles have urged utter discretion). We're more sarcastic and distrustful with one another than ever before: with those who weigh up the chances on each side and are ready to jump on the winning bandwagon; with those who parade their nationalism in the streets only to bring the government down; with those who look prepared to march arm in arm with plundering empires; and with those who generously offer Romanian blood for the cause of France and Russia . . . Each of us has convincing arguments: you and I are the only ones arguing in good faith; the rest are motivated by self-interest; spies and lackeys are crawling all around us!

There's no danger of an invasion, as some evil-intentioned people are implying in their own interest.

Bear in mind, gentlemen, that one false move is enough for our little country to disappear from the map of Europe, as if it had never . . .

The situation is radically different from a few months ago. Then, St. Petersburg wanted us to enter as late as possible so that we wouldn't be able to make any demands of our own, whereas now they've sent Brătianu an ultimatum demanding that he join the war.

But what about France, gentlemen? We should never forget that the French . . .

We know everything and nothing, because of Brătianu's infuriating silence.

So who *do* you think will do a deal with the Russians behind Brătianu's back? Who will sell us down the river? Come on, sir, out with it!

Do you mean France? Our sister country, which has proved so many times . . .

And which is unable to safeguard its own fate!

I still think we should enter as soon as possible, without petty calculations, and without getting distracted by what everyone has to say about it all.

In my view, politics is a practical matter: it's not about passing fads . . .

Why am I getting mixed up in this? If I'm not an expert at politics and find the whole business disagreeable, why can't I refrain from butting in with a skeptical remark or a doubting smile? And when they get around to the Allies' guarantees and their ability to defend us, will I be capable, this evening at least, of keeping my pet fable out of the discussion? What childish vanity could make me relate it, when I've seen so many times before that, however much sense it makes to me, no one else is in the least bit interested?

"A little true story," I'll hasten to assure them with a courteous smile, "from the time when the future of our little country seemed even less secure than it does today."

"Has there ever been a time when our future hasn't seemed insecure?"

An interruption not worth bothering about.

"It takes place during the early years of the reign of King Carol. The crux of it, in fact, is a little exchange of words between two diplomats. I don't want to be too indiscreet, so I won't reveal the name either of the German official in Bucharest or of the Romanian politician, who is still alive today . . . Well, in an attempt to obtain the minimum guarantees for our future, the Romanian politician asked the man from Berlin: 'Will Germany consider any violence to the little kingdom of Romania as an affront to its own prestige as a great power, given that a Hohenzollern also sits on the throne of Romania?' And the pat answer: 'A division of Romania (half to Russia, half to Austria), or even its annexation, would have every chance of gaining our assent if it was in Germany's interests and if the general situation made it seem advisable.' Maybe you think there was a hint of sarcasm in the reply. Well, you'd be wrong: it was given in a perfectly cordial spirit!"

Did my intonation or gestures indicate in advance that it would be a boring story? Perhaps. Anyway, most of the guests will go on talking at the same pitch. Some will try to catch what I'm saying but give up after the first couple of sentences, and no one amid the bustle will understand what seems to me the obvious point of the story—a still topical point for what I call the "sad fate of Romania."

In fact, it would be even more distasteful if someone were to pass a comment. Good old Victor, for example, might say:

"But, *mon cher,* what have I been telling you these last few years? We should enter at once on the Allied side! It's good that, even at this late hour, you've come to realize what the krauts are capable of. I thought you were tending in the opposite direction . . ."

"But it's not only Germany I'm referring to: it's the other great powers as well. I must have expressed myself badly if I gave the impression . . ."

"Is that right, Victor? Did you think he meant only Germany?"

"What was I supposed to think, my dear Sophie?"

In our early years together, I used to be terribly embarrassed when she cut in like that. But she belongs to a generation that likes to trample on privileges of rank or gender (or, to be more precise, pretends to trample on them). It's become quite common for ladies to discuss politics more heatedly than gentlemen. When I think back to our early days, it's true that her interruptions embarrassed me, but I looked on her as a faithful dog, lying muzzle on paws and snarling a little before dashing forth with eyes blazing. What about now? Should I listen to what she is saying, in that slightly affected tone that she adopts when she is playing the coquette? Everyone knows that Victor has a great weakness for her. "I'm still a bachelor because there's only one Sophie in the world." He never fails to repeat that sentence late at night, when the drink has gone to his head.

And she puts on a smile, looking flattered, without a trace of irony! She has that feminine capacity to lap up cheap and insincere compliments, but as soon as we are alone together she laughs and pokes fun at Victor. Meanwhile it's:

"How simple you make it sound, Victor! What our politician wanted to know was whether we can count on Germany, given that our own king is a German. He was imagining an even bleaker future for our country, but the surprise is that Germany, in fact not necessarily Germany . . ."

She recites like a schoolgirl, in her own words, what I explained earlier. When she's in love, she's capable of such touching—one might say total—devotion, a ravishing stubbornness that means she sees only what it suits her to see.

If you no longer spot any of these signs, can you be sure she's no longer in love? So I'll remain on the margins of their conversation, glad that young Ialomiţeanu will be openly seeking out my company. He'll immediately ask me those little questions, with his skilful display of timidity, so that I'll have to deny that I know more than anyone: I'm sorry, Mr. Ialomiţeanu, I've heard nothing about that . . . Looking into his innocent eyes, I shall be far too embarrassed and, as always when I'm hiding something, think that I'm an open book for the other person. But he'll still want to know whether it's true that Brătianu is stitching together a government of national unity, including not only Take Ionescu but even Marghiloman. Feeling under pressure, I'll resort to pulling a wry face and offering a complicit wink, like those *well-informed* gentlemen who stress certain words and accompany them with a tap on your shoulder. They'll be inelegant gestures, moreover, breaking the strict silence that Liberal circles are meant to be observing, and for this reason I'll move away rather brusquely from Mr. Ialomiţeanu.

I find it harder and harder to bear my dissatisfaction with myself, which already used to trouble me as a young man longing for the calmness of a still sea. Ah, that unattainable *sophrosyne* of my dreams! How far off it will remain when I'm busy organizing the whist and *écarté* tables! As the host, I shall then have to go to the little drawing room, where the sound of youthful voices will be heard—the Pallade brothers, no doubt, one the agreeable tenor who usually accompanies Sophie, the other the motorcar driver. There will be *Lieder* . . . A lieutenant will stand in front of the piano—a young man from a good family who has just returned from college in England. Oh . . . what's his name? Ah, yes,

Alexandru Geblescu. Our ubiquitous Titi Ialomițeanu will play the host by asking him some innocent questions. What can he say about the new appointments? Is it true that the king, not Brătianu, is supporting General Crăiniceanu?

From these young people, who in their way are also wrapped up in politics, I shall move on with pleasure to the inseparable Nacu sisters: *pauvre* Ortense and *pauvre* Lily. Another summer has gone by without their managing to find a husband. And the opportunities are becoming few and far between.

"What ravishing dresses! You must have mortgaged your houses and estates for them," I cheerfully joke, bowing to each in turn. "Yes, it's always been like that in your family. Perhaps your adorable grandmother told you about the dramatic scenes during Sarah Bernhardt's visit to Bucharest. No, I'm perfectly serious. I was at school at the time, and your delightful grandmother was still in full bloom. All eyes were on her as she stepped into her box . . . Yes, I assure you. Why do you find it so difficult to believe?"

After dinner, the men will retire to the smoking room. They'll start off by exchanging the hottest gossip and a selection of bawdy jokes, but soon the conversation will turn to the *nouveaux riches:* all those rustics who've taken over Bucharest, dealing in export licenses and the black market; all those crooks who sit around in booths at the Hotel Imperial and quarrel with the waiters over the bill; all those puffed-up parvenus who undo their waistcoat buttons!

Loud roars: a healthy national taste for laughter that, as I've seen all my life, accompanies great disasters such as fire, earthquake, war, cholera, or a breakup of the country.

A memory of a summer evening in the garden of the Fântâna Blanduziei. I was just back from the cholera hellhole of the Balkan front, thanks to an intervention by my friend Jean Athanasiu; I spent the whole evening fidgeting on a chair, unable to hear one line or to enjoy the sausages and hot dogs on offer at the simple popular festival. Poor Sophie had reason to reproach me sometimes! The only free table we could find was in a corner far from the stage. And, on that rare occasion when we were out on the town together for a few hours, when both she and everyone else were trying to forget the horrors of war, I spoiled it all for her with my brooding.

Guffaws, irritable voices, know-all voices.

Just think, gentlemen: a little nation in a world that's going up in flames!

Russia's annoyance with us is coming right into the open during these days.

It has to be said that the public is not at all excited by the news that we're entering the war.

Well, one false move and our little country will disappear, as if it had never . . .

The public is worried and skeptical, and even I am weighed down by a sense of foreboding . . .

That's why, at this late hour, I repeat what I said before: the criminal who is preparing to spill so much blood, with such criminal negligence, is that man Brătianu!

Even if I recognize the voice as Victor's, it would be rash to jump down his throat and shout like a neurasthenic: "But, my dear sir, haven't you been demanding for two years that we should do precisely that—enter the war at once? Weren't you arguing just a moment ago that we should get stuck in and throw aside all petty calculations? Aren't they your very words?"

"Extraordinary!" Victor would exclaim. "Quite extraordinary! Forgive me, old chap, but I was arguing that we should enter at a different moment. At the time of the Russian advance on Lemberg, maybe! Or at some other moment, one of the many there have been and will be, but not now! Anyway, certainly not the criminal indifference with which we sat by and watched guiltless Serbia being throttled, nor our passivity when our own little country was being strangled by one side and abandoned by the other! I, and many like me, have been arguing for us to enter at a different moment! Not with Iliescu running the show—a man who's drunk day and night. A different time, and with different men! Not those who've grown fat on our neutrality, on railway concessions and export licenses and all the rest of it."

"Just a minute! I thought we were talking about entering the war. If you thought there was a better moment, doesn't that mean we'd have entered a year or several months earlier? And, since we are all so skeptical and pessimistic, isn't it good that our country was spared a little longer?"

"Excuse me, that was then—but I'm talking about now. Why is there this petty distrust of our great Allies? Brătianu is as suspicious as a peasant from Argeş at the market."

He'll go on arguing like that, of course, and you'll watch his skinny little chin, the yellow patch on his iris, his thick fingers beating out the sentences, and all the other peculiarities you've come to know over the last twenty years without learning anything special from them. You'll listen to him, and it won't occur to you to suspect him of bad faith. God, how boring it will be: how tiresome that everyone will talk so heatedly and intolerantly, convinced that they alone are right! What will have been the point of our exchange of harangues, when each of us concludes by restating the position he had before we started?

Sick to death of it all—and so so tired!—you'll walk over to the card tables. What serious faces, what smugness as each asks to be dealt another card!

You will leave unnoticed by this door, already left slightly ajar, and breathe some fresh air on the terrace among clematis petals swollen by the night. The smell of warm earth, still rising through the wisteria and the thick burdock leaves, will break in on your keen, analytic consideration of the competing arguments.

Then your thoughts will turn again to the mirror-like surface of a calm sea. Ah, that unattainable *sophrosyne* of which you have dreamed so long! Leaning over the balustrade, by the honeysuckle, you will try to remember when it blooms—May? June? anyway some time ago—and its scent will seem like a message from a celestial realm; its delicate blossoms are much sparser now, in the form of pious hands with fingers glued together.

It's one of the last nights filled with the heat and dust of summer, before the feast of the Assumption brings fresher air and a different light. As you stand there, feeling more and more remote from the fiery discussion and the wooden responses that sprouted on your tongue, it will seem a night like any other in the suffocating capital city—except that you're one of the very few who know the real situation. And, like any higher man halfway through life, eager to improve your vision and understanding of things, you will see nothing but darkness out there.

Darkness, darkness . . .

Yet your logical, opaque, and optimistic nature will not resign itself. You will reproach yourself for neglecting your duties as host, and you will feel surprised that you grew bored faster than you had expected, but you will go on contemplating the rise of the mighty rural moon over the

limes on nearby Kiseleff Avenue, and think that in less than a hundred
years it will be eclipsed by the bright lights of a real metropolis.

An aural hallucination? Or is that really the doorbell? Shaken from
my daydreaming, I prick up my ears and listen to the sounds that float
through the domestic silence: a squeaking door, a creaking floorboard
somewhere upstairs, steps as light as a cat's on the staircase. But the bell
doesn't ring again. Maybe it was a prank: maybe a boy fascinated by the
new electric bell gave a quick ring and ran off to the wasteland, to boast
to his friends about his courage. My hearing sharpened, I probe the
silence for a few more seconds, in the same way that a microscope looks
for forms of life teeming in a drop of water.

And close by, so close that I jump, the clock begins to strike.

Yes, it won't be long before the bell rings without a break. I reach out
and take some silken envelopes from the bronze vase. Over there the
printed words *Tavernier à Paris* look down from the dial of the clock.
How can I reconcile myself to the idea that a trip to Paris has become
an impossible adventure? Does a curtain of fire now really separate me
from the colleague who scribbled his name on the back of this envelope?
Explosions that scatter bleeding heads and limbs, shells that decapitate
schoolchildren and the statues of saints in great cathedrals: I'm incapable of imagining the hell described in the newspapers. But it's already
two years since my last trip abroad, when I went to Vienna to choose the
phonographs and all the accessories I need for the phonetics laboratory
that I'll set up in the university basement as soon as I get my strength
back.

Nothing must stop us from carrying out our duty! So let us keep
looking straight ahead, neither left nor right, like a horse with blinkers.
Even if our skin cracks and bleeds under the harness, even if our tail
cannot drive away the dark-green flies that swarm around it, even if the
bit makes our mouth bleed and we stumble more and more often under
the lash, we must continue to drag our burden. However grim the future
that lies ahead, we must press on with our plans for the laboratory, asking advice from those who have had one for a long time already—from
those I used to go out strolling with in the old days! Ah, those walks of
our youth, on Cologne's Hohestrasse and the Zülpicher! How wonderful
it was to be in Europe! How wonderful Europe was!

I fumble for the paper knife, my eyes fixed on the stamp on the envelope I am holding. The cancellation marks have made the cathedral's lattice work even darker, but they would have to be much darker still for me not to recognize it, with this wrenching feeling in my chest. I slide the knife earnestly into the envelope, but I have a frozen smile on my face. What strange pity a grown man feels for the image of himself in his youth!

A skinny youngster, his voice already broken, but still with boyish rosy cheeks beneath a downy growth, awkwardly puts on a bored look as he passes the janitor . . . As soon as he enters his room, however, he hurries to the blackened mirror in the wardrobe; what unsettles him is not the drawn face, with its thick eyelashes and prominent nose, but the navy-blue frock coat, the yellow waistcoat with dark little flowers, and the duck's egg color of the trousers. What is there that still bears marks of his East European origins? Although *pauvre maman* was pained at the thought of his departure, she went with him to the Quatre Saisons shop on Strada Vămii, to dress him from head to toe in an outfit perfect for hot weather or cold.

His searching eyes run once more from the black silk bow tie down to the soft boots with uppers and the socks matching his yellow gloves. So, what is missing? Why does he still not look like young people here? Is the cut of his clothes out of date? Does he already look old-fashioned? Or maybe it's the awkward way in which he holds his body? How could the concierge have guessed which part of Eastern Europe her new tenant has come from to study philology and epigraphy? It's true that there was a flicker of doubt in her eyes: no, he's not Polish, unfortunately, nor Greek or Serbian, certainly not Hungarian, and not even Albanian . . . If she hasn't heard of the little Balkan kingdom, he has no wish to enlighten her, nor will he blush at her questions, as he did in the first few days. He will reply to everything in monosyllables, so that she can't detect his insecurity or his delight to be here. In just a few weeks he has ceased to be a child, but he still gets too worked up over trifles to be a grown man. No, he's not pretending, he really is breathlessly short of both time and money. So, he lays his reading aside only when tears of weariness fill his poor myopic eyes. Disheveled hair protruding from his nightcap, tongue held childlike between his teeth, he sits cross-legged on cold sheets and begins to jot things down.

As the ancient Greeks knew their myths only too well, what interested them in a tragedy was not the plot or the characters, but how the poet

justified events of long ago in accordance with the new way of thinking.
For people had in part forgotten the old way of thinking, and in part no
longer understood it. This means that the poets' imagination only ever
gives us back the present. But, in that case, is each instant lost in darkness?

Lunch: table d'hôte, boeuf à la mode . . . , *French fries, escalope with*
spinach, 15 crowns.

Money borrowed: 85 crowns. Repayment date: 26 October.

Books borrowed: The Iliad, *translated by Voss.*

Note. I have the impression that the very core of the discipline in which
I want to work is changing, while the shell remains the same as before. As
for my own research, it offers me no security—on the contrary. Most of the
time I'm terribly ashamed of it, and I feel like scrapping it all. But I fear
that this reaction proves beyond all doubt my essential mediocrity.

Does that notebook in which the poor youth stared at the unfinished
page still exist in some drawer of my old filing cabinet, or on one of the
rickety tables in the attic? Had he managed to squeeze all he could from
the little time and money available? His nose cast an imperious shadow
over his long face, which was pathetic in its gravity; he was alone and
had arrived so late, unable to afford sinking into disorder.

Performances seen: The Huguenots, Wallenstein's Death, Egmont.

Found other lodgings, with a separate entrance. Furniture: writing desk,
bookcase with mirror, dressing table, bed, armchair, washstand with mar-
ble slab and an attached tap, carpet, curtains at the windows. Included:
morning coffee, lighted fire at all hours, laundry and brushing of clothes.

For the exam: study Meyer and Lübke.

Unforgivable guilt: a week late writing home.

He yawns, lets the notebook fall from his knees, swings his feet onto
the floor and pokes around with them for his slippers. A strange laziness
is sapping his Spartan resolution and making him careless in the way he
moves his hands and feet. He abandons his search for the slippers too
easily, shuffles over to the wretched little washstand, turns on the tap
and drinks directly from it, then shuffles back to the bed, avoiding the
clownish figure in the mirror with nightcap and downy beard and chest.
Ah, if only he was better-looking!

What strange compassion I feel for that young man, whom I allow,
almost without caring, to rush blindly toward future troubles! Yes, and
as I do it, I have the crazy idea that it is in my power to turn the clock
back to the beginning. But I move the pencil toward the draft and write:

Lieber Karl . . . I write the draft carefully: all my attention is focused on it, not on the poor youngster I once was, who may bear some resemblance to me. How thin my eyebrows have become! How little hair is left on my head! It's only a vague resemblance—except for the astonishing fact that no one, not even the Almighty, knows more about him than I do.

At the time he gave French lessons to two young ladies at the boarding house, having learned the language at home and sat exams at the Romance languages faculty. And on Sundays, when the city plumbed mysterious depths and books lost their fascination, he fought off tedium by dreaming of their rosy complexion and implausibly bright hair. He allowed himself no other friendships than with his dear Karl: he despised the frivolity of ordinary conversation, and sought neither amicable companionship nor success in amorous conquests or society gatherings. And in the evening, of course, he continued to write in his old notebook.

Kölnisch Anonym: Christ in the Garden of Gethsemane. *Since the artist knew neither the laws of perspective and anatomy nor those of drawing, I really cannot work out where the artistic effect comes from—especially as here the colors do not help either, having been degraded by poor conservation. I could also say the opposite, however: that the color degradation is largely responsible for the artistic effect. At a later date, the gold of the crepuscular sky has been filled out with dark patches that seem symbolic and portentous.*

But can unintended effects that have come about by chance really be described as artistic? You could think that the little Garden was an animal pen, since it has only a couple of stunted trees and is surrounded by a crooked fence. Christ looks misshapen, as if he has suffered from water on the brain. The soldiers have dull, ridiculous faces. So, the spectacular golden sky with dark streaks is due to changes in the paint and wood over five hundred years. The terror that has brought Christ to his knees—he is truly a pitoyable bonhomme, *for whom the idea of martyrdom for others seems an unjust absurdity—is lacking in any grandeur. With its lack of beauty, the scene may inspire the same kind of pity and repulsion that unkempt and malodorous old people arouse from close up. As for the bloodthirsty soldiers, the fear that one feels on seeing them by the fence is mingled with disgust and hilarity, because they are so grotesque. Like the forces of good, evil too does not here have the solemnity you would expect . . . Nevertheless, Christ does right to pray on his knees beneath a sky that will grow darker over the years, because glowing patterns surround him on all sides, shrill red plumes flutter overhead, and halberds flash in the dark.*

Some notes cannot fail to bring a smile to my lips.

As soon as I went in, I was struck by the fairy-tale atmosphere emanating from the colored paper lamps and the garlands hanging from trees with photographs attached. But then I was caught up in it as well, especially during the tableaux-vivants, *and afterward I tried to find the unknown woman and to make sure she saw me. I finally succeeded only when the ladies appeared in all their finery, adorned with real flowers in the manner that—as I was told later—this season's fashion dictates. More original and more sincere, in her renunciation of both aristocratic orchids and bourgeois roses, she decorated her décolletage with no more than a bunch of fresh violets.*

I am sure I know everything about him, but many years have turned up nothing about her . . . I break off writing and rest my chin on the palm of my hand, thinking of the question as on so many other occasions: who could she have been? Why, on that evening, did an attractive woman who had people crowding around her accept a gawky student so rapidly? Which world did she come from, which did she belong to now? Her manners were impeccable, as were her sparkling teeth. But what of the house he entered, as excited as someone in love? If you don't have experience in these matters, but only a young body tormented by bad habits and shameless daydreams, the unbearable tensions of love strike you like lightning in the most modest of circumstances.

Or anyway, that's how it happened for him.

The window in the little drawing room, which is permanently open, is not enough to dispel the odor of damp coming from the poorly maintained walls, or the all too human smells—food, dust, eau-de-cologne to cover the rest—which probably entered long ago into the worn, once light-blue, carpet with a pattern of flowers and twigs. Here and there, however, are signs of a more prosperous past: a beautiful Japanese cloisonné dish on a wall, a fine old clock on the marble of the white-tiled stove.

How long did you sit talking there, on the little sofa with worn springs? Your memory has retained only the next scene, and retained it miraculously well, as if an all-seeing outsider had observed it: he moving slowly toward the bed, on his long bean stalks of legs, vainly trying to cover his nakedness, breathing faster and faster, his vision increasingly blurred. And then, suddenly impatient, he buried himself in the still

fresh roundness of her body, his hand trembling so much that he could
scarcely feel her soft, loosely hanging breast. But what a miracle! What a
miracle she performed, by showing him that his body—which until then
he had despised as a dangerous unclean beast, always ready to pester and
humiliate, and carelessly groomed in lodgings so cold that dressing was
a Spartan test of endurance—was actually capable of bringing happiness
to his soul. Was her friskiness in that old bed a practical lesson for his
benefit? But no, he no longer had to learn how to move, hobbled by his
own self-consciousness, like an adolescent at his first dance lesson, or a
ballet dancer paralyzed by the stage lights.

What a greedy, impetuous debut! The path now opening up for the
first time brought a lofty detachment, in which he lazily floated along,
relieved of the weight of his own body. Was his life in fact just an insig-
nificant fragment illuminated by a chance ray of light, a corner of a vast
tapestry from which you had to stand back to see the whole? A deep, perhaps conclusive, understanding hovered before his closed eyelids, while
he lost himself in the spasm of love that cast him ashore as an earthly
creature with atrophied senses.

What a bright morning entered through the open window, over the
roof slates of the old city! Nothing would darken it during the next few
months . . . With dressing gown slung over his shoulder and hair carefully enclosed in a net—he now respected the time she spent ironing for
him—he stroked his newly grown moustache and sank into the armchair, a prey as so often before to memory. A lustful dizziness in his
mind, a buzzing in his ears, a wave of blood that made his bones feel ever
lighter, ever spongier, and in his belly the same hot spike of desire . . .

Bent over the pedestal table, I now make a clean copy of the letter. Again
I see myself as if I were a stranger looking in from outside, but how different everything is! My weak, crooked shoulders give me a slight hunch,
my chest is narrow, and my innards protrude in a little embonpoint. I
see a whitish wart in the corner of my eye, and a nervous twitch rhythmically shakes my long, emaciated legs, the pointed kneecaps sticking
through my trousers. How can *he* be *I*? Only a vague resemblance—like
between father and son, only less. Actually he could be *my* son: that's
what I would say he was.

If he were my son, I'd close my eyes in terror. No, I'd cry out, if it be
possible, let this cup pass from you! No, I'd cry, going on my knees before

him . . . How could I leave him alone in that two-day train journey, pale and with rings around his eyes, shaking with fear at the window, looking out but oblivious to the landscape?

Restless hours in the carriage, teeth chattering, hands and feet frozen, repeatedly pulling down the window to lean out and shout: "Faster! Faster!" to the driver. And someone inside him pleading that the journey will last as long as possible, even infinitely long. But now there he is, climbing the entrance steps and the endless wooden staircase, staggering up and breathing with ever greater difficulty, and then suddenly the smell . . .

Already in the dimly lit corridor, where the tips of his shoes found every bump in the floorboards, the smell became more and more overpowering, until he gently pushed the half-open door to his mother's bedroom and suddenly understood. Instead of the fragrance of lavender and basil that usually wafted from fresh sheets and cupboard drawers, there was a shameless odor of rotting flesh and urine. And his restrained mother, who had arrived late to see him off at the station, and still had her helpless eyes hidden beneath a veil when the signal was given for departure—my God, how could she have sunk into this terrible state in such a short space of time? In the flickering candlelight, her face seemed black and shrunken to the size of a fist on the colossal white pillow, eyes blinking icily, lips purple and parched. She was motionless, barely breathing in a strange whistle, as if struggling with something on which she had concentrated all her attention. "It's me, you know . . . ," he whispered stupidly, and the black pupil contracted in those eyes that no longer saw anyone. Did it really contract, or was it just an illusion? The whistling sound had not ceased for a moment to come through her half-open lips, and she had still seemed wrapped up in one all-important thing that concerned her alone, requiring the same conscientious attention that she had brought to bear on other matters throughout her life. Be a little patient, she'll deal with it in a minute and then the two of them can sit and talk normally.

"It's me, you know . . ." A smell of pure wax and incense, covering the shameful odors of flesh. Doors opening and closing behind him. Suppressed tears. Steps on the wooden staircase. The jolting of a carriage on the bumpy street outside. The clanking of empty milk cans on a cart. All these ordinary sounds came from a world that, by remaining the same, had ceased to be warm and welcoming. Where had it been hiding this dreadful, obscene smirk?

Steps of people around him. The strange whistling sounded weaker on her purple lips, and the look on her face was even more concentrated— but also more unconcerned, as if she had forgotten that she still had to complete the pressing matter so that the two of them could then sit and talk. Incredible though it might seem, it was as if she no longer cared that he had made the long journey back after such a long time away, as if she didn't think it necessary even to glance at him.

Again the door bell, again steps on the wooden stairs. The shouts of a water carrier outside, immediately covered by the rattling of his wheel-barrow on the broken paving stones. *You,* who used to sparkle with life. The voice of an old man, dry and plaintive, immediately covered by the grinding of a barrel organ. A door opening, suppressed tears, and he not knowing what to do with himself, shifting from one foot to the other, his eyes dry, *when you and I were alone in the world,* an old man's voice, unbearably dry and plaintive, and he standing awkwardly, almost impatiently, not even realizing that his whole existence had ceased to be what he alone thought it possibly was: a natural and pleasurable ascent to sweet harmony and well-deserved abundance . . . For, defying all sense, withholding all encouragement, she had left for him there no more than the demeaning odor of rotting flesh, the incongruous whistling of half-open lips.

It therefore seemed no less natural to him when the whistling suddenly stopped, the half-open jaws stiffened, and all that could be heard was the usual sluggish silence.

If he had been my child, I would have been incapable of pushing the envelope firmly aside while this picture of his woes lingered in my mind's eye. Nor would I have profited from the lack of a witness to yawn heartily and stretch my arms and legs, and then search my pockets for the little silver box of Vichy fruit pastilles, *traitement rationnel de la constipation, migraines, dyspepsies, maladies du foie, de l'estomac, de l'intestin*—ah, yes, found it at last. The familiar sweet-and-sour taste on my tongue, a sigh of relaxation and pleasure, the peaceful blue sky beneath cotton-wool clouds, an unexpected breeze—thank God!—that animates the tops of the poplars in the garden opposite. Their bright green body is breathing, and I breathe in time with it, a happy look in my eyes.

But how is such a thing possible?

How can someone ring so disrespectfully at this time of day? And how is it possible that there's no one at home to go and see who it is? Have things reached the point where the servants are all out, leaving Sophie to look after the garden and me to open the door instead of Grigore? Can't I have a minute alone with myself until a new day dawns tomorrow? Isn't it enough that I'll reel into bed at daybreak, after a long grueling night? Do I have to put up with their assaults even now, offering false smiles and tactful conversation? Wonderful! So anyone passing can just ring the bell and stroll in, without sending their card or telephoning in advance? Does it make no difference if I sit tight in my chair? Are there no rules in the world anymore? I keep quiet and sit still, my heart pounding with emotion. How can anyone dare to ring three times and push open the door ever so gently? But look who's standing there in the doorway!

"Ah, Mr. Ialomițeanu, do come in and make yourself at home. We've talked about these things so often, haven't we? Protocol is out of place in the modern world: everything is getting simpler and simpler . . . Please, sit down or stand, as you prefer. Of course you're not disturbing me, not at all, my dear Ialomițeanu. On the contrary! As you well know, I always have people around when I'm dealing with my correspondence. You might say it's a little habit of mine."

Sophie

I was doing nothing—just sitting there. The sky was a stony white, with a streak of blue at one end. I was looking at how ivy hangs over the window of the room where we agreed I'll mostly sleep from now on. Our bedroom window is completely covered with ivy, but I like there to be plenty of light. That's the reason I gave for not wanting us to sleep in the same room any longer . . . So I'd given up the idea of going to the attic again to shake that good-for-nothing Grigore. I was doing absolutely nothing, just waiting for my malaise to pass so that I could go back into the garden.

All that could be heard was a distant cooing of pigeons and, more distant still, the sound of a tram. The sun came out from behind a white cloud, suddenly throwing the sharp contours of dark and shadow onto the wall, and I became agitated as the memories flooded back. I felt I was choking: blood piled up in my chest and in the veins on my forehead. I

saw and felt the raw and velvety contact of our skins and, oh, our bodies glued together, issuing from the same thigh. The sun disappeared,
together with the clear demarcation line on the wall, and I could hear
the little anxious, fearful, beats of my heart. A cock crowed hoarsely a
long way off, little green berries peeked out from the ivy in front of the
window—all that remained was fear. I thought I could hear a carriage.
I didn't want to be late, so I got up and inspected my dress; the ivy was
eternal in its immobility.

"Spurning prejudices, the modern mind recognizes that women desire
men, to a similar or comparable degree."

The sentence echoed in my head as I crept down the staircase and took
the basket, gloves, and garden fork from their usual place. I could hear
the exact intonation with which it had been said, only I had seen things
very differently at the time. I honestly wondered whether Lisette had
similar fantasies, several times a day, since she made it up with Georges
after the maid gave birth a month ago.

I heard the carriage again as I went into the garden through the back
door. What a summer! The leaves on the trees no longer seemed green—
more white, as if covered with fine salt, and as shriveled as if it was a month
later. I didn't want at all to think of how life would be in a month's time,
of what would have become of us all. Nor did I want to hear that unseemly
sentence echo in my head, or to imagine things several times a day that
are usually shrouded in silence. Least of all did I want to see Ștefan's eyes
and the purple rings around them. I've come to fear their constant scru-
tiny, all the harsher for their hostility and lack of understanding.

Life is meant to be a joy, not a burden. It is this idea that allows me to
drive out dark thoughts so effortlessly. Since the leaves on the trees were
so dusty, I turned the hose on them: it's sheer madness to water trees in
broad daylight, but so what? Life has no pleasure if you don't spice it with
a few little follies. It was very easy for me to stop thinking of the things
I wanted to drive out of mind—including that indecorous sentence. I
pointed the hose at one of the young apple trees and watered it bit by
bit. Little apples, not yet ripe, glistened beneath the silky white leaves. I
simply couldn't hold myself back: my mouth suddenly filled with saliva.

I stood on the tips of my toes and stretched full out to reach an apple
above my head. The water pressure made the hose wriggle out of my fingers onto the path, but I left it there because I was busy trying to get
at the apples. It was just then that the carriage passed the house. Life is

meant to be a joy, not a torture, and none of its troubles will affect me if I don't want them to. I was just about to reach the branch, but I gave up and turned my head to look toward the carriage. It was not the one I'd been expecting—probably the driver had taken a wrong turn, because he drove on past our house. I calmed down and managed to grab the branch with the apples. The first one was so unripe it made my eyes water, like when someone annoys me; its little white seeds burst between my teeth, and for a while I felt a bitter taste in my mouth as I looked toward the clematis terrace. I wasn't surprised to see Ştefan standing half-hidden there, scouring the yard, the street, the garden with his piercing eyes. He'd like to get inside each of my gestures and thoughts—what a vampire's instinct! What did surprise me was that he had the strength to force the door open. Pretending not to notice him, I bent down over the hose. So this is what it's come to: forcing a door that no one has opened for ages, and lurking there to spy on me! The sometimes troubling idea that I might be hurting him vanished there and then. No one on earth has a right to take possession of your every thought. To be constantly spied upon is an abuse that you have to defend yourself against—alone ... And the first step is to stop thinking. In the eighteenth century, which carried the art of living to perfection, amorous adventures were considered a right. Life requires you to make compromises discreetly and graciously, because it's not just about applying principles *sans queue ni tête.* "That's a big mistake," Ştefan said, when I reminded him that he had once explained the same idea to me. Afterward he also said, quite unconvincingly, that such frivolous notions were not his style at all: he had simply wanted to put me on my guard against falling in love with him! *Il ne désirait pas s'attirer des histoires . . .*

When I looked at the terrace again, it was empty. Maybe he was spying somewhere else, behind the curtain or from the half-open door. To reassure him, so that he wouldn't waste any more of his time, I went on trimming the roses and putting the waste in my basket; I didn't care if he saw. The roses weren't so wilted as to be no good for jam, and such a delicate operation can't be left up to the servants. That cow Margot would do well to take an interest in it herself, instead of spending the day dolling herself up in front of the mirror. In fact, I ought to feel sorry for her: she's as ugly as ever, despite all her efforts. As for her character, it's worryingly superficial, as they wrote in this year's school report. I also remember this: ". . . makes great demands of others, wavers in her loyalty."

From time to time, I take an apple from a secret pocket in my garden dress and nibble at it until my lips pucker. Were I still in any doubt, that urge would be argument enough—plus the fact that for weeks now the house has been filled with smells. When I went into Margot's dressing room earlier, there was a smell of burned hair; Madam Ana, as usual, stinks of fried onion and stale sweat; there's a stench of cat's pee under the divan—she's certainly been keeping that wretched tom Pițurcă there at night—and I saw Margot's stained knickers in a corner. Ugh, how disgusting girls can be sometimes! Not even a good education can make sex less dirty. I rushed out, to avoid vomiting, and that was the worst sign of all: I began to throw up as soon as I got to my room and closed the door behind me. I leaned over the washstand and kept vomiting for a long time, and in the end even spat out a streak of blood. I got Maria to clean up, even though I know she hates me and watches my every move. But I know Ștefan's also convinced she hates me, so he doesn't believe anything she says.

"Clean it well," I told her. Then I lay down in bed.

I knew this would make her hate me even more. After she'd finished, I got out of bed, gargled, rinsed something dry and yellow from my face, then lay down again and, for fear of falling asleep, kept my eyes fixed on the ivy branch that cuts the window into two.

Everything could have been avoided, I thought as I lay there, if we'd left in time to go on vacation. Whose fault had it been that we spent the dog days in Bucharest? Whereas everyone else, because of the war, was off discovering how nice the beach is at Constanța, we had to stay here and suffocate along with all the slum dogs, amid the dust and sausage smoke of a city that's simply unbearable in July. Oh, if only I had a kindred soul I could open my heart to about this impossible situation! There are only whims and recriminations when Ștefan and I are alone together, and in company all I hear are rude words or discourteous remarks that betray a foul mood. Ignore who else is there and speak ill of your nearest and dearest: that seems to be the name of the game! And, when proof of virility is required, egoism and weakness rear their heads instead. So, what if one fine day I no longer have the strength to "keep up appearances"? Neither the strength nor the inclination . . .

Ah, to feel so young and alive, with nothing but obstacles in your way! To have no other future, no other prospect, than looking after a sick and crotchety old man, a spoiled sister who thinks only of herself, and a war that seems about to break out any minute.

And if you want to taste a natural pleasure for a moment, as your young heart urges you to do, you have to face all the troubles of womanhood . . .

Lost in my thoughts, I feel myself becoming wet. I get up quickly, but it's nothing: all is as before. This seems to happen ten times a day, and each time I immediately realize I'm mistaken. I feel bad about it, and to keep my spirits up I look again at the ivy cutting the window in two. If I'd left in time, none of this would be happening—because I wouldn't have had a chance to go to Titi's room. Like this, we remained alone in the tedium of an empty Bucharest, with no other distraction for me than Ştefan's crystal-ball-gazing about the war, which changes each time you listen to him. One day he wants to persuade the doctor to let him enlist, the next day he wails about the bloodbath and the horrors that lie ahead, and the day after that he's so unwell that, war or no war, he won't make it till next summer. Finally, he asks what people will think of him, now that so many reservists are being called up. His opinions change with the days of the week. Only one has remained the same for more than three months: "I don't want to hear the word 'vacation'!"

This leads to his usual refrain: the war will catch us en route, weighed down with a nurse, a baby, and a maid, trunks and hatboxes and the inevitable chamber pot . . . How vulgar can you get! I'd never have imagined my future would look so grim!

"But how come all our friends have had the courage to leave?" I ask each time.

"Recklessness is not the same as courage!" he answers.

His illness and fixed ideas have unbalanced him so much that he immediately launches into a real speech. He sees himself on the platform of a philanthropic society in the provinces: the guest speaker from Bucharest, who has to impress the ladies staring at him through their lorgnettes. So, without wasting a moment, he introduces his pet subjects: the Phanariot Greeks who left their mark on our state administration, their disorder and primitiveness, a country that was then and will for a long time be rotten to the core . . . On and on he goes, *à tort et à travers,* before finally priding himself on his illness and his ignorance of practical matters.

In fact it's a major defect, which he won't even recognize as a defect, still less correct it.

"Why do you try to drag me into your jaunts? Can't you see I'm sick and frail?"

That's how he ends most conversations, and so, on the verge of a breakdown, I retire to my room so as not to give the servants more cause for laughter. Now that I can go to my own room, I know that he won't come two hours later and start pestering me, as if nothing has happened, as if it's normal to "make it up" in a way that can only disgust me. I can't have that done to me in whatever state I'm in. On the other hand, I'm so gentle and patient by nature that everyone takes advantage of me—even the servants and that impudent Margot.

When I drew this conclusion for the thousandth time, the basket was three-quarters full of wilted roses. Then I suddenly realized that I'd moved away from the hose and left it on; it was twisting around like a snake, in a little pool of water and petals, but I hesitated to pick my way back over the sodden ground. As I never lose track of time, even at the sweetest moments or even in the dark, I thought to myself that it was already a quarter past the hour I had told my dear Titi it would be convenient for him to come. To go and switch off the tap would mean getting my shoes dirty. Still in two minds, I forgot the hose again when I heard the sound of the carriage.

Until then I had remained calm, as I always try to do. I hadn't been worried how dear Titi would react when I told him the news. Nor had it unsettled me, when I spotted Ştefan on the terrace, that he might see us in the garden together.

But now, on hearing the carriage, I felt a knot rise from my chest and grip me by the throat, so strongly that I was afraid I might feel sick again. I understood that there could be only one reason for it: it will be a more difficult pregnancy this time. Didn't my godmother, Fănica, tell me as much? No two are ever the same.

Last time I didn't have a lot of nausea, and once it was past and my tummy should have become visible, I put on a tight corset and no one noticed a thing. I went to balls and picnics, to the races and wherever others went, and no one guessed I was expecting Yvonne.

"Well, well, *ma chère*," old General Praporgescu teased me later, "so where were you hiding it?"

What a nice polite man, with manners like in the old days!

It came as such a surprise to him that, for all his refinement, he couldn't help mentioning my hourglass figure to all and sundry: *je l'écoutais sans mot dire,* keeping my secrets to myself. How Madam Ana struggled with the straps of my corset! She'd bend her knee into the base of my spine, then push and pull, push and pull . . .

"Ay, you're weighing my soul down with sins, Miss Sophie!" she complained.

She complained, like they all do. They think it makes them sound more distinguished! It's true, though, that when I was in labor and shouting the house down Doctor Rădulescu said to me: "What's this I heard about a corset? How could you have been so mindless?" And at the end he added: "You weren't far off killing the poor creature, you know."

So this time it's more difficult, I suppose. Maybe it's a boy . . . The smell of a rotting carcass suddenly hit me from the wasteland on the other side of the fence, and I realized that there'd be a disaster if I waited a second longer. Fortunately I didn't have to worry that a servant would open the door for him: Madam Ana was still putting Margot's hair in curlers, and Maria was looking after that crackpot Grigore. Not being the kind of person to hesitate after I've made a decision, I told myself that everything would sort itself out in the end and that the first thing I had to do was go and be sick.

So that's what I did.

I looked a waxy yellow in the mirror, and my legs were trembling as they always do after I throw up. I didn't have time to fix my hair or makeup, so my appearance was perfect for the part of a dedicated gardener.

I again took the back door into the garden, where the hose was still running, but I didn't have time to turn the tap off. If Titi took it into his head to ring at the front, God knows what it would lead to! His sweet innocence and awkwardness with women—which moved me at one point—are nevertheless a major defect for a man. In fact, I still wasn't sure whether to run away with Titi or not; it was the kind of situation where you want to see what he has in mind. It wasn't easy to resolve things *sans tambour, ni trompette,* but my nature is such that I can't stand half-measures. All this was going through my head when I saw Titi—before he saw me.

He went slowly down the steps, staring at that wretched cat Piţurcă, who had been whistling for some time to lure birds. Calm and collected, as I like to be, I walked up to him without making any sign. I was sure of the feelings between us, so I thought that the unfavorable conditions for a talk wouldn't bother him too much. He looked his usual gentle self, and it occurred to me that the things I loved in him and found such a relief for my nerves were the exact opposite of the ones that disturbed me in Ștefan. On the other hand, Titi's meekness is also a sign of weakness, since he looks helpless precisely at moments when he is flushed with anger. I've seen him put on a wounded air when he should have been really letting fly. So I can tell if he's annoyed if his face suddenly looks creased and he walks with a more hesitant step.

It's always surprised me how he can turn a blind eye to things that anger him. I'm not like that at all. I can't forget it if someone is guilty in my eyes, but the effort I make is to stop myself getting too worked up about it. In the end, other people's attempts to get at me usually fail, because it is I who decide what to get worked up about.

Titi, on the other hand, is affected by everything. I often say that other people's opinion matters to me, but if I don't want it to matter then it doesn't. He has admitted to me that what people think about him always counts enormously. Well, I thought, as I listened to him, that's how good qualities can turn into faults. I thought the same about Ștefan when he started to irritate me, but then I understood that in his case I was talking about pure faults, and I lost interest in the whole subject of Ștefan.

At first, when I saw *cher* Titi going down the steps, I was sure he'd come and look for me in the garden. But no, he set off down the path to the front gate. Was he angry that I didn't go out right away to meet him? I was very sure of his feelings, and I thought that, being the kind of man he was, his gesture in coming here two hours before the other guests was little short of heroic. When I saw him walking back to the street, obviously in a bad mood, my heart softened again. His meekness had opened up feelings of tenderness in me, as in a flower that opens out late. This idea occurred to me at least twice, in those very words, which I'm almost sure were mine. I liked the formulation, but I still had my doubts. Why had the words come to me so spontaneously? Had I not read them somewhere?

I decided to write them down in my diary, when the guests have left and I go to my nice new bedroom. I'll feel like a *jeune fille* again. Like ten years ago, alas! I'll wait for the noises in the house to die down, then clean the candle wick and note the sentence down in a newly begun diary. My life has been so terrible up to now: I've lived my youth less than anyone, after that ghastly accident that left me an orphan at such an early age. And I long to be a girl again, surrounded by suitors at the ball, flirting with each one in turn, because such things are natural unless you want your life to be a torture and a burden.

Of course Titi's lack of skill with women is a defect, but it made me feel even younger than I am. What I also liked was that he felt embarrassed to talk about himself. That touched me deeply, coming as it did after the other one's self-conceit. I couldn't bear it that Ştefan thought of himself as the center of the universe.

That's what particularly touched me about Titi.

Obviously he couldn't accept the cruel idea that we'd have to wait for the other guests to arrive before he could be with me. So he turned around at the gate to see if I was there. Of course he tried hard to ensure that the feelings lighting up his face could not be read by anyone, even at the moment when he caught sight of me.

When he turned, he suddenly saw me walking gracefully toward him, a smile on my face. It didn't sadden me that he was already so near the gate: I was convinced that I could send him a signal to turn around, and I concentrated hard to achieve this. If my spiritualist effort failed, I could always shout when he reached out to open the gate: "What's with this incognito visit, Mr. Ialomiţeanu?"

I mentally rehearsed the tone I would use, but in the end my stare proved sufficient—another proof, it seemed, that our spiritual bond needed no words. He turned his head and walked back toward me with characteristic discretion. It's hard to describe the expression on his face; his suit had a defect at the shoulder that I spotted immediately. As I'd planned, I didn't say anything at first, but offered to show him a new variety of rose in the garden. I felt he was disappointed, as he'd certainly been expecting something else from me, but I walked ahead of him at a respectable distance, swaying my hips like a true gardener. I knew how my blonde plait lay on my neck, above my beauty spot, which he couldn't fail to notice. Piţurcă came up to me, arching his back, and I stroked him with the tip of my shoe.

"You see what shiny fur he has?" I said. "Well, that's thanks to Madam Ana, who looks after him as if he was her patient. One day he came back full of scabs—God knows how he got them—and she caught him and soaked him in kerosene. And when he finally struggled free, was he a sight to behold! I'm not exaggerating: I nearly fainted on the spot. Georges Ioaniu, who happened to be around at the time, suggested that we put him out of his misery and offered to get his orderly to do it. Believe me, the poor thing looked like a monster: just tufts of fur and raw flesh, mewling terribly and rolling on the ground in pain. What uproar there was in the house! But, with his animal instinct, he probably realized that his life was on the line, and so he vanished before we could make up our minds. We were all missing him terribly when he finally returned with the glossy fur you can see now, a real Prince Charming of the feline race. He must have been living in the Herăstrău woods. That's where he got into the habit of whistling to attract birds."

I was very relaxed and talkative, like when I have to entertain guests. My nausea had gone and strange effluvia ran through my body, as if someone had taken me by the hand. But the ground became wetter and wetter as we continued down the path. This must have bothered him, because he looked *mal à l'aise* and kept wiping his brow with a handkerchief. There were red patches on his face again, like when some emotion stirs in him—which, for me, is a sign that his skin is as sensitive as his soul. When I saw his far from spotless handkerchief, it moved me to think that he had no one to look after him: his mother and sisters live in another house, and I'm sure they don't care what becomes of him. Another reason why I felt touched was that I once scolded him for not paying attention to such details. What does life really mean? I mused, as we advanced over the slippery ground. What does life mean? What is living about? You liked something yesterday, and now you can't stand it. And vice versa.

"My dear Madam Mironescu, couldn't we perhaps stop here, as our feline Prince Charming has done? Because if we go on . . ."

He looked increasingly uneasy, increasingly awkward. I know that my presence unsettles him, and that he can't act naturally with me in company. But there was something else as well: *il se fait du souci* more than any other man I've known. So, quite lucidly, I decided two things: I won't let myself be influenced by his anxiety; and I won't look at him through the eyes of a narrow-minded woman (if I did I'd find him cowardly and repulsive). I have considerable presence of mind: the *dames patronesses* at the Queen Elisabeta Society told me a long time ago that I take more trouble than anyone else over school festivals or fund-raising events for orphans and the needy poor; other ladies do no more than parade in national costume, trying to get a mention in the official report and taking any opportunity to flirt, but each time I show that I'm more useful and more skilled. Now, though, my presence of mind was beginning to desert me, and I realized that he didn't think it much fun to traipse down flooded paths. At some point he splashed his trousers really badly and bent down to wipe them with the same handkerchief, like a child who's been brought up by a slovenly nurse. Maybe it was a chance for him to end our walk—a walk he found rather unbecoming, as he put it, with a smile that I know and don't approve of at all.

"You know Pasărea monastery, don't you, my dear lady? And its guest rooms that are used for secret liaisons lasting a couple of days? I remember, when you first heard about them, you were amazed that it's possible to stay there, even for just a few hours. Yes, yes, I know, you reflected that the beauty of the natural surroundings would make up for the discomfort and the plague of mosquitoes. And then, later, you kept suggesting that we spend a night there. Well, according to trustworthy sources, the church authorities offer those facilities in collusion with the secret police; they keep an up-to-date list of the people who've slept there. No, they don't have more tangible proof than the empty candy packets, slices of dry bread, and bottles of perfume, which, as you may remember, lie around in all the drawers. What I want to say is that you can't feel safe anywhere on earth. Of course, I know what I'm saying doesn't worry you: all the police in the world couldn't do anything against you, because you're always calm and in control of the situation . . ."

I don't like that kind of chatter, which I find distasteful and unmanly. Those are two characteristics I've often had occasion to deplore in him, the main occasion being a few moments later, when he stopped and was reluctant to walk any further:

"Dear Madam Mironescu, if we went any further I think it would be like venturing into the desert . . . So what I'd suggest is that we look at your new roses another time: I have no doubt that they're absolutely wonderful. Of course, it would be different if there wasn't all this mud, but the conditions are not right at the moment, don't you think so?"

Possibly noticing my look of displeasure, he began to ramble in a way that irritated me. So I stopped listening and decided to clarify the situation.

Afterward, looking back at the gesture I made at that moment, I thought it had frightened him more than any of my words, which he anyway no longer seemed to hear, so sudden was his reaction. Still rambling on, he pressed the mud-stained handkerchief to his face, so that he was dirty when he finally stopped speaking and put it back in his pocket.

"No," I said in a low voice, pulling him closer and reaching out to wipe the stain from his cheek with my own handkerchief, "we can't go back until I've talked to you . . ."

He jerked violently, as if my words or my hand had burned him. He glared at me, his eyes suddenly cloudy and obdurate, then looked away. He was flushed, either with embarrassment or from the sun, and his whole body seemed to have shrunk in size, as if to fit into a hiding place should one offer itself. But, when one failed to appear, he uttered a half-good-bye and hurried off down the stony path we had just covered together. His flight would have made him seem guilty rather than innocent in the eyes of an onlooker. So I concluded that it wasn't a sign of cowardice on his part, since a moment's reflection would have told him that it would do him no good—and he wasn't the kind of man to do anything without reflection. But my argument didn't change the fact that he left me alone, not knowing how to get away quicker. I walked slowly toward the tap at the bottom of the garden, my nostrils under assault from the stench on the wasteland. Over the fence I could see dusty thistles, a huge clump of belladonna on a garbage heap, a furless dog with raised paw, and a few wooden stakes pointing skyward and rotting away.

But I wasn't suffering, and, if I so wished, the whole thing would cease to bother me. The sun was much too strong. Afraid of another bout of nausea, I put the hat back on my head without tying the cord under my chin.

"In a world full of tricksters, you have to keep your eyes peeled, even if you don't cheat yourself . . ."

He said that to me one day at his place, when I was sitting on a rickety old chair that he kept warning me not to use.

Suddenly I felt an urge to throw away the basket of wilted roses, to stamp my feet and shout, even to scream and have a fainting fit. I'd come around much, much later, between fresh sheets smelling of sweet clover, in a room with closed shutters, my forehead and temples in a muslin headband soaked in aromatic vinegar.

And at my bedside I'd find a dish of coffee ice cream, in a pail full of ice cubes that I'd use to cool my feverish hands.

I looked again at the sky, which was now darkening at the approach of night. My feet were wet, something odd and repulsive was scraping against my chest, and I'd decided that I'd wasted enough time already. I needed to freshen up a little, to change my clothes and see to my afternoon toilet. Then I'd be ready to go down to the drawing room with the tiled fireplace, where I'd assess what, if anything, remained to be done, and "last but not least," as Georges Ioaniu would say, calculate the number of guests and the portions of ice cream.

Chapter 8

The Clematis Terrace

"There's no doubt about it," Professor Mironescu said. "My illness has forced me to scale down my household duties, and many of them now fall on Sophie's shoulders. They've clearly been getting her down. That's one reason why things are not functioning as well as they used to—another being that Grigore has come down with mumps, now of all times. Close up, and with man's limited logic, one often has the illusion that there's some causal chain. But when you look back later, from a distance, the process of deterioration will look very different. You'll see the wider picture, with the awesome divine eye above it. *From those who have nothing, even what they have will be taken away.* How will you resign yourself to such a message? But you're right, *ma chère,* such speculations are completely inadequate—especially now, when the months ahead look so gloomy . . ."

"I suppose you've heard that the Russians have crossed the Danube at Isaccea?" the guest cut in.

"My dear young man," the professor replied with a friendly smile, "you're more up to date than I am. What interest in the affairs of the polis! Believe me, I'm really full of admiration. Even when I was at my best, I had limited curiosity and limited powers in that domain. And now I rarely set foot outside the door. As there are no courses at this time of year, some of my colleagues have boldly gone on vacation."

At the other end of the room, irritated by the reference to a vacation, Sophie snapped her fan shut. She was sitting upright on the sofa, her nostrils flared, while the professor, his glasses lower than usual on his nose, struck his pile of letters with his paper knife. He didn't need to glance over at Sophie to know how she looked at that moment. He knew too that his "young friend" was sitting there, legs crossed and showing white silk socks that were the height of fashion that summer; a welcome casualness had chipped away at his formal, civil-service style of dress. Someone must have taught him that a hint of nonchalance adds spice to an immaculate costume, the professor thinks, with a gently ironical smile. A real patrician will avoid showing himself *tiré à quatre épingles* and affect a sovereign disdain for such matters.

The professor senses that he is too talkative this afternoon. A murky, slightly unpleasant feeling impels him to speak—a feeling he has had for some time, which he might ponder on and analyze.

But he avoids examining it too closely.

"Various difficulties do a lot to explain it. But it's true that explanations don't excuse anyone."

The professor breaks off suddenly and, with a radiant smile and outstretched arms, goes up to little Yvonne, whom Nela has brought in without warning through the half-open door.

"Come, my little one, come!" he says hesitantly in the middle of the room.

The little one takes a few steps, then takes fright at all the people and, with a little cry, scurries back to the folds of Nela's dress. The professor's arms fall again slowly, like the ribs of an umbrella that is being folded shut. He looks confusedly toward his wife's chair. Yes, sensible Sophie must be right again: you have to respect the child's mealtimes, even on an evening like this, when Mademoiselle Lisette, driven wild by the latest rumors, is crying as she packs her bags upstairs. What's more, servants shouldn't be encouraged to shirk their duties by playing on our good nature. Otherwise, they'll end up dictating the times when it's convenient for us to see the child—which, to be frank, is what has been happening recently . . .

The professor runs his eyes irresolutely over Margot and Titi Ialomițeanu. Less susceptible to logic and educational theory, as young people are nowadays, they both ask for an exception to be made this evening. And in this way the professor receives permission to keep little Yvonne, given *à contrecoeur,* as he can tell from Sophie's aloof manner. He sits himself on his chair, holding the precious bundle on his knees and stroking her wispy blonde hair a little heavy-handedly.

"As for the Mamornița incident, have any new reports explained exactly what happened?"

What a pointless question! But young Ialomițeanu enjoys the professor's indulgence.

"What could there be new after all this time?" the professor answers patiently. His indulgence is directed toward the least brilliant of his spiritual children. Yes, he has had many other disciples in his long academic career, each capable of original thinking and displaying clearer evidence of a vocation than Mr. Ialomițeanu does. He still sends books and encouraging letters to a good number of them, and if he is able to, he gives a helping hand for a grant, an appointment, or a transfer. But sometimes he admits that illness and old age have made him less generous than he used to be.

At such moments he invariably opens a parenthesis to underline the falsity of a certain Christian, or optimistically humanist, belief that poverty, loneliness, and unhappiness develop the good qualities in people; that honesty and generosity are found in the most underprivileged, whom God, out of love, has afflicted with the trials of Job. That, he argues, is a preconception that blinds modern man. And, in closing the parenthesis, the professor admits that sickness, old age, and so on have made him less able to tolerate the passing fads and insufferable vanity of intelligent young people. What he doesn't recognize in public is that some of his most gifted disciples have begun to challenge him, in ruthless appraisals of his work, and that others are reported to have said highly unflattering things about his person. In short, he has received a number of blows to his human pride.

This is one of the reasons why it is the meek Alyosha, rather than the shadowy Ivan, who has remained at his side—to cite the fashionable novel, by a Russian called Dostoevsky, which he read recently in a bad German translation. At least this Alyosha has a welcome practical sense. He has only to see his chubby, childlike cheeks turn red at some indiscreet remark, and he feels a surge of trust and fellow feeling toward him.

"Yes, indeed, so much time has passed that it seems strange to wonder about such things! But our regiment was put on the alert, and it looked like we were going to war."

Why does this young man suddenly rise from his chair and assume the posture of a parliamentary orator? Is it true, as Sophie mentioned *en passant* one day, that although young Ialomițeanu feigns an interest in philology his real dream in life is a diplomatic career? It must be true, if she heard it from his lips. Poor lovers—here an indulgent smile on the professor's face—always confess things to married women, relying on the discretion of a *donna angelicata* who doesn't exist in reality. Poor young men, whose experience is limited to the bedroom, where lovers usually speak only of themselves! It's hard for them to imagine that an uncontrollable instinct will lead their angel to pass on any tidbit she hears to her lord and master, usually truncated or skillfully modified. Which woman, warbling inoffensively, has failed to change her husband's mind about his relatives or best friends, basing herself on facts visible to her innocent eyes alone? That's how solidarity blossoms between a couple, freshening the air of their conjugal bedroom once the wild perfume of their early embraces turns stale and threatens to suffocate them.

But why, the professor wonders, does young Ialomiţeanu want to go in for diplomacy—a profession for which he is obviously not gifted? Doesn't he realize that he's not cold-blooded enough, that he lacks the spirit of repartee, and that he has neither a personal fortune nor family connections to make up for these evident handicaps? Why, at an age when he should be thinking of a doctorate magna cum laude and a well-earned professorship, does he start hobnobbing with second-rate politicians, as if his only aim in life is to accumulate bits of absurd tittle-tattle? It's as futile a pursuit as filling the pitchers of the Danaides, and it arouses the suspicion that he is of an essentially frivolous nature.

But what is the reason for—or, to be more precise, the source of—the joy that freshens Professor Mironescu's emaciated face as he reviews the young man's defects?

Two souls are dwelling in my breast, as the poet so rightly said . . .

"Yes, they were the last days of your call-up. A week earlier, on a Sunday, you came to see us on leave and said you were going to slip away."

But something in the album on Margot's lap seems to have attracted the guest's attention, because he tries to look over her shoulder. Obsessed though he is with the rules of society, he thereby commits a second unforgivable act of impoliteness (after his coming unannounced): he ignores the words that Sophie, the lady of the house, addresses to him.

The professor can't continue his meditations, because Yvonne climbs onto his knee and tries to cling to his lapel with her little nails. And when the patient father puts her down and lets her take a few steps around the table, all the time holding her carefully if awkwardly, she still doesn't deign to behave as a guest at a party should. What a tasteless show! the young mother remarks. It's turning our drawing room into a fairground. But it would be equally tasteless to argue in public with Ștefan over one more thing that they don't see eye to eye about.

Sophie hides her disgruntlement behind her fan and predicts that the child will soon do something so silly that they'll regret having let her into the room. She stands up gracefully and walks slowly over to the sofa. She's not going to get involved, but will devote herself entirely to her duties as hostess and pick up the threads of the flagging conversation.

"Tell me, Mr. Ialomițeanu, do you know *en gros* how things went at Mamornița? From what I know, the king was cruising on the Danube at the time, and when he heard that the Russians had invaded he hurried back despite the queen's insistence that they keep on going. Actually, quite a few people blamed her for that . . ."

Her gentle, patient tone has the effect of a stinging rebuke. Turning bright-red, young Ialomițeanu changes his posture with military alacrity and presents the lady with an elegant bow of apology. As for the professor, his eyes have for some time been turned toward the clematis terrace. Through the crystal-clear windows, the blue-velvet corollas stand out against the opaline luster of a green and red sky. And, as at daybreak, the sparrows keep up their deafening squabble.

Shouldn't that be enough for you to feel an impersonal joy that wards off all the pettiness of existence? The famous state of grace that this hour of day offers, with its illusion of an eternal terrestrial beauty . . .

The professor's eyes light up as they focus again on Yvonne. Gripping the mechanical pencil as tightly as she can, she tries to raise it to her eye and look through its little window at the end, as Papa once taught her to do. She's unsuccessful, however, because her arm is too shaky and uncertain. Papa works miracles by picking it up between his long warm fingers, and she gives a few yelps of joy when she suddenly spies a little world through the pencil window.

For a while the professor continues to watch the girl with tender indulgence. Then he feels obliged to join the conversation.

"But it's impossible that Mr. Ialomițeanu doesn't know these things!" he points out to his wife irritably. "After all, the papers were full of them."

"Of course they were," the young man says, "but when you're posted near the top of a mountain, as I was . . . Besides, it depends on what kind of general you have. General Prezan, for instance, forbade his officers to read pro-German papers, particularly *Steagul*. Didn't you know that? Haven't you heard it from anyone?"

The professor remained silent, accepting that he hadn't heard it, and shot a glance at his former student. He didn't look happy with him.

Perhaps it's simply the young man's equivocation that led him to confuse matters by courteously leaping to Sophie's defense. Isn't generosity the trait he displays most often, causing him to dissipate his energy all over the place? He always seems to be busy: whether it's to fix up a grant for a jobless friend, to save a civil servant from redundancy, to find private lessons for a student with no other means, or to take medicine to an old lady he happens to know . . . He never stops running around, keeping up relations in a way that is both charitable and useful to everyone. That's Titi Ialomițeanu: a kid from the provinces who still only knows a quarter of the people you know, but who's capable of putting you in touch with the right man at the religious affairs ministry, or at education, foreign affairs, or internal affairs. He doesn't forget anyone and can guess (or find out) the best way to approach a contact: perhaps by offering a little present, by playing on a weakness for the fair sex, by drawing on a third party, and so on. That's a simple enough formula, which you could apply yourself, if your instinctive dislike for such things didn't make you feel that you never have enough time for them. As it is, you sometimes feel pity for poor Ialomițeanu, who agrees to involve himself in vexing little matters, out of a love for his fellow man that you are unable to understand, and which you can reciprocate only by enduring the mechanics of his childish questions.

"Besides, even if I'd been able to read a paper, it wouldn't have been enough. You have to read two a day: the pro-German *Steagul,* and *L'Indépendance roumaine* (whose French title speaks for itself)."

"No one's ever right all the time," the professor replies, with brooding indulgence.

He too can feel two souls dwelling inside him. At times like now, when benevolence toward his former student seems to have the upper hand, he remembers an old hypothesis of his: namely, that the sensitive young man hides his vulnerability behind a plodding, stereotyped conversation. That would fit the professor's charitable way of looking at other people, although sadly reality doesn't often bear it out.

"Someone told me, in connection with the Mamornița incident, that the governor was attacked for not disarming the Russians. His answer was always: how can we disarm our great allies of the future? So I wondered if, with the passing of time, some new light has been thrown on things . . ."

Titi's loquacity is fueled by his conscientious nature, which keeps pushing him to improve on his rather uninspired formulations. Still thinking of the vulnerable soul hidden under his guest's tortuous syntax, the professor feels like an impatient child tempted to open a pastry shop wrapping to see what is inside.

A demon of curiosity springs out like a genie from the lamp—an uncontrollable curiosity, stemming from a confused feeling that resists analysis. The professor offers his disciple an inscrutable smile that is still relaxed.

Still satisfied.

With lightning speed, Yvonne takes an unopened envelope from the bronze vase and clutches it in her little fist. Whispering gently in her ear, Papa tries to take it back without being noticed, but she no longer pays him any attention, as if she has eyes and ears only for the paper rustling so agreeably beneath her touch. Maybe another reason why it is so pleasant is that it excites the people around her. Glowing with contentment, she shows them all the now soiled envelope, as an executioner breaks off torturing a martyr to display his twitching body to the assembled faithful, overjoyed by their impotent shudders of indignation.

"Ah! non, j'en ai assez!"

Driven by Sophie's irritable muttering, or perhaps suddenly losing patience himself, as one can even with one's nearest and dearest, the professor tries to prize open the little fist. He is amazed by the strength in those pale thin fingers. And, confident that nothing bad can come from her Papa, Yvonne lets out a long shrill scream that fills the room like a fire alarm.

Mr. Ialomițeanu laughs and exchanges complicit smiles with Margot. Meanwhile Madam Mironescu, balancing between victory—she did predict something silly!—and irritation, is about to ring for Nela to come and take the child back to her room, so that the salon can resume its civilized existence. But, when the others plead for the culprit to be forgiven, she makes a gesture of acceptance that reveals her firm white arm through the opening in her dress.

"You encourage her to be naughty," she censures Titi, playfully raising her finger. "Everyone does the same, either because it's easier or because they couldn't care less, and I get nowhere when I warn them that she'll grow up spoiled."

"I'm much more innocent than you suppose . . . As usual . . . ," he protests with a smile.

A confusion has arisen. Mr. Ialomițeanu has the impression that her rebuke was directed at her sister, with whom he has been chatting separately. Hence the artful shine in his eyes. Contradictory feelings are present in his soul, making themselves visible in a lively twitching. Blushing, he politely holds out a chair for the lady to sit on, then looks over toward the pedestal table.

It is obvious that Professor Mironescu holds the most interest for him right now.

But the professor is still engrossed in little Yvonne, who has finally found a quieter way to spend her time. Sticking out her finger, she prods Papa's nose, eyes, and eyelids, until he takes fright and protects himself.

"Innocent? *Pas du tout*! There are many things you could be blamed for," Sophie insists. "For example, knowing you as I do, I've often wondered why this gentleman bends over backward to keep all his acquaintances happy. What's the point of taking on obligations to people that you owe nothing to? And, at the same time, you don't do enough for those who . . ."

Sophie fans herself and frowns a little as she looks down at a print of Rubens's *Daughters of Leucippus,* as if it holds the key to the riddle she is trying to solve.

"It's true," the young man says, a bold, self-satisfied smile on his face, "I don't do enough for those closest to me. The closer someone is, the more my behavior is . . . I'm afraid . . ."

"The worse it is, you mean."

Sophie's smile—slightly resigned, slightly acerbic, slightly offended— crosses his jokily triumphant smile. They don't meet, but rather pass each other at different speeds, made of the same substance at different stages of disintegration.

"I still don't understand why you insist on being liked by everyone: the doorman at the Vanicus, Marghiloman, Nela, Nicu Filipescu, Madam Ana . . . , everyone without exception. What kind of character can you have?" she asks, showing no more than her reproachful eyes from behind the fan.

"It's a question of my political principles, dear lady. Politics, not my character." And, as if he has just given testimony that compromises him, he nervously retreats a few steps.

As he does so, he reaches out mechanically and brushes his fingertips against the gleaming bronze Apollo and lyre on the mantelpiece.

A little vibration, due to memories from a time when his blood gushed through his veins and his natural sensitivity found an outlet only in the study of Greek pottery, with its scenes of imminent rape, its leaf-clad or leafless statues, and its naked bodies that his trembling hands longed to touch. Obscene primitive symbols, explored *à bout des nerfs*. And, hovering above it all, a comforting certainty that he'd always be capable of bowing to the precepts of reason; that he'd never do anything reckless that he knew would harm him; that fear of disease, scandal, and unpleasantness would protect him from the real temptations that he kept at arm's length . . .

Little Yvonne doodles while the professor admires the flight of the house martins; their zigzagging black lines intersect between the walls of the soft ivory sky, on which the setting sun has begun to cast its reddish glow. An intense golden light gradually lengthens the shadows in the room, much as water rises and falls in two communicating vessels.

Sophie's voice, still talking spiritedly about the Mamorniţa incident, brings the professor back from his reverie.

"Of course King Ferdinand didn't want to hear the official version: that the Russians had crossed the frontier by mistake. 'A mistake across sixty kilometers?' he asked. 'It would be insulting to suggest that map-reading is beyond the powers of a Russian general!'"

What's happened to Sophie? She used to shed tears over a romantic novel or go into the garden loaded with brushes and canvases, wearing her black cloak and that quaint hat slung over her back. Now, all of a sudden, she knows all about politics and discusses it with her usual self-assurance! Is it the pleasures of vanity that enliven her young face? Or is it just that double chin, still so sweet and graceful, that low forehead, aquiline nose, long thin lips—an egoistic, one might even say petty, nature? Our family sentiments, so stable, so mediocre, seem to give us no knowledge of the creature who breathes the air next to us—just as we know nothing of the body that we routinely make use of!

Mr. Ialomiţeanu throws out another question, in such a low voice that the professor doesn't catch it. All he hears is his wife's reply:

"Of course, everyone assumed that from the word go. Didn't I tell you that Brătianu dashed back from his estate? And, already on the ship, the king was gripped by emotion—maybe it was rage, maybe fear, but he didn't stop shaking for half an hour."

"Well, I never!" the professor cut in. "The king shakes for half an hour, and we all get to hear about it right away! God, what people! What a country!"

To show his indignation, he lifts Yvonne off his knees and puts her down. He doesn't need to glance at his wife to know the expression she has on her face: the look of a sullen child unable to defend herself. An innocent blue strip floats for an unpleasantly long time among the heavy mahogany furniture, while Professor Mironescu remains stubbornly silent.

"But even people in his inner circle told us," Sophie persists. "Don't you remember Georges saying so? You were there, weren't you?"

A plaintive sweetness in her voice triggers blind fury in him before he can think any further. For some time now she's thought it more fetching to use that tone in company.

Of course the professor doesn't remember that Georges Athanasiu said anything of the sort; nor is it his style to spread that kind of information. Besides, it's six months to the day since they've seen their friend Athanasiu. He knows that better than anyone, because loneliness weighs on him so heavily that he even looks forward to visits from Titi Ialomiţeanu. People who used to present their visiting card on their way back from an evening walk on the Avenue stopped doing it more than a year ago. And even their friend Georges does no more than telephone. If Sophie doesn't think about that, it's not only because she has a bad memory, as everyone knows, but also because she hasn't had to endure the same isolation. She hardly ever misses a Battle of Flowers on the Avenue, or a dinner with Miza and Radu afterward at the Flora; she regularly has an ice cream with Lisette Athanasiu at Riegler's (that may be where this bit of gossip came from!); and lover-boy Ialomiţeanu takes Margot and her to the theater from time to time—in fact, they've got tickets for the French Theatre tomorrow, although there's a rumor that it's packing its bags in readiness to leave for France.

The conclusion is that Sophie hasn't been as neglected as she makes out during the time of your illness. If she gets things mixed up in her memory, it's not only out of a general confusion but also because she has a lot of things to remember. That's how she can claim that Georges first told that story about the king in your presence, when in fact you, her husband, are only hearing it now for the first time.

That means she must have heard it separately, somewhere else. There's no point asking her where: she probably wouldn't remember, even if she was willing to tell the truth. Hasn't the whole of Romanian society embraced café culture, in keeping with the fact that nations that have just emerged from barbarism have no other wish than to indulge in sordid luxuries and to scoop up the latest vulgar gossip? In the Red Cross, the League of Orthodox Women, or the Society for the Protection of Gardening, the ladies nowadays talk politics with the same passion as the gentlemen.

The professor rests his neck on the back of his chair and, in removing the glasses that have been cutting into his nose, manages to hide the rapid blinking that has turned half his face into a grimace.

A sign of controlled irritability.

There are moments in a room with many people when you'd think you were moving among psycho-electric currents—which is only a step away from Doctor Charcot's much-heralded theories and the world of spiritualist séances. But the rational mind, and the positive thinking in which he has been trained, make Titi Ialomițeanu mistrustful of the vogue for such ideas. There are enough ordinary explanations for the tension between the two spouses: the heat of the day, the rumors of war, the professor's illness, uncertainty about the months ahead . . .

While trying to find a way to revive the conversation, Mr. Ialomițeanu sits down beside Margot on the sofa. It's not clear why she avoids looking him in the eye and sits frozen with the album on her lap. The young man stays there for a while, his hands awkwardly placed on his knees. Something like consternation has buried itself in his translucent blue gaze, in rather the same way that, in fine weather, you can sometimes glimpse the rusty hulk of a sunken ship under hundreds of meters of clear water, encrusted with shells and surrounded by green and red algae.

Suddenly he comes out with the most candid of exclamations:

"Oh, my God, what will become of this country if we one day put politics in the hands of women?"

His presence beside her finally prompts Margot to enter the conversation. Her thin voice exhibits the slightly spoiled tones that you find in most young girls, at an age when they are suddenly becoming aware of their power and think that a few infantile flourishes will enable them to rule the world.

"But what about Queen Victoria? Or our Queen Elisabeta? Didn't you say, Ştefan, that this is the century of science and progress, and that we'll soon see a new type of woman emerge? Do you remember? You came to pick me up one Saturday from school, and you stopped on the way back for a woman in trousers to get into the hired carriage. How frightened she was—a little made-up, and so frightened! *Elle tremblait de peur,* the poor thing. Go faster, you told the driver, faster, faster, and she huddled up on the front bench; the hood was up, but it made no difference, as people could see her anyway. How they threatened her with their sticks! Faster, driver, faster, you called out, and they went on shouting and hooting. They even hit the carriage with their sticks, you told me to wrap something around my ears, and at one point a heavy object landed on the hood. How we screamed! *Soyez tranquille,* you said to us, *il n'y a plus de danger,* and later I understood that they'd already thrown everything they could lay their hands on . . . It's too soon for Parisian designers to send models in trousers onto our streets, you said, when we dropped her off at her fashion house. But you'll see, it won't be much longer before it's considered very *chic* to go around dressed like that!"

"What an adventure! That's the first I've heard about it!" Sophie said curtly.

"What do you mean? I told you the same day—we both did," the professor countered sourly.

He suspected that his wife wanted to put her younger sister in her place. But Margot's remarks hadn't struck him as at all impertinent, and his teaching experience had made him opposed to severity at any price. As a man, he thought that a touch of frivolity suited young girls, that it was in keeping with their naïveté and freshness. Of course, Sophie's attachment to her sister wasn't in doubt, but her behavior sometimes went too far in the direction of rigidity.

Another silence followed, in which all that could be heard was the swishing of fans. Then, blinking with surprise, Sophie held out an olive branch:

"Ah, yes, now that you mention it . . . My famous memory seems to have been playing tricks."

And she laughed. Her usual pearly mannered laugh, which might well have been less false than it appeared to her husband.

"As far as politics is concerned, I don't claim any special understanding. All I did was repeat what others have said to me."

Ah, yes, this is now her speaking as a normal simple woman—a role she plays in her rustic *tableaux vivants,* or at a popular festival when she dresses up in the beautiful costume they wear in the Muscel region. How submissively she replies to her guest, even though he wasn't at all friendly in the way he spoke to her! On the contrary! Would it be a morbid fantasy, or perhaps a sign of neurasthenia, for her husband to detect an element of displaced coquetry here?

"So, I leave politics to the suffragettes . . ."

Of course, neurasthenia means that when he imagines something it seems real in every fiber of his weakened, petulant being. Otherwise, how is one to explain this new welling up of rage, despite his wise decision earlier to hold it down?

"I wouldn't be at all surprised, *ma chère,* if you became a suffragette one day. Your various societies have been taking up too much of your time, with the inevitable result that you have less and less available for your ordinary female duties."

No more than five minutes pass, however, before he is doubting the truth of his assertions. As for the wisdom of rebuking a young spouse in public, the less said about that the better. But the rage that made him want to lash out at her for the last half-hour, whatever she said in her defense, has now vanished without trace.

Used to his excesses, Sophie goes silently over to her armchair, with the submission of a domestic animal. In the corner of her trembling lips, the dejection of a harmless creature who doesn't understand why she has been beaten fades away imperceptibly, like a ripple in a pool of water . . .

It is a sight that would soften the heart of a professional hangman.

While Professor Mironescu runs his fingertip along an embroidered water lily (or lotus), and while Margot prattles away with Yvonne, young Ialomiţeanu clears his throat in preparation for another question. And as he looks at you gravely, with the submissive look of a dutiful soldier, doesn't he dispel your last doubts about his loyalty?

"Regarding the explosion at the Dudeşti powder factory . . ."

The two leaves of the door finally open on Madam Ana's starched bonnet, and she wheels in the tea service on the special trolley kept for the purpose. All heads turn to her at once. Only Professor Mironescu, his neck resting against his chair, waits with a kindly expression on his face for the guest to finish his question.

Madam Ana's starched bonnet moves across the room to the little long-legged tables by the fireplace. She places a five-arm candlestick on each of them and, after a slight hesitation due to the fact that it's not yet dark outside, lights the stearin candles.

Behind Mrs. Mironescu's chair, the flickering light reveals the bust of an ancient god on a white column-like base. Poseidon? Or Jupiter Tonans?

Again Madam Ana's muffled steps, the unhurried solemnity of hands reaching out to trays and plates, jaws moving without hunger, without haste, without greed. The blessed aroma of tea.

With a light swishing sound, Sophie moves from one guest to the next. Her grave childlike face floats in the shadowy part of the room as she gracefully holds out a steaming cup, so precise and so thoughtful that no one could think that anything she does is wrong—that she ever makes a mistake . . .

"Oh, Ştefan, please!"

She takes the sugar tongs from his burning hand, irritated by his awkwardness. The look she flashes at him under her long eyelashes speaks volumes about the authoritarian, possessive manner of her care, and with another gesture that brooks no contradiction she points to a slice of cake that he must eat.

Ah, those solid, mediocre family feelings! It seems you are unworthy of them, since you can't stop yourself watching the one closest to you—and committing the sin of judgment as you watch.

How bitter the tea is this evening! Or is it just your palate?

"Careful, Yvonne, that's not a toy," Madam Ana says, stopping the child from pushing the trolley. "Here, eat your biscuit . . ."

Without looking away from the figure of his wife, the professor pulls a childish face as he swallows his last piece of cake . . . Look at her, so good-naturedly acting the hostess, showing no sign of her irritation. Of course, even later she won't reproach you for raising your voice at her; the most that will happen is that she'll have a headache or one of those female disorders that keep her in bed. She'll lie there white as a sheet for hours on end, her forehead wrapped in a band smelling of aromatic vinegar, a hot water bottle pressed against her feet. And you'll regret more than ever that you offended her, in front of others! You'll remain alone too, in your cheerless study, working unproductively on your language atlas but unable to keep your mind off her. Cold comfort that you're the only one who makes her suffer, that she doesn't even seem to hear incivilities when they're spoken by people she doesn't care about. Take our young guest, for example. She doesn't seem bothered by his lack of attention— which she certainly would be if the absurd suppositions you sometimes make were well-founded. Then her tender, sensitive heart would be broken by the way he is courting her own sister!

As for the young man, look how nonchalantly he takes the steaming cup from Sophie's hand. Does that same hand stroke his body, moving lower and lower, all the way down? What an absurd idea!

There is a soothing buzz in the room.

"The explosion at Dudeşti obsesses me because I found myself having to go to the funeral service . . . Imagine the hundreds of coffins, one after another! This made the most painful impression, especially as I'm sure everyone thought they were attending the prelude to much worse things to come. Such a crowd there was, with officials, speeches, and suffocating heat. Well, Professor Mironescu, I'm sure I wasn't the only one to ask himself the question; many other decent Romanians there must have been wondering like me whether it was a criminal act, an act of sabotage, with a foreign hand behind it."

Mr. Ialomiţeanu bows, in his exaggerated way, as Madam Ana offers him a dish with his favorite ice cream.

"Foreigners undermining our joke of war preparations?" the professor smiles. "Since our artillery hasn't received the deliveries it ordered, why should the enemy bother? I won't even ask which enemy you have in mind, my friend. Brătianu's still keeping mum, so we can't know whether we're about to end our neutrality and, if so, whether we'll side with the Germans or the French. Shouldn't we be wondering more about ourselves than about some dangerous foreign hand?"

A drop of malice mixes in with the amiability. Despite his ashen appearance, he seems to have recovered his good humor. Perhaps he is trying to make up for the bad thoughts he had about his guest half an hour ago, when he took it out on Sophie.

"Still," Titi continues naively, unaware of the master's complicated thought processes, "I have a feeling that the investigation only scratched the surface, as if the police weren't really interested in discovering the truth. And do you rule out sabotage?"

"Maybe the ones who killed King Carol were also behind the explosions," Margot suggests.

Titi, surprised, looks up at her in amusement, then nervously gobbles some more ice cream.

"I remember that evening very well," Margot continues. "You were visiting us at the time. Sophie went to the telephone and was so bowled over by the news of the king's death that she gave birth to Yvonne before she was due. You left soon afterward, and godmother Fănica came and tapped her palms and said there was something fishy about it all. Alecu, our godfather, told us he'd bet the king would be poisoned sooner or later because he'd signed a secret treaty with the Germans . . ."

"What nonsense!" Sophie exclaimed, now also sitting on the sofa, beside Mr. Ialomiţeanu. *"Tu prêtes comme d'habitude l'oreille à toutes les bêtises. Ce pauvre Alecu est bien gentil, il fait de son mieux, mais . . ."*

"Come now, Yvonne, stop your playing, and don't bite any more biscuits. A good girl should eat properly. Who will want them if they've all been started? Come on now, do as you're told! And don't look at me as if I was the big bad wolf!"

Madam Ana's scolding made everyone smile—except the young mother. Only she expressed concern that, in such hard times, when foreigners were packing their bags to leave, it would be more and more difficult to find someone suitable to look after the children.

"Yes, dear Madam Mironescu, the German and French governesses will leave, and, what's worse, the servants will disappear. Food supplies will become a problem—which they already are for the poor, who have to stand in line all day and can only buy meat on two approved days a week. It'll soon be like in Germany, where people of good birth have to line up too. Ah, yes, my dear lady, much worse times are in store for us."

The young prophet's voice is cheerful enough, and there is a twinkle of satisfaction in his eyes. But an uneasy silence has spun its web among the shadows, in this hour *entre chien et loup*. Professor Mironescu's face has darkened most of all: he mops his receding brow, and his burning eyelashes tell him that his temperature has risen dangerously. He'll stay a few moments longer, then go and lie down in his room until he has to dress for dinner.

"Did you see Colonel Albu's young wife at the funeral? Everyone's talking about her."

Mrs. Mironescu holds out her unfinished cup of tea to Madam Ana.

"Yes, my dear lady, someone pointed her out to me. But on such occasions you don't look at women too closely, and even if I'd dared I wouldn't have seen much, *parce qu'elle portait grand deuil.* Her veil was so thick that you could only guess at how she looked, and I don't think those who rave about her beauty saw more than I. Of course she looked overwhelmed by her loss, and that made a deep impression on everyone, but I could say without exaggeration that you had the same impression wherever you turned your eyes. So many families devastated, each standing by its coffin! And, of course, all the coffins were sealed. You can imagine what they were like inside: scraps of bodies, a shoulder here, a leg there ... forgive me, dear Madam Mironescu. Don't worry, I won't give any gory details—but it's a fact that you had to hold a handkerchief over your nose ... I know, you accused me of exaggerating the seriousness of the situation. But, well, I've heard it from reliable sources that from this evening there'll be no more passenger trains for Sinaia. And I've also heard that doctors in the provinces are being made to train for army service."

"May God grant that what you heard is right—I mean, that enough doctors are being trained. I hope we've learned something from the last Balkan War, in 1913, when lack of hygiene and general disorganization led to so many casualties and it did us no good that there wasn't any shooting. I saw with my own eyes how our poor soldiers were happy to be given Bulgarian uniforms, not knowing that they would turn out to be real shirts of Nessus. One young doctor, just back from Heidelberg, insisted that captured uniforms should be put through a sterilizing closet. But everyone asked where they were going to get a sterilizing closet from. There was plenty of scope for sarcasm, but the men also showed our usual lack of respect when faced with a different opinion from our own. The doctor's youth didn't help either, so that even those who might have agreed with him pulled a wry face and said: 'Come on, man, forget about it. Give us a break! Open your eyes: can't you see you're in the Balkans, not in Heidelberg!' And it didn't take long for him to see: he was one of the first to die of the cholera that came with the Bulgarian uniforms!"

Gripping the arms of his chair with damp hands, Professor Mironescu shakes his head and smiles wanly. What youthful illusions had made him volunteer then, to endure boots that peeled the skin from your feet, backbreaking marches in fierce heat, foul drinking water, bits of dirt that crunched in your mouth as you ate, the stench of latrines next to the field kitchen, and the constant presence of other people? As the memories flood back, he takes out the box of pastilles he always has on him: *Fructines-Vichy, bonbons laxatifs purgatifs dépuratifs, inoffensifs antiséptiques de l'intestin, A. Pointet, Pharmacien de première classe.* His fingers shake as he fumbles inside and takes one out.

"Come now, Yvonne, leave that trolley alone, it's not a toy."

Madam Ana takes the girl's little fingers and manages to lead her to the door, just a few steps away. But when she loosens her grip to turn the handle, the child, as slyly agile as she is unsteady on her feet, immediately disappears behind the furniture, to the great amusement of Mr. Ialomițeanu.

"Yvonne! You know where you should be at this time of day! She gets tired and confused when there are strangers in the house, and that makes her all the more difficult . . ."

A little interlude has developed. Mrs. Mironescu asks Yvonne to go straight to bed, Mr. Mironescu compliments Madam Ana on the cake, Miss Margot talks in whispers to Mr. Ialomițeanu, and Mr. Ialomițeanu, laughing playfully, suggests that she voice her puzzlement aloud.

"Maybe that's why the king didn't want to go to war at the time; maybe he knew the country wasn't ready . . . Yes, Mr. Ialomițeanu, you told me that yourself. You said they shouted from the street for him to order a mobilization but he wasn't having any of it. Afterward, he bowed to the people's will, called in his ministers and, with tears in his eyes, signed the order. When he'd done it he said 'poor country' in German—*armes Land*! But he did let the people have what they wanted . . ."

"The people, huh! They know so well what they want! By the way, do you remember how much an agent cost last time? Twenty lei! I'm talking about an agent provocateur who stirs up war—or whatever you'd call them," Mr. Ialomițeanu laughed.

"How can you talk like that? You saw yourself how the streets were full of demonstrators calling for us to join the war on France's side."

Sophie's voice was trembling with greater indignation than the incident merited. And, since Mr. Ialomițeanu simply went on laughing, she stood up, took a biscuit from the tea trolley, and went back to her chair at the other end of the room.

Speaking softly, the professor isn't about to give up.

"Perhaps we've learned something for once. I've heard that we now have ambulances and horse-drawn pharmacies and sterilizing closets—even hospital trains, with bathrooms and every comfort. Well, we shall see. Hygiene has always been this country's Achilles' heel."

He patiently fulfills his duties as host, ignoring the childish disputes and reintroducing a more edifying theme into the conversation, so that the dangerous electric charge in the air disperses unnoticed. Then he'll be able to retire to his room, safe in the knowledge that he has left a pleasant atmosphere behind.

"Unfortunately, though, none of the positive measures that could be taken to clean up the country is within our power." His voice is throbbing with sincerity. "For all our good intentions, we idealists don't have now and never will have anything but words at our command. We find ourselves so often alone and impotent, and it's well known that loneliness brings fear and a selfish desire to protect yourself . . ."

During that other war, he'd often wake with a start and wonder what he was doing there, his weak lungs scorched by the heat of long marches, his body constantly exposed to flies, dust, and a host of microbes, among crowded ambulances and stretchers covered with white sheets. What good would it have done anyone if he'd given up the ghost in such circumstances, no longer strong enough to complain, his body too dehydrated to sweat out another iota of blood or pus? It had been a stroke of Providence when Georges Athanasiu appeared on horseback one day. *What are you doing here, old boy? It's crazy to get mixed up in all this. Go back to your phonograph recordings and your language atlas!*

"I had an opportunity to see things up close in 1913, in the last Balkan war, until the Almighty helped me to escape with my life. Providence dictated that Georges Athanasiu rode up one day alongside a much more important volunteer, the past and future prime minister Ionel Brătianu, and after an exhausting journey over hundreds of kilometers I suddenly found myself back in a hot and sultry Bucharest, where everyone was planning their summer vacation. Even today Sophie scolds me for my morose state when, soon after my return, we went out for the evening to the garden restaurant at Fântâna Blanduziei. But I admit that the national appetite for laughter amid catastrophes gets on my nerves. Some claim that it's helped us to survive, but I wonder whether it hasn't somehow been our undoing."

The professor tidies up his papers on the table, his hands shaking a little as he does it. But, following a long tradition, his guest begins to pace up and down the room. Probably—the master thinks—he's waiting for me to come out with what others see as my excessively severe judgment of this country and its people . . .

How can we know what others think of us—even those who agree with every word we say so as not to hurt our feelings? The most modern theories, at odds with the positivist mainstream, would claim that we can know it intuitively. (Professor Mironescu regrets more and more not having ordered Bergson's much-discussed books in good time.) If this is true, intuition should tell him the exact degree of condescension that his former student feels toward him—intensely, as in the flickering of a light. But since it's a rather troubling insight, he avoids giving it free rein. Otherwise, how can we prevent ourselves from committing a mild form of indiscretion toward others?

So the professor puts on a kind face and adjusts his glasses on his nose. A soothing buzz in the room, a diamond brooch sparkling on a dress, frilly lace breaking up the shadows . . .

"Look out! Oh, my God, look out, Yvonne!"

Rustling skirts, loud shouts, tramping feet, cups banged down on saucers. Yet it is he, the four-eyed dreamer with slow reflexes, who gets there first. Detaching Yvonne's tiny hands—how can they be so small?—from the edge of the trolley, he smiles with pleasure when her fingernails dig into his skin. He caresses her thin wispy hair, through which her rosy scalp can be glimpsed here and there. He takes her little fists away from her eyes, but she immediately puts them back with unsuspected force.

"It's all right," he says, "nothing has happened. She just got scared by our loud voices."

This is indeed the truth. Nor was she ever in danger, for the simple reason that tea had already been served. Nevertheless, he's been waiting for some time to play the role of savior, and he proudly raises his trophy that smells so sweetly of milk and softness, dressed in the tiniest navy-style shirt.

Ah, those family sentiments, so stable, so mediocre, give you the strength to start each day anew, and to put up with everything as each night falls.

"I'd have preferred not to be proved right so soon. *Mais c'est une véritable folie de la faire confier à Nela . . . Cette fille trouve tout le temps des moyens pour se dérober . . . Et toi aussi, chéri, tu laisses aller les choses.*"

Sophie's reproach to Ştefan sounds harmless enough, but she looks at him with a fixed stare. Again he has the sensation of becoming transparent, of being constricted by a lie. For, in the end, it's a lie to hide the bad moments from her, when she guesses that something's wrong but doesn't understand what it can be. She can't help letting it get on top of her, until she ends up thinking that he's a semihypochondriac, a semineurasthenic. After all, he never has any treatment, never sees a doctor . . .

Swallowing his displeasure, Professor Mironescu settles the child on his knees. The worst of his fever seems to have passed, because he feels refreshed and therefore able to talk more. The same disagreeable sensation keeps pricking at him, but his voice is loud and clear, his eyes sparkle, and the green of his iris looks fresher than before.

"You see, people in our country are born weary and resigned, as if they have already lived many difficult lives filled with disappointment and long given up opposing the power of evil. Disorder, stopgaps, and primitive behavior grow spontaneously—like microbes in dust. It's as if there's a fermenting agent for disorder in the very air we breathe . . ."

"An enzyme, no less!" the young guest laughs.

"Yes, if you like—a superbug of corruption, chaos, and slipshod work . . . Evils that my father complained about, and that we too never stop complaining about. All this together produces a terrible inertia, so that our energies lose themselves in a sticky morass. You've seen how gifted our young people are, haven't you? How wonderful our children are, and how disappointing our adults!"

He gently winds his arms around Yvonne, who doesn't realize how well Papa is protecting her and, with a little yelp, shows that she would like to climb down.

"So, my young friend, how do you explain that we all complain about the same things to one another, and that we've been doing it for so long? If so many of us are really discontented, as well as honest, how could the evil continue to grow—from generation to generation, it would seem . . ."

He pauses and lets Yvonne down, suddenly feeling that his guest is staring hard at him. Maybe he doesn't entirely agree! Well, the thing to do is to invite him to express the doubts that his original mind has come up with. This is precisely what Professor Mironescu does: indeed, he asks him a question to get him going. As the representative of a younger, more cultured generation, which makes greater demands of life, how would he explain the persistence of these national characteristics? How do we transmit our indignation together with the evil, ready to adapt as soon as our own person is at stake, but to accuse, run down, and slander once it's a question of someone else.

As if taken aback, the young man blushes and his ears turn bright-red. His generation, he answers, is younger but by no means more cultured. It has greater pretensions, yes, as well as being more pretentious. But it's hardly destined for the bright future that is often predicted for it, since, if we go by what we see around us, we might call it the "sacrificed generation." Its pretensions are futile, since the die is now cast and we're talking about the first "sacrificed generation" after not such a long period of peace and prosperity. It remains to be seen whether the sacrifice is worthwhile . . . As a representative of the younger generation, he is the first to recognize its superficiality. But that's nothing yet: we shall see how eager for compromise and hungry for gain are those who come after!

Young Ialomiţeanu is now at the end of the room where the tiled fireplace faces the terrace door, leaning against the fireplace and running the fine tips of his fingers along its edge. How could the professor have spotted, right across the room, the keen emotion that the young man felt a few moments ago, when he was idly pacing up and down and saw that the door to the clematis terrace was slightly open.

Amazing! It's always been their habit to keep the terrace door shut, and now here it is a hand's width open. That means it must have been open an hour ago, two hours ago. Someone went onto the terrace to look at the street, or the yard, or even the garden. And that someone could only have been the professor, since he was alone here dealing with his correspondence.

Titi Ialomiţeanu's heart booms with emotion, like a gong of ill portent, but he still replies amicably to the professor's unanswerable question. Unfortunately he hasn't considered this point before, but in the future— if any of us have a future—he'll find the right explanations. Meanwhile he'd like to ask a question himself. Concerning the recent writings of Constantin Stere . . .

The professor blinks hard. So, he was wrong when he interpreted his young friend's uneasy stare as a wish for dialogue! A *malentendu*? Yes, of course. But, obvious though this is, he isn't really satisfied. So this is one of those—and not the worst!—in whose hands we must leave the world. Or is he just an example of the egoism and superficiality of youth? Perhaps his immaturity is sufficient explanation for the mediocrity of his company—company that the professor awaits with embarrassing relish, but finds no less irritating for that. He shouldn't deceive himself: his solitary life is the real reason why he can't drag himself away from this idle chatter, which leaves a bitter sense of futility in the depths of his being.

"You are too young to remember the Maiorescu article in *Deutsche Revue*," he says with a smile. "It was the first that openly argued for a rapprochement with Germany. Even old Brătianu had got a cool reception when he went to meet Bismarck in Berlin, even though Russia had been putting a lot of pressure on us. Public opinion here was not in favor of a pro-German turn either, mainly because of doubts about Austria and the situation of our brothers and sisters in Transylvania. Otherwise, why would the king have kept our treaty with Germany secret for thirty years? In my view, then, we should also look differently at Stere's writings . . ."

Hot air blows through the slightly open door, causing the off-white net curtain to flutter above the mirror-like parquet. However much he thinks, the young man can't find an explanation that puts his mind at rest. If the professor opened the door himself, it's possible that he went onto the terrace and saw Sophie drag him along on that wretched walk . . . But he doesn't dare to continue this line of thought . . .

Since anxiety is his constant state of mind, he has learned to be always on the alert. The professor's last sentence was in effect a question. It requires an answer. So, nearly choking with emotion, he begins:

"I wouldn't insist, not by any means, but I seem to remember that two years ago in Constanța some surprise was expressed that Stere had agreed to be present at the meeting with the tsar of Russia. Do you think he should have done that, having been one of the tsar's victims in Siberia?"

"Well, my friend, I don't think it right that I should express an opinion about Siberia and the tsar. I've never spent one day in a prison cell, thank God! Who knows? Maybe it was a good idea for him to be there, precisely because he'd suffered at the tsar's hands in Siberia. But, as you put it, I haven't had an opportunity to reflect on this. On the other hand, let's all give some thought to what the postwar world would be like if Russia called the shots and extended its rule to the mouth of the Danube."

The professor hears his voice ring with an emotion that embarrasses him, especially since he cheapens his thoughts by giving way to salon demagogy. But he can't suppress his wish to go on talking, driven by that unpleasant sensation he has never managed to analyze. It's like a fox cub hidden in his breast, under his starched shirt and collar.

"Well, now, I'm sure you will say that, *en ce qui concerne la politique,* things are no different in civilized European countries. But it's not quite like that, my friend! We all agree that there's a greater lack of seriousness in Romania—greater indifference, greater volatility. People care less about keeping up appearances. Yet practical skills and a sense of when to compromise are the very stuff of politics. It's not serious to wash your dirty linen in public and then claim to be believed when you raise the banner of lofty ideals!"

An unexpected cough drowns the professor's voice, forcing him to hold a handkerchief to his mouth. Bur after a few moments he rolls it up guiltily and continues:

"Maybe it's my age, but I tire easily and no longer get worked up over everything. Although you were away at the time, you must have heard about the rumpus at the club, when the most honorable men, some at a ripe old age, got into a shameful brawl that left them with crushed hats, bumps and bruises, twisted collars and broken sticks."

He has slipped down low in his chair, trying to find a more comfortable position. Sickly red blotches mark his forehead, cheeks, and jaws.

Fever.

As he speaks, he keeps his eyes on Titi Ialomițeanu's face, both wanting and not wanting to see whether there is something between him and Sophie. Of course he can't simply excuse himself and leave the two of them together, without his supervision. He'll have to stay longer, as if waiting for something to happen, though well aware that nothing can happen while he's there. The more he is disturbed by that unpleasant sensation, mixed with a vague tenderness toward the two of them, the more considerate his tone of voice becomes—so gentle, in fact, that only he can detect the few false notes.

Did I say false notes? No, that's wrong. Rather, the two souls dwelling in my breast, as the poet put it so well . . .

"The famous letter in which Carol complained to foreigners about us contains a few interesting passages. How can you deny that an overdemocratic constitution was granted too early to a people that, not knowing the meaning of liberty and democracy, made wrong use of them? A man of the future who looks at our newspapers and memoirs might find the din truly deafening: all that sarcastic raillery and backbiting! An ant heap of grotesque shapes—puppets pulled by the strings of ambition and greed! That's the picture we paint of ourselves, with our constant shouting, our impudent challenges in the Chamber, our sabotaging of good legislation simply because our opponent proposed it, our fancy speeches in support of things that are indefensible! What lawyers we've landed ourselves with, in just a few decades! What a parliament—one of the first in this part of Europe! Rioters who take themselves for revolutionaries, and who scatter as soon as the mayor sends in a few policemen or some bullyboys he's swept up from the gutter! Groups of people who find any pretext to gather outside the palace and shout: *Down with Carol I, Romania's shame! Down with the government of murderers!* Students who waste their youthful energy putting up barricades and making incendiary speeches at the foot of Michael the Brave's statue! That man of the future will surely fail to see that everything around him—apartment blocks, laws, boulevards, everyday expressions, loan and insurance companies, contracts, banks, highways and bridges, schools and railway stations, picturesque allegories at chariot parades—that all this was achieved, despite the brouhaha, by hearts and hands, especially hands, building with solid bourgeois material . . ."

The unpleasant feeling inside him is producing verbal diarrhea. And the frozen smile on his face is beginning to give him cramp!

Dark-blue rings around his eyes, and sparse hair already nearly white.

"No one in this country would agree that anything can be done disinterestedly, for the public good. Maybe I'm a dreamer, maybe it's true that nothing like that is possible. But how many generous souls, how many matchless intellects, are future generations likely to uncover among us? Of course, you might tell me that no one is a prophet in his own country, or that the present has always been unjust, ever since the beginning of time. But I'd reply that there's something absurd and repulsive in everyone, so that each of us is inevitably at the mercy of those who observe us. That's all we are: the image that others form of us. But why do we make our fellow men the butt of our irony? Why such dizzying arrogance? Why are we so ungenerous, so lacking in tact and fellow feeling?"

Outside, behind the clear windows, the blue velvet of the clematis stands out against a gold and pink sky, while below it a thick undergrowth of wisteria twines itself around the knots of the old walnut tree. All around, glistening scales of ivy give the walls a pompous garb, leaving just a few patches of naked white at the level of the lion-headed gutter. Out there in the darkness, stone slabs covered with greenish-black moss lie half-buried in the rich soil.

Here in the room, where the mahogany furniture has lost most of its shine amid the soft shadow, Professor Mironescu willfully breaks the rules of polite society, which require that conversation should be pleasant, sparkling, and superficial. Under his starched shirt, the fox cub's bloody claws still work savagely at his flesh.

However, like the little Spartan of old, he won't give himself away with any trembling of his voice. He'll continue to wrap his words in lace netting, so that he can get as close as possible to his rival—no point in denying that that is what he is—and study his inner workings.

"That's the lack of fellow feeling, or even elementary courtesy, with which our upright citizens treat one another. Each day another scandal breaks out, another case of sordid scheming by people who had seemed above suspicion, another swindle involving men for whom we've written glowing character references. Something is said in confidence one minute, and an hour later the whole of Bucharest hears about it, yet there is no end to the speeches denouncing corruption, fraud, venality, and treachery. All the chatter and gossip leaves no one untouched by at least subtle insinuations. And, as if enemies weren't enough, we also have to worry about absent friends, since evil is never found only in the other camp, that's for sure. We have seen the contradictions between words and deeds in each of the people around us, the vile displays of cowardice, the little base acts, shameful alliances and unspeakable ambitions. We could say a lot about each of them—and we do say it, because we see them close up."

But why, at an age when illusions usually crumble, does he still find it so troubling to witness evil tongues at work? Is it because of his structural inability to imagine evil, as much as of his credulous nature? *Calomniez, calmoniez!* he hurls at his calumniators—but he knows all too well his own propensity to believe what he hears. His defiant smile is that of a puny kid afraid of not being taken seriously because he knows how little strength he has . . .

He is so caught up in his own sentences that even the familiar striking of the clock makes him start. The others, who for some time have been stealing glances at it, also jump a little. But their faces do not return to him until the echo of its last chime has fizzled out.

"Of course, there are quite a few of us who deplore the waste: so many subtle observations, flashes of humor, and memorable formulations expended on base trivia and destined for oblivion! But, in my view, no one is sufficiently bothered that *il en restera toujours quelque chose.* It's not we who invented that proverb, because we are never guilty of calumny! We are sure that at every moment we know the truth, the whole truth, about others."

A slight stutter confuses his thoughts and warns him of the ridicule to which he is exposing himself. Lecturing in one's own drawing room: what poor taste! how impolite!

Professor Mironescu removes his steamed-up glasses, cleans them meticulously with his handkerchief, and continues more hesitantly:

"We men of honor, unversed in these things, also tend to think that what we see in others is only intrigues and machinations. I'm not speaking of you, my young friend, but of Bucharest in general. We have an extremely skeptical and materialistic way of looking at things: the world is a basket of crabs, in which you have to use your elbow, close one eye, lower your head, ally yourself with the devil . . . This is often how the legendary passive intelligence of Romanians is frittered away, by discrediting what others do before they have managed to finish it. We throw out the baby with the bathwater. By constantly harping on the human failings of our fellow men, we end up abandoning the principles as well."

Suddenly worried, Mr. Mironescu rests his eyes on little Yvonne, who for the last few minutes has been circling around the table with the photographs, threatening to overturn the candelabra with its lighted candles. But, sensing his disapproval, she runs and hides under the pedestal table, from where she peeks out through the silk tassels and waits for him to say "Boo!" He scarcely has time to furrow his brows before she crawls back with the speed of a wild animal, laughing shrilly until she begins to hiccup. Then she reappears, still hiccupping, and crouches on her knees in a way that dirties her openwork stockings and navy skirt.

By now, however, Papa has forgotten her.

"If we swallow every bit of gossip, believing that it simply confirms our way of looking at things without illusions, and if we reduce every good deed to grubby self-interest, is it any wonder that we remain so skeptical and unfeeling?"

But why does an old memory well up, unconnected with anything he is saying? It was a glassy-gray February morning, and he was forced to walk down Strada Sfântul Ionică because he didn't have a cent in his pocket to get even the most wretched horse-drawn cab. Huddled in a thin coat, constantly slipping on the ice in his dainty ballroom shoes, he clutched a heavy old locket studded with diamonds and rubies that he'd inherited from *maman*. He'd spent all night playing cards and losing— no longer on credit but *au diable*. He was hurrying to the pawnshop, so that he could draw a line under the whole unfortunate episode. He knew himself too well to be sure that he'd be capable of burying the memory of his profligacy and avoiding a repeat in the future. So, shivering in his elegant costume, making utopian calculations about how much money he'd need to buy a long-coveted sable overcoat (so necessary for a being such as him), he continued to grip the locket in his icy hand as he walked down Strada Sfântul Ionică, on that glassy-gray February morning. The biting cold stuck to his red nose, and his eyes were smarting with tears. Being young and vigorous, he thought it only natural that he should pawn a deathbed locket to make up for a night he had spent frittering away his life. But now, no aberrant ideas are there to still the painful memory he has kept buried deep inside him. His mother's love is still hovering and protecting him, but she no longer has any way to scold or praise him, or even to understand . . .

"So, my friend, don't you think it's hard for national illusions to grow out of so much pragmatism and sneering? And, if they do, can't we expect to lose them at the first major test of history? No sooner does the sky clear than another cloud comes along and blots out the sun. A fine morning ruined—and wasted!"

Although young Ialomițeanu mumbles something in agreement, the professor is sure that he's wondering what political disappointment the master has suffered recently to be launching such an *attack*. Yes, "attack" is the right word, or anyway the one that the disciple applies to the master's speech.

But, the professor asks himself, what is the point of this exhausting attempt at a meeting of minds, if it is doomed to failure from the start?

The prejudice inherent in the act of speaking, which he has been studying for the past twenty years, then loses its essential element, much as water is lost when it is held in a clenched fist. How little of what exists inside us do we manage to convey through words! And how little of that little is received! Yet we go on speaking (look at us!), in the belief that the sun of reason will enlighten our soul. What would become of our lives if we saw an exchange of words as the difficult transfusion that it is in reality? Such a suspicion overcomes us only when things go badly wrong, and even then we forget it at the first opportunity. Only after we have let all the sincerity drain out of our soul, and the other has proved incapable of receiving a single word, do we glimpse in resignation the obscure laws to which human beings are subject when they try to draw closer to each other . . .

Such thoughts occur to the master at the moment when he comes under the disciple's gaze. The shine in his eyes flickers inexplicably, as clammy as in those of a cornered animal. But the professorial vocation, calling as it does for perseverance, prevents Ştefan Mironescu from capitulating, as he is tempted to do.

"Besides, we have enough critical sense to be aware of this defect. We speak with amused resignation of our lack of fellow feeling. That's what Romanians are like everywhere, at home or abroad: they quarrel and tear each other to pieces, more ready to believe a foreigner than one of their own people. Maybe it goes back to the time when they informed on each other to the Sublime Porte. Yes, that must be the explanation! Otherwise, would it be natural to feel closer to representatives of the Great Powers—Blondel or Bussche, Czernin or Poklovski—than to other Romanians who happen to be your political opponents? I don't know, my friend, I'm just asking. But if you insist, that's what I'd say. Anyway I think it's wrong to lean too much toward either France or Germany, Russia or Austria-Hungary . . ."

The others look uneasily at the little table and the lighted candelabra wobbling on top. Mr. Ialomiţeanu has already hurried over to it. He blows on the candles, then bends down and uncovers the culprit lurking beneath it in the dark.

"Good children are in bed by now. Time for 'Twinkle, twinkle, little star,' no?" he asks, bending down further and further to coax her out. "Twinkle, twinkle, little star . . ."

Everyone there knows that baby talk requires a special talent, and his realization that they know stifles his thin little voice.

"Attendez-moi un tout petit instant, je viens vous porter secours . . ."

With the majesty common in tall women, Mrs. Mironescu walks over to the table. A sulky little girl, who can hardly resist grabbing her doll by the leg, throwing it into her basket, and drawing the little checkered cover over it: this is how Sophie appears when she finally succeeds in catching the pale-cheeked child with the old woman's nose. She places her on her knees and patiently waits for her to calm down. In the end the little bundle does stop thrashing her arms and legs about, though by then a mixture of tears and saliva has dribbled all over her navy costume.

When peace and quiet has returned to the room, Professor Mironescu excuses himself with an embarrassed smile before continuing.

". . . far be it from me to find fault with the light from the West! As you know, I'm not one of those who took to the barricades because a bunch of dilettantes started speaking French at the National Theatre. I hope you will remember the discussion we had at the time, when I described that demonstration as a piece of foolish nonsense. But precisely because I feel a grateful filial love toward France—the love that every Romanian feels—I can't help being pained by some of the ridiculous things it does. On the one hand, veneration and imitation of the West, in so far as that's possible; on the other hand, a benevolent disregard, a lack of interest. Shall I put it more strongly? Disdain, even? But the truth might be too hurtful . . ."

There he goes, straying from the point! Again it occurs to the young man that, when Sophie misguidedly leaned over to wipe away the mud with her handkerchief, the professor might just have seen it from his hiding place outside the terrace door, amid the ivy and clematis. And now he's beating about the bush, waiting . . . For what? Obviously for the right moment to make a scene that will ruin his career and block his future in respectable society. As this mad idea occurs to him, the young man finds it difficult not to say a hasty farewell to everyone, grab his hat and stick, walk down the entrance steps, fly to the gate and out into street, and never set foot in the house again . . . Out of here, yes, as quickly as possible . . .

"A memory came back to me at that moment: the evening when General Pau, on his way to St. Petersburg, was met at the station by thousands and thousands of people. A frenzied crowd, with flowers, flags, the inevitable *Marseillaise,* ovations, and tears. I was in my friend Georges's car, and I won't deny I found it moving. There's a kind of collective

emotion that can grip you, leaving you with no control over it. My critical
sense finally returned over dinner at Mişu Cantacuzino's, when I found
myself seated opposite General Pau himself. There was still a crowd
beneath the window, with flags, speeches, ovations, tears . . . This time,
however, I wasn't so overcome with emotion, because I had the confused
figure of General Pau before me. The rules of diplomacy required him
to express his feelings for Romania, but unfortunately he knew next to
nothing about our country, and our wild demonstration hadn't whet-
ted his appetite to learn more. As a soldier, his greatest respect was for
Germany, and in fact he spoke later about the Germans. Well, my friend,
I hope you won't conclude from this that I'm pro-German. My sympathies coincide with those of the majority, but can you see me waving a
tricolor in the street at my age? Is my temperament the same as that of
your mentor, Mr. Marghiloman? No, my vacillating nature means that I
don't count myself among the men of action . . . I have never felt capable
of adding my voice to those calling for the harsh sacrifices of war. So,
when I hear all the accusations that Brătianu is a petty calculator, weighing up the pros and cons of each possible alliance . . . Petty calculator?
Does that seem to you the right description?"

Mrs. Mironescu hides a yawn behind her fan. Then she looks demonstratively at the clock, and equally demonstratively at her husband.
Adjusting his glasses on his nose, he makes a reassuring gesture: just a
little longer, just a little more patience!

"You'll probably be upset if I tell you the real reason why I like satiri-
cal prose less and less. Some colleagues of mine swoon over the brilliance
of this genre in our recent literature, but for my own part I simply can't
stand exaggerated passion. So I associate the excellence of our satirists
with other signs of our cultural inadequacy. On a closer look, many dis-
parate things prove to be linked to one another . . ."

A golden light suffuses the sky and creates a dark rim around the red-
tiled roofs. How imperceptible are the changes in the soft air outside,
how huge is the variety of its shades! Does our young friend also have a
secret rapport with nature, with the course of the heavenly bodies? He's
been standing by the terrace door all this time, as if keeping an eye on
something out there. The entrance steps? The street? The garden?

"So, my well-known love for the common people doesn't blind me to
the point of imitating those top officials who show nothing but folkloric
displays to foreign visitors, as if that were all Romania consisted of. In

reality, it is often a sign of poverty, primitivism, and an anarchic stopgap mentality. Nor can my love for the peasantry make me overlook that we are more backward than other nations in Europe. Look at how peasants are forced to eat cornmeal porridge and vinegar, or to go around bare-footed and wear shoes only when they are in the city. I agree with the Liberals that reforms are needed to deal with this."

Still holding Yvonne tightly, Sophie sighs and wipes her face with a handkerchief. What a tiresome afternoon! And since her bouts of nausea started she has found it more and more difficult to put up with the little girl's wriggling.

Yvonne doesn't seem to like sitting on Muti's lap. She isn't allowed to rub cheeks with her, in case she disturbs her makeup, nor to take her by the head, because then she immediately grimaces and pulls away, nor to play with her hairpins . . .

When Muti holds you in her arms, what you feel is not a firm protec-tive bosom but unpleasant soft orbs behind the taffeta material of her dress, which keeps rustling drily as if about to tear . . .

"If you don't sit still, I'll put you down this minute!"

Yvonne doesn't wait for this to be repeated, but slides down and runs on her thin little legs into Papa's outstretched arms. From there she looks defiantly at the glass beads hanging from the lamp, at the bronze Apollo, and at other parts of the room. As she breathes in a calming fragrance, she feels with surprising certainty for her age that she, and not Muti, is the most important person for Papa.

"I dare to think that, if we'd carried out a land reform earlier, the country would look different today. And if the king . . ."

"King Carol?" Margot interrupts, with her usual promptness. "But what could King Carol have done? Nothing, if you think about it! Even when he tried he couldn't do anything—and in the end he committed suicide . . ."

"*Tu ne renonces pas à dire tes naïvetés!*"

Sophie's bored protest strikes her as profoundly unjust.

"Yes, it was suicide, that's quite certain. His nerves were terribly on edge, and he wept all the time in his castle in Sinaia. He ripped off all the medals he got from the Empire, so that they only had two left to put on him at his funeral."

"Only future generations will solve the mysteries of history," Mr. Ialomiţeanu mused, with his usual touch of irony. "Let's hope they clear up all the things that puzzle us, although at times I ask myself whether some may be so hidden that the truth will never come out."

"Mysteries are mysteries," Sophie retorted, "but that is just idle gossip!"

Then her voice immediately changed.

"Yvonne! Yvonne! Please sit up and stop looking around like that . . . It makes me worry that she may be cross-eyed," she explains to the others.

Did she notice the confusion on Titi Ialomiţeanu's face?

To avoid having to look over at the professor's table, the young guest picked up the pink Nereid that was voluptuously reclining in a shell, her plump legs slightly apart. Although he had furtively examined her many a time before, he only now wondered whether such a shameful detail of our animal existence could really be made into an object of luxury and artistic contemplation. Shouldn't there rather be a strict separation between poetic things of beauty, rarely encountered in reality, and the prosaic side of life, including the prints that adorn bordellos or the obscene drawings mentioned in a low voice in certain kinds of conversation.

This was only a fleeting thought, because his mind was actually on the problem of how to end today's visit in as polite but expeditious a manner as possible.

"It would seem that in this difficult period . . . er, it frequently happens in discussions . . . in short, people's eyes are often filled with tears."

Sophie looks with irritation at the clock, then again at her husband, who makes her the usual sign to be patient just a little longer.

"Are we talking about King Ferdinand, my friend?"

The professor's attention to the guest's face, trying to imagine the charm it has for Sophie, verges on the humiliating. He beams with a kind of slow-burning cruelty, until an impure tenderness, forgiving and almost fraternal, takes hold of him. Yes, he forgives everything—even the fact that, despite his troublesome sincerity, he hasn't drawn an inch closer to the young man's inner being. The guest says nothing, except when he has an opportunity to tell one of his pathetic stories, with sufficient distance to keep himself protected. What is this? Oversensitivity? Hypocritical cynicism? A bewildering spiritual void?

"Yes, of course we are!" Mr. Ialomiţeanu replies quickly. "Of course we're talking about King Ferdinand. People in his innermost circle told me as much."

How hard it is to be so young, Margot thinks to herself. Adults slight you with their stupid arrogance and swap remarks with each other, in a game in which you, poor shabby Cinderella, with your chapped red hands, have to run around comically on the margins. You don't even exist for them. You don't even have a right to be angry, or to explain properly why you are right:

"I don't remember who, but I do remember exactly when it was and what was said," Margot says in a low, tearful voice. "The point was that people took advantage of King Carol's nervous state and drove him to take his own life."

Looking away discreetly, as if recalling how they used to be at that awkward age, the other three ignore the young miss as they would any child who has gone too far.

"*Ah, j'en ai assez, elle fait tant de bêtises!*" Mrs. Mironescu says, suddenly standing up and going to ring the servants' bell.

"Take her to her room," she tells Nela.

Flushed, sweaty, and disheveled, the little girl keeps up her usual shrill screams as she is dragged toward the door.

Night is closing in. The gas lamps in the street are not yet alight, and the house martins haven't yet stopped their flight. They flash by, swooping like sinister airplanes, and only the double glazing prevents their cries from breaking into the quiet of the room.

"Nevertheless, there is an explanation even for things you weren't expecting..."

Mr. Ialomiţeanu pauses, a little ill at ease, and coughs to clear his throat. But Professor Mironescu, in the kindly way with which everyone is familiar, completes the idea.

"Yes, indeed. There must be an explanation for the fact that we're so taken up with what other countries do! That's why, my friend, I was going to ask you whether you know of another European nation so lacking in self-confidence—I'd even venture to say, so contemptuous of itself. Leave demagogy aside, or, on the contrary, allow room for it, since this self-contempt of ours can reach truly terrifying heights. When we see something badly done, we think it appropriate to say: a Romanian production! And we say it in an inimitable tone, with that inimitable mocking smile."

Margot gets up from the sofa, squeaking her ankle-boots as she does so. What's the point of listening to any more of this endless stuff?

Blague ennuyeuse! Just empty chatter, in which you can't get a word in edgeways. *Sophie se conduit toujours comme en pays conquis*—but take heart, poor Cinderella! Who knows what Prince Charming will appear tonight? Go to your lonely room and pour your heart out in a long letter to Coralie. Just as you finish, Madam Ana will come in and the excitement of dressing up will begin. Ah, what emotion you'll feel at the sound of the first carriage! You'll glide down the stairs, checking your dress and your hairdo in each mirror. "If only I were your age!" godmother Fănica said. "There wouldn't be one minute when I was sad and weepy. People would never lay off a gentleman who was so blind as to ignore our young lady!" Fănica knows everything. So, people won't lay off someone like Titi Ialomițeanu, who started out a ragamuffin and is turning into a moldy old bachelor from hovering around married women all the time. If you look closely, you'll see that it won't be long before he has a potbelly.

She tiptoes across the room, ready to say that she must prepare for this evening if anyone asks. Sad to say, no one asks anything by the time she has opened the door to go out. Maybe no one even noticed her?

The silence in the room is so great that the ticking clock and Mr. Ialomițeanu's squeaking shoes can be clearly heard. He has left the corner of the fireplace and gone up to the professor's table:

"But there's also an explanation for out-of-the-ordinary things—even my unforgivable visit this afternoon . . . , at this inconvenient hour . . . without giving you any notice . . ."

Professor Mironescu raises his arms to protest.

"Come now, my friend, there's no need to excuse yourself. It was a natural gesture on your part, which shows how close we feel to each other. You're more than a friend, more than a regular visitor. We are all extremely fond of you!"

A familiar noise: the dry clicking of ivory on ivory. Mrs. Mironescu fans herself faster and faster, with growing irritation. Won't there ever be an end to this embarrassing situation? What vulgar things she has to endure! And, to cap it all, she can't stop herself perspiring. Although the heat of day has passed, drops of sweat still form on her brow, at the roots of her blonde hair, and in the dimples on her chin. She dabs at herself with her handkerchief, behind the screen of her fan.

"But look, I wanted to tell you earlier, in the hope that you'd understand me. Everything happened as it did for the simple reason that the servant came down with mumps."

The professor smiles, but there is a slight trace of guilt in the corner of his mouth. He saw the darkness on his wife's face as she looked at the clock and then at him. Still speaking, he slowly begins to put his papers back into the vase. No, she isn't fooled by his merry stream of words, nor is the ever deeper silence lost on her. Can he trust her intuition, as he trusts her healthy moral sense (even if, knowing that flirtation is a fashionable society game, she forces herself to attract a suitor so that she doesn't seem like a raw provincial)?

But why keep pretending not to know the reason for his verbal diarrhea—that little fox cub of jealousy gnawing at his breast? It's a simple matter, which only her naïveté makes more complicated. For she is so naive, and so unaware of things around her, that she doesn't even see her suitor's cowardice, in case it should disgust her. Perhaps he ought to leave her alone with him, unsupervised? Of course, he'd give a lot to be in possession of just one hard fact, instead of wearing himself out with this interpretation of every word and gesture. But, despite the humiliating pain caused by his flighty disciple, and despite the doubt that he ever really has been his disciple, curiosity continues to get the better of him, here and now.

Of course there were several other ways—apart from slow-motion filing—to avoid leaving them alone together; more natural and more brutal solutions to this demeaning and, sadly, all too banal situation. But his curiosity kept him rooted to the spot, so that he could observe the restless void at work in the young man.

"Your generosity only underlines my guilt. It makes it all the more difficult for me to stop . . ."

"I thought we'd decided to drop the subject! What's the point of returning to it?"

Ştefan ought to get up first and apologize for having to go and dress for dinner, so that Sophie can then follow him. He knows how long a lady's toilet can last! But he keeps delaying, not wanting to lose contact with her for a second. He'll probably do the same all evening, with the result that she won't have a chance to exchange two words with the shiftless young man and make sure he has understood the problem facing her as a result of their hours of passion . . . *S'il ne veut assumer aucune responsabilité* . . . Then she'll conclude that there's no point in torturing herself and consider what other options she has . . . The fact remains, however, that she skipped her siesta for that ill-fated rendezvous, and that now she risks having her evening spoiled. It's not enough that Ştefan keeps shuffling his papers, while the other one tries to engage him in another discussion. Ah, how is Titi capable of sacrificing her to the laws of prudence? For nothing else can explain why he wants to open an insipid conversation that evidently interests no one. If he'd just turn his head a little, she'd discreetly signal for him to stop!

"The funeral of Queen Elisabeta left a painful impression, don't you think?"

Professor Mironescu probably dislikes that kind of remark, but the young man has promised to sound him out on the question to discover the extent of his Liberal sympathies. And now he can do so with his mind at rest, since he has trawled through his memory and convinced himself that the old man didn't see him with Sophie in the garden. His evidence is that the professor, who's quite incapable of dissimulation, was extremely surprised when he saw him at the door; he smiled, accepted his excuses, and looked at him as at a strange animal—but without hostility, without rancor. Conclusion: he saw nothing, suspected nothing. If he's been rambling on like this, it's because it's in his nature to do so.

He still intends to get away before the party, however, because that's the only way his untimely arrival will be explicable. And, if Sophie hires a cab and bursts in on him tomorrow morning, hiding her face behind a thick veil and sniffing a little at the smells on the staircase, that won't bother him in the slightest—on the contrary. So, for the moment he keeps talking.

". . . rather warm recently, yet Brătianu goes around in his fur hat! It inevitably set people talking, because he was one of the pallbearers at the funeral. There you had rows of diplomats dressed to perfection, while our prime minister . . ."

You take a last look at the clock and decide that you'll get up and go when it strikes the hour. Your character doesn't allow you to give up until you've played your last card, but now your mind is made up: you have only a few minutes left here. Oh, if only this cautious little devil wouldn't try to keep Ştefan here with his stupid chatter! You'll stand up and make your excuses, even if it means you'll never get to have the *tête-à-tête* with him that has been your aim. It wouldn't be too wrong to describe it as that, a simple aim on your part, even though it caused a strange pain that you've managed to banish from your face, your mind, your soul . . .

You'll get up as soon as the clock strikes, even if it means abandoning the hope . . . What hope? Have you considered for a moment what your life would be like with this poor Ialomiţeanu. Could you accept it? Do you even know what you'd say if he proposed . . . but what could he propose? To run away with him into the big wide world? It wouldn't be like you to swap one evil for an even greater one—and you're waving your fan more and more agitatedly. Would it be more correct to say that only curiosity has been driving you on—curiosity to see what he's capable of doing for you? Only then would you reach a judgment about the situation—and about the company you'd have in it. God, how late it is! And how bad you're feeling! Just a few more minutes and the clock will strike. You can last a few more minutes, since that is what you've decided. How patient you can be once you've chosen something, but how you can turn into the opposite in the twinkling of an eye! So, look at them patiently, as if you were listening to their every word.

". . . horses drawing the funeral carriage so fast up the slope at Curtea de Argeş that some people in the cortege began to run, while others fell behind. All solemnity broke down. The king, with the delicate nerves you know, looked very unhappy. My question was whether such things can be fortuitous."

Why this honeyed tone, which seems a parody of politeness? How many times have you heard this young man speak to you in exactly the same tone, which is in fact ironical? You stop him with a bored wave of your hand, and only someone whose mind was wandering could fail to grasp what your sullen voice is saying:

"Well, seeing that I wasn't there at Curtea de Argeş . . . ," Professor Mironescu replies, with a helpless wave of his hand.

Well, what could I say? I wasn't at Curtea de Argeş, and I wasn't at the funeral. Nor have I had a chance to see Prime Minister Brătianu, with or without a fur hat.

But was this impudent drift present in the young man's words? Did Sophie really flash him a smile in the mirror, telling him to be quiet, encouraging him to stay, or doing what? Was there really a smile in the mirror between her and Ialomiţeanu?

An embarrassing honesty does not allow the professor to feel certain, and as usual the shock of the first suspicion soon passes. He doesn't know whether what he saw was true, or whether it was a delusion of his neurasthenic, morbidly suspicious mind.

Glancing out at the clematis terrace, Professor Mironescu blinks rapidly and wearily. In the calmness of late afternoon, unclear shadows seem to pass overhead without touching the earth.

"It seems certain that Romania will soon declare war on the Central Powers, so it is reasonable to assume that Brătianu will come out on top when it all comes to a glorious end. Opposition attacks will do no more than compel him to form a coalition government, so that the laurels of victory are shared round a little . . ."

Your sign telling Titi to stop all this stuff has had no effect; the insufferable man just goes on and on. Oh, how late it is, and how bad you are feeling! But take a deep breath and think how pleasant the mornings once were when you didn't keep open house and no one came visiting—at least not this insufferable Mr. Ialomițeanu. Take a deep breath and think how pleasant the mornings were a few years ago, when you had just returned from that wonderful trip to Italy. You woke up early, as you'd like to have done all your life—oh, that pink sky, those two poplars growing redder beneath the glowing vault, that view from the window in your dressing room, that fire exploding in your breast as you looked forward to the great love of your life, so intense that happiness itself would be painful . . . Take a deep breath and remember riding in the gig, jolting over holes and bumps, gently rocking along smooth stretches of road, the green fields opening out like a fan on all sides, and the red tiles of the guesthouse receding further and further into the distance, and the loud chirping of birds, as if you were driving over heaps of broken glass, and, oh, the bracing fresh air and the tasteless green mulberries that you reached out for as you went along, and the rough leaves that lashed your hand, you let the fan drop beside the sofa, and no one seems to hear your quick apology as you get up and go to prepare for the evening, you'll be back—will you be back?

You hurry toward the door, teeth clenched, nostrils flared so much that you feel your eyes whiten like a horse's. Just as you are pressing on the handle, the strikes of the clock crash down behind you . . .

Sophie's departure, angry or not, makes the professor more relaxed. He looks at his restless guest, in whom evil manifests itself in perpetual motion . . . Look at him there, as elegant as someone like that can ever be, in a new beige suit that he says he picked up only this afternoon from the tailor, and a red tie and white silk socks—a dapper young man, you might say, if it weren't for the signs that he's putting on weight. And that furtive, skulking look he has in his eyes, like a man with unmentionable habits.

Habits not so alien to him, perhaps?

In the end, what is this constant restlessness, and this platonical courting of the ladies and young misses in every respectable house he enters? What else can it be than a way of concealing his real lack of interest in them?

"Please, would you excuse me for a minute," the professor says, standing up with a little sigh. "I'll be with you again in just one moment."

He steps toward the terrace door, his skinny back wrapped in an oversized jacket.

"Of course, go ahead . . . I've imposed on you enough as it is . . . I assure you, although my coming early has put me in the wrong, I wanted to tell you right away . . ."

"Come, my friend, let's be serious! I thought we'd agreed to drop all these apologies and fancy talk. I just want a get a breath of fresh air, before I go upstairs and dress for dinner . . ."

Supporting himself on the side of the terrace, the professor lowers the curtain of ivy and woodbine that he raised when he turned to answer Mr. Ialomiţeanu. Then he breathes deeply and holds the air in his thoracic cavity, where his rotting lungs are choking him. He takes a few steps on the terrace and again rests his arms on the railing. There is a dizzying fragrance of grass, hay, earth, and distant childhood; he can feel that it's summer . . .

Ah, summer, summer . . .

Air enveloped in blue, the soft shade of the clematis, a smell of flowering tobacco and petunias. Sophie's roses in the garden, shining in the darkness, and beyond them two wicker chairs side by side. Their proximity is unsettling, as if they are evidence of a whispered conversation. But, dismissing this thought, the professor again feels a sweet shiver of regret . . . Ah, summer, summer . . .

How many more summers? And what kind of summers will they be?

Close up, even the martins look and sound fierce: their flight is not effortless gliding, more a desperate thrashing. You see the spasm of their wings as they cross the translucent matter, and you step aside for fear that they might pass through you. A few steps and it's surprising how things change . . . How quickly you understand now. You look carefully around, your attention ever greedier with age; you still read, still accumulate knowledge, still classify things and try to deduce more from them, but you don't do it with the same relish, as if weighed down by a sense of foreboding. Maybe you know that your illness will not allow you to share any new knowledge with others, that you will not even be given enough time to write it down. Perhaps all you'll be able to do is look around attentively. And when the illness makes you forget your own body, so that it no longer feels worn-out and vulnerable like an old jacket, all that remains may be a greedy . . .

One vast stare . . .

For a moment, the light in the soft ivory-white sky creates an illusion that his lungs might recover, and with them the bitter taste of being with someone in whose company he should never have found himself.

Professor Mironescu goes inside with a little sigh of happiness.

"What were you saying, my dear man? That you can't stay for the party? Don't even think of such a nasty trick! At least you had the tact not to mention this betrayal in front of the ladies. You realized in time that you'd never be forgiven for it. So, please be so kind as to come upstairs with me, so that we can make sure we're both dressed properly for the occasion . . ."

Don't let this sudden softening confuse you. That's his nature: a few minutes after behaving badly, he pulls himself together and acts the perfect gentleman. It was the same this afternoon. He felt he'd been impolite in expressing such surprise at your presence, so he tried to make up for it by overwhelming you with nonstop chatter. Now he's almost courting you. But you shouldn't be taken in. Bow again and tell him politely how things stand.

"Of course I deserve to be punished for my lack of consideration in . . . But what greater punishment can there be than to miss the dazzling party? Unfortunately, I have these pressing obligations . . ."

After all these years, the professor still finds that electric lighting makes people's faces look pale and unnatural. He raises his handkerchief to his tired eyes and, when he reopens them, the light seems even more artificial and incongruous. So too do the guest's apologies—and what's more they have been presented at the last minute. What's going on? We were talking for three hours, and only now does he come out with the most important thing he had to say!

Suddenly the professor no longer feels tired: he's almost beginning to look forward to the evening. His relief is so sudden that he feels a surge of joy, although he has to hide this when replying to the guest.

"Well, if you speak of pressing obligations, what more can I say? All that's left is to express my regrets . . ."

Fearing that the guest will read his true feelings, the professor avoids making eye contact and looks casually down at the beige suit that screams its newness. He notices a loose thread that the tailor must have forgotten, then a twisted sock, then some strange splashes of mud on the cuffs of the trousers.

Fresh mud! It must be fresh, since he picked up the suit from the tailor earlier today. He said himself that he put it on before coming here . . . But splashes of mud on such a dry day? Splashes of mud on trouser cuffs, two wicker chairs facing each other under the walnut tree, waterlogged paths in the garden, where Sophie was pointlessly watering her roses at the time when there was an inexplicable ring on the bell? All very confusing! He'd been hoping for something more than an endless hunt for the meaning behind words, a little piece of actual evidence—and now here it was, still not certain, but already casting its shadow over the whole evening, regardless of whether the guest left or stayed.

Taking short breaths, the professor raises his crumpled handkerchief to his brow with a damp hand; the blood hammers in his temples as he accompanies his guest to the door, all the time wondering how Sophie and he, both of them, could have made such a mistake. This man, of all people, to whom they'd taken an instant dislike! Can't the clock be turned back somehow, to that day when they first met him? Or at least it should be possible to track down the moment when the mistake occurred. The guest smiles as he takes his hat and stick: how sorry he is that, leaving like this, he's adding the ultimate impoliteness of not saying good-bye to the lady and the young miss!

The professor will convey his apologies, of course, only later, when his eyes are red and he can hardly stand from exhaustion. Then the interrogation of Sophie will begin: she'll wriggle out of it and walk off, an enigmatic displeasure in eyes still as blue as ever behind her long lashes. Light steps, the creaking staircase, doors opening and closing upstairs, a few notes on the piano, a dress fluttering beyond the terrace railings, the guest. He too should get a move on, so that the other guests don't catch him. What a wonderful light in the garden! Sophie's dubious décor: bunches of roses and colored paper lanterns hanging from the trees. The professor nervously rattles the tin of lozenges. Splashes of mud on the cuffs of trousers fresh from the tailor. But why the unarranged visit? At such an inconvenient hour! Why this, why that: a slow review of each fact, each curious-sounding word. The professor pops one of the lozenges into his mouth, *inoffensifs antiseptiques de l'intestin,* to hide the twitch that contorts his face for a few brief seconds.

A sign, though, that his nervous agitation is under control.

He feels humiliated that he can't get those splashes of mud out of his mind; it causes a loathsome, unbearable physical suffering in every fiber of his being. At the same time, he senses a pair of friendly clear eyes looking tensely toward him; doors opening and closing upstairs, light steps making their way down.

"What's this, Mr. Ialomiţeanu? Aren't you staying for dinner? Are you abandoning us?" Mrs. Mironescu asks, gliding majestically down the staircase.

Mr. Ialomiţeanu is a perfect gentleman, as everyone knows. Although he's shy by nature, he delights in the ladies' company: he comes to take them for a ride, by carriage in the summer, or by sleigh in the winter, to the sound of tinkling bells. Sophie and Margot stick their noses out of the furs in which they have wrapped themselves: what giggling, what roars of laughter, during those outings through a snow-shrunken Bucharest, where smoke coils out of roofs and chimneys into ivory-white skies!

In fact, Professor Mironescu has never much liked sleigh rides or carriage outings, and has a special aversion to picnics and parties or dance evenings; in recent years he has simply refused to go out at all, but maybe that's because of his illness. Well, so this evening Mr. Ialomiţeanu has pressing obligations, and that's why he came around early but delayed telling us the unpleasant news until the last minute, and now all he wants is to take his leave of the lady and the young miss.

The splashes of mud on trouser cuffs are still there, an enigmatic certainty, but the professor's face remains inscrutable. His nervous tic has disappeared, and so too has his relaxed smile. The aggressive electric lighting and his misdiagnosed illness are sufficient explanation for the deep lines that appear on his face when he holds out his hand to say good-bye to the guest.

"What, aren't you staying for dinner, Mr. Ialomițeanu?" Margot asks. "Of course: you must be going to see someone else; this visit was just the first on your rounds."

Suddenly united, the two sisters snipe at the deserter with their insinuations, while he politely makes a farewell bow. Maybe they'll talk about him tomorrow evening, each one's curiosity fueled by the other's words, and in this way they'll explain his peculiar actions. On the other hand, this evening's events may be so exciting that nothing about Mr. Ialomițeanu will seem interesting anymore—or in need of explanation.

But, precisely because he has had so many failures in life, the young man is a past master at covering them up and bearing them with resignation. He bows more deeply, and looks affectionately at his good friends more often than is necessary.

No, the professor says to himself, even if my suspicions appear absurd and exaggerated (once I have calmed down!), it's still rather surprising that I disregarded what I felt at every moment: that we have nothing in common, and I dislike almost everything about him.

In half an hour Mr. and Mrs. Mironescu will receive the guests in the reception room. Dinner will be served earlier than usual, and the professor will stick to his own frugal menu: just a couple of aperitifs, followed by cold slices of meat and *Linzertorte*. Sophie's grave voice will rise in the side room, accompanied by the serious Georges Ioaniu on the piano, and she will create a sensation with a heartrending Verdi aria. After some dancing, the young Geblescu, recently back from a stay in England, will give the instructions for a new society game, to Margot's childish delight. In fact it is a simple experiment in physics.

"Please lend me your ears, sweet ladies and noble gentlemen. Now, please pay close attention. Keep your eyes fixed on the black dot in the middle of this circle. You will see—you already see—not one but dozens of concentric circles around the dot, and your eyes have begun to swim. So, your eyes became tired and changed their vision, long before I had time to move the circle—which I am moving only now, do you see it? A misperception wormed its way into your vision, at the point when you were straining to play your part. However hard you look, what you see changes all the time and is never the same as it was at the beginning. We've known for a long time that we can't step into the same river twice. But here is another discovery: we never look at anything in the same way twice."

When the applause and laughter die down, a grave voice will ring out from the smaller side room:

"If we're able to keep to our present position, without risking the country's future through some rash action or another . . ."

Of course, that can only be the voice of friend Victor.

Part Three

Chapter 9

The Journal of Professor Mironescu

22 August 1916

Policemen's whistles, church bells, and factory sirens sounded the alarm several times last night. Then the artillery began to boom without a moment's pause, mixed in with bursts of machine-gun fire. We all groped our way in the dark, sleepless and on edge. Of course it was hard to persuade my servants to go into the cellar (as the police have instructed us to do), since the general view is that there is no danger. It's true that up to now the zeppelins, or "zippiligs," as they call them here, have not inflicted any casualties. We went back to our rooms in the early morning, dropping with tiredness, but it wasn't long before our artillery started up again. Such a night plays havoc with our domestic routines, so that we'd only just finished breakfast when an automobile drew up outside around eleven o'clock.

It was Madam Nicolaid, one of the patronesses of the Queen Elisabeta Society, who had been on her way to the North Station to donate various things to soldiers leaving for the front. Having heard at the last minute that the ladies who had promised to accompany her had pulled out, she nevertheless got into the car with a servant and her devoted husband. After a few meters, they decided to risk a detour via Şoseaua Bonaparte, with the intention of appealing to Sophie's obliging and unstuffy nature. They couldn't stay long—but it was enough for us to have a pleasant morning walk in the summery garden, where Sophie, with her customary pride, showed us her new strains of roses. We had a little chat in the pavilion, enjoying the luxury of a nonersatz coffee, and exchanging thoughts about the feverish night and the phantom zeppelin that the morning newspapers had discussed. Madam Nicolaid knew from the Red Cross that a terrible bombing raid caused more than a hundred casualties in Constanța. I told them what is probably no longer a secret: that Brătianu made a personal appeal to Bussche, the German emissary, not to wage aerial warfare against the civilian population, and that he received assurances in this regard. As it was late, and as Mr. and Mrs. Nicolaid had to be at the station on time, we got up and left the pavilion. Unfortunately, Sophie was unable to be of any help, since she had a vicious migraine that was far more than a headache and caused dizziness and vomiting. Margot most willingly offered to stand in for her, and I had to yield to Mr. Nicolaid's urging that I go with them and see for myself how much the capital had changed after just five days of wartime regulations. Before I left, I had a difficult conversation with Sophie: she categorically refuses to see a doctor, and so I told her, in my calm way, that I'd be forced to call in Doctor Fundățeanu, whether she liked it or not. I have to admit that it wasn't a suitable moment, in view of her state of nerves. In any case she reacted violently, out of both modesty and stubbornness, and I left feeling bad that our altercation had taken place *devant les domestiques* (which is something we both hate). There are times when it seems that everything is over, and I no longer hope for any understanding between us. In the automobile I tried to conceal my true state of mind from the other two, who kept teasing each other and behaving very tenderly. I've heard that *ils ont toujours été raisonnablement heureux en ménage,* and their spectacle aroused all kinds of bitter impulses in me.

Suddenly I realized that what I felt was straightforward *envy*—something I have had the good fortune to experience only rarely in my life. Embarrassment and, above all, the sight of the animated streets calmed me down. Or rather, what I saw from the car replaced my personal disgruntlement with a more legitimate collective anxiety, quite different from the torments of jealousy and discord, which fill you with darkness and are as humiliating (and absolute!) in their control as the pangs of hunger.

Already in our part of town, but more and more as we went into the center, the shops were decorated with the Romanian tricolor and the Allied flags, and the walls were papered with declarations and announcements that I had mostly read in the press. As we slowed down near Piața Matache, my eye caught one addressed to SOLDIERS!

THE NATION WILL HAIL AND BLESS YOU DOWN THE AGES!

I don't think it was nervous fatigue that brought tears to my eyes, but in any case I felt that familiar rush of emotion and idealism that people close to me often look for and reproach in me, creating a permanent sense of shame and guilt. How can you feel like crying over those royal decrees? More lucid minds criticize them in every way possible, while the ordinary run of people pass them by in their dazed wandering between market stalls and bread lines.

The city, almost deprived of its usual transport, has a strange look about it. It was only this evening that I realized how lucky I was, since most of the automobiles, cabs, and taxis have been requisitioned for the front—a sign that things are not going too well there. Against the background silence, the noise that came from passing military vehicles seemed even more strident than before, while the trams are so few and far between that people travel hanging from the steps. The sidewalks are filled with people who have bought up whatever there is to be had, panic stricken that the supplies of eggs, meat, milk, and even bread are running out.

When I reread the notes I have just written, they seem so naive and awkward that they could be the work of a schoolboy. The old story: you feel one thing, and put another on paper. I'll carry on, though, without deluding myself, aware that the essence escapes me.

Take, for example, the stupor on people's faces, the sense that history is playing one of its tricks on *us*. We are indeed a sacrificed generation: that's not just one of those high-flown ideas to which we have grown so accustomed that we pay them no attention. I have felt the same astonishment, hour after hour, since the bells rang on the night of 14 August to announce a general mobilization. Words I have so often repeated to my students—collective destiny, fate of the nation, history—now have a quite different ring, which I would describe as somber and religious. The thoughts that pass most often through my head are not mine, since although we fear for ourselves and our loved ones we all wish and hope for the same thing . . . This is why I thought I could read the same thing on the faces of people in the street: stupor that it's actually come to pass, anxiety about the times ahead, mistrust, and patient endurance—our well-known capacity for endurance, which can serve us either well or badly.

Before I entertained these banal reflections, however, I had felt a state of elation at the North Station. The solemnity emanating from that modern construction, the echo of our steps among all the others, the excitement of the crowd: all this produced the familiar lump in my throat, almost before I saw the first soldiers' faces and bluish-green uniforms. Some of them were standing around, others sat on the edge of open goods wagons. We, who had come to see them off, had the certainty of being present at a solemn occasion, so unlike any other that selfless dedication seemed the most natural thing in the world. At those moments I thought of making a special effort to enlist, but I knew only too well that they would turn me down. Evidently I am not yet able to accept the position on the sidelines to which life has driven me, and to which I will be confined more and more from now on.

Patriotic voices were singing *To arms!*, some boldly aware of their power and melodic quality, others unmusical and shyly restrained, as at an Easter ceremony. I sang too, of course, in a low voice. Many had come with flowers and were offering them to young men hallowed in our bookish imagination, placing the nimbus of our ideals around their swarthy unshaven faces. My gaze shifted from a pure-eyed schoolboy, his cheeks pimpled beneath closely set eyelashes, to a corpulent woman with a half-withered crimson bust held up by the tightest of corsets, and then on to a (probable) schoolteacher, already nearly bald and looking affected behind his monocle, a respectable family group of father, mother, and children, and a pair of graceful young ladies chatting under their parasols. But what's the point of such a tedious inventory of the human types that caught my eye? Can a collective soul ever be born out of such different bodies? How the simplest things can astonish me! And yet, standing on the platform, I could tell that what united us was more than chance and more than *destiny*, an impulse vibrating within us with the same silent cunning, but also the same force, as hunger or the urge to copulate.

Enough of these digressions! Regular services were suspended, and the military specials were packed to overflowing; two hospital trains had their roofs covered in white paint and an enormous red cross, no doubt so that enemy planes would refrain from attacking them. Mrs. Nicolaid and Margot walked the length of the platform handing out cigarettes and food parcels through the little windows; the servant followed them, carrying the supply baskets, while I accompanied them at a certain distance. Mrs. Nicolaid soon got through her parcels and began to hand out money; everyone became excited, because she didn't have any small change and kept fishing out a twenty-lei note and asking several men to share it among themselves. Of course many hands stretched out imperiously—me! me! me!—and her selection became increasingly hurried and random. I was pained to hear the coarse comments of those who were disappointed. They even revolted me, as life usually does when it suddenly drags me down from the clouds. It was also then that Margot caused a regrettable little incident, when she thought she heard the whistle for departure and threw the last packs of cigarettes toward the train. The poor men jumped on any they could see, jostling and shouting at one another, even trampling on hands with their boots. All this scuffling once again confronted me with the poverty and primitivism of our people. Given my general volatility and melancholy tendencies, the beautiful scene that had gone before shattered into more mundane fragments: one man picking his nose, several playing a dice game, another relieving himself in almost full view, a group making crude remarks to our noble-minded ladies, another trying to chat up some Hungarian serving women . . . My familiar bewilderment when I compare life's spectacle with my ideal image of it. But my self-censorship, which I introduced at more or less the same time that the interior minister, I. G. Duca, was decreeing wartime regulations, has had an immediate effect. I didn't allow myself to see anything base in the behavior of these men soon to lay down their lives for an idea, while I rode in Mr. Nicolaid's comfortable automobile, took my constitutional on Calea Victoriei, and drank my usual iced coffee at Riegler's. I would be a long way from the din of the North Station and its packed trains, on which toil-worn hands—you could see it from the awkward letters—had written: *Here come the Carpathian tigers!* or *Long live Greater Romania!*

I clearly wasn't alone in my moralizing. The upright Mr. Nicolaid, disabled from a previous war, waxed indignant when he saw and heard the street spectacle again: crowds out for a walk, terraces with sunshades, ladies and gentlemen making little nods of recognition, blowing kisses or raising hats, or letting off steam about the government ban on the sale of spirits. "How is it possible that nothing has changed here," he said, "on a day when the first casualties have been announced: more than five hundred wounded, and certainly more killed than we read in the reports? I find this fun-loving atmosphere perfectly shameful."—"Okay," sweet Mrs. Nicolaid laughed, "but then what are we doing here, *chéri*?"

On our way back in the car, Mr. Nicolaid told me about the troubles of his sister Nathalie, who married Judge Crețeanu less than a month ago. Honeymooning in Sinaia, at the Hotel Caraiman, not only did they have to worry about their proximity to the front—*pauvre* Nathalie's hat had been crushed and she whimpered that something could happen at any time, in the absence of the usual laws and customs to protect them—but they suddenly found that the only train still running was indescribably crowded. Poor Crețeanu, born into a good family and previously unscathed by life, pulled every string he could to get their luggage put into one of the carriages, but there simply wasn't enough room. In the end they traveled in a goods train as far as Ploiești, where a brute of a soldier waved his gun and forced them to sit on the floor amid horse dung, respectable people mixed up with bad, the air impossible to breathe, complete chaos, fear of the itch and of catching something from all those unwashed bodies. Then a whole night in the station at Ploiești, without so much as a bench to sit on. When a train arrived, people nearly trampled on them in the mad rush to climb aboard. I asked Nicolaid to repeat his story over the lunch we later had at my house, but Sophie pretended not to see its relevance to our bitter quarrels over the wisdom of a summer vacation, and after the Nicolaids left she stopped speaking to me again.

In the afternoon I tried to get down to some work, despite the hostile atmosphere around me. With the future so uncertain, it seems a fault to put off writing any page until another day. For at least five years the Damoclean sword of war has been hanging over our heads, preventing us from settling down to anything really important. And, although I see my work as essential, I am not exempt from a nagging guilt that my slow, painstaking, utopian effort is at the expense of a book that could be brought out more quickly—or, to be more precise, could have been brought out more quickly. I remained in my study until dinner, being spared the labors of correspondence, which have anyway become much lighter recently. My general state is surprisingly good. Nothing major to report as I finish these notes. I have decided to do all I can to keep my *sang-froid,* and as for Sophie's distance I'll try to find a solution at a calmer moment.

23 August 1916

The weather is still fine. Victor Apostoleanu broke my total isolation with a long-threatened visit, which he made today because the courts still aren't open and the ban on alcohol has spoiled his habit of an aperitif at Mircea's bodega. He rang our bell at half past eleven, but we didn't hear it because of the artillery columns that had been passing for hours on end; the trotting of the horses on newly laid paving and the rumble of the carts caused our windows to rattle. However, there was no danger that Victor would remain unnoticed, since the rhythm of marching boots drew all the female servants to the windows. He had the excellent idea of offering the soldiers some water, and we shall try to make this a regular practice. Like many people, Victor is obsessed with the thought that spies and informers are among us, the clearest evidence being the bomb attack on Take Ionescu's house at the Atena corner of Piaţa Lahovary. He had just been there to inspect the damage. The curiosity of the local population had turned the bomb site into a free show that they visited when they went for a walk. Friend Victor said that Marghiloman, who supports an alliance with Germany, met with a hostile reaction when he showed up there, but it remains to be seen how much he was exaggerating. He's the kind of person who can be blinded by political sympathies.

He witnessed another scene today, when the king passed through the city center in a car, attracting a spontaneous display of support from the crowd. Pedestrians and shopkeepers, plus some old drunks who can't bear to abandon the bars, even if it means sipping lemonade, came out waving their hats and cheered *Long live the Romanian army!* Victor contrasted it with the Tenth of May, when poor King Ferdinand had gone among a silent and indifferent crowd, and when he himself—as he put it in a high-flown moment—had felt at one with the population at large, believing until the last minute that the Germans would never march in. Otherwise, he was in his usual foul mood, especially concerning the government and Brătianu's actions. But, unlike others he had heard today, he wouldn't go so far as to say that a defeat that allowed us to choose new leaders would be preferable to a victory that left us with the same old crew. (I omit the names he mentioned, because I'll publish these notes one day and wouldn't like to give the scoundrels even that much fame.)

How far can Romanians go in their lack of solidarity? My heart sank when I remembered the *mal à propos* speech I gave on the subject, on that tiresome afternoon just ten days ago. It wasn't so much what I said as who was there to hear it . . . Titi Ialomiţeanu!

When we looked at the map I've set up in the side room, on which little flags mark the shifting frontline in Transylvania, we were both suddenly struck by the length of our frontier. What army would we need to have to defend our borders *alone*? Alone, because General Saraille is stuck in Salonica, even though our entry has helped the French out at Verdun by diverting German troops here! Alone, because the Russians haven't sent as many troops as we wanted and aren't having much of an impact—just look at the situation in Turtucaia, where fierce battles are still raging.

Alone, on such a long front—a newly awakened people, whose organizational defects we know all too well! What if all Brătianu's plans, leaving nothing to chance, are blown sky-high because the agreements we made are not respected? What if the Allies lose interest and leave us at the mercy of an all-powerful enemy?

After lunch I worked quite hard, despite a sense of unease that crept over me, whether because of the general situation, or because of the situation in the house. My temperature is a little higher, for no apparent reason. On coming back down at five o'clock, I happened to be near the telephone when it rang. Mr. Ialomiţeanu—wanting to know whether it would be right to have his usual game of tennis with Margot! I decided to say nothing to the little one—who's anyway worried about the dangers facing her new heartthrob, Geblescu, at the front—and told him that I thought such a distraction might look frivolous in the present circumstances. There was also the problem of getting to the courts in Cişmigiu, since the few trams are completely packed, while private carriages and automobiles are not only difficult to find but can be requisitioned at any minute and sent off to Turtucaia. How can I, as Margot's guardian, allow her to go so far from home in these conditions? Ialomiţeanu behaved well throughout, as he usually does, although it should be noted that for the first time I didn't invite him to pay us a visit. I'd be relieved to know that he understood more than I actually said, and that this was our last conversation, since I realized afterward what a drain on my nerves it has all been. The fever grew worse after dinner: a shiver shook my whole body, I had a terrible headache that still hasn't cleared up, and I feel nauseous and generally weak. Sophie made a short visit to a friend this morning—still being *en froid,* she gave me no details—and has spent the rest of the day in bed, allowing no one but Madam Ana into her room. I insisted on entering myself and practically forced Madam Ana to open the door for me. But in fact I had nothing to say, except that Mr. Ialomițeanu had telephoned, perhaps telling her this in an unpleasant tone and forcing myself to watch the expression on her face. She was terribly pale—ashen, I would say—and looked at me *comme une bête traquée,* although her eyes had that stubborn look that infuriates me. The air of mystery surrounding her complaint—which, I have no doubt, is female—also infuriates me: her refusal to see a doctor, the primitive remedies she probably resorts to, my inability to control the situation except by shouting at her, and her egoism that adds new sufferings to the ones connected with my own illness. She didn't say a word all the time I was there. An hour has passed since then, during which I wrote these notes and went to bed, although I am unable to sleep. I can hear muffled sounds in her room downstairs, which makes me think that something is wrong; doors keep opening and closing, unusually for this hour. As I can't even smoke, the waiting is unbearable. Oh, my God, why is life sinking so easily into this unnatural agitation? Why do I have to live with my nerves on edge, when all I wanted was a little peace and quiet?

27 August 1916

I haven't been able to write a line these past few days, in which the defeat at Turtucaia has come on top of the problems at home. Minister Athanasiu suddenly took it into his head to call me this morning; he could tell from my voice that I'm a complete wreck and found time later to drive over here. I was alone, since Margot had gone with Madam Ana to the Central School (where a large number of the wounded had been taken), and Sophie was in the hospital for something that no one knew anything about; nor did I fill him in with any details. He's always liked being busy as a bee, but this time I didn't suspect him of putting on an act, especially when he told me that preparations were underway for a possible evacuation of Bucharest after the spread of panic from the Oltenița region. Yesterday they gave up the idea, but he's still suffering from the effects: it's not at all easy these days to be part of the government that took us into the war. As always, my unbearable state of tension eases a little when I am forced to come out of my shell and look around.

Georges was also in a bad state of nerves—worse than I've ever seen him
in the thirty years we've known each other—and he implored me not
to tell anyone how pessimistic he is about the way things are going. The
defeat at Turtucaia is first of all a material disaster: he claims that he still
doesn't know the exact number of prisoners, but it's quite possible there
were as many as twenty thousand. Plus all the artillery, machine guns,
and so on. But the demoralization is also very serious, and we all know
where that can lead. It will be necessary to bring troops here from other
fronts, he said, chain-smoking, and that could undermine the advance
in Transylvania. Well, I exclaimed, but someone must take responsibility
for what happened! He said that General Aslan and General Teodorescu
put the blame on each other, but that both of them have now been
removed. He's sure that our equipment is not up to the needs of modern warfare; our field artillery, in particular, is very poor in comparison
with the enemy's, and the other side also has airplanes for reconnaissance and fire direction—even a captive balloon. But low morale also
weighed heavily in the balance. At first our troops were numerically
inferior, and although sixteen infantry battalions and two howitzer
batteries were transferred from the strategic reserve in Bucharest, they
arrived too late and made little impact because of the lack of commu-
nication between the various field commanders. Precisely because they
knew that reinforcements were on the way, General Headquarters gave
the garrison a tragic order to fight to the last man! Later, with the battle
already lost, they failed to take measures for the army to retreat from
its position in enemy territory, its back to the Danube and lacking any
means to cross it. They completely discounted the possibility of a retreat
to Silistra, even though the solution evidently lay in the strengthening of
that city's defenses. So, panic took hold of our inexperienced forces, and,
worse still, of their commanding officer, who fled across the river on a
launch, leaving them to be killed or captured.

This was the situation he asked me not to mention to anyone! For
my part, I asked him to persuade Lisette not to visit Sophie in the hospital, since she will be out very soon. Despite Georges's tragic reports
and the general climate of uncertainty, our conversation was a source
of some comfort to me; we were as close to each other as in our youth.
I sometimes hear bad things about him, especially since he joined the
government, but I don't even try to ascertain whether there is an ounce
of truth in them. What would be the point? Having remained friends

with him for so many years, I am not going to start judging the man, any more than I judge my own family. I doubt whether we'd become friends if we were to meet for the first time today: I suspect that the mature Georges wouldn't be at all to my liking. But for me he'll always be the one who thirty years ago . . . twenty-seven years ago . . .

Since this journal concerns the present, not the past, I refuse to enter memories in it. Nor would I have the strength. This is the third afternoon that my temperature has been above thirty-eight—for reasons that I know all too well. Only today, profiting from a new apathy, have I managed to follow the diet recommended by the doctor. I ate lunch alone, feeling incredibly calm. Margot's enthusiasm for the war wounded has become excessive, and I had to remark on this to Madam Ana when they came back very late. I'm surprised at the stamina of these delicate *jeunes filles,* who faint at the merest trifle yet can spend hours among mutilated bodies and open wounds. Of course she's carried away by romantic energy, and over a coffee on the terrace—where I've been going in the afternoon since I opened the door—she told me of a Captain Feraru or Heraru (a battery commander, I suppose), who fought to the end at Turtucaia and committed suicide with some fellow lieutenants, rather than be taken prisoner. She was very affected by the story, and she claims that she met one of them, Ioachimescu, at a skating rink last winter. Even allowing for her excitability, it would seem that there was not only panic but also moving acts of heroism at Turtucaia. But I don't think her place is in the midst of so much suffering, and besides life is showing her a vulgar and absurd side that children of her age normally don't even suspect. Mrs. Nicolaid, who called round with her husband in the evening, said much the same things. They are affectionate people—perhaps a little lonely, like Sophie and I, since they are going out of their way to cultivate our friendship. They were overawed by what they saw and heard: Lucia Nicolaid, in particular, sat with the wounded they brought by tram from Obor Station, whom they are keeping in a vacant plot until conditions are right for them to be taken in. All their stories from Turtucaia spoke of hell on earth—for example, the one about a ferry loaded with wounded soldiers which, just as it was leaving the Bulgarian side of the river, was overrun with able-bodied men in flight from the enemy's withering gunfire, panic-stricken, climbing over prostrate bodies, jostling, crushing, trampling everything and everyone in their path. I shuddered at the thought of the groans and shouts, the swollen corpses in the water, the infernal shore packed with desperate men, some hurling themselves into the vast river, others fighting over a flimsy, holed boat or trying to float on a plank or box, still hounded by enemy shrapnel and bullets. What devastation, what waste! Then I remembered the names of the heroic officers who tried to resist the general panic, amid a crowd that could see no way out and thought only of saving their skin. What exemplary individuals we have, and how lightly we sacrifice them! How quickly the memory of them fades, trampled by the animal herd! What's the matter with us? Who is to blame for this curse? What will become of Romania?

I felt the familiar lump in my throat as I put one question after another to Mr. Nicolaid.

7 September 1916

I have made no entry for more than a week, living in a strange spiritual numbness, only occasionally stirred by pricks of shame and bitterness. But paradoxically, and despite the many air-raid warnings, I have managed to press ahead with my work. In these moments—what a strange utopia!—I imagined that Sophie would remain in the hospital and that my life would continue in this tranquility of which I have dreamed for so long. Someone might think it cruel or pettily selfish on my part, since God has already punished her for the harm she did me, but the fact is that I wanted her to be far away *pendant des mois*. I suddenly realized what a torture it has been, and felt surprised at how I have borne everything almost without noticing it. I also find it surprising that her absence seemed such a relief. Incredible! No regrets, no nostalgia! But how is it possible to suffer so much for someone whose absence does you such good, and who therefore gives you nothing through her presence? I didn't want to continue this dangerous line of thought, so I went out for a few hours, taking up invitations I had refused in the past and doing various other things. And, although the city was dark and empty, I felt unexpectedly good. *J'avais le coeur léger*—even a sense of a new beginning (which I have experienced a few times before), as I fought off the shameful ache in my soul. Again I reached the conclusion that, if my conventionality hadn't prompted me to start a family at a time that already seemed late in life, and to give myself up to feelings that were actually quite lukewarm at first, I would have been able to lead a more adequate existence, free from any servitude of the heart. Ah, the dream of serene indifference!

As I reread what I have just written, I wondered whether my new sense of relief was due not to real indifference but, on the contrary, to the fact that Sophie is in an isolated place where I am no longer forced to watch her. I couldn't make up my mind whether this was the case or not. I have often observed the impurity of affection, in both myself and others, struck by how quickly it can become mingled with hostility, boredom, escapism, or emotional links to long-lost feelings, not to speak of (sometimes violent) urges that drive you out of yourself, or the kind of need for a beautiful idyll that born dreamers feel. People rarely allude to this tangle of feelings: it is considered somehow unseemly to mention it; we all know it exists, but we don't bring it up in conversation.

I have resumed my journal today because my peace of mind vanished on my way home with Sophie; *mais c'était à prévoir,* even though things seemed to start off well enough. How politely I helped her into the automobile, and so on, taking care to ensure that others weren't able to read what was on my face. In fact I hated her terribly, with a repulsion that didn't stop me from suffering terribly at the same time. The mere sight of her produced a physical pain, in the same way that an old wound sends toxins all through your body. I tried not to think of the man whose kid might have killed her, and still less did I ask her anything about it. Normally, after such an episode, a marriage of this kind is dissolved by the Good Lord. But was that really what I wanted? When we reached home, she said that she didn't want her suitcases to be unpacked: her idea was to leave for Buzău with Madam Ana. Impossible—I said to her, laconically. In peacetime I would have accompanied her there myself, as wayward young ladies used to be taken to a nunnery! But now, when it's almost impossible to leave Bucharest in an acceptable way, and when there's a risk that you won't see anyone who does leave for a very long time, her insistence seemed to me a stupid and tasteless game of blackmail. She kept repeating the same demand, in an artificially cheerful tone, and Madam Ana's constant wailing made it look as if I was a crazed tyrant. Angry at the falsity of the situation, I said she must need to rest and left them there alone. But for the next two hours I paced up and down my study, unable to do a stroke of work. Perhaps I could have done some if I'd started at once, but I was shaking like a leaf and couldn't get our conversation out of my head. It can't go on like this, I muttered several times through my teeth. I was also suffering because I was unable to smoke. They called me to the table, so I managed to resist lighting a cigarette. Five weeks now since I gave up! Before setting eyes on her, I decided not to go to her room again or to start any conversation, except, of course, when there was someone else present. From now on, at least, appearances must be kept up, because the servants' gossip is one of the things that make me suffer. How humiliating it is that Madam Ana knows—perhaps not the truth (the whole truth?) but incomparably more than I do. On the morning of our return from the hospital, when I got out of the carriage and the old woman started her wailing again, I couldn't help pointing out that she'd nearly been the death of Sophie! But over the next few days I wondered whether I wasn't blaming her too much (she's just an ignorant creature, after all), so as to avoid heaping guilt on the one whom, even now, I often imagine to be innocent. But what makes the situation truly unbearable is the vulgarity of it all, which drops on my head like water thrown from an attic window onto a passerby. I suffer because I disgust myself much more than others disgust me, and because I know that my weakness keeps our trivial conflict alive. The proof is that, despite my earlier resolution, I accepted at once when she asked me rather timidly after lunch to accompany her on a short walk in the garden. The only excuse I can give is that Margot was also there at the time. Besides, a love of the garden is probably the only feeling I wouldn't doubt in Sophie. As I walked along the path, bending now and then to snip off a wilting rose that she pointed out to me and carefully putting it into the basket, I made great efforts to engage in idle chitchat without mentioning any sore points. Unfortunately, I wasn't able to keep this up until the end. Although she came quite close, so that our hands sometimes brushed against each other, I didn't feel the slightest stirring of desire (her virgin-like timidity has always stopped me getting carried away physically). Nevertheless, her proximity had an effect and caused me to go back on what I had decided. It flashed through my mind that the answers to the questions that had been tormenting me—however much I had put them aside during this unhappy month—were to be found right here, in the being who was resting on my arm. So, plagued by curiosity, I said to her:

"If I could understand why so much mystery was necessary between us, after we'd become so close...I don't think the reason can be excessive shyness, or . . . To forgive what happened, I have to understand it . . ."

How would any rational being have reacted to such a tactful approach? She'd have answered in a few words, *voilà de quoi il s'agit,* and everything would have been all right—or as right as propriety permitted. But instead her eyes began to blaze with fury, and she sneered that she'd been expecting such an *attack. Qu'est-ce que cela veut dire?* I babbled in astonishment, unfavorably impressed that she had used one of that good-for-nothing Ialomiţeanu's pet words. I therefore repeated what I had said before, only more slowly and deliberately, almost certain that she hadn't understood it. *C'en est trop!* she shouted, with that lack of self-control that I find so vexing. She threw down the basket with the rose trimmings, no longer caring whether anyone saw us from our rear windows. *C'en est trop! C'en est trop!* she repeated, gesticulating wildly. I struggled in vain to keep up appearances by picking up the roses, as if she hadn't thrown them down on purpose, but I eventually gave up—partly because she was shouting so loudly that she must have been heard at some distance, and partly because I kept pricking myself on the thorns. I angrily took out my handkerchief to wipe away some drops of blood, encumbered by the basket on my arm, irritated by the mud on the path (it had rained heavily overnight, sparing us an air-raid alarm), and exasperated by her hysterics, whether feigned or really as crazy as they sounded, and her absurd charge that I had brought her here to stop her going home to Buzău, so that I could lock her up and drive her mad by interrogating her all night long! So, she wanted to go to Buzău, even if it meant risking starvation and death en route! "As you wish," I said, cutting her off. When I pointed out that she was again exposing us to the servants' ridicule, she seemed to see red at my concern for appearances and began to scream and sob even louder than before, accusing me of egoism and a coldness that had spoiled everything and broken her heart even before we married, etc., etc. . . . Well, if that was so, why had she gone through with it? What frightened me most wasn't the list of all my evils (which I mostly attributed to her malevolence, although on other occasions I had admitted to some in order to keep the peace), but the fact that her reproaches didn't seem to lose any of their vehemence through repetition. It was as if she dipped into an arsenal of weapons, then carefully replaced them for the next time, and the next, and the next . . . Disfigured by fury, looking ten years older, her face ashen-gray, she opened her mouth so wide that you could see where she'd lost a tooth after giving birth and neglected to have a false one inserted. Her lack of interest in her appearance, as if she couldn't care less how she looked in my eyes, was another source of annoyance. I asked her to calm down, but this seemed to have the opposite effect; her bad upbringing was evident, despite everything she claimed. She shouted that it was too late, that I could have avoided it but there was no point in asking her now ... The fit of hysterics, her swollen face, the spite on her thin lips and pointed nose, the contortions that accompanied her outburst and aroused in me both pity and rage, remorse and disgust: all this made me completely beside myself, as if a red shadow had descended over my face. I felt my blood boil, and I must have looked a dreadful sight as I gripped her by the shoulders and shook her. Shut up, will you be quiet! I think I shouted at her, feeling a deep need to lash out but trembling at that very need. But although the urge was dizzyingly strong I didn't allow myself to do more than pinch her—I think it is vile to strike a woman; if I'd begun it would have been very difficult to stop. I already saw her in my mind's eye, lying on the ground and silently beseeching me—in vain, though, because her weakness would fire me up even more. How much cruelty there is within me! Yet it remains an unknown quantity—except for those early childhood years, when I can remember torturing earthworms. I should never have confessed that to *her*, because she'll always use it to string together the most absurd accusations.

It was as if I'd opened a door just a little and, glimpsing something I didn't want to see, had closed it again immediately. Do such depths of cruelty lie inside every innocuous man of culture, or do I have the humiliating privilege of being a degenerate form of humanity? When I thought about it afterward, I didn't know what to reply. Yet that moment when I held back and contemplated the cruel spectacle in the making— I'd never have recovered if I'd actually lost self-control—shows that I am capable of mastering my impulses.

But what was I to make of her animal reaction, which threw me off balance, and which I cannot describe more closely? Acting in a way that came naturally to her, without my sense of scruple, she threw herself at me and lashed out wildly—not pausing to consider that, whereas men often raise their hand to strike, a woman who does the same flouts the image of her sex. At the same time, she shouted the lie that I had hit her, so that my scornful riposte, much stronger than is my wont, was fully deserved.

I have no more strength to write, nor any wish to add further details to complete this ignoble scene. She ran off to the house in tears, shouting to me not to follow her—which I had no intention of doing. As I walked on to the pavilion, I realized that to spend any longer with her could only mean further humiliation and suffering. I felt nothing but disgust for us both, almost without differentiating between her and me, whereas she, in her obtuseness, persisted in seeing herself as the victim and me as the tyrant. Her judgment is so skewed that I no longer suspect her of deceit. Things might work out again if she made a tiny effort. But no, she keeps heading toward destruction, so blindly that I'm seriously beginning to think she is mad. I've become almost certain that she inherited a form of neurasthenia. But what hope can there still be once we start treating each other as neurasthenics?

It was unpleasant in the pavilion: a few damp autumnal days have been enough to leave a musty smell; spiderwebs cling everywhere; and there are heaps of dust and dried leaves. A bird left its droppings on my head as I passed under the walnut tree, and I kept trying to wipe them off with a handkerchief; we used to find that kind of thing amusing as children, when we thought it would bring good luck. I immediately had a fit of coughing and, to my amazement and shame, I found myself regretting that I was here alone, instead of sitting with her at lunch or dinner. Does this mean that, utterly disgusted though I am with her, I would still like to blackmail her with my illness? To obtain what?

The upshot of our fifteen-minute walk together was a wasted day for us both. When I calmed down, I went to my study and spent the time until dinner filling my *Papierkorb* with crossed-out sheets of paper. The only agreeable time in this hellish day was the half-hour before dinner, when it was still daylight and I walked hand in hand with Yvonne down side streets leading to the Avenue—the same ones that Father used to take me down. (Once—it must have been a year or two before his death—he was feeling happier than at any previous time in his life, mostly because the house had recently been finished in accordance with his modest plan, but also because the job of internal decoration was over.) It was nice and peaceful today, and the blue-painted street lamps hadn't yet been lighted, so I thought for a moment that the war wasn't happening—nor, of course, my personal drama.

Sophie didn't come down to dinner and sent word that she was feeling unwell. I had a sense that Margot was also acting coolly toward me, but it's possible that my hypersensitivity was playing tricks. In any case, I was feeling calmer after my walk, and she and I went into the side room after dinner and, as usual, moved the little flags around on the map. Sighing, we had to surrender the town of Petroșani to the enemy. Things are still at a standstill outside Sibiu, for reasons that are as incomprehensible as ever, unless it's because some of our troops have been switched to the front in the south. Mackensen's offensive on the Rașova-Cobadin-Tuzla line seems to have ground to a halt, after a victory of sorts. The minutes we spent following operations, now proud, now anxious, were almost normal. My temperature has risen, but less than one might have expected on such a grueling day.

As I finish these notes, I am suddenly hit by the doubts that come over me especially in the evening, when my nerves are at their weakest. What if the aborted child was mine after all, and Sophie is blameless? If she's guilty, then things are more or less as I described them. But what if she isn't guilty?

11 September 1916

Today it was Spiridon's turn to leave the hospital. That means he'll be going back to his regiment—which is why Madam Ana has been bawling and squalling, as they say, this last week. Margot has added her own pleading, and even Sophie came after lunch to discuss what can be done. Although she denies it, I'm convinced that Spiridon's illness was cooked up with Mr. Ialomițeanu so that he could get three days' leave, since this has been very difficult to obtain since the mobilization began. In fact, she volunteered the information that Mr. Ialomițeanu had a hand in it, and that that was why she was so attentive to him on the afternoon before the party. Now, however, the doctors are so overwhelmed with the real sick and wounded that I imagine they're afraid to keep Spiridon in the hospital any longer. All that's left, then, is to make another appeal to Mr. Ialomițeanu. But, although I left her free to do as she wishes, she has promised not to meet the gentleman again and is putting pressure on me to approach him.

Why should I be more inclined to do it? I suggested contacting Georges Athanasiu at the ministry instead. But she immediately came up with the irrefutable argument that he's never given that kind of help, even on much simpler occasions. So, feeling that she was trying to force my hand, I said that I wouldn't appeal to anyone. The next day we were quite frosty with each other. I can tell that she thinks of me as selfish, heartless, and even vengeful. Has anyone stopped to think how difficult it is for me to get involved in these things, which seem to them simply a fact of life, whereas for me they entail demeaning and humiliating myself? Besides, whom am I supposed to ask? The man I assume to be her lover! After moments of resolute refusal, I began to waver a little today, especially when I saw Spiridon looking so glum, and not at all like a convalescent. Although he's young and sturdy, the poor fellow hates the army and the war. But can I say that I ever loved them? When I thought of how he grew up in our midst, like a little domestic animal, I even softened toward his faults. If I refused to help him in any way, it would be as if I were signing his call-up papers. In the end, they're only asking me to give it a try. Margot's argument seemed the most sensible and finally clinched the matter: namely, that life has become increasingly difficult but that, since Grigore was mobilized, I've been the only man in the house, and not exactly at the height of my powers. *Bref,* I suddenly found myself picking up the telephone, at the time of day when I knew I'd be most likely to get through to Mr. Ialomiţeanu. I certainly didn't enjoy doing it, but I also felt a kind of morbid attraction and curiosity, coming as it did so soon after I had decided to have no more to do with him. The attraction was very weak, though, and I wouldn't have given way to it if the aforementioned positive emotional arguments hadn't been so cogent. It seems idle to waste any more ink on this nonsense.

The gentleman wasn't at his desk, but I left my name and he didn't take long to call back. He apologized for his long silence, which he explained by his huge workload at the present time. This was how I discovered that he worked at the censor's office: it surprised me, but not really that much. His heated speeches in our salon, blaming the government for missing better opportunities to enter the war, had suggested he was on the side of the opposition, so it was quite an eye-opener to learn that he was a *government man,* with a job that meant his much-vilified Liberals had complete trust in him. How could a petty man such as he, a salon oppositionist, end up in the censor's office, surrounded by political secrets? It suddenly occurred to me that the stupid little questions he persisted in asking on every social occasion were not at all superfluous. Was it possible that we'd had a *mouchard* among us? Who exactly had he been snooping for (assuming, of course, that my suspicions are well-founded, not just due to resentment on my part)? Everything is so unclear, so much based on suppositions. Who was he working for—well, we shall see! In any case, certainly to feather his own nest!

Keeping my surprise to myself, I told him about the ladies' request for help in relation to Spiridon. Eager as always to be useful, he said he would see what he could do: we both knew, though, that such things were not easy at the moment; I must have heard of the police checks in the last few days to catch draft dodgers, sometimes without any legal cover, simply taking advantage of our usual chaos. I interrupted him to ask, with boorish pleasure, whether it didn't bother him personally to have to carry his papers around all the time. In so far as I could tell over the telephone, the question wasn't much to his liking. He flashed back that quite incidental responsibilities kept him in the capital, but that this was a temporary situation that wouldn't last much longer. The vagueness of his language reinforced my suspicion that there's something *louche* about him—as did the fact that, with typical adroitness, he then switched our conversation to the latest rumors. Despite my impoliteness, there was no change in his voice or his language. He always sounds diffident at first, but in fact he's capable of the most incredible nerve, swallowing absolutely anything, in what seems like a tactic to smother human dignity in the way he responds. It's an effective weapon with people like me, who are thrown by such a mean trick. In any case, contrary to the image I used to have of him (making allowances for his low intelligence), I now realize that he is in no sense a good man, and that he's capable of almost fiendishly disguising his resentment. Okay, that's enough! We discussed the practical steps in relation to Spiridon, and I insisted that I would personally take the application and the necessary certificates to the ministry. (He kept saying that he would collect them from my house, but I've had enough of being manipulated.) He didn't seem to be in the picture about Sophie's illness.

12 September 1916

An infernal day, despite its auspicious beginning. The mutual indifference that now governs our relations can change into hostility at any moment. Such is my mental state, at least, which I perhaps unjustifiably attribute to Sophie as well. As she is still convalescing, she wastes too much of her time on household matters. Maybe out of gratitude for what I did in connection with Spiridon, she has been behaving in a more civil way, showing various signs of affection. Today (as I shall describe) she even tried to show that she cared about me. It's not the first time I have noticed that people who bear you a grudge and even act badly toward you are capable of suddenly forgetting even quite major things you have done, and then on the following day going back to square one, without seeing anything blameworthy in their erratic behavior. This is not only true of women, whom you don't expect to be logical or consistent. Men also display the same tendency, which fills me with disgust.

Sometimes I think that life is like that (though Sophie sometimes strikes me as an allegory of life!), and that my desire for things to be neat and proper is too rigid and artificial. I try hard not to show anything, but the murky, confused state of our relations is continuing to gnaw at me. I fear that events have done irreparable damage, because my will and logical mind no longer have any power over my changed feelings. My fear, I repeat, is that there may be no going back. Fortunately, she can't read my mind at all—and in the end that suits me. But it is unforgivably frivolous to keep dwelling on this subject, at a time when air raids and bombs put us *en danger de mort* at any moment, and we constantly hear of the death of someone close to us.

Mr. Ialomițeanu and I agreed that, when I go to the ministry, I should use his name to make things go more easily. I left home quite late—later than I'd intended—because a journey to the center has become quite an adventure. I'd understood from Mr. Ialomițeanu that my audience with the minister would be confidential, but for whatever reason—either because he'd been exaggerating, or because exceptions to the rule are normal in this country and special intercessions happen all the time—I found myself in a waiting room filled with people. Although he'd said that I shouldn't line up like everyone else but go in as soon as I saw the door open, I didn't have the nerve to do that. My natural timidity and my principles together held me back, so I sat on a free place on a sofa, put my stick, gloves, and hat next to me, and started to wait. The problem was that everyone who went inside seemed reluctant to come out again, so I began to panic, especially as I had to go and arrange for some firewood to be collected. The others couldn't have been in such a hurry, because they seemed happy enough and chatted softly with one another about their reasons for being there—which, as far as I could make out, were the same as mine: to obtain provisional exemption from the draft. Some argued their case in confusing detail, while others gesticulated and looked nervously around them, knowing that the place was crawling with spies. Increasingly irritated, I pulled my watch out of my jacket pocket, counted the minutes that each one spent inside, and tried to make a little calculation—a futile effort, if ever there was one! Apart from anything else, many simply barged in or took an official inside with them (as I'd been advised to do); no one saw any point in protesting about this, because they feared it would count against them when their turn finally came. It was going to be hard enough anyway! And the outcome was so important for each applicant.

To keep calm, I forced myself to pay more attention to the conversations around me, thinking that I might hear something of interest to note down in this journal. Unfortunately, however, they were all so boring and full of platitudes that I'd have preferred to have my ears stopped up. I was amazed at the complexity of relations in our society, if such motley company could become party to a private audience with a minister. Or had Mr. Ialomițeanu lied to me from the beginning? The others spoke assertively, and in profuse detail, of the exceptional circumstances they had invoked for X's son, Y's nephew, or Z's son-in-law. In fact, X, Y, and Z are all well-known figures, who persistently called for Romania to enter the war and are now trying to get their relatives safe (I won't give their real names even here, because I know these pages will be published one day, and I don't have the heart of a Saint-Just). But what else were the rest of us hoping to achieve here, with our various supporting documents? Perhaps we had better reasons but fewer chances—and therefore more venom in our tongues. It's natural that one exception should bring ten more applications in its wake, and so on, and so forth. Sure, the war had to be waged, for the sake of Romania's territorial integrity, but each of us had the right to get our loved ones out of the way of danger! I couldn't help but note the illogicality, just as I couldn't help taking out my watch and pointlessly looking at it one more time.

At one point a young man who looked like a court clerk came and sat next to me, his neck slanting crookedly over his left shoulder; he had ink-stained fingers and dirty fingernails, coarse, unsightly features, and stupidly dreamy eyes. He could have been a university student, who copied documents just to earn his keep, since he took a few newspapers

(*Adevărul, Steagul,* etc.) and a novel (Anatole France's *Thaïs*) from the pocket of his loose, shabby, grease-stained jacket.

He put the papers down and began to read *Thaïs*. His head slipped even further to the left—toward me, that is—and I noticed that a peculiar smell was coming from his half-open, obscenely purplish mouth, mixed together with an implausible perfume, *Heliotrope blanc,* that he had sprinkled onto his handkerchief and lapels. I immediately recognized it as the perfume that schoolchildren used to rave about in my youth, such a long time ago!

From time to time, he shook the shiny black curls on his head into place, sending some more dandruff onto his shoulders. The disgust I felt also gave me a kind of perverse pleasure, and I thought that perhaps I should be more indulgent toward this well-educated, good-mannered young man. But it was no more than a thought: in the end, I moved away slightly instead, unnoticed by my studious neighbor, only to hear someone else say: "Excuse me, would you mind?" I therefore had to move back closer to the young man, who put his papers on his lap and shifted to his right, while a stocky aging woman on my left almost knocked me out with a cloud of strong perfume that I was unable to identify.

For a while she was taken up with her huge and cumbersome hat, which she loosened and then refastened on her oversized bun of hair, moving so forcefully that I, with my delicate nerves, imagined she was packing it into her brain. Though tightly corseted, her large bust overflowed and put the buttons on her dress under severe pressure. A fur stole (completely out of place at this time of year, when a bright blue sky still shone through the window) partly covered the grayish-white locks at the back of her head and the hump of fat that gave her back its rounded shape. When she had finished adjusting her hat, she began to tell a white-goateed man opposite her how she had had to fight to keep the concession on her newspaper kiosk, when her husband, may he rest in peace, passed away in February, and many others had wanted to trample on her rights as a widow. Now everyone was saying it wasn't worth her while to keep it, and, to make matters worse, her son had been called up for military service, even though he'd already been declared unfit once before. So here she was again: please, mommy, you go and ask, I'm no good at these things! Well, what about her? Wasn't she so shy that she'd nearly faint when she was called in for the interview? And things were so difficult at home: a daughter to be married off, another older one, given for adoption at an early age, who'd married a man from Oltenia and was living in the Pantelimon area of town, although now he'd been called up too and left her with a string of brats to look after.

By now a bundle of nerves, I took my watch out again and looked at it. How can you love humanity when you're surrounded like this and have no way of escaping? To get away from them, I'd have had to stand up and remain on my feet for God knows how long, which wasn't possible in my state of health. It also annoyed me to think that Mr. Ialomiţeanu had been right to advise me not to line up. I couldn't help noting that my principles had deserted me once I was in the same position as everyone else. Although I might have subtler arguments, and look with a "cold and clinical eye" at those around me, we were all in the same wretched boat. What was the difference between me, who was opposed to special favors in theory, and those who thought it natural to try to get some for themselves? We were all seated on the same plush sofas, looking at the same little square gold-edged mirrors on the same door, and noting the same anxious looks on each of our faces. I told myself that I wasn't trying to flout the law for my own sake, that I was helping out the son of a widow, that I was already at an advanced age, and so on. But, in comparison with a dubious altruist such as myself, wasn't it easier to pardon the woman beside me, who, like any other mother, found it impossible to understand a law that put her children in harm's way? Or wasn't it easier to sympathize with a young man's fear of death, even if he had bad breath, a misshapen face, and crumpled clothes?

More and more desperate in front of the firmly shut door, I struggled to ignore my constant wish to see myself in a more favorable light. The truth was that I no longer had any wish to see either myself or the others. No need to look at my watch to know that, if I didn't make up my mind in the next quarter of an hour, I wouldn't for the rest of the day either. As for collecting the wood, it was now out of the question. Here I was, sitting on the sofa like a sick pensioner and letting bolder ones walk all over me! Seized by this thought, I stood up so resolutely that I crushed the hat of the woman next to me—after all the trouble she'd taken, at the risk of piercing her little brain. I muttered a feeble apology, grabbed my stick, gloves, and hat, and surprised even myself by directly approaching a secretary who—*oh, Fortuna!*—happened to be crossing the room at that moment.

Five minutes later they registered the application, along with the medical certificates, and promised to look into the matter. Happy to have fixed it, I who can't stand "fixers" felt like a virtuous woman at a ball who has managed to flirt as well as the rest! I then set off for the firewood depot, in a cab that had appeared from nowhere, as if from the bowels of the earth. Fortune was smiling at last, and my mental state was calmer all the time. Usually, the poor districts on the edge of Bucharest depress me with their monotony. But today my heart softened at the sight of the hovels, with their tiny windows and muddy flea-infested yards, their dogs and chickens, their sniveling children dressed in rags, and their mothers worn by toil, hair carelessly tied in a shell shape, skirts fluttering as they bent over a stewing pot or a washing tub. The poor women, left alone with a brood of children, waiting for husbands away forever in the army, or, without knowing it yet, having no one to wait for anymore.

Soon I caught a first glimpse of the endless line outside the firewood depot—mostly women, though some were older and more hunched. The crowd was far larger and far more desperate than the one in the minister's waiting room, so I realized that there could be no question of slipping in round the back. The people waiting there resignedly would have turned at once into a hydra and torn me to pieces, their pleasure all the greater because I wasn't one of them! I tried hard to recall the name of an official who had served me promptly once before. *Je lui donnerai sa pièce* right from the start, but what the devil was his name? I remembered his face and the precise occasion, but not his name. As I thought and thought, I breathed in gulps of fresh air that felt like in the country (albeit with a little dust in it); the carriage hood was raised, and the soft midday light sparkled in the red and yellow trees that hung over the crooked wooden fences. A pleasant breeze had been stripping them bare, but I noticed one leaf that was suspended in the luminous air, no doubt held by some strands of spiderweb. It suddenly struck me that the blue September sky beyond was changing rapidly: I looked up and, yes, greenish-white puffs were racing together and expanding like balloons, not at all like the inoffensive clouds that form in fine weather. The people in the crowd, to which we were drawing ever closer, must have realized that something was amiss, because many pointed up at the sky, hands covering their eyes. The happy shouts of children reached me from the houses we had left behind, and the general euphoria increased when five silvery toys appeared gleaming in the festive sky: five Taube airplanes.

Before I was even aware of the danger, the earth shook with a deafening roar. All that frightened me at first was the excitement of the horse, which bolted into a field in the opposite direction from the explosion—as I later realized—threatening to overturn the carriage, and flinging me around so violently inside that I'm surprised I wasn't thrown out. I'd heard that the key thing in such situations is to take a firm hold of the reins, and I remember thinking desperately that no one was able to do that. Black smoke filled the air, and the sound of screaming gave me the sensation of being in hell.

How long did this last? I don't know. Acting on instinct, either the driver or the horse brought the carriage to a halt. One of the wheels had flown off, leaving it in a terrible state. The driver was still shaking, as I was too. I had bumps and bruises all over me, and blood was trickling from somewhere on my face, but none of this really concerned me. The horse was covered with foam; the driver kept patting it with the palm of his hand, then took out a blanket and threw it over its back. It was becoming quite chilly.

I asked questions and made some pointless suggestions of my own, moving around and talking excessively in a strangely nervous state. I was shocked, of course, but the infernal day wasn't over yet. I wanted to hurry away to find someone willing to help the driver. First I scoured the sky for the little toys, which were no longer to be seen, then I set off for the alleyways of the nearby slum district. Once I got there, however, I realized that the yards of the houses were deserted, and that every woman, child, and old person was running toward the wood depot, where (as I only now saw clearly) the bomb had fallen. I decided to follow them, bareheaded and not caring about how I looked, limping more with every step, but driven on by an emotion that was neither curiosity nor pity, rather the terrifying fascination that draws you to the edge of an abyss. I didn't see much for quite a while, since people were milling around and obscuring the scene of the tragedy. *Tout à coup, j'ai demeuré pétrifié, mon sang s'est glacé dans mes veines:* I thought of the danger I'd have been in if I hadn't arrived later than I'd intended. Fate is blind, I said to myself. It chooses its victims at random, as when a number is picked out at a lottery.

One part of the depot was in ruins: the force of the explosion had shattered all the windows and wounded the officials inside. The first I saw had a gaping hole instead of an eye, and fresh blood was pouring out of it onto the congealed layer already on his face. Groping his way in the painful darkness around him, he was led by several women to the place where other victims were waiting to be taken to the hospital, many in such pain that they uttered chilling screams.

Feeling unsteady on my legs, I supported myself against a poor stunted cherry tree. I wanted to leave for home, but I didn't have the strength. What should I do next: cover my eyes or my ears?

Those who ran over from the slum district—women, children, old people—were shouting for their loved ones, but their voices were lost in the eerie expanse of the field. It was a swarming mass, some moving forward, others turning on their heels: occasionally you heard a shout of recognition and saw people in tears embracing one another. Everyone's eyes were pulled magnetically to those who found their loved one among the wounded, either at or on their way to the hospital collection point, whereas I for one didn't even look at the area at the other end where the still unclaimed dead were provisionally laid out. Quite a few were still searching for a relative or friend, looking more and more wild and dejected as they blindly knocked against others and kept returning to the spot where the bomb had landed (very close to my halting place). There, on the upturned soil stained with dark blood and gray matter, body parts lay waiting to be identified. I can still see, as if in a terrible hallucination, a man's leg with an army boot on the end, a severed hand, a bare-breasted female torso sliced in two diagonally, a bleeding heap that might once have been a baby, and a boy whose thin body was still intact, but whose head was completely crushed, toothless, and smeared with his brains.

Ah, how his poor mother must blame herself for sending him to line up in her place! The worst casualties had been at the front of the line, beside the wall that the bomb had flattened. Some helpers were trying to dig with spades or bare hands, while others shouted for them to slow down and take greater care, since there could be quite a few buried underneath. And in fact, shortly afterward, I saw two hands emerge from under the rubble. I shook with horror and vomited on the spot, not bothered about who might see me: all the artificial conventions of civilized existence disappeared, leaving me face to face with life's bare, cynical grin.

Pondering thus on our illusory way of living, my legs still shaky beneath me, I stepped aside as a truck and two cartloads of Boy Scouts arrived to take the wounded to the hospital and the unidentified corpses to the morgue. I turned around to avoid the sight and raised my hands to my face. Traces of tears, congealed blood, dirty marks, and bruises: I must have looked really ghastly, and indeed a woman carrying a pitcher of water stopped beside me, thinking that I was one of the luckier victims of the explosion.

She was one of the many who came to help with fresh water, clean clothes, and candles for the dead and dying. She held out a tin can to me, and I washed my face, rinsed my mouth, and drank thirstily. I then staggered on my way, but after a few steps I pulled up before a woman I had at first thought dead, who lay on the ground in one piece, not groaning but puffing slightly and staring blankly upward. An older woman, either a relative or just a compassionate soul, was bent over her, holding a baby who was fast asleep, its face covered in tears and dirt, two fingers wedged between its lips. Two scouts who had come up behind me tried to lift the prostrate figure, but they took fright when they saw a pool of blood beneath her skirt and heard her let out an unnatural shriek. As the old woman struggled to light a candle in the wind, the child woke up, took a look around and began to scream. I walked on, feeling sick at heart, until they were out of sight.

Why, for God's sake? Why? I wanted to shout to the bright blue, festive sky. Eventually I met up with my carriage driver, who had somehow managed to find someone to help him fix the wheel. It looked as if this would take some time, but I decided to stay and wait, because otherwise I'd have had to leave with one of the funereal carts. How would I have got another carriage driver to come out in these circumstances? Although it had been a warm day, the cool of evening was rapidly setting in. The hubbub at the depot across the field had slackened a little, and people from the nearby slum district were wandering back home. By the time the carriage was repaired, the only traces left of the disaster were in the wall and the earth. An eerie silence hung over the field.

In the carriage, shivering with emotion and tiredness as we made our way through bomb-spared streets, I suddenly felt I could see the world of convention and illusion spinning its web again. Ah, I don't know how to express this terrible sensation, which I've had before at times of great misfortune, when I've suddenly realized that this is the truth in everything we experience . . . It was after five when I reached home, dropping from exhaustion. I heard doors, shouts, steps, and on the clematis terrace

I could see Sophie's face light up amid the glorious red and green of the ivy. *Elle bondit de joie, comme un enfant.* They knew there had been a savage air raid: the house had had two alerts, and she had waited for me on the terrace, some sewing on her lap, as she used to do in the past. She almost ran up to me. *Quand on s'y attend le moins,* she said, laughing. And she threw herself into my arms, not caring who was there to see us.

I stroked her face, for the first time after a month of estrangement, but a strange coldness remained in my breast. We all dined early, and I had much to say, but I don't think I was very coherent. I kept shifting from one thing to another. No doubt it was an effect of the shock.

After dinner we went into the smaller room, where I read the papers and commented on the situation, while we moved the little flags around on the huge army map that Sandu Geblescu gave Margot before his departure for the front; I certainly made an effort to take an interest in something other than the bombing. It was being said there had been five hundred killed and a thousand wounded, but the injuries were such that the death toll was likely to rise. Bombs had fallen in many places, including Covaci, Piaţa de Flori, and Piaţa Sf. Anton. Seeing the effect the news had on me, Sophie insisted that I lie down and rest, because no one could tell what the night would be like. She stayed with me a little and made me take my temperature. While we were talking, she drew my attention to the fact that I'd come home without my hat and stick. She remembered how I'd looked when I got out of the carriage, and the sight of me had made her overlook this detail at the time. But, although I'd been in a confused state, I don't think I forgot them in the carriage; most likely, the man who had helped the driver to fix the wheel had made off with them. I tried to console her, especially about my antler-knobbed walking stick, of which she'd been very fond.

After she went out, I got down to describing the day in all its details. If I've given so many, it's only because of a fear of what I would have to relate at the end. But now, as I finish, I can hear the cathedral bells, and my heart is leaping in quite a different way from before.

15 September 1916

Dazed after three days of air-raid warnings: the zeppelins, or "zippiligs," at night; the bomber airplanes by day. I no longer feel so safe in the cellar since Victor confirmed what I've heard elsewhere: that some bombs can blast through three floors of reinforced concrete. We don't even relax after the all-clear siren has sounded at the Arsenal, but simply wait for the next alarm. Now we know what bombing means.

Clearly the enemy knows that the defenses in Bucharest are inadequate: we only have short-range artillery, and our aviation is up near Sibiu, where the situation seems really bad. The countless spies in the capital have passed everything on. That is why bombs fell near the houses of Filipescu and Take Ionescu, near the Brătianu estate, and so on. Marie-Liliane heard from General Averescu's wife that he intends to send a personal letter to Mackensen protesting about the bombing raids: it would seem that they no longer distinguish between military theater and political theater, basing themselves in both on active intervention.

Today I felt and looked less shattered, so I reluctantly went back to the center with the aim of trying again on Spiridon's behalf. All he's received so far is an order to report for duty within forty-eight hours. Although everyone in the house thinks that I've done all I can, my conscience reminds me that I didn't have the patience to submit the application in the required manner. I have therefore decided to see whether there might be a *porte de sortie,* no longer having any scruples *pour graisser la patte de quelqu'un,* if that's how the game is played. Mr. Ialomiţeanu, more unctuous than ever, told me that none of the applications presented at the audience has been accepted, even though a lot of pressure was exerted in many cases, and he intervened personally on Spiridon's behalf. I'm completely skeptical about all this. I have the feeling that for one reason or another he's no longer interested in us; it may be that he's now cultivating other contacts for his own purposes. On the other hand, he confirmed my hunch that the general staff is in a constant state of alert, that we don't have enough troops, and that the Russians are giving us little or no support. When the enemy breaks through at one point, men have to be sent there from elsewhere on the front. In these conditions, it's obviously very difficult to obtain an exemption.

Mr. Ialomiţeanu put on the jolly face he usually has when he makes grim prophecies. I asked him mischievously what reasons he had to be in a good mood these days, but he replied that it was just a nervous jollity. He went on to add that something is bound to crack at various points, and even become critical. *Bref,* the retreat will begin soon, the country will be occupied little by little, and we'll try to take shelter under Russia's protection—which will mean the end for us. He paced up and down his empty office, speaking in a low voice and looking nervously around him. But why did he insist on having this dangerous conversation? Eventually he took me outside: "*Savez-vous ce qu'on m'a raconté? Quelqu'un très haut placé . . .*" And he confided in me that most of our wounded in the last few days were caused by our own side; the shells we fire at German airplanes are of such bad quality that they explode only when they fall to earth! How depressed I was to hear this report, which I fear was all too accurate.

All the time, however, I thought there was something fishy: I couldn't put my finger on it, but I had no doubt that he was up to something. Whereas he used to be interested in finding things out from me, he now seemed to be dishing out information so that I would pass it on to others—all of it catastrophic and demoralizing. Otherwise, why would a man working for the government—a man who is prudence incarnate—run such risks for the sake of some idle chatter?

Although the news that all the applications had been turned down took a weight off my conscience, it was no pleasure to go home and tell them that Spiridon had no chance. I could imagine how Madam Ana would react, *qu'elle allait pleurer toutes les larmes de son corps,* and I decided to put it off by taking a short walk in the center.

We were spared air-raid warnings today. The city again looked different: gaping holes indicated where the bombs had fallen, but the special kind of energy released by a disaster had mobilized the survivors, uniting them not only in fear but also in the relief that they had escaped this time. Trucks and carts were carrying the rubble away. But tramps and other shady characters were also combing the ruins, where pieces of paper blew around and rags or torn clothing fluttered in the wind. Hammers and saws were at work on all sides, giving the impression of stability that comes from any normal work activity.

I walked glumly in the warm soft light of midday. Here and there a collapsed wall indecently offered a torn picture of domestic intimacy. As I neared Strada Covaci, I stopped and stared at a space cleared of rubble between two intact houses, like a gap after a tooth extraction. And on this newly vacant plot, candles arranged in the form of a cross were burning in the loose soil, while dahlias and zinnias rose out of stoneware vases. Passersby suddenly assumed a dull, terrified expression, probably similar to mine, as they sensed that this was not wasteland but an open grave.

A carriage drew up and an elegant lady wearing a thick veil got out and came closer; I helped her to place her bunch of white camellias in one of the vases, from which I had removed some withered zinnias. Standing quite still, she thanked me in a hoarse voice. No doubt she would have remained like that if an aged gentleman—his face was familiar, but I couldn't place it—hadn't come from the carriage and offered his arm to lead her back. She followed him without demur, while I too walked away, feeling a morbid pleasure as I imagined some personal drama.

Feelings high back at home. Margot profited from my absence to skip out for a bicycle ride on the Avenue. The impropriety of her action was as great as the danger to which she exposed herself, since all the shops close their shutters as soon as the alarm sounds and she would have been left in the open. Besides, the machine gun on top of the new museum rattles off bullets, and one of them can easily go astray. Just think: a young lady out unaccompanied! On a bicycle! I know it's the modern world, but we can't turn everything upside down. So I told her she would spend two days in her room—a big punishment for someone who can't stand being alone.

In the evening Mr. Ioachim, a former student of mine, called round. He's a shy, dedicated man, who's been exempted from the army because of his extreme short-sightedness. He's working at the Red Cross with Marghiloman (I recommended him, through Marie-Liliane).

He gave me news from the pro-German circle that sometimes coincided with what Mr. Ialomiţeanu told me this morning. For example, he'd heard from Mr. Marghiloman—who'd heard it from Petre Ghica—that our own shelling was responsible for many of our casualties. Mr. Ioachim seemed disinclined to believe it, though. As the newspapers become more laconic, there is a steady supply of rumors: some prove to be true, but I suspect that others have been spread to trigger reactions such as extreme fear, collective panic, and so on. A rumor that my critical faculties reject out of hand may serve someone's purpose, by latching on to our national tendency to self-deprecation, and there's always a suspicion that it might contain a grain of truth. When I said these things to Sophie, precisely in connection with the rumors about our artillery that I first heard from Mr. Ialomiţeanu, she flummoxed me with the information that Titi Ialomiţeanu has been on the best of terms with Mr. Marghiloman since the old days in Buzău. It even crossed my mind, quite absurdly, that he may be on the payroll of the German Legation.

However, neither his old view that we should join the war on the side of the Allies, nor his new position as a trusted government functionary, argues in support of such a hypothesis. On sober reflection, I thought that fantasy and resentment probably played much too great a role in Sophie's judgment. She puts on a disdainful look when our former family friend is in question. Such a radical change in one's way of looking at somebody usually points to something more than friendship. Everything suggests that *ils ont rompu l'amitié,* and if I really had a forgiving nature that would be enough. But is it?

No longer prepared to waste time on idle speculation, I have tried to see Sophie's new attitude to him as the result of his failure to act over Spiridon. "That was the least he could do, once you'd asked him," she said to me, as the lanky kid walked from his mother's arms toward the train door, carrying a backpack and stamping his heavy army boots along the platform. Although I have diligently made inquiries, I haven't been able to discover anything about how the case was handled.

A sullen atmosphere at dinner, with Margot confined to her room. In the end, I couldn't bear to deny her the pleasure of our game with the little flags on the map. She also went feverishly through the foreign papers, not only the Romanian ones, looking for details about our Lieutenant Geblescu and the Sibiu front. The supreme commander in Transylvania is the famous Falkenhayn, who was recently replaced by Hindenburg as head of the German general staff. During the two weeks that our forces have been holed up outside Sibiu, neither shelling nor occupying the city, Falkenhayn has brought major reinforcements from every front in Europe to teach the treacherous Romanians a lesson: a punitive war that will, I fear, be *sans pitié.*

A comparison of the foreign and Romanian press shows that our situation is worse than dramatic. Now we know that we're not prepared for mountain warfare, that we don't have the necessary weapons and equipment, such as mountain artillery and airplanes, and that our forces are fighting with heroic desperation to escape encirclement. All we can do here is wait with bated breath. A rumor is circulating that there will be another defeat like at Turtucaia, and of course many are criticizing our dilatoriness at Sibiu. Nothing new from the Allies. Mr. Ioachim said today that Brătianu is so unhappy with the Russians' passivity and disinterest that he's threatened to sign a separate peace if they don't send us help.

18 September 1916

Many casualties from bombing near Filaret. I was also sad to hear of the death of the eleven-year-old daughter of Ştefan Iosif; his great poem *To Arms!* is much loved by everyone. The disastrous end to the battle of Sibiu has deepened the mood of pessimism, even though most of our forces managed to break the encirclement, with inevitable losses of men, weapons, and supplies.

We know from the wounded that we put up fierce resistance, despite the enemy's huge superiority in machine guns, airplanes, artillery, and so on. We even lack telephones and have to rely on horses to convey orders in the field—which often means that the results of our reconnaissance never reach headquarters, and that reinforcements aren't sent in time to the right place. Bavarian mountain troops (a whole army!) were able to outflank us and begin to encircle our army group on the Olt river, before we realized at the last minute what was happening. Given this appalling muddle, the best we could have hoped for was to save ourselves by retreating.

Some still place their hopes in Averescu's offensive in the south. Our friend Victor, for example, argues that if it's successful the whole theater of war will change: Dobrogea will be freed from enemy control, Mackensen's army will be pushed further south, we'll continue our advance to join up with the army of Salonica, and that will finally open the long-awaited front in the Balkans. What mad dreams! Superstition even makes me regret having put them on paper!

19 September 1916

A special day in the calendar of the war. Despite the bad weather, I had to go out this morning for some humiliating negotiations over household supplies. It's the first year I've dealt with this personally, but otherwise we'd have risked going without wood in what will undoubtedly be the worst winter we have ever known. The general unease also makes things more difficult. Around lunchtime, revived by promises but tired of wandering in the pouring rain (no cab anywhere!), I was making my way home down Mihai Vodă when I noticed a crowd around a newspaper seller on the opposite sidewalk. As usual, I had been lost in thought and hadn't heard what he was shouting. I had just arrived in front of the Café de Paris. I hesitated for a moment, shivering under my umbrella and fearing the effects of the damp and my wet shoes, then hopped over the water-logged gutters to the other side of the street.

People were almost snatching the paper from the seller's hands. There were shouts and laughter, and I even saw two friends embrace each other. The remarks and exclamations more or less told me what had happened, but I bought a copy for myself, put my glasses on and stood in a doorway.

Our troops have crossed the Danube between Rushchuk and Turtucaia!

No less! Fuel for our imagination. Averescu's southern offensive at last! If only God would be on our side from now on!

It was after two o'clock when I finally got home, soaked to the skin. Sophie had been out all morning at the Society of Orthodox Women, and I sneezed nonstop as I shivered and waited for her to return. I was worried that the weather might have been bad for my health, so I had lunch served at once and went upstairs to rest. When I came down again later, refreshed by my nap, Sophie still wasn't there. My state of nerves was still good, however, and I donned some warm clothes and went onto the terrace. The air after the rain had a fresh, mellow quality, which I thought would be good for my health. I asked for the little table and wicker chairs to be brought out, so that I could have my coffee there. The downpour had left gleaming drops on the rosebushes, which have been blossoming these days for the second time. The most glorious sight, however, was not the garden—with its cover of yellowish-green leaves battered by the rain—but our modest curtain of ivy that covered the house and the whole terrace in perfectly divine shades of red, orange, and yellow-streaked green. How could one believe that such beauty is blossoming forth on the very eve of defoliation and death? Or that the murderous Taubes might appear at any moment in the clear blue sky?

Margot came and sat with me, wearing that new expression of melancholy resignation she has had since reports from Sibiu convinced her that Sandu Geblescu—her "fiancé," as she thinks, without much justification—died on the field of battle.

We were discussing the day's events when an automobile stopped at our gate and a spotless white-gloved hand waved to us through its lowered window. Then a sturdy but incredibly graceful form stepped out, curly-haired beneath her hat, smiling in a sardonic but friendly way: Marie-Liliane! Almost at the same time the other door opened on Sophie, radiant and waving a folded newspaper.

So there I was, surrounded by members of the fair sex demanding coffee and cakes and launching into heated conversation about the war. Detailed strategic considerations, realistic descriptions of battle wounds—pausing only to pop a candy from a Meissen bowl into their mouths, when they seemed no more than greedy children. Of course, they hastened to tell me the latest gossip from Mrs. Averescu about the crossing of the Danube: that we built a special road through the marshy plain of Flămânda and crossed the river on boats and pontoons; that the bridge is now complete; that we came under attack from the air and, as usual, did not have enough airplanes of our own. As I listened, I was struck by the frivolousness of the situation. I took on the comic role, completing my map of the war from the ladies' chatter—a grotesque, impotent figure on the sidelines of the tragedy.

Bowled over by my self-critical spirit, I turned my sarcasm toward the two ladies who share my soul, inviting them to have lunch, even though it was already late. They'd evidently lunched already at the officers' mess: they'd soon be receiving a uniform as well, I sniggered! Sophie paid no attention and continued her war stories; she thinks highly of General Popovici, who staged a careful retreat from Sibiu along the Olt valley. I was irritated by the starry-eyed manner that has become so familiar with each of her passing fads: Meyer-Lübke, Grigorescu, Kimon Loghi, Anatole France, Paul Bourget, Wagner, universal suffrage, Senate debates, constitutional amendments . . . Now it's the latest Austrian trench mortars, war of movement, survey instruments—what a waste of fresh energy! Petty jealousy drove me to ask her what was behind this sudden new interest in things, er, military . . . It even occurred to me that it might be Georges Ioaniu, but I can't believe that Sophie would be interested in someone with such a lack of imagination . . . Anyway I argued that, in the view of one not exactly old-fashioned man like myself, the sight of wounded soldiers is too shocking and indecent for the innocent eyes of ladies to behold. As for their charitable activity, it seemed to me pointless, because such respectable ladies were incapable (*que Dieu nous en preserve!*) of performing the humble and repulsive actions required by the suffering of these unfortunate, and mostly lowborn, individuals. So it would remain limited to not much more than a society game.

Was this a selfish outburst caused by jealousy? Who knows what Marie-Liliane made of what I said? I had the impression that a hint of sadness appeared in her eyes, remaining there until she stood up to leave. Sophie, who is rather less shrewd (but so attractive since the end of her conva-lescence!), *fut celle qui me répondit, et pas un moment n'entra en colère, comme elle avait l'habitude.* But, although she spoke in a gentler tone, she completely ignored my argument. "If you saw such a terrible sight you'd send me yourself to help out!" she exclaimed. Then, with a laugh for Marie-Liliane, she said that she'd been accused more than once of neglecting her wifely duties, and that this time—*hélas!*—it was not without justification.

I felt more and more uncomfortable as the conversation went on. Not only did Sophie seem unable to understand any of my reproaches; she countered with tiresome details of how she and Marie-Liliane had organized a Red Cross clinic in a school in the poor suburb of Bariera Vergului, because the public hospitals were no longer sufficient to handle the growing numbers of war wounded. This was how I found out where they had been and why they had come back so late, but I'm still in the dark about who arranged for them to go there . . .

Our conversation began to flag. But then it suddenly picked up again when we mentioned the alarming report, confirmed in the morning papers, that objects infested with germs or toxins had been found in the streets. Marie-Liliane asked me whether I thought enemy airplanes had dropped them, or whether killers might be lurking among us? I can't help feeling that there are spies and traitors all around us, I said.

When I looked at the two of them together, I felt so worried that it almost gave me the cramps! Yet I knew it was nothing serious, only a vague fear arising out of my conventional nature, and I didn't feel at all guilty when I looked inside myself. The only bad idea had been to bring the two of them together, but I'm the only one who knows why . . . Suddenly I remembered an unpleasant incident in my early youth, when my extreme innocence led me to enter a bedroom that was famous in Bucharest at that time. For years I suppressed all memory of those awkward embraces, of the faded charms that did nothing for me, of the semiadulterous hard labor that sullied the moral and intellectual esteem I bore for *her* husband. I was terrified that the foul deed might become public knowledge. On the other hand—what innocence!—I felt surprised that something so embarrassing, and so blameworthy by any acceptable standards, had aroused no regrets in me other than a cowardly fear that the truth would out. The heavens didn't look as if they were about to punish me: nor, in the monotonous days that followed, did the earth has-ten to swallow up this wicked Don Juan.

Marie-Liliane fell silent in the last few minutes before she left. Afterward—oh, the perfidy of the conjugal bond!—I came out with my well-rehearsed accusation that Sophie had come home with a friend because she had felt guilty about being late. What a mean ruse to discover the real reason for her visit! But it was effective, since Sophie replied that Marie-Liliane had simply wanted to celebrate with me a possible turning point in the war. I was flattered—although, when Marie-Liliane left, I couldn't but feel a pang that her face was becoming more wrinkled, her figure more rotund.

23 September 1916

Everyone is thoroughly disheartened. The picture of what happened at Sibiu looks more and more disastrous as reports come in from those who escaped the encirclement, either through forced marches over the Făgăraş mountains carrying the sick and wounded, or in the main part of the army, with horses, heavy weapons, and food supplies, risking an enemy ambush at every turn in the Olt valley.

Today the irrepressible Sandu Geblescu, Margot's official sweetheart at present, gave us his eye-witness account of the nightmare. Having been sent to the general staff with the tattered colors of several decimated regiments, he had to wait a few hours for a reply to the envelope he was carrying and, since his parents live in Craiova, he decided to use the time to visit his closest friends in the capital. I was a witness to the moving reunion of the two young people. The young man, who has studied law and economics in England, then recounted the night a week ago when, after days upon days of exhausting combat, they stumbled more than marched through inhospitable territory beside the roaring waters of the Olt, constantly forced to stop by screams of agony, by the terrifying sound of vehicles crashing into the ravine, by the lowing of pack oxen, sometimes as many as eight pairs, attached to the field guns and crates, and by the crackle of gunfire. The high valley walls echoed all the noises threefold, and our young lieutenant was convinced he would never see the end of the hellish night. He had only caught snatches of sleep for three days, and now he sometimes nodded off with his eyes half open, dreaming that the narrow valley might open out soon. A few times, when this did seem to happen, he sat on a rock by the wayside and slept for half an hour. It might be the finish of him, but it was all he cared about at the time. "Really, all?" his little friend protested, and there followed an interlude of *marivaudage,* in which, with all the boldness of the younger generation, they exchanged tender looks and meaningful smiles as if I simply hadn't been there. "So, how come you didn't remain fast asleep?" I asked, tactfully reminding him of my presence.— "My orderly, the faithful Ion, pulled me up after a while. Pure instinct made me strike out wildly, but the next day I regretted that I had been so brutal."

At this point we were interrupted by an air-raid warning. Once we were in the cellar, Sandu Geblescu told us about the Romanian refugees from Transylvania who have taken the uncertain path of exile; the Câinenii region is full of these poor uprooted people, who have left all their possessions behind and risk starving to death.

Our guest left immediately after the all-clear sounded, on the pretext he had some urgent matters to attend to. In reality, though, he was going to have lunch at Enescu's with a good friend he'd met at the general staff (as he told me in confidence when I was seeing him to the door). It seemed unforgivably frivolous of him to turn down our invitation to stay for lunch, after all the horrors he'd been through, and I was shocked by the lust for life that his whole being exuded. But then, as so often, I thought that I was being unjust. Didn't he deserve to enjoy a *jambon de Prague sauce madère* or a *dindon veau truffé* that he'd dreamed of when living off army biscuits? A fine spread, washed down with Pommery champagne and accompanied by a good-looking *chanteuse,* wasn't such a sin for a lieutenant who had proved his bravery and was the only surviving officer in his battalion, forced to take the command of exhausted and demoralized troops.

Of course he didn't mention the lunch at Enescu's to Margot. But isn't the essence of love to see yourself idealized in another's eyes, even if it means keeping quiet about a few prosaic details?

After he left, I was obsessed by the dark scenes he had described, and even more by the implications of the defeat. This was the beginning of our withdrawal from Transylvania! Our troops entered Transylvania to win it back from Austria-Hungary, but now, after no more than a hundred days, they are in headlong retreat from the land for which we've suffered so much. There have been reports of reprisals against our brothers and sisters there who welcomed in the Romanian army. How can you not become disheartened when you hear things like that? All we have left are our victims, our depression, and our dashed hopes.

It breaks my heart to think of the blood spilled in vain. There were a few little victories, in which our men fought with bayonets against airplane-guided artillery or managed to save a cavalry unit under fire, but more often than not this meant briefly occupying a position that should have been abandoned, had the orders arrived in time and a sense of reality prevailed. As it was, there was no point in the bloodbath and in all the suffering endured by mothers and wives who will remain forever inconsolable.

How can you raise your head when such cruel blows of fate are raining down? And why blame the gods, when the fault lies with us alone? From what I've heard, much the same has happened at Porumbacu and Bărcuți: hard-won positions that we abandon soon afterward on our own initiative.

Brătianu's fear of an attack from Bulgaria, and his calls for the Russians to send reinforcements for the defense of Dobrogea (which we dismissed at the time as petty and indecisive), prove to have been well-grounded. The Russians have sent far fewer troops than they promised, and have generally displayed a suspicious inertia. In the south we have therefore had to rely on our own meager forces, which are anyway not of the best. It looks to me like another defeat. Yet the accusations against Brătianu are coming thick and fast, more even than in the days when he refused to break with a policy of neutrality. "Why did he enter the war if he knew that Romania couldn't hold out?" my friend Victor asked yesterday.—"Do you think he's to blame for everything wrong with the Romanians?" I countered. "And for the Allies' desertion of us?"

I'm one of the few who still defend Brătianu against the flood of sarcasm and invective. What mockery we read in the press and in his opponents' speeches! In my eyes he's a real martyr, exposed to insult and injury whether he deserves it or not. All this betrays a provincial mentality, incapable of distinguishing between an illiterate and incompetent demagogue and a politician who weighs every step carefully for the good of the nation. I'm not going to heap the responsibility for disaster on his shoulders, even if I'm the only one who refuses to do so.

But maybe my pessimism is getting the better of me again. Maybe our retreat will stop at the mountains, where Margot planted her little flags this evening. Maybe our troops will hold out in our wretched fortifications, until the long-promised Allied offensive allows them to advance into Transylvania again. What else can we hope for if we are left alone to defend our huge frontier? Under massive attack on all sides, how can we keep shifting men from north to south and back again, wearing them down and sending them help only when it's too late? How can we not turn in desperation to the Allies, from whom we have so far received only unreasonable lectures, stinging criticisms, and unfulfilled promises? We wonder what they are playing at, but they still show no sign that they'll send us the promised assistance. Our entry into the war helped them out at Verdun, by making the Germans divert forces from the western front to attack poor Romania. And what have the Allies done in return? What's happened to the Russian offensive? What's going on in the Balkans?

For the last couple of days there have been rumors of an exodus to Moldova. Those who have the possibility are packing their stuff into trains and automobiles, and it seems certain that the banks are planning to move.

Part Four

Chapter 10

Geblescu

"Poor Niki! How happy he is when he goes into town and can meet someone he knows. Still youthful and vigorous: it's terrible, Madam Delcă, to
see how a man bubbling with energy like that can suffer from inactiv-
ity . . . In the old days, he'd have had regular clients by now and made
a name for himself at the Bar. He'd also have had a place in the world
of politics: parliamentary deputy, undersecretary of state, maybe even
a minister—you remember what that used to mean! It was something
you could put on your visiting card for the rest of your days: SO-AND-
SO, FORMER MINISTER . . . Sure, let's face it, it wasn't easy to become one,
even then. But it was different: people could get ahead in life, in a different kind of way, without having obstacles put in their way all the time,
until they got sick and tired of it all. Ah, poor Tudor! Poor Niki! And
poor Mr. Delcă, forced to keep slaving when he was already old, for the
sake of a measly pension! Poor creatures we all are—yes, Madam Delcă,
I often think that when I see how much we have to bear . . . I used to be
a happy-go-lucky soul, but now I've lost all hope. When I was young, I
used to dream of traveling and even fixed myself up with a grant—but
then the war came, and Muti refused point blank to let me go abroad. I
gave in, because I was beginning to go out with Niki. I was sure there'd
be plenty of time: what's a year or two at that age, when you think you're
immortal anyway? That's how we all used to think. I was also sure that
Niki would make a career for himself, what with his gift of the gab and
his way of getting on with people. Besides, I could get Sandu Geblescu to
pull a few strings for him. Yes, I tell you, Niki would have had chances

if the times hadn't changed in the way they did . . . And now would have
been the time to enjoy the honest fruits of all his efforts, instead of his
joke of a pension, on the scrap heap after a lifetime of hard work without
any satisfaction. Retirement is no fun for women either, but for men it's
a real catastrophe . . . But, apropos of Niki, since he's obviously tied up
with that acquaintance of his, why don't the two of us have a little coffee?
No, don't move: I'm as good as anyone when it comes to making coffee,
even though I say it myself. Even Niki says he hasn't drunk anything
as good anywhere else. It's true he hasn't been able to travel much, any
more than the rest of us have, but he's got around a bit in his time."

Oh, yeah, got around a bit, has he? Just look at Ivona: the dumb broad's
had the table laid for him this last hour and she's still Niki this, Niki that
. . . I can't believe she's for real sometimes. Him a minister? Maybe in the
Land of Nod. She seems to lose her marbles when it's a question of her
Niki-Wiki; that's when you can see how batty she is. She's not a bad sort:
look at the way she's fussing around to make it up to me. Only there's no
more mention of those fifty lei. Maybe she'll remember when the coffee's
ready. Ah, poor Ivona! She may have a few screws loose, but here she is
with the coffee cups on a tray—like with special guests. She's even dug
some biscuits out from somewhere.

"Really, Madam Ivona, you should have let me do it. To think that I've
known you since you were this high! Your father had just died, and your
Aunt Margot sent me to fix your dress. I sewed some tucks for you and
took up the hem. We sat alone together, except for that German governess of yours, and you never said a word but just kept looking out of the
corner of your eye. I remember how red your eyes were, and puffed up
like fists. The poor thing, I said to myself. What a house she has—like a
palace, with everything anyone could need. But she looks so shattered. I
didn't need anyone to tell me how cruel an orphan's lot is."

As I say this, I see the winter when Mummy died. I can hear the wind
blowing outside, and in the house it's really cold and dark, with no oil
for the lamps and no candles—only a little votive light still burning in
her memory, because it's only a couple of months since she died, the poor
thing. How I jumped up from sleep when I heard knocking on the window. Come on, Vica, time to get up and go to school! And I groped my
way to the kitchen, lifted the lid from the pail, broke the layer of ice with
a soup spoon, and scooped up some water as best I could in the hollow of

one hand. Whatever you do, my poor mother told me, you must never go out in the morning without a quick splash. I still feel that water burning my face and my chapped hands . . . Get a move on, Vica, stop dawdling like that. Tincuța, my poor neighbor, was afraid of going out after dark. She'd knock on my window and, still half-asleep, I'd wrap myself up in some tattered clothes that Mummy had left behind. Then I'd bend down and tie some rags around the cracked soles of my boots; I might have been little, but I knew that if I didn't look after myself no one else would. I can still see myself as I was then, frozen to the bone, teeth chattering, as I crept out to buy some bread and slowly pulled the house door shut so as not to wake my sleeping brothers. It was even darker and colder in the line outside the baker's; everyone stood hunched up, dozing if they could, or else talking nonstop about so-and-so who's croaked or is lying half-dead or has just been buried or is due to be tomorrow, or about a woman in the next street who's shacked up with a German and for a few lei will darn clothes or get you firewood or permission to sell plum brandy—on and on they gossip, cursing and hardly pausing for breath . . . Trembling with cold, I clung as much as I could to Tincuța. I pressed my hands to my breast, inside my dress, but they still felt like two ice cubes, and the cold made my eyes water as if I was crying. So, when I say that I know how bitter is the orphan's lot, I still see myself lining up for bread in the dark and cold of winter. And, oh, ho, how many lines I've stood in since then; it's as if I've spent all my life lining up! There only had to be a crack of daylight and I see myself holding that horrible bran-stuffed block, more like a lump of rock than a loaf of bread, frozen solid in my arms, then racing home because I knew what was waiting for me there. I knew what was in store when I got back home with it. My kid brothers, all awake and screaming, would fall on me and shout so much that I wouldn't know which one to start with. Wash them, give them some grub, open the door to let in some fresh air and drive out some of the smell, then fetch some wood from the shed to light the fire, with those little red scratched hands that I seem to have before my eyes right now. Running a house or collecting firewood on your own isn't a piece of cake when you're eleven, in a winter that's come early and brought snow and sleet. That's why I counted the rows of logs in the shed, and why an icy shudder passed through me when I realized we'd got through another one. The neighbors started pulling things down—an old fence here, a hen coop there, soon it would be the turn of the trees. Then we heard there was loads of wood lying around on sites where they hadn't put the roof on before war broke out, so off I went with everyone to the new areas in Mihai Vodă and Vama Poştii. I remember two posh ladies wearing hats and Astrakhan furs, one hand in a muff, the other dragging a beam by a piece of rope. There they were, pulling it over the bumps and potholes on Strada Iancului; who knows where they picked it up from. I also remember an old man, a real gentleman with whiskers and everything, trudging in the snow with a wooden pile under his arm. Well, so I stopped and thought about it: if they can only just carry the stuff, I'm not going to walk any further and freeze to death for nothing.

Yes, I can see myself there on the corner of Strada Iancului, remembering how much I used to love going for a walk there in winter with Mummy and Daddy, and how Mummy would give me a few coins and I'd run and buy some roast chestnuts. But then there was no longer any brazier or roast chestnuts, nor any Mummy and Daddy, only a man propped up against a fence, once well-off no doubt, because he held out his hand without daring to open his mouth to ask for a few cents . . .

So I let everyone go downtown while I ran catching my breath to get back home before dark. I was afraid of passing Capra church at night: they bring so many coffins out and hang so much funeral drapery by the door, and then there are all the fresh crosses in the graveyard— God, was I afraid! I walked along the outer wall, eyes shut and using my tongue to make the sign of the cross in my mouth. I was afraid of the cemetery, although how long was it? a month or two, since they'd taken poor Mummy there. And there'd been so many others since that you didn't know who was where any longer. When Daddy came back, we couldn't tell him where Mummy was buried, or whether she'd got a cross or not . . .

"Yes, that's it, no one can give you back your parents or your health; once they're gone, they're gone. And you're left with no one to protect you, no one to complain to. Who'd believe you anyway? Even now, when I'm an old woman, the thought of it soon gets me going . . . My husband makes fun of me. 'What are you doing, Vica? Shedding tears for the mice to drink?' That's why I remember you so well when you were little. 'Go and fix my niece's dress, Vica,' Madam Geblescu said to me, 'because misfortune has come when we weren't expecting it. My poor brother-in-law, Ştefan Mironescu, is dead, and we don't even have the right clothes . . .'"

"Do we ever see misfortune coming? Poor Margot! Did anyone warn her of her misfortunes? I can see her so well as she was at the time: urchin cut, attractive-looking, slightly eccentric, the way people were in the roaring twenties. I was so fond of them, both her and Uncle Sandu. Yes, Uncle Sandu, Alexandru Geblescu—a real man about town. But he still had the patience to play with me. When I heard his car engine I ran and threw my arms around his neck. How nice his cheeks smelled, so soft and smooth after shaving, and how his wavy hair shone under the brilliantine! He always brought a little cake box up to my room, with Suchard chocolates and glacé fruits. I stuck to him like a shadow and giggled at all his jokes, which Muti said weren't all that good. Muti was never keen on the *chic* type of man, and wasn't very tactful in their company."

"No, I don't agree with you there. I never heard Madam Ioaniu say a thing about Mr. Geblescu. Not a word about how he and Madam Margot separated . . ."

"They didn't separate, Madam Delcă. I mean, not in the way you mean. He heard they were about to arrest him and managed to escape to the West. Didn't you know?"

"I can't remember everything. It's possible Madam Ioaniu never told me. And what she didn't tell me, I didn't ask."

"Well, now, how about a little drop of something, Madam Delcă? A coffee and a cognac, what do you say?"

"What a question! Will a cow eat clover?"

"Well, Madam Delcă, I see things rather differently when I look back from a mature age. For example, why wasn't Muti smitten by Uncle Sandu, whose seductive powers were obvious wherever he went? He was in the Clark Gable mold. All women felt drawn to him, like to a perfect stud."

"Oh, ho, I was pretty keen on Clark Gable too, not to mention Jean Marais—but not to have around the house!"

"No, believe me, not all women think like you do. Once charm and sex appeal kick in . . . And Alexandru Geblescu was certainly a charmer. All women went for him: none more than Tante Margot, who because of him forsook Mr. Ialomiţeanu's steady affection for her. He was terribly affected when he asked for her hand and was turned down: he never got over it. Ah, men used to love differently in the old days: it was one woman till death do us part! Of course they had their men's world—acquaintances at the Café Charmant, flirting at various salons, sometimes an arranged marriage—but if they gave their heart to a woman it was for ever, like in a novel. And, however late in life they met again, he loved her as on the very first day, as Mr. Ialomiţeanu did Tante Margot. In my opinion, though, the only man she ever loved was her husband. After they married, she had to put up with so many things. All those banquets that were the talk of Bucharest! Anyone who wanted to see Uncle Sandu didn't go to their home but to the Hotel Boulevard (he was crazy about French cuisine). He had no prejudices when it came to women and having a good time. You could even come across him at low-life dos, listening to a melancholy gypsy band and sticking a banknote on the singer's forehead!"

"What did I tell you? A womanizer, and full of airs and graces! Not the type to get mixed up with at all. They can keep their charm and waltz off with it . . ."

"Tante Margot put up with everything. His larking around, his mis-tresses . . . Niki's right when he says they were both one-offs. They were alike in some ways: she was also a spendthrift, and although a fortune passed through her hands she'd never have invested a cent if Muti hadn't given her advice. It was thanks to her that she bought their villa and vineyard at Otopeni, although as things turned out she'd have done better not to have had them. Everyone's fate is decided in advance. You think you're in charge, but in fact the Good Lord lets you go down a path that's already been laid for you . . ."

I wouldn't say this to Vica, but the truth is no doubt that Margot reached a point where she no longer cared about Uncle Sandu's esca-pades, and that she had some compensations of her own. She probably liked to have lots of money—otherwise what excuse could there be for a well-bred woman going into business! Her fashion house did have a select clientele, but still, what an idea! Besides, another husband would have simply forbidden it. Did he perhaps have more liberal ideas than other men at the time? Or did the indifference in their life as a couple leave each of them considerable freedom of action? That's what Muti thought. But I'm still inclined to think that Niki's right: that her fashion house was useful cover for Uncle Sandu's own rather murky dealings. Tante Margot traveled so much, had so many contacts in the fashion world abroad! And he went with her on each trip! Was he so attentive to her needs in this area, though he'd forgotten how to be a thoughtful husband otherwise? I've never discussed these possible explanations with anyone, and of course Vica's the last person I'd float them with. And nowadays it's healthier to know as little as possible about someone.

"Well, now, Madam Delcă, how about another little drop of cognac?"

"Well, yes, I'm looking at my watch because we have to go to a wedding this evening. When Niki went out, I told him he mustn't forget the church! But something in his look suggested that he had masses of things to do. As you know, you can read a man like a book when you've spent your life with him . . ."

"That's right. All I have to do is start getting ready and my old man's squirming around in bed. You should see the look in his eyes. The poor creep can't stand to see me going out any more. You're off and leaving me alone, he starts. Make sure you don't come back late, or I'll get worried! One day after dark, there I was on my way back from Niculaie's, shuffle-shuffle on my poor legs, and who do I see but my old man, waiting for me on the street corner. I couldn't sit around at home any longer, he said. I thought maybe you got hit by a tram. The things he gets into his head! And, you know, if you come back late again, I won't let you out of the house any more; look how my heart's thumping. Come on, you old creep, I told him—but it was true, his heart was really going boom-boom. He's like a frightened mouse since his hair turned gray. Come on, you old creep, I said, now you're afraid I'll pop off, but you've spent all your life giving me a hard time. There are others much worse than me, he said, because otherwise we wouldn't have been together for forty-nine years . . . Ah, may God grant you and Mr. Niki as much! Whatever you say, you can't keep your eyes off your watch! You're just like my old man."

"I'm just thinking that he won't have time to rest before the wedding. We don't have to go to the party afterward, but we must be at the church. Clemența—you know who I mean, Clemența Vrăbiescu, the bridegroom's mother—insisted on having it at the Boteanu church. The reception will be at home, with a smaller group of mostly young people— a lot of fuss and expense, and the girl's parents will cover everything. So Clemența didn't feel able to dish out invitations, or at least that's how she excused herself. Personally I understood this and accepted it. But Niki—you know what men are like—never says no to a bit of feasting . . . Anyway, Madam Delcă, you don't need to hurry off. I don't know how much longer Niki's going to be."

Don't you worry, I'm not going anywhere yet. My legs are like jelly after all that cognac, so I couldn't go even if I wanted to. Anyway, you don't seem in a hurry to cough up those fifty lei. So I think I'll just sit tight. You're so dopey that you mightn't remember to give me them until you've closed the door on me. Why shouldn't you do it now, since we're only a week away and then you'll have to put it in the mail? Why give the postman an extra five? Whew, my face is on fire, and what's this buzzing in my ears! I guess I'd better take a Hiposerpil: I don't want to keel over here! For God's sake, my head's all fuzzy, and she's still rabbiting on! That's why that jerk Niki is never home. She just can't keep her trap shut!

"I'm not worried, because what does poor Niki have left apart from a little tennis and an occasional chitchat? It's no fun retiring when you're still . . ."

"My husband's not like that: he blessed the day when it came. Now others can get up at four-thirty to start the six o'clock shift. Let them stand around shivering for that goddamn tram. He's happy waiting for the postman to deliver his pension: that's all he worries about now."

"If you don't mind my saying so, it's not quite like that, Madam Delcă. I'm sure Mr. Delcă couldn't wait to call it a day, and the poor man was right: the years had already been creeping up on him when he had to switch from being a tradesman to a factory job. But things are different in the case of Niki—or of Mr. Cristide, the engineer, you know who I mean? I can still see him down there in the street, on his way to work, punctual like clockwork for thirty years. What do you expect, Madam Delcă: he studied in Germany and got a doctorate, then worked there for a while; it was that that got him into trouble later . . . He doesn't talk about his time in prison, or about the years afterward when, as he hinted to me, the Securitate kept a close watch on him . . . They also tried to get him to inform for them, but he's a man of honor and wasn't having any of it. He never mentioned it to anyone—except to *her*, and of course she spread it around in no time. Yes, she's a nice enough woman, but he's irre-proach-able . . . Now I'm the only one he still talks to when he comes across me in the street: he feels there is a kind of rapport between us . . . No, no, how can you think that? What a funny idea! I've never given Niki any reason to be jealous. Ha, ha, ha, what a scream you are, Madam Delcă! Here, have another cognac, just a tiny little drop! Yes, of course I will too. Now, where was I? Ah, yes, Mr. Cristide, the engineer. He had to take his pension, because although he'd have liked to carry on . . . you know how it is, with restructuring and all that—although, come to think of it, you've never actually had a job, have you? For months before he retired, the others were plotting what to do with the job. What do you mean who? His colleagues, the management, men itching to take his place. So, in the end the poor man had no choice. One day he confessed to me that, although people had told him it would be hard to adjust psychologically, the reality was far worse than he'd expected."

"If he gave his pension to my husband, you'd soon see how easy it is to adjust. He'd say thank you very much and wag his tail; you might even see him give up his football match on TV to go burn the money. He'd stuff himself with pastries and fizzy drink at the nearest stand, like he's been doing all his life . . . If I didn't clamp down hard, there'd be nothing left of his pension . . . It's just a pity it took so long for me to see sense! My sister-in-law's right to point these things out, the old shrew. Think of all the money that's passed through your hands, she tells me, and you don't have a home of your own for your old age. Yes, look how I've ended up. He gave to everyone to show how generous he was, and I gave some here, some there, to my brothers and nephews, laying the table for anyone who called around; and if my man had dared to say a word, I'd have scratched his eyes out! But the old creep, who's sure got an evil tongue, just kept his trap shut. So I'm stuck in this hovel for my sins, going to the toilet at the bottom of the yard in all seasons, swallowing all that bellyaching from the bitch of a landlady, old Pug Nose. It makes me sick to think of it . . ."

"What can be done, Madam Delcă? You stayed there because times were hard, but it's also what fate had in store. As I said, my dear, I believe everyone has a fate. Think of all the people who had land and a house of their own, until the state took them away. How many died as poor as church mice, while some upstart took over their house! How many scraped and saved for years to get the home they'd set their hearts on, only to have to start all over again! There's no point thinking how your life might have been, after the things that all of us, without exception, have had to bear. Apart from the bootlickers, tell me anyone of our age who hasn't suffered? A sacrificed generation, you might say! Two world wars, confiscated property, a devastating earthquake, arrests, crowded jails, terror and misery! When I think back to the terrible winter of '52— do you remember? It caught us without any firewood, and I'd go with Muti to a depot where they allowed us to pick up some shavings and put them on my sled. I rummaged in the snow until I lost all feeling in my hands; they were so swollen and painful that I couldn't move them for days after. But dear, wise Muti—like the mother of the Gracchi—kept our spirits up by telling us that we live for one another and have no right to think of death! Even if dying would be easier for us personally, we must think how the ones we'd leave behind would suffer. So, Madam Delcă, may the Lord give you a long life—because you have someone to live for. The ones you've been giving to all these years. Feelings are far more important than possessions, so, believe me, you haven't wasted your money! You say enough has passed through your hands to buy a little house. But how much passed through Margot's hands, and she still ended her days in a basement . . ."

The poor dear: how she ended up, wearing a child's dirty fluffy pink bonnet, pulled down over her eyebrows! In that terrible July heat! At least I didn't put my foot in it and urge her to take it off. Yes, of course, Muti had warned me not to; she'd also told me not to be surprised if I found her skin and bones, with a pale-yellow face, the color of Vaseline. My God, what a terrible illness! But how could she have let herself go like that: an intelligent, cultivated woman, not seeing a doctor until the last moment? When any drop of blood after the menopause is suspicious, how could she have kept going like that until the pains began? And the radiotherapy that burned her skin and caused her hair and teeth to fall out. Poor Tante Margot! Maybe she knew what was happening to her, but didn't want to go straight from prison to the hospital. That would make some sense, no?

"What were you asking, Madam Delcă? Ah, yes, when did Uncle Sandu leave? He left in 1947. Why didn't he get Margot and Riri out of the country? Because it was too late: the Iron Curtain was falling. No, Margot knew nothing until the last minute. That's the truth, believe me. Margot didn't know."

She doesn't believe me. No one believed then or believes now that Margot knew nothing—except, that is, people who imagine he told her nothing for fear that she'd inform on him. That's certainly not how it was. He was in the habit of telling her bad news only at the last moment. After all, something unexpected might happen to change the situation, so there was no point in jumping the gun. That's the sort of excuse he gave. Yes, given his difficult profession, it could have been an excuse.

And I'm convinced that, if he didn't tell her until the last moment, it wasn't because he feared that she might inform on him.

"That last evening he told her they were going to split up forever, but he didn't explain how exactly. He also said he wouldn't write, because it would only hurt her. So they said good-bye and never saw each other again. Very rarely, he still sent news through someone or other, but no letters or packets. Not once! Did she bear him a grudge? No, Madam Delcă, there was no question of that! Margot never blamed him for leaving. He hesitated for a long time, too long, given the risks he ran here. I can still hear the annoyance in Margot's voice when anyone criticized him; she always found a way to cut the conversation short."

Poor Margot! It's funny how people seem to take pleasure in hurting others in delicate situations . . . And what point is there in telling someone like Vica about the Securitate interrogations Margot had to endure? But they didn't get anything out of her, for the simple reason that she didn't know anything!

"When Margot moved to a smaller place in the suburbs, to Otopeni, we thought it was to save money. Muti would have been very upset with her if she'd known that it was in order to keep Mr. Ialomiţeanu there in secret. Yes, the man you see here in the photo! Of course Muti knew him, from the days of their youth, and you couldn't say she was very keen on him. He'd asked for Margot's hand in marriage, and been refused. After the Great War Alexandru Geblescu, the youngest deputy in parliament, was a much more suitable match than Mr. Ialomiţeanu, whose reputation had been ruined by his collaboration with the German occupiers; a "kraut lover," as they called him. That had been in the autumn of 1916, when the Russians left us in the lurch, and the royal family, the government, and anyone else with the possibility took refuge in Moldova."

"Autumn 1916? No, I'm sure it was winter. You've read about it in books, but I saw it with my own eyes. Some things I remember, others I don't, but my childhood memories are as fresh as yesterday's. Do you know how close the artillery sounded? You'd have said it was just a street or two away. My poor mother used to complain that, what with the guns and all the other worries, she hardly got a wink of sleep at night. The guns boomed during the day as well, but it's not the same as hearing them in the dark. We kids would play all day and fall asleep as soon as we hit the deck, but Mummy went on chatting with the neighbors into the small hours . . . One day the Germans had been given a hiding and the war would soon be over; the next day it was the opposite and the Germans would soon be in Bucharest. Who said all this? Well, the women from the neighborhood! What did they know? And what did I know, a little girl of eleven? If I'd known how many days my poor mother had left on earth, I wouldn't have taken my eyes off her for a moment, but as it was I spent all day playing in the street; we only got together at home after dark. Once I even went as far as Obor Station with that crazy Niculaie; I remember it was winter, with a cold wind and snow and sleet. I'd never seen such crowded trains: there were men on the steps, on the roofs, some hanging on with only one hand or leg, others sticking their head out the window to breathe. A lot must have been crushed to death there and then. They said afterward that many women and children died of heat or cold or typhus, whatever, before they got to where they were going. And do you think there was anyone to bury them? It seems they just pulled the window down further and tossed them into the fields. I don't know if it's true or not: I'm just passing on what I heard. All I can swear to is what Niculaie and me saw with our own eyes—the heaps of people jammed together in the trains for Moldova, or the desperate crowds on the platforms, soaked by the driving sleet, who had left everything behind but had no chance of getting on. We also saw a goods train now and again, and you should have seen all the plush stuff in the open wagons! Nothing but sofas and armchairs, fancy tables and barrels of wine, windows and bird cages, copper pots and pans, hatboxes and rolled-up rugs and carpets—what a treasure! All that money thrown away on things lying there higgledy-piggledy! And what would be left of it, if there was a layer of snow over everything even in the station? What a waste, what a crying waste! But that's what I think now, after all I've seen of the world. In those days I didn't have a clue about anything. I just stood there goggling; I'd never seen the likes of that before. And, as we stood there, there was suddenly an explosion like it was the end of the world. We were used to bombs, but this was something much worse. Later people said the gunpowder factory had gone sky high, not far away in Dudeşti. Who did it? Our people? The Germans? It was all a mystery to me. All I remember is people saying the powder factory had blown up. Anyway, we got the hell out of there and didn't stop running until we were back home. My poor mother had been looking all over for us, with Vasile in her arms and the twins clinging to her skirt. But, when she saw we were safe—I won't describe the walloping we got. Maybe that's why I still remember that mad crush in the station so well."

"Of course, it's different if you saw it with your own eyes. The easiest way to go to Moldova was in a team of officials that went there with the government. But it was only people with connections in high places who enjoyed that privilege. Our family, like yours and like so many others, had to live through the occupation in Bucharest—for two years, I think it was. It was then that Mr. Ialomiţeanu joined the new administration, no doubt banking on a German victory in the war. Of course, our people didn't take kindly to that when they came back in 1918. But it wasn't long before they calmed down and let bygones be bygones. What was there to hold against him, after all, except that he was suspected of having been one of countless informers in the pay of the Germans? The problem was that their names were never published, so there were all kinds of rumors. But it's not as if there wasn't any evidence. For example, at the height of the evacuation, someone came across the secret papers of a German agent in a safe: Günter . . . yes, I think it was Günter something . . . and what do you think they contained? A list of collaborators, and of the sums of money given to each of them. Romanians, of course, including some well-known names . . . Why can't you believe it, Madam Delcă? Why should it be invented? Do you think things like that only happen in films? Well, I hope you won't mind if I tell you you're wrong. It's just a pity that those names weren't made public; that's always the way it is. So all we were left with was rumors, and you can't condemn someone only on that basis. Anyway, I remember that this Mr. Ialomiţeanu wasn't received in our house after the war, because he'd been a senior official and a parliamentarian under the occupation. But Papa also said that, after the government and the royal family fled to Iaşi, when the Germans were expected to arrive in Bucharest at any moment, Mr. Marghiloman, the head of the pro-German faction—you must have heard of him, anyway I'm telling you now—was inundated with people. His waiting room was chockablock, as so many who'd cold-shouldered him or gossiped about him or even openly attacked him in recent months came and asked for his help. Papa got upset when he told us this. Mr. Ialomiţeanu came from quite an influential family in Buzău and had got to know Mr. Marghiloman there. So why shouldn't he have asked for his help, or anyone else's, in hard times? According to Margot, that was the explanation for Mr. Ialomițeanu's record during the years of occupation; it didn't mean at all that he was a dubious character . . . But you don't seem very interested in politics, Madam Delcă!"

"To hell with politics! When I see the news on TV, I tell the old man to switch it off so we won't have to spend another hundred lei on that thief of a repair man. Did Margot keep this Ialomițeanu hidden at her place in Otopeni? So, that time Madam Ioaniu sent me there with a demijohn to pick up some wine and I had no idea who I was going to meet . . . Do you think Madam Ioaniu didn't know he was there either? And to think I was angry with her afterward because she could have landed me in trouble!"

"No, Muti didn't know that Margot hid Mr. Ialomițeanu there after Uncle Sandu left the country. Muti was so shocked when she found out! She thought Margot had been unforgivably reckless, with a man who didn't even seem well-bred and whose behavior during the war had left a bad impression. Muti was patriotic, like Papa, and had favored the alliance with France for the sake of Transylvania. During the occupation she worked as a hospital nurse, like many other ladies, although few of them took the work as seriously as Muti did. She used to leave home at five with Madam Ana, while it was still dark, in order to be at the hospital when the sugar and rations were weighed for the patients. She knew how much stealing went on! Once she went to the old people's home, where soldiers suffering from camp fever had been quarantined. Lice were crawling all over them, even on their eyebrows, even on their eyelids, so she had to make them wash in wooden tubs and then pour Creolin disinfectant over them; the lice went down the drain with the water. No one could say it wasn't dangerous. In fact Marie-Liliane Botescu, a friend of hers from a very good family, caught the fever and died as a result. Yes, just like you say your mother died! Muti used to tell me that they made silk bonnets for themselves, because the lice couldn't crawl on them. The hospitals were short of everything: heating fuel, oil for the electricity generator, cotton wool, bandages . . . It was so cold that the doctors operated in their overcoats, by candlelight! In the end, after Miss Botescu died, Papa told Muti to stop going there. But, although she was badly affected by her friend's death, she was never willing to give up the work. Papa had to accept this, and anyway the Germans soon took him hostage, after someone—who could it have been?—reported his association with the Liberal minister Georges Athanasiu. When Muti got worked up, she used to say that Mr. Ialomițeanu must have informed on him. Of course Papa was never really active in politics. But plenty of others, who'd published anti-German diatribes and beaten their breasts in support of Transylvania, now strolled around declaring that they had always been against Romania's entry into the war. That's always what it's like! Papa hardly ever appeared in public, because of his illness and his general character, and yet . . ."

"He took the rap!"

"That's why I think someone must have denounced him. But who?"

"Some evil little devil, like the one who snitched on Cabbage-Washer, my father's brother. The Germans showed up one day and went straight to where he had his shed; they cleared the wood he'd put in front of it and dug around inside until they got to a little bricked-up section where he'd stashed away sacks of stuff from his business—sugar, rice, you name it. Who could have told them except some neighbor who'd seen him laying the bricks? The Germans carted off everything they found, and took Cabbage-Washer along with them. It was a year and a half before he came back."

"I remember a story that Papa used to enjoy telling. In 1918, when the Germans were in a great hurry to leave and everyone was waiting for our troops and the French to arrive, Papa happened to be at the German commandant's office for some reason or other. Maybe he'd gone with one of the medical certificates that allowed him to stay out of custody on conditional release. Papa knew German very well, from the time he'd studied there as a young man, and he was chatting with the officer who usually dealt with his certificates. Well, suddenly the officer began to open one drawer after another in his desk and to empty the contents onto the floor in the middle of the room. Finally he pointed the tip of his boot at the heap of papers, which were covered with all kinds of scribbling, and said: 'You see, all these denunciations come from your fellow countrymen. We didn't pay much attention to most of them, but how couldn't we have picked you up after all these denunciations from other Romanians?' Papa didn't live long enough to see the dust settle, when people stopped blaming Mr. Ialomițeanu and he could gradually improve his situation. Later he married an ugly, ill-bred woman who had some money, and it seems that her relatives helped him to become an influential figure—although I don't know exactly what kind of politics he

was mixed up in. Also pro-German, I think. Anyway, he didn't lose any
ground when Antonescu took power—on the contrary. You do remember Marshal Antonescu, don't you, Madam Delcă? You were staying with
us at the time of the Iron Guard revolt."

"Yes, I do. I also remember the ones they shot here at Ţăcălie hill;
no one was allowed to take their bodies away. And old Pug Nose's husband was packed off to a camp, leaving her to tremble and shake till he
returned. He told me later, though, that he used to makes chess sets out
of wood or bread or whatever, and swapped them for cigarettes and other
stuff from the prisoners' packets. Pug Nose also used to send him packets, so he doesn't seem to have had such a hard time. After the war, the
communists had another good grope in his shed, and he found himself
cutting reeds in the Danube Delta for a while. That was much, much
worse, he said."

"Yes, it happened to a lot of people, including many who were innocent. Even Margot—who, I'm convinced, only hid Mr. Ialomiţeanu
because she was alone and disoriented."

Her eyes suddenly looked huge in her emaciated face . . .

. . . "'Please, don't bother,' I called out, when I saw how difficult it was
for her to open the sideboard door. But before I could say any more she'd
taken out that dish of rock-hard Turkish delight. I can still see the green,
red, and orange cubes encrusted with sugar. It was obvious that she kept
them only for guests—since God knows when! And even that little effort
exhausted her. She slumped into her rocking chair, which didn't budge
an inch beneath her weight. Then she asked me to get two glasses from
the dresser and some water from the ice chest. 'Riri gets ice for it every
two days,' she said. And it was true. My cousin Riri was meticulous
about it, although the main reason was so that Margot could apply compresses day and night in a vain attempt to stop the hemorrhaging. God
knows what damage all that ice did! But she refused to stop, so long as
she remained conscious . . .

"I brought the glasses from the dresser. They were terribly dusty, so I
realized that no one ever came to visit her and Riri. This was probably
the first time she'd used them since she'd moved there. I wiped them
with some faded table napkins, then forced myself to swallow a piece
of the rock-hard Turkish delight. My teeth began to ache. She said she
had no appetite at all and apologized for not joining me. I already knew
from Muti that she wasn't able to swallow, so I didn't try to persuade

her. To amuse her, I told her about Uncle Sandu again—how handsome and charming he was—and she immediately perked up. When he was a young lieutenant in the Great War, she told me, he gave her an army map that they used to keep in the little drawing room; they regularly moved the flags around to mark the army's advances, and then its retreats. I noticed that the story of his escape to the West had changed: he risked his life by delaying his departure until 1947, because he couldn't tear himself away from her and Riri. Had it really been like that? I can't see why such a clear-sighted man hadn't left earlier, when it would have been possible to take his family with him."

Like so many others did . . .

"Poor Margot! She found an unconvincing, sentimental explanation for everything that remained unclear. One thing is certain, though: Uncle Sandu realized early on which way the war would go, and toward the end he played a role for which he hoped he would be rewarded afterward. That's one explanation for why he didn't take the opportunity to get Riri and Tante Margot out of the country while it was still possible. Did he hope until the last minute that things wouldn't work out so badly? For some time I've thought that everything he did must have been premeditated. Maybe the image people had of him as a spendthrift was wrong, since Margot later found some notebooks in which he had jotted down his expenses, using initials and some kind of code. Not for nothing had he been minister of the interior at one point . . .

"What are you doing, Madam Delcă? Are you looking for something?"

"I'm looking for my ragbag, to take a Hiposerpil. I'm burning all over, and my head's going round and round . . ."

"Don't worry. Spirits aren't bad for your blood pressure. If you're feeling dizzy, I'll make you a coffee. A little one for you, and a bigger one for me, because I want to smoke a cigarette. We'll drink our coffee, and you'll feel better. Meanwhile Niki's bound to show up."

"Please don't get up, Madam Delcă, I'll bring it over! I think I told you that, when Papa was alive, we had tea served at five in the main drawing room. No, nothing's the same anymore. The room was split into two, as Muti thought that after I married we could go on living together, only on different floors; their incomes weren't high enough to make buying another house a realistic prospect. As it turned out, however, we merely prepared the house for our famous new tenants, who contributed more than their fair share to the imperfections you can see everywhere. Muti tried negotiating with Petruța, and even invited her to have a coffee when she could get hold of a few spoonfuls, but it was all to no avail. Between you and me, the whole idea made no sense anyway, since Petruța hadn't a clue about drinking coffee properly. It wasn't yet the fashion to drink it in mugs in every office . . . I can still hear Muti telling her how attached she was to the trolley and sideboard that had been left in his bedroom . . . 'Please be careful how you treat them.' . . . In fact, she wanted him to avoid putting wet plates or hot pans or bottles of oil on top of them."

"Petruța . . . She's the one who got too big for her boots?"

"That's right. But don't think she didn't have an answer for everything. You're like my mum, she'd say. How many times have I told her to chuck all that junk of hers out! She can't even keep it clean. But she just goes her own sweet way. That's what old people are like: they hang on to all kinds of stuff in the house, because it reminds them of one thing or another . . . You might think she said that because she was badly brought up. But no, it's their way of shutting you up—by acting more stupid than they really are! A kind of cunning that stands in for intelligence. You could also see it in her husband, who quite liked Muti but not the rest of us. He used to joke with her and call her the Old Lady! It's possible that Muti steered him in that direction, when she had that fit of hysterics after Uncle Georges's death. But, on the other hand, we'll never know if he really liked her, or if he was simply acting on orders from the Securitate. Maybe he thought he could find other things out from her. Anyway, they moved out in the end, and here we are again in the old drawing room where it seems I used to get up to all kinds of mischief. Apparently I'd dash over to Madam Ana's trolley and give it a push. By the way, I don't know if you ever met Madam Ana . . . Yes, she was old and broken. Do you know her story? Her son, Spiridon, was taken prisoner by the Russians in 1942, and she kept waiting and waiting for him to come back. In the first war—what bad luck!—he'd been taken prisoner by the Bulgarians, suffered extreme cold and starvation, caught typhoid fever and dysentery and spent time in a field hospital. But, well, in the end he managed to escape."

"Yes, that's how it is. You escape if your time hasn't come . . ."

"So he finally reappeared, weak and in tatters, a shadow of his former self. At first they thought he was a beggar. There was chaos everywhere: the Germans had set fire to the warehouses before they left, and things looted from houses were being sold for next to nothing. There was one long celebration on the streets from morning till night, with flowers and Romanian flags. People were singing and shouting as everyone waited for our troops to arrive. Of course, I only know this from what others told me."

"But I lived through it and remember it very well. What madness there was all around! One night some tramps came and broke into Cabbage-Washer's shop—God knows who they were—then threw a match and left. I can't describe it. People came out of their houses with buckets of water and poured more and more onto the fire, but it kept spreading, as if they were pouring gasoline rather than water. We thought the whole neighborhood would go up in flames and burn us all like mice. How scared we were! After all, we were just poor orphans. But some neighbor eventually took us in."

"Yes, I remember hearing what feverish days they were. There was no sign of the police or army, so everyone really let their hair down! People went into the streets in the morning, flying the tricolor and singing patriotic songs. Papa went out too, unable to refrain from taking part in the explosion of joy. Romania's morning at last! he shouted, burning with emotion. But then he took his hat and stick and went off. It was rumored that the French had arrived and that our own troops were entering the capital. It was late by the time Papa got back, his clothes in disarray, without his hat and stick. Some Germans had appeared from nowhere, there had been a skirmish, and Papa (the hero!) had hidden in a doorway. The people inside, all women, saw a ragged-looking man and wondered what to do. Give him some alms? Keep perfectly still, so he'll think no one's in? As you say, Madam Delcă, everyone in those days was afraid of being robbed, and the well-to-do lived with the thought that people from the slums would come and invade their home. But none of that came to pass. Anyway, while they were wondering whether to go to the door, Spiridon—Madam Ana's son—stood there afraid that some Germans might be billeted inside. Later, when the war was over, he became an office worker, having studied at the Business School, and married a young woman who worked at the telephone exchange, and had a child with her . . . But the poor baby died when the Americans bombed Bucharest in April 1944; that was another blow of fate for Madam Ana. She was still living with us at the time, as part of the family . . . I don't think Spiridon got to hear about his son's death, because he was then a prisoner-of-war for the second time. Or maybe he did hear about it? Yes, I think he just had time to. Yes, if I think about it—the bombing was on April 4th, and the army surrendered at Iaşi on August 25th, or maybe the beginning of September . . . Yes, Madam Delcă, the armistice had already been signed with the Russians . . . But so what? Haven't you heard of cases where people out for a stroll were picked up by the Russians and taken off somewhere for years and years? You know what things were like when the Russians came in '44."

"Sure as hell I do! Any woman who wasn't old enough to be dribbling put some soot on her face and a scarf on her head, 'cuz she knew what would happen if the Russkies got hold of her. I did the same. Didn't I draw the shutters on the store and turn out all the lights? But do you think that put them off? They banged on the door all night with their rifle butts and shouted in that language of theirs. What a racket! What a hullabaloo! I didn't get a wink of sleep, and the next morning I bowed to all the icons and gave thanks that me and my husband were still in one piece. But they still showed no sign of going away, so we decided to open up. My husband said to me: open up and give them something to drink. Who cares if they pay? Just give them something to drink and maybe they'll clear off. So I opened up. But first I hid all the watches, in case one of them wandered in and got his hands on them. Well, none of them wandered in, but we were still in a pickle all right. My husband had been wearing a watch on his wrist, and as it was summer he had a stripe there from the sun. He was my old darkie—only a strip on his wrist was still white. Well, you won't believe it, but the Russian stood there waving his gun at him for two hours, repeating all the time *Davai chas*! I'd have given him the goddamn watch, so he'd go back to where he came from. But my poor creep of a husband? You've got to pull the mule by the tail if you want him to move an inch! So what did he do? He kept telling the Russki in signs that he'd sold his watch. The Russki wasn't having any of it. *Davai chas, davai chas*! he went on repeating. Waving his pistol in the air . . . I was at sixes and sevens, but I gave him something to drink, standing close to him, trying to get around him all the time. But the Russki was only interested in one thing: *Davai chas, davai chas*! Then what do you think happened? Two soldiers and a boss man appeared out of the blue, with guns and Kalashnikovs, and you should have seen this guy turn as yellow as wax. He dropped his pistol, and the boss type barked something at him and marched him off double quick. And if you never saw him again, I certainly didn't . . ."

"You mean they actually arrested one of their own men?"

"They sure did. I saw it with my own eyes. I don't know how they knew what was going on. Did one of his comrades snitch on him? Or was it a passerby—because everyone thought the world of me, and a lot had got credit from me over the years! In fact, I haven't a clue. As for *davai chas,* only he knows what the Russians did to him. Some say he was shot, others that they beat him with leather straps . . ."

"Yes, that *davai chas* business—what a story! You remember our great cabaret artist Constantin Tănase? They kept threatening him, but he just wouldn't give up! He was back on stage the next day, with watches around his wrists and neck, and whispering tick-tock, tick-tock, with his finger to his lips? 'It was bad enough with *Der, die, das.* But even worse is *davai chas.*' And two days later he was dead, the poor man. What dramas the war brought with it! But now it's so much water under the bridge . . ."

"Ah, life goes on! And time heals all things. I used to say that to Madam Ioaniu . . ."

"Yes, life goes on, and all anyone remembers is what has happened in their own little circle. That's why we were talking about Madam Ana. When the war ended and everyone returned home, except for her son, we saw her decline more and more each day. And then suddenly she was a helpless little babe again."

"Yes, of course I remember that. She used to sleep upstairs in the attic, and there was a smell of piss everywhere. A baby's piss smells of milk, but an old geezer's is worse than a tomcat's. Madam Ioaniu put an oil-cloth under her, but the smell still spread everywhere. Me, I wouldn't have kept her in the house for a pot of gold. When I was least expecting it, I'd suddenly see her there in her nightdress, eyes bulging, a few tousled white strands still sticking to her head. An apparition like that at night is enough to give you a stroke! Sophieee! she'd call out. That's what she called Madam Ioaniu. I've gone and wet myself: you'll have to come and change me! . . . One day I asked Madam Ioaniu straight out why she kept her there, 'cuz it was no life for either of them. You should put her in a home or somewhere, I said. But no. I couldn't do that to her, she said. The poor thing brought me up after all . . . If it had been me, I'd have been out of there a long time ago. Then, when I dropped by one day, the cleaner Leana told me that Madam Ana was dead and buried. I still don't know. Did you put her in a home in the end?"

"No, how could we have? Muti always said you can't know how some-one will end their days. Madam Ana had been such a skilful woman, running seven houses, and look how she ended up. Muti worried the most about her, of course, and I spoke up for her with Niki—because, as you know, men like a quiet life more than women. Like you, he thought more of the practical side, but we kept her at home until she died. Poor Madam Ana! How her mind went toward the end. She was even expecting her son to appear: she was sure he was still alive! As you can imagine, no one took her seriously. But, a year or so after Madam Ana died, we had a visit from a man who intrigued me as soon as I saw his short stocky figure from the window; he looked around so suspiciously before he decided to ring the bell! We were still living crammed together in the attic, so it was no pleasure to invite him upstairs, and for his part he didn't want to say who he was or what he wanted. He only asked us to tell him something about Madam Ana. He'd been a lieutenant in the Iaşi army and gone to the same camp in Russia as Spiridon, then worked down the same mine. When they were separated and sent to different camps and mines, they exchanged addresses and each solemnly prom-ised to visit the other's family if he was ever released. This relaxed us a little, because in those days all kinds of shady characters tried to get something out of you by telling you good news about one of your family in prison: maybe a lunch, a coat, even some money. Isn't that so, Madam Delcă? And the Securitate also sent people to worm secrets out of you. That's where we thought this man was from at first, so Muti and I were on our guard. But we opened up when he said he hadn't found anyone at Spiridon's home address, that his wife had indeed remarried . . ."

"Well, what's a woman supposed to do? Live alone like an owl? As if that would bring him back! You can't blame her for wanting a man and a proper home."

"Yes, you see things practically. But not everyone . . ."

"Do you think he wouldn't have remarried if she'd been the one to kick the bucket? Look at Reli's brother next door! He lived for thirty years with his wife, and brought another one home just three months after burying her. Reli didn't blame him at all. Didn't he need someone to wash and iron for him? she said. Was she supposed to look after him? She couldn't even if she'd wanted to, at her age . . ."

"That's what Spiridon's wife thought too. Maybe she was right, Madam Delcă, but I'm convinced that I wouldn't have the strength . . . Another husband, another child: God forbid! Anyway, as I listened to the lieutenant, I became more trustful and invited him to stay for lunch. We had to insist a lot before he accepted. He spoke in a low voice, looking all around him, because he knew they were watching us. But we didn't ask him any questions: he said what he wanted to say. That's how it was when one loose word could land you in prison for years, wasn't it, Madam Delcă? We didn't want to get the poor man into trouble, and the fact is he didn't say a word about how his life had been in Siberia. All he did was say something about the camps he'd been in: first the one in Roman, in this country, which filled up with peasants they wanted to get out of the way; some told him that in fact the Russians had grabbed them at an opposition rally addressed by a priest, and then shipped them off somewhere. The next camp was for Germans and Hungarians: it had originally held thirteen hundred, but by the time the Romanians arrived death had reduced this to a mere three hundred and fifty. He and Spiridon made friends with a Hungarian there, a tall architect aged around sixty, who had a double chin. He'd gone with his wife one day to the theater, and the Russians had pounced on them as they came out. They said: ladies home; gentlemen *syuda*—that is, 'over here.' I've often imagined how that tall man must have looked: impeccably shaven, an overcoat with a fur collar, a fashionable hat, a cigar in his hand . . . Gentlemen *syuda*."

"Oh, ho, I've heard other stories like that! There was a guy in our street who came back quite late, in '49 or '51, and who said that a lot of others had stayed put in Russia. They were married, but they had another wife there, and other children, so what was the point of returning? That's why I say that only dumb broads sat and waited. That's what men are like . . ."

"Poor men! Do you think they were there for fun? I think Spiridon must have been one of the ones who stayed . . . But I heard of someone who came back in '69. He'd been sent to work in a mine near the Chinese frontier, and while they were there they all thought the war was still going on. But then there were armed clashes at the frontier, as you know, and the Chinese crossed into Russia for a time. So the workers were sent home from there too, as someone else also told me. Spiridon's friend became more and more relaxed, and he chuckled to himself now and again as he spoke. He'd developed a bit of a belly and sat with his legs apart on his chair, laughing and pulling what little remained of his hair to cover his baldness. He'd lost the best years of his life and returned almost an old man."

"I've also heard things like that. Do you know who from? Madam Cristide. How she used to pester me to pay her a visit: Please come, Madam Delcă, please don't avoid me. You don't know how much I like sitting and chatting with you, like you do with Ivona and Madam Ioaniu. Well, I wasn't sure what to do, because I had enough clients already. I went to see her a few times, no more. I'd ring on the bell, once, twice, ten times, like I did on yours today, but no answer. But, when I'd made up my mind to leave, I heard a voice: Come in, Madam Delcă, please forgive me! Oh, ho, I thought, the devil might forgive you, lying in bed like that till midday. And when I went in, it was pitch dark; I had to grope my way, taking care I didn't break a leg, scared I'd never get out of there alive. Yes, I bumped into tables and chairs, banged into walls, and when I tried to find a light switch you should have heard how the mad old woman yelled. No, don't do that! Please don't switch the light on, Madam Delcă."

"Yes, I know, that's how Madam Cristide sleeps. She has insomnia at night, since the menopause, but she doesn't want to take anything. She only manages to get some sleep in the morning. That's why she blacks the house out. It's good for her nerves—and for the insomnia."

"It's good for her laziness! Believe me, that's why she stays there in the dark, so no one can see how frowzy she is. But I've seen her there in her lop-sided shoes and that dirty rag of a blouse you wouldn't fancy wiping the floor with. Come on, Madam Cristide, I say to her, come and open the sewing machine for me! Show me what needs mending. So then she turns on a little light in her bedroom and powders her face. Seeing me behind her, she stops the makeup and starts going through her cupboards and drawers, banging and slamming them because I wouldn't let her get on with painting herself. Like she's got the devil inside her. Then she comes with an armful of stuff and flings it at me. She looked so wild I didn't say another word. There was so much powder on her face that she didn't look yellow anymore—more like a clown at the circus. You should have seen how the skin on her neck hung down. And she didn't seem to have any eyebrows. Then back she went to the mirror to put on some more paint, pulling faces in front of it—like this she went, like this . . ."

"Ha, ha, ha! What have you got against that? She was just trying to work out what looked best."

"You can't imagine the stuff she gave me to mend. Stinking rags, which fell apart as soon as you opened them out! I joined and patched and darned, but it all probably came apart at the first wash. A pity about the hard work! No, madam, I thought, you won't con me another time! And how stingy she was with the food! Only with the chatter was there no holds barred: blah blah blah, putting everyone down, one after another, so my ears were ringing by the time I left."

"Really? Is that what it was like? Did she gossip about us too?"

"She spoke about that brother-in-law of the woman at the end of the street, that Iron Guard boss man who ran off with the Germans. The Americans got him in the end, though, and handed him over to the Russkies—then off he went to Siberia! What a film that was: *The Ballad of Siberia*! How it made me cry! I'd sit whirring away at the sewing machine and singing 'The Ballad of Siberia.' And Madam Cristide said they got him pulling a plough in Siberia. And when he came back in '54, she saw the marks it left on his shoulders. I didn't believe it myself— that's Madam Cristide for you—but she kept repeating that she'd seen the marks with her own eyes. To hell with you! I said to myself. And what did you show him of yours? Your big fat pussy?"

Ivona opened the door, and the sound of the clock came in from the semidarkness. Both of them counted the chimes: Vica from her chair, Ivona standing, one eye on the old clock on the sideboard. It had a blue enamel face, surrounded by golden lacework. The hands of the clock were also golden, as were the roman numerals indicating the hour.

"Two o'clock!"

"Two? That's impossible. It must be later than that."

Ivona went out, and she could be heard running on the stairs. She brought back a Soviet alarm clock and put it on the sideboard; its loud ticking soon filled the room.

"Now that's what I call a real clock! I've got one of them at home too: it's enough to waken the dead. That other one's only good for its looks . . ."

"No, it still works, Madam Delcă. But sometimes it stops or goes slow for no reason, even if you wind it up properly."

"It's had its day—that's all there is to it. Nice-looking but an old crock inside. They last as long as they can, then off to the garbage with them."

"How can you say that, Madam Delcă? Old clocks are as precious as jewelry, you know."

"Well, all I meant was you should sell it to the secondhand shop or whoever wants to take it. If it doesn't tell the time anymore, what's the point of keeping it and taking up space?"

Ivona turned the little wheels on the back of the clock, pursing her lips in a posture of attention and dissatisfaction. She didn't put her glasses on. When she put the clock back, she noticed some marks she had made in the dust with her fingers. She went to the kitchen, came back with a piece of cloth, and quickly wiped the surface of the sideboard.

"My childhood clock . . ."

"Hum, what a load of dust you've got: here, there, in the corner. And over there! I'm the same without my specs. As if I'm blind: what I don't leave behind when I sweep the place! My mother-in-law's moustache . . . You've probably never heard the saying: if you don't notice something, it's probably your mother-in-law's beard and moustache . . ."

"Forget the dust! Believe me, it gets harder and harder to cope with everything. A big house, Madam Delcă, especially an old one that's been left for some time, is hard to keep clean these days."

"Yes, you'd do better to get the hell out and move into a block."

"You're just like Niki! Don't think he hasn't told me the same—that we should sell the house and buy a two-room apartment in a block."

Ivona took a cigarette from an opened pack and flicked her lighter with a forced smile. It was an unpleasant memory . . .

"For some time now," she'd said, taking care not to raise her voice, in case Muti should hear her from upstairs, "you've seemed prepared to throw everything to the winds. Just like that, in a couple of hours. The house, the family, the past . . ."

"Such are the times! What do you want?"

He'd laughed uneasily, not looking her in the eye, as he always did when he felt she was alluding to the person whose behavior seemed more and more to resemble . . .

"It's the times we live in, and there comes a point when you've got to start adapting. For God's sake, must we keep having the same old discussion?"

Her outburst had had no other effect than to send him straight to the front door. Soon his steps were heard in the hall. He reached out for the sports bag and tennis racket. Again she'd be left to wrestle with the familiar sense of anger and humiliation. After years of forcing yourself to hold it in, you can't suddenly give free rein to your unhappiness.

She sat still, struggling to control an inexplicable panic. Hot flushes burned her cheeks, and she began to scratch herself mechanically on her arms and neck, not caring at all that this might aggravate an allergy that had recently appeared from nowhere. The last year had been very difficult, and Niki, who knew this and should have supported her, had been as unhelpful as usual. He'd never given her any support—on the contrary, he'd chosen these difficult years to leave her more and more alone. And now he'd come up with the idea of selling their house, in which so many hopes and so many years of waiting had been wasted. It must be what that figure in the shadows was urging, who'd had her heart set on a car for such a long time. He'd use the difference between their house and a smaller apartment to buy it for her, and would be at home even less than now . . .

"I'm not thinking only of myself, but of you and Muti, who find it so difficult to heat this big old place. Your life would be easier. Nowadays that's what everyone wants . . ."

"Move Muti into an apartment? It would a nightmare for her: to be at the mercy of a janitor who'd set the heating either too high or too low."

"Well, there are advantages and disadvantages."

A scornful smile on Niki's face as he nonchalantly searches for his keys. And her despair, which makes her look pathetic—and ridiculous.

His scornful voice. His hands carefully lodged in his sweater pockets, one foot planted a little forward. Only outside, in the sunlight, will tears become visible in his bloodshot eyes.

"You'd wipe out a whole past in twenty-four hours, even though you know how attached we are to this place. To be swallowed up in a part of the city where you're not sure if it's Bucharest anymore, where people should go after they first arrive from the country. We've been living in this street for a hundred years, in this same house, and a hundred years means a lot for . . . But no, it means nothing to you. All I hear from you is that we have to adapt."

"Come on, don't exaggerate. You make a drama out of everything. Let's drop it—or talk about it another time."

And before she could tell him everything she had on her mind, he went into the hall and reached out for his sports bag. End of discussion— just when she had cast aside her doubts, in a surge of irritation that made her voice strident and brought tears to her eyes. She knew well enough that he'd wait for a better moment to renew the charge. Had he perhaps sounded Muti out already? She hadn't been the same since her beloved Tudor went away, and it wasn't impossible that she'd even consented to Niki's creepy plan. That was hard to believe, though. He'd go and ask Muti, but only after the storm had passed . . .

"Please, don't start one of your scenes! I beg of you, don't let's have a fit of hysterics!"

She can't stand the thought of Muti's scornful, authoritarian voice, interrupted by that smoker's cough of hers. She'll go on cleaning her fingernails with solvent, pick up her cigarette from the edge of the ashtray and, still coughing, take one last puff, then remove the stopper from her little flask of cheap pink Romanian varnish. She'll concentrate on each nail in turn: one stroke, two strokes. And, if she feels it isn't right, she'll quickly wipe it off with some cotton wool she keeps handy. Her movements will be precise and measured: her eyesight seems to have improved recently.

To help the varnish dry, Muti will wave her gnarled hands in the air, their thin layer of skin looking mauve and spotted on top of swollen veins. And finally she will look up at her daughter with her usual expression, unsurprised and mildly disapproving.

Ivona paced up and down the dining room, which had once been the salon. A corner of her mouth twitched with annoyance, and she could feel her head throbbing. She would have liked to scream, to slam doors and burst into tears, driven by an anger that kept rising together with a strange, unexpected heat. How terribly hot it was! Only her feet were ice cold. Niki had left: she could hear his familiar steps in the front garden and felt like opening the window and shouting after him. Come back this instant, talk things over properly, face to face! But she did nothing, only paced up and down the room, scratching herself with her sharp oval-shaped nails. She heard the ticking of the hall clock through the half-open door, and the scratching speeded up, becoming more and more vigorous, mixing pain with pleasure. Reddish marks, oozing blood here and there, remained on the soft flesh of her arms, and on her long legs, which never saw the sun anymore, yet which still held their shape despite the burst veins that left dark patches on her pale skin. . . Slender legs of a former skater, a former tennis player, a former . . . The mysterious hot flush passed, and she now felt so cold that her teeth chattered. She pulled a leather-backed chair toward her, sat down on it, and lit a cigarette, impatiently drawing the first puff. Then a vision of what lay ahead suddenly rose up crystal clear, so loathsome that it wasn't she who envisaged it, but an omnipotent, omniscient gaze that reached deep inside here. She realized what she had left out of account since Tudor's departure. Now she would have to take Muti's place, fending for herself as she watched over the house and the family's affairs.

Life with Niki would be increasingly difficult; he would tend to leave her by herself more and more, taking less and less responsibility for things. There would no longer be Tudor's presence to help keep a kind of balance. Nor, before long, would there even be Muti, who had exerted her influence until now with such tact and delicacy. She would be left alone with this slippery egoist of a man, beside whom she would unfortunately have to die as well as live. From now on she'd have to decide everything herself, doing no more than consult him from time to time, and try her best to become independent and put her life on an even keel. Despite the unease and bewilderment that his behavior aroused in her, she would have to act as if nothing was ever wrong.

Keep calm, then. Calmly climb the stairs, calmly knock on Muti's door, and go up to the big leather armchair where she would certainly be polishing her nails.

"If you knew how often I had to fight them, Madam Delcă. I say them, because Muti surprisingly agreed with him. Yes, imagine selling our house and moving into an apartment in a block. Or, to be more precise, she didn't oppose Niki's suggestion—which came to the same thing. Two against one!"

"What could have been going through Madam Ioaniu's head? She had some brains, after all. Maybe she thought that, with the boy gone and no one else to leave the house to, there was no point busting herself up over it. We're like that too. If we'd had children, maybe we'd have put some money by, maybe we'd have said it would help them buy a house of their own, and we wouldn't be living now in that dump where I have to put up with old Pug Nose's poison when I head for the toilet in the freezing cold yard. That must have been what Madam Ioaniu was thinking. But I've seen from my sister-in-law that it's hell on earth living in a block."

"Perhaps you're right, Madam Delcă, I don't know. In any case, Niki's pleading gradually persuaded Muti that it would be best for all of us, that it would mean less work for me (which was important for Muti, since she knew how I hated cooking and all the rest of it). But I put up with those things—and they are getting more and more of a problem—because I can't bear to leave the house. I'm as attached to it now as Muti ever was! But I had to put up a fight, with both of them. It really shook me that Muti sided with Niki, and when we were alone I raised my voice with her for the first time in my life. I regretted it later, because the poor dear was suffering from pneumonia at the time. But how was I to know?"

I only found out when the doctor came, but even then I was furious with her, like with a naughty child. "Pneumonia's an illness that old people get," I said. "I've always told you to beware of the cold, to dress properly, to avoid people with flu, to take vitamin C tablets, to drink hot lemon . . ." As she lay there flushed with fever, white hair uncombed, her eyes suddenly seemed to have turned deep blue. She had a guilty look, because instead of making my visit easier for me—as any parent is duty bound to do—she was complicating things even more . . .

"She became delirious and kept losing consciousness. One day I even called the priest, as the end seemed to be just a matter of time. By chance Niki happened to be away, and it was I who had to hold her still by force so that she could be given Communion. She hadn't been able to swallow anything for some time . . ."

. . . that moment of confusion when, holding her wasted shoulders, I felt that she was giving up the struggle. But, of course, it was no longer the authoritarian Muti but a poor child forced to take some horrible medicine . . . Even now the scene makes me feel giddy: it seems to have an artificial quality, because we'd already been through it a number of times before. The same rattling of a spoon against clenched teeth, the same honeyed cajoling, *come, now, just open a little, you won't even notice, there it's over,* as on the numerous occasions when Tudor had been ill. Who was this ignorant, impotent creature, weaker and more defenseless than any child? Certainly no one other than Muti, yet a completely different person . . . And there were moments when her look, strangely youthful, distant, and mysterious, gave me a glimpse of how young and dreamy her face had once been, before an all-conquering hand cruelly disfigured it . . .

"Poor Muti! I'm sure she knew she wouldn't last much longer—the way that animals can sense the approaching end. I'm not superstitious, but all kinds of things happened around the time that Muti passed away. First of all, the door to her room fell off its hinges. Then that clock simply stopped for no reason. Then the kitchen was invaded by red cock-roaches—which we'd never had before . . ."

"Ugh, those disgusting creatures! Kerosene's the only thing I know that sends them packing, otherwise they take over the whole house. I go around sprinkling all the corners where I know they're hidden. My featherbrained sister-in-law turns her nose up: oh, no, it smells awful.— What of? I ask her.—What of? Kerosene, that's what.—Well, just leave it alone: the smell will go away, and I trust it to work because there isn't a trace left of the little buggers at my place. I don't know what I'd have done otherwise in that old dump, where all the woodwork is rotten."

"Kerosene, eh? I used some Romanian insecticide, but I have a feel-ing that cockroaches thrive on the stuff. What's up, Madam Delcă? You seem to be looking here, there, and everywhere. Are you looking for something?"

"My ragbag. I need to take a Hiposerpil and a Carbaxin, seeing as I've been drinking one coffee after another and I wouldn't want to . . . No, please don't get up! I'll just get some water from the kitchen."

She puts her bag on a chair and shuffles off, holding the tablets tight in her left hand. A glass tinkles in the kitchen, then the fridge door clicks. She comes back licking her lips.

"Okay? Do you feel calmer now? So, what were we talking about? Ah, yes, the red cockroaches that appeared after Muti died. I was at the end of my tether that summer and, after a lot of trouble getting a visa to travel abroad, I went to visit my darling Tudor. When I got back, there were no more cockroaches. Vanished into thin air. And that clock, which I couldn't get going and no one had done anything about . . . one fine morning, when I was having a coffee with Niki as usual, I wound it up again without thinking, and it started working just as it always used to. I don't mind telling you that, ever since then, I get upset if I see it's stopped. On the other hand, it brings back my childhood just to look at it. I remember one afternoon in particular, when I was punished by being locked in Margot's old dressing room until six o'clock. I'd have given anything to be able to read the time, so that I'd know how much longer my imprisonment would last. The room was chockablock with things: a couch and umpteen cushions, velvet stools, vases of various sizes, night-lights with shades fraying at the edges, which seemed more and more menacing as darkness closed in . . . And that mirror: you know the one I mean, with mother-of-pearl encrusted in its frame. A mirror feels strangely threatening in the dark, don't you think so? Or maybe it was just me, because I was a particularly sensitive child. As soon as they turned the key in the lock, the room began to fill me with terror. I'd have given anything to read the time. I kept trying to work it out, but I never got anywhere. Anyway, they didn't free me till the stroke of six, because I'd been really bad that day . . ."

"I don't know what to do with her anymore," Muti said. "What she did today was . . . completely abnormal! I've noticed that the games she plays aren't normal either. She's got all those dolls, but she prefers to play with leaves, moving them around and getting them to say weird things . . ."

There was a curtain of morning glory in front of the window, and I used to play with its leaves, discovering a different person's face in each one . . . Then I crept up the stairs and went into Papa's study without knocking; I was the only one allowed to do that, and was I aware of the privilege! Well, he'd just taken me in his arms when Muti burst in, also without knocking . . . I was annoyed that he didn't quarrel with her. "Just a second, sweetheart!" Papa said to me, putting me down again. I waited, more than a second, and soon lost patience . . . He hurried over to her and kissed her on the forehead, then the two of them stood there talking. He'd obviously forgotten about me. I kept hovering around them, but they didn't even realize I was trying to get them to take notice. Muti had both hands behind her back and almost doubled up with laughter as she told Papa something or other. I looked for a long time at her pink hands, at her beautiful nails, and then I sank my teeth into her little finger, which was a little apart from the others. What uproar! Muti crying with shame that she had such a child. Everyone talking about it and making comments. And poor Papa, usually so pale, turning red and speaking so shakily. He obviously felt embarrassed: such an intelligent man couldn't fail to realize that it had been a little fit of jealousy on his account. Hoping to prevent an escalation of the incident, he kept hovering around Muti, comforting her, and agreeing with what she said. Yes, she must be punished . . . but he had such a desperate look that you'd have thought he was the guilty one.

How abandoned I felt! What undying shame had fixed itself to me! That's probably why I continued to behave so badly and cast such evil looks at everyone. There was no way anyone could persuade me to ask for forgiveness.

∽

"Oh, for crying out loud, it's stopped again!"

Great, now she's found something to keep her busy, so she doesn't have to go look for my fifty lei. She's so hopeless that everything slips through her fingers, but now she's made up her mind to fix the clock! Fidget, fidget—is she going to go on like this till tonight?

"Forget the clock, Madam Ivona. What's the point of busting your head over it? Mr. Niki will come and sort it out. Or the watchmaker . . ."

Like talking to a brick wall. Nods her head and keeps on with it! I'll give it a bit longer, then tell her straight out. She knows it's only a week till she has to give me the money, but she pretends to be clueless. And my guts are rumbling and growling from hunger, just listen to them. I'm not going to ruin them for a crackpot and a miser like her! A miser who chain-smokes and drinks one coffee after another, and still doesn't get ill!

"You should give it a break, Madam Ivona, you've only just put one out. You're obviously worked up because Mr. Niki hasn't come back, but if you chain-smoke or not you'll still be worked up."

"Really, Madam Delcă, is that what you think? That I'm on edge because Niki's late? I wouldn't . . . That's how we are: neither of us gets worried if the other one's late. I hate families where someone lives in terror. Men also need to breathe some fresh air. It's not right to be cooped up together at our age, don't you agree?"

"That's exactly what I tell my old man! Go take a walk in Cişmigiu Gardens, have a look at the chess players, don't sit in front of the goggle box taking it out on me. If I was him, I'd croak from spending all day indoors. After a while I have to get out and see people: one day here, another there, having a little chat, finding out what's new . . ."

"Yes, you're right. We have to use up our energy one way or another, because we still have plenty of it. It's not enough to go shopping and stand in lines. That's why I think a husband and wife should show some understanding, even if the government doesn't. After slaving away for years on end, not getting any satisfaction from his job, shouldn't a man have some understanding at home? From his wife at least?"

"Understanding, my eye! As if men know anything about that! They're like children: all they understand is fear."

"No, Madam Delcă, you're wrong there. A man also needs to develop his personality. I thought the same when I was young. I always tried to be rational, always put myself in the other's shoes. Now, for example, I try to think like Niki: here I am on the margins of society, though still with a lot of strength in me; here I am, in the sad condition of pensioner, sad in itself, but also because of how things are in this country! Yesterday you were still somebody, to some extent respected, to some extent sought after. Today you don't count for anyone; you're slighted more than servants used to be. Your own children look down on you, feel embarrassed if you spend too much time with their friends, worry that you might say something that makes them feel ashamed. There's never been a child as wonderful as Tudor—yet even he . . . You wait for hours at the medical center, and when you go in they give you short shrift, even though it's only at this age that you have diseases that need to be treated. As for the hospital, they're instructed not even to look at you. Acquaintances who used to phone you all the time for advice, or for help in arranging something, have forgotten your number and don't even send you an invitation to birthday parties or other celebrations. You no longer have a job, but at least if you had some money to your name! Things were done more sensibly in the past, when personal fortunes were not divided up until after old people died. They still had a presence: they were courted and looked after properly—because money always forced others into it."

"Poor Madam Ioaniu, may she rest in peace! How many times she told me: put some money aside, Vica, whether you've got it or not. So that's how I saved up seven thousand lei. But since I retired, as you would put it, I haven't managed to save a single leu."

"Yes, it was a real feat to save seven thousand from what you had coming in. Do you think we have more than that put aside for a rainy day? And we can't even say we have much fun. We've lost interest in everything, long before our time . . . In the West, people still have a real lust for life when they retire. They're determined to do all the things they couldn't do when they were young and had to work hard. We work too, of course, but you have to admit we don't exactly stretch ourselves to the limit. There you're paid well but you have to make a real effort—otherwise you might lose the job you fought so hard to get. What I'm saying isn't propaganda, Madam Delcă. On the other hand, once people in the West retire, they can begin to relax a little. They travel around the world, because there aren't any restrictions over there . . ."

"Huh, I can't see the point of traveling so much. Why throw your money away?"

"Come on, Madam Delcă, don't say that! They get to see the world, educating themselves at the same time as having fun."

"Wandering around is no fun when you're old. In fact, I wasn't very keen on it when I was young either. What's the point, when you can see everything on television anyway?"

"You see one thing on television, but quite another in reality. And the simple fact of moving around keeps you young and healthy—both mentally and physically. People of our age go to dances, to festivities . . ."

"That's all I'm missing! For my old man to get the hots for some floozy. He used to be a famous dancer, it's true, and we waltzed like nobody's business when we were young. Everyone would stop and stare at us! But why stomp around at our age, when you're getting doddery and can't do the things that youngsters do? Only that crazy Reli likes that kind of thing: going to dances and chasing after men. She says she needs a man, and hers stopped functioning when he hit fifty."

"I'm not just talking of people's sex lives, Madam Delcă, although in the West they do have a completely different attitude to such things. Incredibly free and easy! I'm pretty tolerant, but even I am shocked sometimes."

"Let them get on with it! We're not short of amusements here."

"I understand your reserve about these matters, but I was thinking more of the life of a man who's not yet too old to play sports. Over there everyone seems to play tennis or swim or climb mountains . . . why not, after all? You think there's something wrong with it, but I'm afraid I don't agree. I mean, why do you think it's better to dress in black like a crow, to go to one funeral service after another, and to look after grandchildren without getting a word of thanks? Why is that kind of life preferable? Just because you get uglier as you grow old, why shouldn't you dress attractively, have massages and face-lifts, and so on? Why don't you try to keep fit, do some sport that's not too demanding?"

"Sure, that's all we need. My husband, all hundred and twenty kilos of him—that's all he needs. What more sport do you want him to do than getting wood and coal from the bottom of the garden? He can't even tie his own shoelaces, so that gives me one more sport to do. I've got more than my fair share already!"

Go stuff yourself with all that crap! Can't you see what you look like: yellow skin, flesh and bones, even with all your makeup and massages? The hell with you. Just stop fiddling with that clock and go get my fifty lei. Hurry up, 'cuz I'm so hungry I'm seeing black. I can only take so much.

And when I reach the limit, I'll give it to you good and proper. Who's the loser if I keep my mouth shut? Me, no? Well then . . .

"No, Madam Delcă, if you don't mind my saying so, you're only coming out with prejudices. Where is it written that Mr. Delcă should weigh a hundred and twenty kilos, at his age? You've forgotten what Muti and I have told you many many times: no fried food, only boiled poultry and veal, or grilled pork. Throw away your frying pan. Don't be angry: I'm telling you this like I would a sister. Diet and exercise! No pasta, no bread, and no thick soups. Some grilled meat, a piece of fruit, and lots of exercise. Because sitting around is . . ."

"What are you saying, Madam Ivona? That's more than we have the means for. I swear we haven't tasted meat the last three months. What with all the fasting we do, you could put me in the calendar with all the saints. If I did like you say, the pension would go up in smoke in a couple of days. No soups, no pasta, no potato dishes, no stews: you're talking about all my basics! I couldn't do it differently—period! Two people living on six hundred and fifty lei, what with the rent, the electricity, the television . . ."

"Yes, I see what you mean. It's certainly difficult, and that's why I've said many times how much I admire you for managing on your income. Still, if you cut out fried food and . . ."

"That's how I eat, and it hasn't killed me yet! I also give it to my husband, and we haven't come down with any illness. It's the skinny ones who are weak and irritable and catch everything going round. Anyway, dieting is only for rich people! I used to say that to Madam Ioaniu, and she said I was right. If you've got two pensions that add up to four or five thousand, you can stuff yourself with whatever you like. But on six hundred, either you eat bread and potatoes or you starve. With four thousand, you can tuck into grilled meat, fruit juice, strawberries, pâtés, you name it."

That's lowborn people for you: give them an inch and they take a mile. I treat her as an equal and behave as nicely as I can, and she takes the liberty of passing judgment on us. Judging us and calculating our income, because that's the main thing they're interested in. They don't lose themselves in lofty ideas, as we do, but keep their feet firmly on the ground and are never satisfied. They think it's normal for you to give them money and things, as if it's your duty, but abnormal for you to have them for yourself. She discusses your pension and her husband's as if it was somehow your fault that you went to university and spent many years out at work. Only I know what I had to swallow for this pathetic pension! I didn't stay at home, although I'd have had plenty to do if I had. She says loudly, for all to hear, that she didn't want to have someone bossing her around. Okay, fine, so you didn't go out to work. But don't start getting uppity now . . .

"Well now, Madam Delcă, if you added up what we have coming in and what we have going out, you'd soon see how little remains. Don't forget we have to heat and maintain this big house, to make telephone calls to my darling Tudor, and to send him packets from time to time. And then there are the medicines, and all the little repairs—a pair of shoes, a jacket, the weekly shopping. When I go visiting, it's impossible not to take a bunch of flowers or a box of candies . . . No, Madam Delcă, don't think they're all trifles: each visit costs close to fifty lei. Of course we don't mind giving: it gives pleasure, and we're happy to do that for people close to us. But it all adds up. By the way, now that you've made the long journey here, why don't I give you the fifty lei that we agreed for next month?"

"No, let's leave it; you don't want to be short either. You've just told me about all your expenses. Mail it to me when you can, whenever that is."

"It's true I'm a little up against it at the moment. Do you know why? I get my pension tomorrow, and the last few days of the month are always tight. Niki and I thought it best to keep our money separate, so we wouldn't have any arguments. But we have a pool for joint expenses. I could dip into the boiler money and put it back when my pension arrives. Niki wouldn't have time to notice . . ."

"No, Madam Ivona, really! I was just getting my things together to leave. It would be too messy for you to start taking money out and putting it back again. Just mail it to me when you can."

"It's not messy at all; it's very simple! For some time we've been saving up to buy a boiler, and each of us puts in what we can from our month's pension. Last summer, Niki needed so much before Tudor left that he nearly ran it down completely. We started saving again in the autumn, and I said to him that he shouldn't be the one who keeps it because he's too tempted to dip into it. And look, now it's me who's drawing on it first . . ."

"I told you: let's leave it as it is. I'm off now. Send it to me when you can."

"Please, Madam Delcă, wait and let me give it to you now. I'll be back in a second, then you can leave if you want to. But while I'm upstairs, please keep an eye on the clock to see if the hands are moving . . ."

She's got to be put in her place, so she realizes she's gone too far. She needs to feel that I'm making a sacrifice by giving her the fifty lei—a small sacrifice, perhaps, but one that no one else would make. To think that she put me in the position of having to justify myself, after I decided out of the goodness of my heart to give her a little monthly allowance! Niki's right: we're not talking here about being charitable. You're letting yourself be had, he says. *Tu te laisses faire!*

But what would he say if he knew I let myself be drawn into justifying my income to her? It was a bad mistake, of the kind I've often made before, because I'm so naive by nature. So gullible! Niki's right to point out that any child can twist me around his little finger. My only consolation is that I at least put her in her place. I was thinking for an hour or more whether to give her the money today, whether to take it out of our savings for the boiler. Was it wise to give it to her a week in advance, with the risk that she'll always come a week early in future? But if I don't give it to her, I'll have to drag myself off to the post office a week from now— another chore, another headache. When I heard her cheek, I suddenly made up my mind to give it to her, but I told her quite clearly where it would be coming from. So there'd be no confusion. I've anyway wasted the whole morning because of her. A wasted morning! Let her feel that's she gone too far this time. I speak to her as an equal, and she answers me like a dog. Muti put up with her vulgarity: sometimes I even think that her way of talking amused her. But that's not my style at all. Not at all.

Ivona put the clock back on the sideboard and went upstairs with the screwdriver in her hand. Vica waited for a creaking sound on the floor-boards, then took a Carbaxin from her bag and went to the kitchen again. On her way back, she noticed a grain-leather photo album in the corner of the table and listlessly put on her glasses and turned the first few pages. She heard a door open upstairs, then the sound of steps on the staircase. Without saying a word, Ivona came and held out a one hundred lei note. Vica quickly put her glasses down on the album, without closing it, and shuffled over toward her.

"What's this? A hundred? I haven't got any change, you know. I can look in my ragbag, but it never happens that there's more than I think in it. I'm never wrong about that."

She picked up her bag and removed everything in turn: empty plastic bags, then her purse. Ivona fumbled on the table for her pack of cigarettes, took one out, and lit it . . .

"Twenty lei. I was sure I had twenty on me, plus a few coins, that's all. But why have you gone quiet, Madam Ivona? Are you upset about something?"

"What an idea! Why should I be upset?"

Ivona stood up and looked at the two clocks: the old one was working, but it was five minutes slow. The cigarette nestled in the corner of her mouth while she adjusted it.

"Twenty-three, twenty-four . . . No, I told you I don't have enough change. That's the lot. I never have more on me than I think. It's one mistake I never make. Well, like I said, mail it to me when you can. You're short yourself; you've had to dip into your boiler money."

"That's not where it comes from. I took it out of Niki's spare cash. Anyway, who knows when we'll get around to the boiler? Take it, Madam Delcă."

"Why shouldn't you get around to the boiler? I can't take a hundred, though. I'll go around the corner and try to change it."

"Where?"

"At the grocery store."

"It's closed until Monday for an inventory. And there isn't anywhere else around here."

"What do you mean? Everywhere can't be shut. I'll try at the tobacconist's."

"It's past four, as you can see, so they'll be shut there too. Don't worry, I'd let you go if there was anywhere open. But there isn't. Just take the hundred: let's say it's for the month after next as well."

"In that case I'll leave you these twenty-four and . . . when the time comes I'll call around and pick up the rest, so you won't have to mail it to me. Yes, I'll come and . . ."

"It's all right, Madam Delcă, you don't need to leave anything. Take the hundred—otherwise I'll get upset. Please take it. Who knows what might happen between now and then?"

"That's a funny thing to say. What's happened? You weren't like that before you went upstairs."

"What do you mean?"

"Come on, you can't fool me. I've known you since you were this high. Come on, count to three and out with it! I've got my things together and I'm on my way out, but how can I leave with you like this? Ah, what a bunch of creeps men are! To hell with them and their dirty tricks!"

Chapter 11

Niki

". . . Even if Niki did lend the boiler money to someone without telling me, it's no reason to get angry."

"Men don't like to go out with their pockets empty. If he took the money with him, he'll also come back with it, you'll see. When you're least expecting it, you'll hear the key in the door, and it'll be Mr. Niki with the money."

"To go out with thousands of lei on him? What an idea! No, the money must be somewhere in his room—in another drawer, or anyway not where it's usually kept. Maybe he hid it intentionally, so that I wouldn't dip into it if I got something into my head. But it was no problem for me to take your hundred lei from his spare cash. I know where he keeps it, but I almost never touch it. Of course I'd have preferred to take your hundred from the boiler money, because it's our joint savings. In fact I've put in a greater share. I spend less and go out less than he does, and since I feel the cold more you might say that I also have a greater interest in the boiler. When winter comes, I feel as if I'm literally freezing to death. And it means I have to keep lighting the fire till May—all those ashes, all that trying to save wood. Coal that burns so badly! But, above all, the bathroom is like an ice box."

"And you're surprised you feel so poorly! No wonder all sorts of nonsense goes through your head. You've caught a cold, that's what. If you keep washing in a cold bathroom . . ."

"If only that was all, Madam Delcă! But I don't think . . ."

"Come on, stop getting ideas into your head! Try to calm down: don't you know how worked up you are? I've felt the same hundreds of times, but who would have noticed? Certainly no one at my place, where the toilet's a hole in the ground. Anyway, everyone knows that kind of thing's due to a cold."

"That's the whole point, my dear Vica. What I've got isn't just due to a cold."

"You're really fixed on the idea, aren't you? But you just said how this big house gets to you, what with all the fires and things. And I know your obsessions—how you're off to the bathroom every few minutes to take a shower. Do you have any stinging? Do you feel shivery?"

"No, neither stinging nor shivering. Nothing. But I can't say I feel too well either . . ."

"Because you're scared—that's why. Because you get all kinds of silly ideas in your head. Because you're having a bad day. Take my advice: when you go to bed tonight, put a hot salt bag on your tummy and a hot water bottle on your feet; put on a pair of thick warm drawers, or better still two on top of each other. That's what I do when this kind of thing happens. Cold is the worst enemy of the human race, so I'm very careful to wrap up well. My nephew Gelu calls me Mother Dochia, the goddess of cold and rain. What a clever, hardworking, sensible boy he is! I say that because he still hasn't had a girlfriend."

"You really think so?"

"Yes, but who knows for sure? He doesn't talk much about himself. You can't trust people who keep their mouth shut: everything can seem to be rosy, but then they suddenly turn on you and screw you over! His mother's the same: tight-lipped and stubborn. But he also takes after my brother Ilie, because he's clever and sensible. Poor Ilie, God rest his soul, had a stroke of good luck when I got married and opened the shop on Strada Coriolan. I had money coming in, so I dug deep and forked out for Ilie's fees—as a boarder, no less. What a nightmare it would have been for him to travel every day from Pantelimon to the Commercial School! How I quarreled about it with Daddy. I'm broke, he said, there's no point asking me! What a skinflint, like they all are in Oltenia! And he left everything he had—houses, shop, money—to the children of his second wife, a real yokel, who let it all go up in smoke. So it was me who got Ilie into the Commercial School. What a find! Daddy said, all bubbly, and we don't even have to pay for it! That's what I told him—that it was a school where you got everything for free, even your board and keep. But I was paying all the time, and it was worth it 'cuz Ilie was a great kid. His son's the same: as clever as they come, always with his nose in a book. Leave that book for a minute, I tell him, when I see him like that. Why don't you go out for a walk? That's why they're all head over heels in love with him: girls, the headmaster, his bosses, everyone! Like they were with Gelu . . ."

"I don't think they could have been that keen on Tudor. Otherwise he wouldn't have gone off as he did."

"Say what you like, but my Gelu, like Tudor, is . . . He just reads and reads, doesn't hear or see anything else. When I was there today, wrapping myself up in all my togs to leave, he said: You look like Napoleyon in Russia, Auntie!"

"What did he say, Madam Delcă? Napoleon in Russia?"

"That's right. So I thought to myself, I'll save that one up for batty old Niculaie. Look at me, I'll say, who do I look like? Who do you think Gelu said I look like? What a laugh we'll have! 'Cuz Niculaie got as far as Stalingrad, where all hell broke loose. He knows a thing or two about Russia, he does! Once, he said, when they were living like rats under the ground, he stuck his bare hand out in the frost—like a frost that cracks walls. And Niculaie, still the little devil, stuck his hand out to freeze, so that with a bit of luck they'd send him home from that hellhole. So he sat like that till his hand was snow-white and stiff as a pole, and when he pulled it back he saw it was swelling up in the warm air. That made his day! Swelling, swelling—only he could still move his fingers. Then, suddenly, the swelling went down. That's been the story of my life, he says with a laugh. Nothing's ever worked out as I wanted it! But that's not really true, 'cuz he had the shop on Brezoianu and some pretty fancy customers. And now he's an old man they still keep him on as head of the cooperative. And people say how lucky he was to come back from Russia alive; so many others left their bones there . . . But here I am talking and talking, and you seem miles away!"

"I was thinking that I didn't look properly for the envelope with the boiler money . . . It threw me so much that I didn't have the patience to hunt for it. After all, it must be there somewhere . . . Maybe it's also because we'd been talking about poor Margot . . . And also the fact that the clock stopped again . . ."

"Ah, all that nonsense! You can see why I might believe in it, but an educated woman like you . . . I never heard Madam Ioaniu ever come up with that kind of stuff. She even used to complain: I can't believe in God, Vica, nor in devils or a life after this. Well, I'd say, no one's ever been there and come back to tell us about it. So everyone believes what they want. My old creep, for example, doesn't believe. But you should hear him go on and on about Adam and Eve and the monkey. He can't stand the sight of priests: they make him see red, and he wouldn't have one in the house even at Easter, the old sinner. Something's rubbed off on you from the communists, I tell him when he starts to snap. But he says that's bullshit: he's always thought like that."

"Well, Madam Delcă, I've believed ever since I was little. How many candles I lit to the Sainte Vierge, the patron of Notre Dame, and how many prayers I said for Papa to come back! Several times in my life I've felt the hand of God above me—even in times of misfortune. I'm not superstitious, but the world seems to me filled with signs, so it rather threw me when the old clock stopped like that . . ."

"Don't you see it's working now? I don't know what you did, but you sure fixed it! Come on, Ivona dear, that's enough of all this flaky non-sense. You really stunned me, you know: I'd never have thought you had it in you to repair some old piece of . . . There it goes, tickety-tick: say no more, I'd better not tempt fate! These old things are like rotten fabric: they fall apart when you're least expecting it."

"Yes, I do have some flair for technical things. Tudor was the first one who realized that. Ivona, he said to me, you chose the wrong career! He used to do all the repairs in the house, but after he left I had to deal with the hard things. You won't believe it, but of the two of us it's Niki who's the poet. He with his ideals, his gift of the gab; I with my skill at repair-ing things . . ."

"Uh, huh, he even wrote poems for you."

"Sssh, Madam Delcă! Please be quiet a minute. I think I can hear someone in the yard."

"Mr. Niki! Okay, I'll go and get my things together: I only stayed so you wouldn't be left on your own. I don't want to be still out when it's dark."

Look how she jumped up and rushed to the door! Well, good or bad, he's her man after all. They've had a lifetime together. Plenty of growling and cursing—but together. And they haven't got so long to go now; Death won't forget any one of us. May God forgive me: I shouldn't tempt fate like that! Something comes into your head, and you come straight out with it. She may be loopy, may be hotheaded, but you can count on her more than you can on Niki-Wiki. Useless at keeping house, but still pretty much of a home bird. Not a bad sort really. She did remember about my fifty lei, for example. After her mother died, it was her idea to give it to me, instead of to the church or every Gypsy hanging around at the cemetery—that crowd of ragamuffins who jump on you as soon as they see you holding a bit of food. And it was a good thing she did it, 'cuz I've never stopped thinking about Madam Ioaniu. If it had been left up to her mother, pigs would have flown before I saw a cent. I've never seen anyone so tightfisted. She'd slip a bit of pie or dried cake into my ragbag, but money? God forbid! All I got was my twenty-five lei, after slaving from morning to night for her . . . Whew, how Ivona rushed to open the door for scumbag Niki! He's her man, her husband. Mine will do the same when he hears me in the yard. The poor old creep! Grumpy, never opening his mouth except to complain, but you know you can rely on him. He did his best, getting up at the crack of dawn, 'cuz otherwise we wouldn't have had a cent in our old age. How he scratched those scabs he got from the factory! His hands were a running sore from all the poisons he carried around with him. And he'd come to me every payday and hand it all over: here, take it! Can you see that jerk Niki doing that? My old creep's not so wrong: you moan about me all the time, he says, but if you knew what other men are like! Yes, there he'd be every payday: here, take it! And I'd count it and divide it up: for the television, the rent, the firewood, somehow managing to save up those seven thousand lei. It was one of the best things Madam Ioaniu did when she advised me to put it aside. That's why I feel so bad when I see the state the house is in now: the pavilion in ruins, the pear tree withered and full of caterpillars, the outside walls flaking, and Ivona thin and pale, no more than skin and bones. I can't stop myself getting wound up. Ah, before you realize what's happened, nothing's left of the past . . . Well, I must be off. I can hear the floor creaking out there.

"No, it wasn't Niki, Madam Delcă. It was the postman, with a letter from Tudor. Stay a bit longer: I'll just fetch my glasses upstairs and tell you what's in it . . ."

So, he still hasn't shown up. But Ivona's lucky: instead of coming back with her tail between her legs, she's got a letter from her son. Now everything's all right again. She's forgotten Mister Good-for-Nothing, forgotten her bats in the belfry... Ah, how crazy she is about Tudor, just like her mother used to be! How they sacrificed themselves! Nothing was too good for him. But he was so fussy, so nerdy. "... give him to me for a month and I'll set him straight. I know how to deal with him." How many times I said that to them! And one day they did go out in the morning and only came back quite late. When I laid the table, Tudor was the same as always: fuss, fuss, I don't want this, don't want that, I'm not hungry right now. So I collected everything up, locked it all in the cupboard, and stuck the key in my pocket... Then, when Ivona and Madam Ioaniu came back in the evening, we all sat at the table and the kid grabbed a chunk of bread and began to gobble it down—like a wolf who can't wait another minute. How we laughed at him! What fun it was! "You're a miracle worker, Madam Delcă," the mother said. "Don't you worry," I said, "I know how to deal with him." But it was the only time I saw him gobble his food. He wasn't a glutton—not at all. Books were his big thing. Everyone would sit down to eat, and he'd polish it off quickly and say thank you for the meal. Then, if he'd finished everything, his granny would let him scamper back to his books, up there in the attic. (When they had a big and a small room downstairs, they were happy to leave him the attic to work in.) He'd often have school friends around in the evening: only they knew where they all came from! They'd put their music on—that thumping noise you'd give anything to be rid of. Even his granny couldn't stand it, and she kept going up to tell them to turn it down, 'cuz she was afraid Petruța and her husband would freak out at the noise. Then it would stop for a bit and start up again. There were girls there too, now one, now another, and one of them was the girl Tudor ended up marrying. Anca, a lean alley cat. She was still at secondary school in those days, and Madam Ioaniu told me that her family had had some problems like the ones she'd had herself. She wondered if the girl's mother knew where she went in the evening—i.e., to see a boy. In fact, there were a whole load of boys and girls up there, but the mother must have known and thought he was a nice boy, with a mother and grandmother around the house, and no doubt fancy carpets and chandeliers, so it would be all to the good if her Anca managed to get her claws into him. And she did get her claws into him. Meanwhile, she often went up the stairs to the attic room, where they talked and laughed and got up to who knows what hanky-panky.

"They're not doing anything, Madam Delcă," Madam Ioaniu used to tell me. Not doing anything—only smoking like chimneys, and drinking liquor that one of them brings along, in the American style that's the fashion nowadays. And they talk when they feel like it, but more often say nothing and listen to music. What's that music you listen to? I asked Tudor, and he laughed and said it was what everyone was listening to. It's barbarian music, I said; we're going back to barbarism. I don't even think he or his friends liked it. After all, there's nothing to like in it: no tune, no nothing, only a noise that splits your eardrums. But they listened to it 'cuz it was the fashion . . .

That's what Madam Ioaniu couldn't stand in her grandson: the music they put on, and their summer treks in the mountains. Only they know where they slept—in shepherds' huts, in tents—or what they ate and how they spent their time. They'd go off with stuff sticking out of their backpacks, bent over almost on all fours, in clothes that were nothing better than rags.

"What fun can that be, to traipse around with a burden like that?" Madam Ioaniu said. "Instead of resting, dressing up nicely, enjoying the views . . ."

"Wild horses couldn't drag me there," I echoed. "If I were those girls, I wouldn't go for the life of me!" But the ninnies could hardly wait. How else could they lure the dumbos into their trap? "No amount of gold would get me to bust my guts for them."

How Tudor would laugh! He wasn't a bad kid, just a bit on the quiet side, like boys are, especially as his Anca could talk enough for two. Ivona this, Ivona that: she soon learned to call her by her first name, so I twigged that there was more to it than met the eye. And in the end Tudor did marry her . . . How he clung to me when he was little, and even later his eyes would light up when he saw me; he had such smiling eyes, neither ugly, nor much of a good-looker; took after Ivona and her side of the family. No, handsome he wasn't, but he was certainly brainy. Anyway, as everyone knows, men only need to be a shade more handsome than the devil . . . He looked worst when he let his beard grow. Ugh, Madam Ioaniu would go, how ugly you are with a beard! He laughed it off, but still got rid of it in the end—not because of what granny said, but because he wanted to join the Party. Things were going well for him at the time:

his bosses and everyone were crazy about him, although Ivona doesn't
like to admit that now. Things were going so well that they sent him to
France, Germany, and wherever. You'll see, he'll stay on and never come
back, Madam Cristide said. But he did come back home, to his mummy
and grandma. Then they wrote to him from where he'd been and asked
him to go there again—either the same lot or some others who'd heard
good reports about him. He planned on going there, wherever it was, but
in the end he didn't. They sent someone else in his place who was a Party
member. So, when he saw that, he thought he'd better get into the Party
as well. He asked them to let him in, but they didn't like the look of him:

"Who do you think you are, coming to us after your stepfather died
you know where? On top of that, one of your grandfathers was a land-
owner, and your aunt spent time in prison for hiding someone in a
cupboard in Otopeni."

They told him one thing after another, because those guys know all
there is to know. They've got a file on everyone: who did what, who your
relatives were, going back to the year one. He kept trying, followed all
the procedures, did all he possibly could, but they still wouldn't let him
join.

Well, he swallowed it in silence but thought to himself: I'll show you!
And, when the time was ripe, he showed them. How do I know all this?
From Madam Ioaniu, Madam Cristide—I'm not too sure. Anyway, these
things always come out in the end. He showed them by taking off to the
West with his wife. But they left everything here—house, carpets, crystal
ware—so the state will get its hands on them in the end. Here we are,
two people trying to get by on six hundred and fifty lei a month, and all
that stuff will go to pot. Doesn't it make you mad? If I were in that batty
Ivona's shoes, I'd sell it all and spend the lot—every last bit, so I'd know
I wasn't leaving anything behind. But you don't feel like doing that, 'cuz
you never know how you'll end your days. That's why Ivona's got even
stingier lately. She's still yes Niki, no Niki, but she knows Mr. Scumbag's
playing games with her. She puts money aside for the boiler, for doctors,
or for some sudden disaster—God forbid!—and he goes off with it to
his floozy. You can bet your life that's what he does . . . But what's Ivona
doing up there all this time? Just a second, she said, I'll be right back: but
there's still no sign of her. I feel sorry for her: she got a fright, and I didn't
want to leave her alone, but it doesn't seem to occur to her . . .

ᖇᖇ

"Are you getting bored alone, Madam Delcă? Why did you jump? It's only me. I'm sorry, but when I was up there I had a dizzy spell and had to lie down for a minute . . ."

"You had a fright, that's why. When that happens to me, I get weak at the knees and can't do a thing for hours. I'm like that today. I left in a rush this morning, on an empty stomach, and now I feel faint all the time . . . I'd bet my last cent you haven't had a bite to eat all day."

"Maybe. But I'm not hungry . . . Let me read you a bit from the letter . . ."

"Who did you say wrote it?"

"Anca. She's in charge of their correspondence. I won't begin at the beginning, because it probably wouldn't interest you. So, here goes:

I don't know why we keep not writing more often, but you know you're always in our thoughts. We talk about you every day, and when I put my earrings on—either the ones from you or the ones I got from Auntie Linica—I always think about you. Everything's okay here. We're happy and very satisfied with things. I worked three days a week in September, but I didn't like it, so I've continued to look for something better and now I'm waiting for an answer from a travel agency. Please ask the Lord to make it happen. It would be really fantastic—the salary and everything else."

"But I thought she was teaching over there."

"It's not so easy to get work teaching, so she's trying to change her job. Let me continue:

I'm behind with all my correspondence, because I'm more and more taken up with my course in economics, for which I have to do a lot of reading and homework. On top of that we're in the middle of moving into a new apartment. It's not a big block—only five stories, plus an underground area where we'll have a huge storage space and somewhere to park the car. We can drive it in through doors that open automatically. The apartment itself consists of two bedrooms and a living room. There's also a big balcony, with a view over some trees that are lit up at night by spotlights. The kitchen is bright, and there's a waste disposal oven on the premises. We've put curtains up in the living/dining room. I bought them here because they have to be the right length for the door-like windows. As soon as we've finished, I'll take some photos and send them to you. We've managed to repair the chairs with straw seats, and now I hope we'll be able to hang the pictures in frames. I've also put the icons up on the wall. We went to Sandra and Şerban's for Christmas; they had their family over from

Germany. They handed out presents and we all had a great time. I made sarmale *with sour cabbage leaves I bought from an Armenian shop, which has lots of Oriental things like salted pickles, Brăila cheese, olives, countless types of halva (really great!), nuts, and raisins. My* sarmale *turned out wonderfully: Tudor even said they were better than Muti's. Your letter, bursting with love and faith in the future, gave us enormous pleasure, as did your phone call for my birthday on January 18th. We also greatly enjoyed the New Year celebrations: we invited a number of guests that we feel grateful to, and we wish them happiness and all good things in life. We think a lot about you and feel very bad that we're not all together. We love you to bits and think the world of you . . ."*

"What are you playing at, Madam Scarlat? Okay, so they're fine over there, we're fine over here . . . what *is* all this? You've been there yourself and seen that they have things we don't have here. And you'll be going again next summer, or whenever it was you said. Come on, Ivona dear, wipe away your tears. Can't you see things are going well for them?"

"I don't know—it's the emotion . . . And I feel sorry for him in particular; it can't be easy. She's doing okay with her courses, waiting for something to turn up. But he's the one who has a hard time of it. You shouldn't think it's easy there until you sort yourself out . . . You have to work hard and keep at it—not like here. And when the poor boy comes home in the evening, he has to study some more, because what you learn here is one thing, and what they expect over there is quite another. No one gives you anything for free. Here we have our own house and everything, but they've got to start from scratch . . ."

"Sure, you don't get anything for free anywhere. Here you're okay so long as you've got something to give, but you're not worth a thing when you don't. It's the times we live in—here as much as there. Come on, don't start getting blue. I know from Madam Cristide that the communists didn't let Tudor join the Party, and that's why he had to leave. But time solves everything in the end . . . Do you know what I've done with my glasses? I'd like to see what the kid writes as well."

"Your glasses? No, I can't see them. But you know what, it's so late there's no more point in saving Niki's lunch. Come and have something. I'll try to get some down myself."

"Yes, times have changed. Madam Cristide has grown old too, but her style's the same as ever: tight dresses with colors that scream at you, wide-brimmed hats, long mauve scarves, cheap gaudy jewelry when a single real jewel, discreetly worn, would be enough. She shocks people and comes in for a lot of criticism, but I've always defended her. Why shouldn't she have a style of her own, like everyone else? If it suits her, what's the problem? But what I don't like is the way she goes around gossiping, and invents something to add to each bit of tittle-tattle. The story with Tudor is a good example. Here, there's a little soup left, why don't you finish it up? Of course you can! No, I couldn't possibly—really. I promise, if you weren't here I wouldn't have had a mouthful. You're so persuasive. You take such pleasure in life that it's catching, although you must have plenty of things to worry about . . ."

"You're telling me! But I don't let them get me down. You're not going to make me lose any sleep, I tell them. And I take a Carbaxin and a diazepam and my other pills you know about, and I sleep like a log through till morning. What would become of me if I didn't take charge? You can bang your head against the wall as much as you like, it won't change what's bound to happen."

"You're right, Vica dear! Would you like a glass of wine?"

"Your very good health! And may everything go well with Niki! What a handsome man he is—and so clever, so sensible . . ."

"He was handsome once, and he may be even cleverer than when he was young. Sensible? Not exactly . . . He has this bad habit of being late, for example. I'm a pretty calm sort of person, but sometimes I get worried waiting for him. Not today, though! I feel quite calm today. I feel there's nothing for me to worry about. You're right, in fact: everything's that's bound to happen will happen . . . But I was thinking about what you said Madam Cristide told you. Things were not like that at all! Tudor's family history meant that he wasn't allowed to defend his doctoral thesis. Do you understand, Madam Delcă? Although he'd finished writing it and even published most of it, they didn't let him defend it for political reasons. So, whenever he applied for a promotion, he was more or less ruled out of court. That really rankled, especially for someone as serious and well-trained as he was. To always see some lout get ahead of you, however hard you tried! To always be the black sheep! To never feel safe in your job, because there's a lot of competition and the number of academic posts is being reduced every year. You swallow as much as you can, and then . . . That's how things really were—not the way Madam Cristide told you. It wasn't that Tudor wanted to join the Party. If there's any truth at all in what she said, the facts of the matter are rather different. I don't know if you understand me."

"I understand you okay. What makes you think I don't? But tell me what else is in the letter."

She's all right, this Ivona, just a bit too flaky. Like her son. He's not a bad kid, but he's also got a few screws loose. He must have, to sit with his head buried in a book all the time. Of course that sends you round the bend. That's why he let the house go to ruin and went off wandering. Just as well I never had any kids! More worries, more sorrows, and all for nothing! The Good Lord knew what he was doing, because if I'd had children it would have been one headache after another. Nowadays, of course, parents are also a headache for their children, who have to pay for the sins of their family since the year one; that's the law for the communists—unless you can find someone to put in a good word for you and get around it like that. I know from Madam Zaharescu that that's how it works. It's a case of the right hand washing the left, she said to me. And she's certainly a sly one, all smart and materialistic, but only caring about herself. Well, at least I didn't have kids: who knows what crazies they'd have ended up as! You sacrifice yourself to bring them up, worrying about them all the time, and when you're in a tight corner later on you might as well not have any. Look at Ivona. She's alone in an empty house; it's getting dark outside, and the floorboards creak so much you'd think ghosts were romping around. She lays the table and sits and waits for Mr. Scumbag. At least until now she did. But in the end she got a wake-up call. Okay, Mr. Scumbag, so you're going to play around with your bit on the side and forget you've even got a wife at home. Do you think you can sneak off like that, then come back when it suits you, for me to wash and iron your clothes and fill your belly with food? No, sir, you can go and stuff yourself as much as you like! Madam Delcă's here now: please sit yourself down, in Niki's place at the head of the table; let me serve you a bowl of soup . . . It's the first time in my life I've seen Ivona acting like her head's screwed on. All you have to do is sit with her for a while, chatting back and forth, and she soon wises up . . .

"Come and sit next to me and tell me what else is in the letter."

On the Feast of the Epiphany we were invited to Sandra's sister's, Mrs. Morand—I wrote you all about her in my last letter. They made a fondue—a kind of Swiss dish with melted cheese—followed by the traditional galette des rois, *which has a little object inside, a* fève, *and the one who has it in his portion becomes the king. Who do you think found it? Why, Tudor, of course, the lucky one of the family!*

"Lucky boy! Mommy could eat him up! But she was luckier still: she got her hands on a clever, handsome young man, who has them swooning wherever he goes. Go on."

As you see, we're not short of a social life. You just have to step outdoors to have some fun; I don't think there's a more beautiful city anywhere in the world. Sometimes we go for a drive in the evening and feast our eyes on the combination of lights and cleverly illuminated stone buildings (houses and churches). But, as I said, it was most dazzling at Christmas, which is a really important day here. It was all so magical, and Tudor had just heard that he'd landed his new job. Now it's the sales period. It's wonderful to see shops all over the city compete to offer fine clothes and shoes at rock-bottom prices. I bought myself two blouses and a pair of fabulous Bally shoes.

"But how careless of me, Madam Delcă, you've been sitting there with an empty plate and saying nothing. Let me give you the next course: chicken with peas. There's not a lot of meat, but here's a wing. Don't worry, you have plenty of time: you can leave after you've eaten. But I'm beginning to wonder about Niki. Of course I'll wait for him until the last minute, but if he doesn't show up I'll have to go alone. It's out of the question for both of us to stay away. I'll have to go alone—and that, Vica dear, doesn't suit me at all. You know what people are like: they find a hidden meaning for every little trifle."

"Ah, who can stop tongues wagging? Let them stick it up their ass, is what I say! But listen, Ivona dear, you just go over there and drink your coffee while I do the dishes. Relax a bit; it's been a tiring day for you."

If, while waiting for your coffee to cool, you sit on the sofa and let your eyelids droop, you'll be surprised how quickly your mind becomes clouded by sleep. Yes, such tiredness . . . An exhaustion you feel in every fiber as your thoughts slow down—chaotic fibers that quiver rhythmically in a black claw. Thoughts breaking loose, sticking together, moving ever more slowly, until you're no longer a bundle of nerves but only a patch spreading over blotting paper, collecting the fibers at its core. Fibers—threads. A black claw opens and closes with a dull pounding, pulling the threads through your weary flesh, sending a current of anxiety coursing through you. It's late, very late. Forget, if only for a moment, that he hasn't come, that it's late; the dull pounding of blood in your temples and ears, in the middle of the taut bundle, pulls the electric threads all the way through you. It's late, it's late, but he'll come soon now, soon soon soon; you'll hear his steps in the yard, hear them soon soon soon. Do you hear them? Will he come or won't he? Soon now you'll hear him in the yard, on the steps, in front of the door. Nothing. Only the ticking of the clock in the hall, like a stranger's even breathing, like an alien presence always there, always unseen, which follows you around; it's so easy to hide among the old furniture, to pursue you in the house's dusty shadows; your heart will burst in the tight black grip, and the threads that tense up rhythmically will send a current of anxiety all the way to your fingertips, to the soft dark depths of your brain. Forget, forget, don't think, don't think, forget the even ticking of the clock in the hall, in the middle of the taut bundle, a desperate struggle for breath in the black claw, a desperate panting, a constant pounding of blood. The window that looks onto the yard gives a glimpse of the night. No pounding on the stones, on the steps, only someone invisible standing and watching you. Not even the telephone ringing. Only the creaking of the old woodwork, the staircase, it's night, still night, still quiet, he still hasn't come and, of course, he never will . . .

Her thick eyelids sank lower and lower, but the thin lashes did not mesh together. A little opening remained, through which her eye, blind and lifeless, looked at the dining room without seeing it. And yet, behind the lids, she did still see the room, with its chairs arranged around the Dutch table and the still steaming coffeepot. What did this solemn invitation mean, as if the chairs had a sense of duty that they would by no means be allowed to . . . ? It was a grave, dignified waiting, in which anxiety was hidden in immobility. Hard to believe we'll ever leave here, watched over as we are by the phalanx of chairs exuding a sense of order and duty. Hard to believe we'll ever go into the hall, or that our feet will ever again resound on the cracked paving in the yard, on the three steps leading up to the front door, each of us will go separately to the Boteanu church, sure we'll go to Boteanu, but not the two of us, not at the same time, oh dear, how much longer is that racket in the kitchen going to last, that clanging of dishes, that wretched gushing of water in the sink, that terrifying roar of an aquatic beast struggling to escape from the pipe where hot water is scalding its shiny bald head beneath a dirty pink hood? The gushing roar of the water, and that black claw that tightens grimly on the threads, exasperating yet soothing, someone's washing dishes in the kitchen, someone's washing pans and plates, and chasing the clock away: Muti. Muti impatiently wipes her fingers, stained black from potato peeling, and throws the rusty half-blade onto a pile of clean dishes, the last of which is piled high with bones carelessly stripped of meat that will feed the spider now descending from its smoky nest high above the sink. Muti removes the jagged varnish from her nails with a cotton pad, she doesn't realize that the cigarette in the corner of her mouth has gone out, why don't you tell her? No, don't tell her! Don't! In such cases, you never tell the truth to the person in question.

"Before we do the decorating, in the days before Easter, the spider will have to be helped to spread its webs in each room, and as for the first floor someone will have to help it discreetly up the stairs . . ."

Muti points at the threads of spiderweb gently shaking above her head. By now it has spun the whole ceiling. Muti crushes her smoking cigarette in the ashtray: look at the smoke coming out of the side, look how the paper's come unstuck. Is that a worrying symptom? A bad sign? Could it be serious, doctor, a . . . ?

". . . since you insist, I'll tell you my fears as a doctor," he says hesitantly. "But you must promise to be discreet, because, if Niki finds out, Madam Cristide will too—he often gets caught up with her till late . . ."

And it's clear to you that Niki is there right now. They are sitting at the kitchen table with Madam Delcă. It's our kitchen, therefore it's the truth: Niki's at Madam Cristide's, and that's where he always goes.

"Rest assured!" the doctor says. "After the operation we'll go together in the carriage and pick Niki up from Madam Cristide's. As for the diagnosis, in my experience blood in the urine, constipation, and swelling are all symptoms of . . . But will you have the strength to face it?"

You curled up in the dentist's chair, his round lamp shining into your eyes, your hands cold with fear. But you gave a sign that you were strong enough to face it, because that was precisely why you'd come to see him: to be told the truth. "Yes!" you shouted, as loudly as you could. But the doctor didn't hear you: it was unbearably irritating. However much you tried, you couldn't get a sound out, because at that moment his drill was boring into one of your teeth.

"Would it be right for me to tell you the plain truth, in the American way?" the doctor asked, pacing up and down the room. "Is it or is it not the normal, human, correct thing to do? I don't know. But I'll tell you all the same, because you should know my medical opinion in time—not like Margot. I'm almost sure you have inflammation of the glands."

What a relief! It's obviously serious, but you turn your head in relief. It could have been something more serious—but what exactly? You can't quite remember. You turned your head before he opened his mouth, so you caught Margot making a sign to Mr. Ialomiţeanu, yes, it's Margot, none other than Margot, that's her dirty-pink bonnet pulled down over her eyes. At the same time you can clearly make out her round bald head, as shiny as a child's marble ball. Margot is making a sign for Mr. Ialomiţeanu to say nothing, but Mr. Ialomiţeanu seems not to notice.

"Swollen glands," Mr. Ialomiţeanu says. "So we're preparing for . . ."

You huddle with fear and cold in the high-backed chair. The two of you are alone in this semibasement filled with rickety furniture, a legless daybed, a dressing table with a black hole instead of an oval mirror, some armchairs placed on top of one another, and a massive chest of drawers that is used to keep the door shut, because this too has a black hole where the handle should be. What bric-a-brac! How cold you feel! And what will you do if Niki doesn't come really soon? How will you escape the operation that Mr. Ialomiţeanu and Margot are preparing? If only Niki would come now now now now! With his back to you, the doctor fiddles nervously on the trolley, shifting around the china cups and gold-plated teaspoons that you now remember, perfectly clearly, having sent to the West for Tudor. What an effort it took, though! Of course—that's why you have blood in your urine. A reassuring explanation! It means no operation will be necessary, so you'd better tell the doctor right away. Go on, tell him! How infuriating to lose your voice just now! Your eyes bulge out of their sockets, saliva dribbles onto the collar of your school uniform and you wipe it away discreetly, preoccupied as you are with trying to shout out. Your throat strains hard, but not even an unnatural cackle escapes from it. No point in torturing yourself any more. Give it up! And you give it up, having just remembered what you quite unaccountably forgot: that you no longer have a voice, because you no longer have any teeth. The radiation caused them to fall out. But it doesn't matter. You calmly run your tongue over your moist bare gums: the important thing is that you're still alive, that you'll live for years and years to come. A year and a half, thank God! It's even possible to live without a voice, thank God; you've got used to it so easily. Only the doctor is still fiddling around on the trolley, and you can hear all kinds of sharp tinkling sounds. And Niki, oh, if only Niki would open the door and walk in! The doctor has found what he was looking for: a gleaming nickel-plated box. Look, he's opening it and starting to take out scoops, forks, lancets, forceps, swabs, and you look despairingly at the door kept shut by the massive chest of drawers. You're cold and frightened. Over at the sink, wearing glossy gloves, Mr. Ialomiţeanu washes the pans of sauce and blood, while a smoky spider's nest quivers above his head. Suddenly he shouts out:

"How much longer are we going to wait here, in this cold and uncomfortable basement? Until it's too late, like it was with Margot?"

"Just a little longer," you shout despairingly. But, however much you strain, only little cackling sounds come out. Just a little longer! Niki will be here soon! He has a bad habit of coming late, but he always comes in the end.

"All over!" the doctor says, moving toward you with a cheap kitchen knife in his hand.

You try to climb down from the high chair, but you are so small that your legs hardly reach over the edge. They put three cushions under you so that your chin reached the table, ah, if only Niki would come now! In the dark hall, bed jacket wrapped around her shoulders, Muti puts her hands over her ears so as not to hear you scream.

"Why do you scream if it doesn't hurt you? Tell me, do you feel any pain?" the doctor asks severely.

Nothing hurts, and you feel ashamed that you are behaving so badly, dressed in your nightdress under the stern, accusatory eyes of the Guests. They all sit, solemn and grave, at the round Dutch table. You're left alone here, you and Mr. Ialomiţeanu, and you speak to him in whispers, because in fact you are keeping him hidden. Shush! Don't let the Guests next door hear you! How cold it is! How quiet! What a horrible light! You're not hungry, but you force yourself to eat properly, chewing the cake without taking your eyes off Mr. Ialomiţeanu. Why have you hidden him here, when you know Niki will come any minute and that he always gets upset when he finds him in the house? No, Niki doesn't like him, and he has good reason not to! Look at how he sticks a finger in his mouth and digs out a piece of meat with his nail. Horrible! How uncouth! What a lack of manners! But you won't be able to tell anyone, since it's you who've hidden him here. "That's not charity," Niki says, "you're being had!" And, as always, he is right.

You sit still and rest your neck against the high back; its worn leather cracked long ago, and yellowish-brown sawdust trickles out into your hair, but you don't move. The Guests who are washing the dishes in the kitchen might hear you. You chew the cake with growing difficulty, conscientious as ever, because the chairs drawn around the table are anyway watching you and leave you with no escape. It's chewing gum that sticks to your teeth and tongue; you chew, desperate that your throat has begun to twitch, you chew, fighting back tears that well up from your throat. A grimace has begun to lock your face in a kind of paralysis, and a little grunt throws the sticky mouthful into the middle of a dazzlingly white table on which the silver and crystalware glisten. You squeal, vomit, and cry into your plate, and your tears and the bitter rejects cover your face like an astringent mask.

"Take her out of here! This minute!" Muti shouts, stretching out a white finger that still preserves the marks left by your teeth.

What dizziness, what confusion! Such a long time has passed since you bit Muti's finger. Aren't you perhaps dreaming, lost in the land of sleep? Wake up! Thank God you've woken up. Thank God you're in the carriage going to pick up Niki; it's moving too slowly, and from the bench you have no way of hurrying the driver up, but you'll arrive soon now, soon soon. The week's provisions lie at your feet: Suchard chocolate, caviar in which you accidentally trod . . . Psst! Don't let Muti see that you trod in the caviar with your sandals! Or that your fishnet stockings are smeared with dog mess. Margot's poor little Pekinese has been hiding in the carriage since he was left alone in the world—since Margot hid herself in her villa in Otopeni so that Ialomiţeanu wouldn't see she had gone bald and wore a dirty-pink velvety bonnet day and night.

"Shall we take Yvonne with us to the theater?" Uncle Georges asked, as if you weren't there yourself.

"It's closed today," Muti said, bored.

Then, turning to you, in quite a different tone of voice:

"Sit up straight and stop gawking like that! When she looks that way I think she must be getting a squint."

"So, go back to the theater!" Uncle Georges exclaimed, prodding the driver with the end of his stick.

"But what about Niki? Aren't we going to pick him up from Madam Cristide's?" you want to shout, in desperation.

You open your mouth and lean over to them—again? again? as if it has happened once before, but when?—and again no sound comes out. There's so much noise all around you: car horns, ticking clocks, horses' hooves from the other carriage.

"Four rolls for ten bani!" the street vendor says, running along with a pile of newspapers under his arm.

And the carriage turns around. You sit on the bench, mouth open, forcing yourself to shout, but no sound comes out. A black velvet bow hangs heavy on your head, and sharp hairpins bore through your skull, deep into your brain, ah, Niki! Niki! But no sound comes out. A pale little girl, nose too long, legs too long, sits on a carriage bench as all the boredom of Sunday washes over her . . .

"Stay like that! Close your eyes and rest some more. Ah, Ivona, Ivona, mommy's little darling, how tired she is! What a tired little girl! Stay like that. I put my coat over you when I came in and saw you curled up with all these drafts around you. If you doze off like that, you're bound to catch cold."

"Did I doze off? Yes, I must have done . . . But not for long, only a couple of minutes. I didn't even start to dream. But I felt cold—I seem to remember that. Thank you for covering me. I'm so exhausted. Mmm, how nice a coffee will be. But what are you doing there?"

"Looking for my goddamn glasses!"

"Maybe you left them at home. Or here, in the kitchen. Bring yourself a cup and have some coffee too. A little bit won't do you any harm."

Ugh, what a disgusting smell! Mold and kerosene. She means well, the poor thing, but unfortunately all her clothes smell like that; I have to air the house whenever she's been here. She's a poor old woman, who hasn't discovered any other way of fighting poverty. Her hygienic solution is kerosene, her medical solution Carbaxin, and so on. In fact, if you think about it, she's quite a character; that's probably why she's attached to me, like she was attached to Muti, because I can't deny there's a certain affection there. Maybe that's also the reason why she comes here more often than she should, although who knows how many more times she'll have the opportunity. Who knows what the future holds in store for you? In her case, nothing good. You can't expect anything good to happen at that age. Like so many others, she deserved more from life, because she has a loyal character.

"I can't see a thing with my glasses; these belong to the old creep . . . He must be blowing his top right now! When I started to get my stuff together, he says: What are you doing? Are you off again? Well, just don't leave with my glasses, will you? And he lies there staring at me like this. What are you getting at? I say. Why should I be interested in your glasses? Haven't I got my own? I don't need your junk or the string that holds it together. He shuts up when he hears me argue back, but as

soon as he turns his head, hoops, I quickly stick his glasses in my ragbag!
Well, but I can hardly see a thing with them; they're way too strong. It's
also a small photo, so I haven't a clue who the people are in it. Just that
one in the armchair: it looks like Madam Ioaniu."

"Yes, that's who it is. The fat man next to her is Uncle Georges. And
those fantastic legs are Tante Margot's. Look how young I was then! I
can hardly believe I was ever so tiny. The whole family's there—only
family. No, I lie, there's a woman in the corner, I can't quite make out
who she ... Would you hand me the magnifying glass, Madam Delcă—
there on the sideboard, a little more to the right, it used to belong to
Uncle Georges, yes, there, thank you. Yes, that's much clearer. I'm quite
sure now who it is: Larisa Peşel. Larisa Geblescu. I'll show you her in
some other photos, so you can see better ... With her curly hair, dyed
mahogany-red, her clear white skin and black eyes: quite stunning! How
well I remember that blouse and its veil sleeves, ending in those hands
with very long, very red fingernails, but without jewelry of any kind!
No rings, no bracelet, not even a wedding ring! She claimed she'd left
it all in safekeeping in Bessarabia, and they never gave it back to her.
She regretted not having taken it with her when she fled with the other
refugees."

"Refugees? What refugees?"

"Don't you remember the trains that brought our refugees from over
the border in the East, after the Russians annexed Bessarabia? The first
time, I mean, in 1940."

"I didn't hear anything about that. Really."

"I remember that summer of '40 so well, and my sense that we were
all going through a difficult moment. I was an idealist, the way young
people are, and patriotic like Papa. In fact, everyone in the house was
affected by the events. One day Uncle Sandu came by in a car and took
me to the North Station. The trains with refugees were arriving, and it
was announced that the one with his cousin, Judge Geblescu, was about
to pull in from Chişinău.

"What an impression the bedlam at the station made on me! All those
puzzled, helpless faces. It gave me some foreboding of what lay ahead.
What will become of us? I wondered, suddenly finding myself in the
middle of a crowd that couldn't care less who you were. As if reading my
mind, Uncle Sandu leaned toward me and said: 'The war won't pass us
by, that's for sure.'

"Our poor relative, Judge Geblescu, felt terrible when he got off the train. He had a heart problem, and he really suffered as a result of the high emotion, the heat, and the lack of comfort in the train. I was seeing him for the first time, and to tell the truth I thought he was pretty boring. His wife, Larisa, had a much greater impact on me—as she did on nearly everyone.

"Everyone apart from Muti, who for no apparent reason took an instant dislike to her. She was spiteful toward her in many little ways that Larisa pretended not to notice. I remember one scene, for example, a year or so later, when Larisa complained that she hadn't got back her jewelry, carpets, silverware, and everything else she'd had to leave behind in the rush to leave Chişinău. We'd heard Uncle Sandu say, though, that he'd made timely moves to ensure that his cousin got his belongings back. I kept characteristically quiet, and even looked away. But Muti commented dryly: 'Anyway, you got back more than you had in the first place.' Or something in that vein.

"Larisa certainly landed on her feet at North Station! Her husband stayed away from all social occasions, on the pretext of his poor health, so that Uncle Sandu and Margot took Larisa with them whenever they were invited somewhere: to parties, to restaurants and beer gardens, to poker games, to friends' mansions. We began to think the poor judge was a hypochondriac and a real oddball—but then he died suddenly. I think it was winter—yes, I remember Larisa in a magnificent fur coat at the funeral. And a toque that looked very nice on her . . . Phew, Vica, how I'm going on! How much I've talked this afternoon! Once it used to give me pleasure, but now I talk more because of my nerves. How can you not be nervous when you have to wait and wait and wait? Is it normal for a man like Niki to behave like a child? And what a child! Tudor never took the liberty of as many pranks as his father does. I can tell you, it's not a subject I enjoy talking about! I just meant to say that I go on so much because of my nerves—no, I'm not anxious, but I certainly don't find it amusing either. What was I saying? Ah, yes, poor Geblescu's death. To be frank, I think we all did him an injustice. That often happens, even in a family. Haven't you come across it, Madam Delcă?"

"Well, in my case alone, I can't remember how many nights I've lain awake worrying about my people. But do you think they're the same? Do you think they worry themselves sick over me? Ay, Ivona, everyone looks after number one! My poor creep's right when he sees me on my way out and says: Why is it always you going to see others? Why don't they come and see you for a change? Oh, stop that, I tell him, but I know he has a point. But that's what people are like. They're happy if I go see them, and just as happy if I don't."

"You're exaggerating, Vica dear. Your brothers and nephews are all very fond of you, as I know from what you tell me. But nowadays people are so busy that they don't see as much of the family as in the past. I remember how thoughtful we all were with Larisa, after her husband passed away like that. Margot, especially, went everywhere with her—on social visits, to shows . . . They became inseparable. It's true that Larisa had a great talent for getting people to like her, and you could see she was well-educated and came from a good family. Presentable, a good figure, fantastic legs, always neatly turned out . . . A wonderful voice as well. She was a huge success at parties."

"Parties? She sang at parties? But, Madam Ivona, didn't you say her husband went to his grave?"

"Yes, that's right. But so what? We all heard Larisa's voice before she went into mourning. How long was it since they arrived in the refugee train? Maybe a year, maybe a few months: let me think. Geblescu and Larisa came in June, then we went on holiday to the sea, at Balcic, then we came back in a hurry because of the disturbing rumors—rumors that turned out to be true. It was our last summer in Balcic. I was back in Bucharest when we were forced to give up northern Transylvania, and we all thought it would come to war. Surely it's not possible that you can't remember that!"

Back in Bucharest, yes, perhaps in this very room. Uncle Georges paced up and down nervously, hands behind his back—a rigid way of walking, like a professional soldier. How we all trembled when the phone rang! He continued pacing up and down, more and more irritated that no orders had come through. "The army has never had such a head of steam. Everyone just waiting for a sign to defend our stolen lands!" And then, when we sang *Arise, ye Romanians!,* we all had tears in our eyes— even Muti. But the one who cried most was Larisa, before going off to prepare a real punch for everyone to drink. Poor Uncle Georges: "The army has never had such a head of steam . . ." That's all he could bring himself to say. But the tension inside him was so real that it transmitted itself to the rest of us. The sign he was waiting for never came: the cowardly king and his government accepted the Vienna diktat that broke up the country. But it was then, for the first time, that I caught sight of the General Ioaniu about whom people spoke with such respect in military circles, behind the portly, withdrawn man who hadn't known how to be close to me at any time in my childhood.

"How can you not remember that, Vica dear? A national day of mourning, which the whole country lived through."

"I'm not sure I understand what you're saying. What mourning? I remember the mourning when King Ferdinand died, and how they put on mauve instead of black for the death of Queen Maria. What a loony she was—may the Lord forgive me!—man-crazy all her life! Those are the days of mourning I remember. And then there was Stalin and our own Gheorghiu-Dej . . . The one I remember best of all is Gheorghiu-Dej: I saw his funeral on television. The poor guy: how I cried for him! I only have to see a dead man and I'm off. What's up, Vica, my old man says, sprinkling some more water for the mice? He's a tough brute, as hard as nails. I've only seen him cry once in forty-nine years, and that was a day of mourning. So maybe it's the one you're talking about. I really couldn't say."

"How's that possible, Madam Delcă? Even people who were little children at the time remember that summer when we lost a quarter of the country."

"I told you, I've never given a monkey's toss about politics. Whether it was this or that, I didn't want to hear about it. All I know is that, if I don't look after myself, no one else will. Politics is a pain in the ass I can do without. If you take it seriously you lose customers: this one supports one party, that one another, but you've got to look after your own interests. That means you have to support all of them and none of them. How many times have I said that to my old creep! You haven't got anything to share with anyone. Let 'em side with anyone they like: you're on my side, that's all! If one of them blurts something out, or gets worked up when he's had too much to drink, you just close your eyes and ears. So long as they pay what they owe, and so long as they don't spew up like pigs or start fighting and smashing things, you're better off just letting them get on with it. Forget politics if you want to keep your customers. That's what I tell my man. There was a time when he went a bit funny in the head himself, but he soon piped down and started looking for some way to cover his ass . . ."

She obviously hasn't a clue what the country's been through. Some of the things she says are so wild that all you can do is laugh. To be fair, though, a lot of cultivated people are not so very different. The character you inherit counts for a lot, but so does the education you receive. As for my own interest in politics, I certainly owe it to Uncle Sandu. A couple of years before that terrible summer, he already predicted that it would be Romania's turn after Czechoslovakia—and later, that Romania's turn would come after Poland. I remember his voice, his carefully groomed hands, and all kinds of other trivial details—because the fact is that I don't know much about him. But I'm convinced that, in the last part of the war, he used Margot's travels to take and send messages between Maniu and the anti-Antonescu opposition and the British. Why else would Margot have needed to go to Egypt or Sweden? Her fashion house wasn't that grand!"

Ivona looked at the Russian clock and lit a cigarette.

"But how late it is! Terribly late. Tolerant I may be, but Niki's gone too far this time. I should really go upstairs and get myself ready, so we can leave as soon as he comes, but I don't feel like it at all."

"Come on, let's just sit and chat a bit longer—we might hear him at the door any minute. Tell me some more about . . . you know, whose husband died."

"Larisa? Well, Uncle Sandu arranged an acceptable pension for her, but the upheavals after the war, the currency devaluation, and all the rest of it meant that he thought it wouldn't hurt for her to have a job. At first he got her into the workers' supply institute, but there was something about it that she didn't like, so then he helped her move to the National Bank. It was there, at the National Bank, that she got to know a Swiss man, who developed a real passion for her. Of course he wasn't young: his children were all married with good jobs in Switzerland. But he was a serious type, widowed or divorced, who could hardly have been a better match. Marriage soon followed. Just then, however, there was a decree that all foreigners had to leave the country, and that they could take a Romanian spouse with them only if they had been married at least five years. The Swiss made huge efforts, all to no avail, and in the end he approached Uncle Sandu in despair and offered him a fabulous sum of money if he would use his contacts at the interior ministry to get permission for Larisa to leave . . . Probably around this time, Uncle Sandu was tipped off that a huge wave of arrests was in the offing, and that his own position was threatened."

"And?"

"He took the Swiss man's passport, replaced the photo with one of his own in profile—no doubt fearing that someone might recognize him at the frontier—and left the country with Larisa by a perfectly legal and convenient route. As if they were man and wife."

"But didn't you say she wasn't allowed to leave? Didn't you say . . ."

"It didn't matter. Uncle Sandu had enough contacts at the interior ministry to get her out. And that's what he did."

"And what about him?"

"Who?"

"Her husband. The Swiss man."

"He went to the authorities the next day and reported that his wife had stolen his passport and run off with someone else. Maybe they had come to an understanding. Or maybe Uncle Sandu didn't fill him in completely about his little trick. All I know is that, as a foreign citizen who had personally done nothing wrong, the Swiss was able to leave without any problems. Once he was in the West, he met up with Larisa and probably handed over the fabulous sum of money."

"So they didn't stay together? I mean, Madam Margot's husband didn't marry Larisa and get her to run away with him?"

"Oh, no! Larisa stayed with her husband in Switzerland—as I know from the letters she sent to her mother. Larisa's mother lived nearly another year, paralyzed and in the utmost poverty."

Ivona stood up and, with the cigarette in the corner of her mouth, went over to the sideboard to deal with the old clock, which had stopped yet again.

"And Madam Margot?"

"Margot? They pestered her at first, interrogating her for a few months or maybe even longer. Then she moved to Otopeni, where . . . I told you. She hid Mr. Ialomiţeanu there. His wife denounced him, there was a trial . . ."

"And him?"

"Who?"

"Geblescu. Her husband."

"What about him?"

"What's he doing in the West? Did he marry again? What does he get up to?"

"What *did* he get up to, rather. In fact he's dead. Vica dear, I've been asked so many times before what he got up to over there. But it's an absurd question. How can you know here what someone's doing there? You might as well ask what's happening on the moon."

"No, it's true, you can't know from here. But what about Tudor? Tudor could have gone to see him. So could you, when you went to the West last summer."

"But I told you, he's dead. He died quite some time ago. None of us saw him alive again, and he was no letter writer. He didn't even correspond with Margot."

I won't tell her that Tudor went to see Uncle Sandu on his first trip abroad, and that that was how we found out he was dead. The concierge told him he'd died of a heart attack two or three months before, and that none of his belongings had been kept. No documents, no papers, none of the memoirs that only his few friends had seen—brilliant pages, it seems, with sensational details about diplomatic initiatives during the war years. That's what pains me the most when I think about it, and I can't understand how they didn't end up in the safekeeping of some friend, as usually happens in such cases. As time goes by, Tudor's hypothesis that Uncle Sandu was a double agent—which struck me as an absurd fantasy of a child hooked on mystery novels—no longer seems to me so far-fetched. But all I have found out is that he lived in Paris, in the fourteenth arrondissement, that he had a car, a huge dog, and a young mistress of low birth whom he trained to keep her mouth shut. He kept incredibly fit for his age, which no one there knew, and he looked splendid right up to his last few days on earth. But little details like those are only good for guesswork.

Tudor's idea of a double agent, which would explain the frequent trips abroad, as well as the disappearance of the documents, memoirs, dog, and lowborn mistress, seemed to me increasingly plausible . . .

"Can you hear? Someone's ringing the bell."

"Niki! At last! Do you see how lazy he can be? What's happened to your key? I always ask him. But he never bothers to look for it . . . Excuse me just a moment, Madam Delcă, I'll just open the door for him."

Niki, like hell! That's not Niki: it's a woman's voice. If she's come too this time, I'll make tracks fast. But I seem to know that hoarse voice? Whose could it be? Just listen to Ivona: do pleeease come in, pleeease! Huh, speak of the devil: it's Madam Cristide! Still wearing that three-quarter coat I turned inside out for her, and my scarf. How she bugged me: I beg you,

Madam Delcă, please make me a scarf. As if I was into ties and scarves, for God's sake! Please take a little up here, a little down there, whatever you think best, but make me a scarf that matches the coat. So that's what I did—otherwise I'd never have been rid of the loony. So here she is, still with the scarf, and still with that hat as big as a carriage wheel. All dolled up, and painted like a carnival queen. And still with that habit of kissing you on the chops!

"Well, hello there, Vica dear. That's what Madam Ioaniu used to call you, isn't it? I can almost see her sitting there with you."

"The Lord knows that a day never passes without me thinking about her! She shrank and shrank till she was little more than a dwarf, but the house still feels empty without her. So, how's life been treating you, Madam Cristide? How is your dear husband, Puiu?"

"Oh, you've got a bit of my lipstick on you, Vica. Not there—a little more to the right . . . Please forgive me. It shows how lousy is the stuff from Mrs. Niculescu's. You know Mrs. Niculescu, in Strada Brezoianu, don't you, Ivona darling? Well past forty, but a doll's head, clear white complexion, not a wrinkle in sight! Whereas me, I've always saved money for my husband! Sometimes I tell him: Puiu, darling, you've no idea how other women get through their husband's money! Nothing but Helena Rubinstein, Elizabeth Arden, Max Factor: all stuff from abroad. And me with my cheap knickknacks and Niculescu lipstick! I make do with them because that's how I am: a modest woman of the people. But you should have seen me when I was sixteen! If anyone had told me then that I'd end up with plastic bags weighing ten kilos in each hand, or that I'd spend my day in lines and scrubbing the floor! It's got so I don't even recognize myself in the mirror. Some women send their husband to the canteen, and their children to the crèche: I can't waste my life on you, they say. They're the really clever ones. That's what a woman should be like—not like me, who sacrificed myself for the family. The real me was different, but I gave it up when I became the lady in the ivory tower. It was Puiu who shut me away there, Puiu who set about creating new habits for me, a new nature that's not my real nature. He kept pestering me till I was putty in his hands. Working in the shadows, he systematically cleared all my suitors from the scene, until he had me locked away in his tower. He caught me when I was a second-year literature student and soon tied the knot. So, being with him all the time, I suppose I got to love him; he was my husband, after all. I began to carry shopping bags around, to pinch and scrape, to make do with lipstick from Mrs. Niculescu. But I beg you, Ivona dear, go and get ready! We must get to the church in time, so we can have a proper view . . . Excuse me, Vica dear, you asked me something, and it's gone clean out of my head . . ."

"Nothing special. I just asked you how you were. And how Mr. . . ."

"Fine, thank you. Don't you know what a moaner Puiu is, and how often he complains of feeling ill? He's having some work done on his front teeth right now, and he wouldn't dream of letting people see him in that state. But I can't let Clemenţa down, I said. And I thought of going to the wedding with Niki and Ivona. But now the gentleman isn't home, and the lady can't make up her mind. Now's our big chance, Ivona. We've got rid of our husbands, so let's take advantage of it. Get a bit of fresh air. What are you waiting for? We'll be too late for the ceremony, and Clemenţa doesn't deserve that from us. Nor does her darling little Ţuţu deserve it. I've known him since he was knee-high. But you don't like him, do you, Ivona?"

"Why shouldn't I? He's a hardworking boy, devoted to his mother. I was very happy when Clemenţa decided to let him marry. Maybe I influenced her a little: she had some doubts at first, but I pleaded hard for him. When you have a child, I said, you must think of him, not of what's best for yourself."

"Exactly what I've done all my life! Sacrificed myself. Even though you had a job and a life of your own, I see that you agree with what I did in giving everything up for the family. On the other hand, how often I've told Clemenţa that I regret not having a job and money of my own, to make a life for myself! Anyway, I understood Clemenţa's doubts when Ţuţu brought his girlfriend home to meet her. I understood her and thought she was right in what she said. My dear children, Clemenţa told them, I see you've made up your minds to marry and that you've now come to ask me what I think. You are announcing it to me. If you'd asked me before, I'd have advised you to wait a little. Yes, I can tell you that from experience, having myself married when I was eighteen. In my day, though, certain things didn't go down so easily, whereas now girls first live with their boyfriends and get married later—which is quite normal, since there are no longer those closed houses where men used to be able to go. Attitudes have changed too, and boys usually behave correctly and end up marrying the girl they live with. If not, the girl marries someone else, who presumably doesn't hold her past against her, since those kinds of scandals are a thing of the past. Maybe you think I'm condemning the girls of today—but no, on the contrary! If I was young I'd do exactly the same. In fact, I wouldn't get married at all! Marriage means drudgery, children, so although you just told me without asking first I'd advise you to think it over well before you take the plunge. That, more or less, is what Clemența said to them."

"Yes, I know. She told me so herself—which is why I felt I had to express my opinion."

"Ivona, if Clemența goes too far with you, you should stop her. It's like when I travel by tram, which is full of common people, so the fact that I dress quite sexily means I sometimes feel in real danger. Well, their coarse jibes go in one ear and out the other. I go on acting nice and friendly with them, and that disarms them!"

"But you misunderstood me. Did I say anything about disarming anyone?"

"I know, my dear. I was just making a comparison, and you're a clever girl who should understand that. So, as I said, you should just ignore Clemența's insinuations. Come on, let's get moving."

"No, you misunderstood me. I wasn't angry. Clemența and I have known each other for ages . . ."

"Sure, Ivona my dear, I know you wouldn't make a fuss about something like that. You're too intelligent to . . . But there was a little hint of anger in the way you spoke of Clemența—not unjustified, I hasten to add. Why don't you be frank and admit it? Anyway, now there's no way we can . . . You must go upstairs and get ready: you look so pale. Go up and get yourself ready. I promise I'll carry the can for everything with Niki! If he gets upset, I'll tell him how much I insisted on dragging you along. I'll also say that you're not at all as independent and in control of your time as Clemența thinks. I know how angry you got when she said that."

"Me angry? Not at all. I already told you . . ."

"Okay, if she didn't make you angry, at least she upset you, didn't she? I wonder why, though, because she wasn't really being nasty. She just said what she thought—said how she saw you. Clemența's not a bad woman, but she's not capable of understanding certain things. She finds it especially shocking how you can bear Tudor's absence: she told me so once, and we talked about it. Unlike with Ivona and Tudor, she said, I couldn't stand knowing that my Țuțu was all those miles away in the West, seeing him only once a year, or every two years, and always worrying whether I'll be given a visa. But Ivona's a modern woman, I tell her, who consoles herself with the thought that Tudor is much better off there than he would be here. She's happy that he's landed on his feet there—although I don't know too many details, except what I've heard from Niki, since he's the more talkative of the two. But I guess he's got a good job there, I explain to Clemența—certainly better than anything he'd have had here."

"Oh, I see . . . I didn't realize there was such interest in my . . ."

"Why do you take it like that, Ivona? You're an intelligent woman, exceptionally intelligent, but in my view you're a bit too ticklish. Tick-el-ish! People are afraid to open their mouth in case you get them wrong. You zoom in on every little shade of meaning. You also tend to be suspicious—yes, yes, you are. Don't deny it! Look how you took what I said just now. That there's such an interest in your affairs . . . That's not it at all, please believe me! But you must admit that people talk when someone leaves the country for good. It's a subject that . . . So, without meaning to, they can end up . . . Take me, for example. I told Clemența I wouldn't dream of leaving unless I could go with the whole family. After sacrificing myself on the altar of the family, at least I should know what I did it for! But, as you know, they almost never let everyone leave at the same time. So, although the idea once crossed my mind, you might say that I've given it up now. Once you're past fifty, it's not easy to find work there: they prefer younger people . . . Anyway, it wasn't like you think. I got to considering your position by starting from my own . . . Clemența said that, if she was in Ivona's place, she'd have died long ago. So I said: don't forget that Ivona's an intelligent woman; she's always had a life of her own, not just slaved away for the family. And anyway, if Țuțu did leave for good, you too would get over it sooner or later. Me? Clemența shot back. Me who got his army service postponed, who sent a telegram calling him home urgently from vacation? I couldn't live a week without him . . . Well, Ivona dear, to show how little you know me, I'll admit that you're right on this score. The truth is that Țuțu is a martyr. Clemența's men have also been martyrs: that Nanu, who you never had a chance to meet, and Barbu Vrăbiescu . . . Everything can be explained, as I think you'll agree. Clemența has remained as selfish and spoiled as when she was eighteen—except that, in those days, she had some men buzzing around her, whereas now the only one buzzing around her is that wretched son of hers. She doesn't do what she does out of spite. It simply doesn't occur to her that she harmed her boy by trying to blackmail him into not marrying. Maybe you're not aware of it, but I know how she tried to blackmail him, and what terrible rows they had. Out of selfishness, she ended up doing harm even to herself. She ended up alone, and with a child on her back to help bring up! But she has only herself to blame."

"Well, if the husband leaves, the woman's always the one to blame. No man walks out if things are going well."

"Yes, Madam Delcă, you're right. I never knew Nanu, but Barbu Vrăbiescu, Țuțu's father, was a lifelong friend of Puiu's. That's how we met, in fact—through the two men. We all used to form a little group. I was the dancer, of course—foxtrot, conga, Charleston, Argentinean tango—I picked everything new up in no time, just like that. And my ideal partner was Barbu Vrăbiescu! Clemenţa, on the other hand, had a developed artistic sense, which was obvious from the minute you set eyes on her. She showed it even in the kitchen. A *salade de boeuf* or a chocolate cake prepared by Clemenţa was sheer delight. What blouses and dresses she would color, just for the fun of it! She'd certainly have been a great painter if she'd set her mind to it—as great as, who should I say, Grigorescu, or Luchian. I don't think there's ever been a greater painter than Clemenţa might have become! But unfortunately she's lazy. I get up late too, but it's never happened that the house is still untidy and the table unset when Puiu comes home for lunch. You should see what Clemenţa's house looks like sometimes. What an incredible shambles! And poor Barbu always eats at diners, so she doesn't have to go to any trouble . . . That must be how he got involved with his secretary, by going to restaurants and the rest of it . . . Ever since I've known him, poor Barbu has been the maid and the nanny, on the days they have off. I can see him before my eyes, holding a potty in his hand, or crawling on all fours and barking to make the little one laugh. But, however undemanding a man may be, you can't complain about losing him if you never satisfy one of the few demands he does have. Clemenţa herself told me that she never stopped calling Nanu her 'man of the forest' because he came from a poor background. Okay, it's natural to find some things irritating, but why did she accept him in the first place? In the end, both Nanu and Barbu Vrăbiescu packed their bags one day and walked out, as you were saying, Ivona dear . . ."

"Me?! Did I say anything like that? About men or packing bags? It's not the kind of . . ."

"Maybe you didn't actually say it, but you implied it. Or, if you didn't imply it, I'll say it myself, okay? I'll say it because it's the truth, not to criticize Clemenţa. Puiu knows I never put my friends down: they're my friends, and I stick by them whatever they're like, whatever they do. But the truth is the truth. One day Clemenţa's men packed their bags, and only poor Ţuţu was left at her beck and call."

The telephone rings. Ivona jumps and, regaining control of herself, goes to pick it up with measured steps.

"If it's Niki, tell him to go straight to the church. Hey, what's this photo doing on the table, Madam Delcă? Who did you say it's of? Professor Mironescu? I've heard a lot about him, but it's the first time I've actually seen a picture. Madam Ioaniu sort of kept him hidden, so that her second husband, the general, wouldn't see him. There'd been some rivalry between them. Yes, I assure you, half of Bucharest knew that Mrs. Mironescu was sleeping with Ioaniu—and that it had been going on for a long long time. And I'll tell you something else, though promise not to . . . They say that Ivona isn't really . . . In short, it was really with Ioaniu that she . . ."

"I don't believe that for one minute. Just take a look at Madam Ivona and then at her father: thin, balding, long-nosed. Look carefully. They're alike as two peas. That flat head . . ."

"Yes, there's a resemblance, I can't deny it. And Ioaniu had a different shape . . . Eh, can we ever know for sure? We weren't there at the time, and in the end I only believe what I can see with my own eyes. Ha, ha, ha! So, that's what Madam Ioaniu looked like when she was young. Presentable, yes, but not what I'd call beautiful. Still, she had a certain something. It's a pity Ivona didn't inherit it . . . Ah, there's her sister, who had such a complicated life. And that man sitting on the chair: wait a minute, don't tell me. Yes, how extraordinary, it must be Titi Ialomiţeanu. Well, I never! How much I've heard about him from my mother-in-law! The Ialomiţeanus and my parents-in-law used to visit each other quite a lot. Otherwise I wouldn't have recognized him in this photo, where he's still so young. Just think: I wasn't even born. I recognized him because my mother-in-law has often shown me photos of him and I've been struck by how much he changed: he was thin and fair-haired in his youth, but I got to know him as a fat, aging, gray-haired man—a completely different person. Why did he appear in pictures with my mother-in-law? You must be wondering if there was something between the two of them. Well, between you and me, Madam Delcă— and I know how discreet you are—I'd say that it's definitely a possibility. There's no doubt that my poor mother-in-law was a bit of a flirt. My Puiu can't stand my saying such things, but I do think my father-in-law had reason to consider himself a cuckold. It doesn't seem to have bothered him, though, as the fact that he's still alive would tend to show. But what a charming man Titi Ialomiţeanu was! What graceful compliments he used to make! Ah, Madam Delcă, young men today aren't worth two figs. What do they know about love? Even men of our generation were no longer like the men of old, who knew how to appreciate women. They were sly little devils: they knew how to twist and turn things, to sow confusion, to . . . Ha, ha, ha! How funny you are, Madam Delcă! Why don't you drop by when you have the time: we can chat some more, and . . . Why did you say Ivona put the photo here?"

"How should I know? She came across it and . . ."

"What a coincidence! To come across Titi Ialomiţeanu! I remember him from the time when he was working for Explora—and making a fortune. It went on booming until the day the communists took over. Then he panicked, went into hiding at his mistress's villa, and . . ."

"You mean the two of them were lovers?"

"Yes, Madam Delcă, I assure you they were, even if Ivona doesn't want to recognize it! She has a ticklish character—you heard me tell her as much just now. Ticklish and not well suited to Niki. Life's like that sometimes: it lands you with someone you're not really suited to. What a sweetie Niki is! So witty, such a fine temperament: I get on wonderfully with him! Like I did with Titi Ialomiţeanu, although, of course, he's from a different generation and has a different character. A few years back, I often used to meet him taking his dog for a walk in the public gardens— a very old and very irritable Pekinese, who tried to bite you on the sly. I had to be careful not to get too close, so it wasn't so easy to chat. All the same, we did talk a lot. He'd been in prison, but had been far luckier than most. I can't remember what happened exactly, but he was soon back with his wife and able to work as before. By the time I met him, though, he was drawing his pension. Modest as ever, he didn't like to talk about himself, but he was a walking encyclopedia and had certainly seen a lot in his time. What an extraordinary mind he had! Listening to him was a

real delight, the kind of opportunity you don't often get in life. I praised
him as a model to Puiu, but that probably wasn't a good idea. Look at
him, I said, he's been in prison like you, and although he's twenty years
older he doesn't complain nearly as much. Maybe that's why Puiu didn't
want to hear another word about him. To keep him out of the way, he
was even capable of inventing all kinds of stories about poor Titi; all his
life Puiu's been such a jealous man. For a time Titi Ialomițeanu became
an obsession for him: he was too clever by half, he'd made a deal with the
communists, he couldn't have got an exit visa for himself and his wife
otherwise. On and on he went: the kind of thing jealous people come
up with. I told him not to peddle such crap just so he could keep me in
his ivory tower. Yes, I really laid into him. Come to think of it, I said, I
first met him in your mother's house, and anyway what's wrong with us
going for a stroll together in the park, taking the air, and exchanging a
few words? And that's all we ever did, Madam Delcă! What else could
we have done at his age? But I liked him, because he was always well-
informed about everything and everyone. Only a born exaggerator like
Puiu could have blown it up into anything else. I forbid you to breathe
a word to that man about either of us, he said, especially as you've
got such a loose tongue and he's spent all his life double-dealing and
worming secrets out of people . . . Ah, how jealousy can cloud people's
judgment!"

The telephone rings again upstairs.

"Listen, Madam Delcă, you know that I'm a decent woman, that I'm
pleasant and friendly to others. You also saw today how patient I can be
with Ivona, even when she keeps slipping things into the conversation.
God, how she looked at me toward the end! Well, I suppose it's best if we
change the subject, because I don't want her to think I'm criticizing her
. . . As a matter of fact, we were talking about Mr. Ialomițeanu—a man
who had more contacts with people than anyone I've ever met in my life.
Whoever he met, he always took an interest in what they did later on.
He's that type: curious about others, and naturally affectionate. I'd even
say tender . . . He kept in touch with people who went to live abroad: he
showed me some letters he'd got from them, and a pile of color photos.
He knew where each of them was and what he was doing. He and his wife
traveled all over Europe in his little car, and on some of their last trips,
when he was really getting on, they took his grandson along with them.
He was over seventy when I met him in the park that day, so you can see

how absurd it was for Puiu to be jealous. It's quite a while now since I last saw him. I wonder if he mightn't be ill . . . Ah, thank God, here comes Ivona at last! Can you hear her on the stairs? . . . I think he must still be alive, because I haven't seen a death notice for him in *România liberă* . . . We were just talking about Titi Ialomițeanu, Ivona dear. I saw his photo on the table. But you know, if we don't leave in five minutes we might as well give up the idea."

"I don't want to cause you any more bother. But what if Niki appears five minutes after we leave? I think it's best if you go on ahead. I'm really sorry I made you wait for nothing . . ."

"Don't worry about that, my dear. It doesn't matter at all. I just want everything to end well. So, let me just repeat that, precisely because Clemența upset you during your last conversation with her, you, as a cultured woman . . ."

"Please, this is beginning to get on my nerves. I keep trying to tell you that what she said made no difference to me, and you keep trying to blow it all up."

"No, look, that's the exact opposite of what I've been doing. You've got it into your head to suspect me, and I know when and why it started. But it's very wrong of you, because I've always praised you to the skies and defended you if someone or other said they found you hard to get on with. You've decided not to go now because you're waiting for Niki, but who apart from me will know that that's the reason? No one. All the others will see you're not there and pass comment on it."

Ivona dashed to the telephone again.

"If it's Niki, tell him to go straight there! . . . Well, Madam Delcă, I think we really should be going . . . Why don't you put the telephone here, Ivona, instead of running backward and forward with it? So, wasn't it Niki even now?"

"Yes, it was Niki. He was on his way home and told me to be ready to leave."

"Excellent! As soon as Niki arrives, we'll be off."

"No, Ortansa, no, my dear . . . It makes no sense for you to wait here. We're bound to be late."

"What's the time, in fact? Yes, you're right. Still, maybe I should wait just a little longer, in case Niki doesn't come in the next five minutes . . ."

"No! You'll only get worked up. And you didn't come here to fall into a bad mood."

"I won't get worked up if I stay and wait for nothing, Ivona dear, or if I'm nice to someone who isn't nice back. Not even if what I say is misunderstood. I've become wiser with age, and I know I shouldn't take things like that to heart."

The clock strikes in the hall. Ortansa Cristide jumps from her chair and buttons up her coat.

"Well, it's a pity we're not going together, Ivona dear. I always enjoy chatting with you. But please promise to get a taxi to take you there. Poor Țuțulică deserves no less, after all the trouble he's had sorting himself out. He certainly had a hard time with his exams—not like your Tudor. Which I suppose is understandable . . ."

Ortansa opens her handbag, takes out an old makeup bag, and adjusts her lipstick.

"You have no reason to feel surprised that Țuțu didn't do as well at school as Tudor: that he had to re-sit some exams and didn't go straight to university."

"For God's sake, Ortansa! I never made any such comparison."

"No, you didn't, because that sort of thing isn't done. But if you had, it wouldn't have been so far from the truth."

"But it didn't occur to me for a moment."

"No, of course not. No one's saying otherwise. I'm the one who drew the comparison. But how couldn't I have done, since it's such an obvious thing to do? Anyway, it's entirely in your son's favor, so I don't see why it should bother you."

"That really is the limit!"

"Why do you say that, Ivona? The truth . . ."

Ortansa Cristide quickly returns her makeup to her bag, slings it over her shoulder, then puts her gloves on and adjusts her hat—a tiny bit down, a tiny bit up.

"Don't forget that nature is objective and balances one thing against another: it makes an ugly duckling intelligent, a fiery beauty so modest that she loses out, and so on. Țuțu didn't have Tudor's sharp mind and capacity for hard work, but on the other hand he was a devoted son toward his mother. What a tender, caring soul! The truth is that children who aren't too pampered by their parents turn out kinder and more considerate than those with parents who sacrifice themselves like you and I did. The ones we work ourselves to death for usually show neither respect nor feeling. You don't believe that, do you, Ivona dear? Again you think I'm barking up the wrong tree. But just think about it. You sacrificed yourself for Tudor, but as soon as he got a chance he put himself first—himself and his nice little wife."

"That's how you see things. I can't stop you interpreting them any way you like . . ."

"Taking offense again? You know, I'll end up never saying what I think to your face. Never ever. Everyone knows you have an exceptional son, who's well-educated and . . . But I was talking about inner feelings, and the fact that parents who think of themselves get more back from their children. It's a simple scientific fact. You should think about it from now on. Yes, look more closely at people around you and think about it. Maybe you'll change your mind and agree that I'm right . . . Well, I'm off. So long, Vica dear—that's what Madam Ioaniu called you, isn't it? Let me kiss you: it doesn't matter if a little rubs off. You see how well it suits you! With that complexion of yours . . . fantastic for your age . . ."

"You've really tarted me up. With a bit of luck, an old charmer will pick me up on the tram and take me home with him."

All three of them laugh.

"Incredible! Have you ever seen anything like that before?"

"Ha, ha! It's not the first time. Do you think I don't know how loopy she is?"

"You can laugh and joke! But I'm shaking with irritation. It's been a dreadful day, and I didn't think I still had all that to go through. What a splitting headache it's given me!"

She sat on a chair and pressed her hands to her temples.

Vica rummaged in her ragbag and took something from among the plastic bags. She shuffled to the kitchen and came back with a glass of water.

"Here, take this! Come on, swallow it, and if you're no better in half an hour . . . Listen to me, Ivona, swallow it down. I'm older than you and know about these things."

Ivona massaged her temples, keeping her eyes shut.

"What a stupid, terrible day! I noticed long ago that, if a day begins badly, nothing you do can make it go well."

"Yes, there are days like that, when you get out of bed on the wrong side."

"Well, enough of that! I can put up with a lot of things, but today Niki has gone too far. He's ruined everything: his plans, my plans, everything. We absolutely had to go to church for the wedding, but he exposed me instead to the flood of insults you've just seen and heard."

"I'm not sure I know what you mean."

"What?! Not a word she said was accidental. Nothing but poisoned barbs . . ."

"Try to calm down. Why do you keep jumping up and down like that? You shouldn't take everything to heart. If I'd let every little pinprick upset me—and there have been plenty of them—I'd be pushing up daisies by now, next to Mother in the Capra churchyard. When my blood starts to boil, I pop one or two of these and immediately feel calmer. You've got a good head on your shoulders, so why do you let that loony wind you up?"

"If only that's all she was! The problem is she wants to know everything, to find everything out about you. I kept dropping hints, but still she wouldn't leave."

"Maybe I've been imposing too, since this morning, in fact. Look, it's already getting dark: I'll have to grope my way through the potholes of Puişor. And what's in store for me when I get home? My old man on the street corner, with a stick to beat me with."

She gets her things together and prepares to leave.

"Well, God willing, I'll be off at last! In any case, Mr. Niki will be back in a few minutes."

"Please don't mention him to me. As I said, he's gone beyond the limit today. We're both at an age when you can suddenly have a bad turn, like mine this afternoon, and you then feel shaken and in need of encouragement. Your presence here, your simple presence, did me a world of good. And, well, even a telephone call counts for a lot, and Bucharest is not without telephones. In the end you can find one that's working—if you want to, that is."

"But the poor man did phone you in the end, just before Madam Loopy hit the road."

"What? Niki phoned this afternoon?"

"What's the matter with you, Ivona dear? You're beginning to scare me. Didn't you come and say that Mr. Niki had called?"

Ivona puts on a quizzical look, a little theatrical perhaps, then fumbles for a cigarette and lights it.

"Niki didn't phone at all. Two friends of mine called, but I put them off. And there was a call *for* Niki: a man who wouldn't say who he was. That was all."

"Huh? But didn't you say . . ."

"Yours is an uncomplicated nature, Madam Delcă, without any hidden corners. As I said, she just wouldn't go away . . ."

"Cristide?"

"Who else?"

"Ah, so you said it just like that?"

"The penny's finally dropped! I did it so she'd go away, though I found it rather disagreeable, as I always do when I lie. What really drove me up the wall was that then she still didn't move."

"She was stuck to the chair, that's all. Why should she move her weary legs?"

"Is that what you think? It's out of the question. As soon as I opened the door I told her I was waiting for Niki, but no, she wasn't going to be fobbed off so easily. Sometimes she even stops me in the street, or drops in on me without the least sign of embarrassment, because that's the kind of person she is. She creeps in everywhere, looking, listening, spying on you. And she takes a malicious pleasure in hanging around, knowing that I'm not exactly crazy about her—a feeling that's mutual, I have no doubt."

"That's not the impression I got. Didn't you see how she kept sucking up to you?"

"Is that how you'd describe her constant jibes? You're too naive, Vica dear, or too inattentive: one or the other. Didn't you notice how she kept getting at me? Apropos of Tudor, apropos of my character . . . All that impertinence about Niki, pointlessly bringing him into the conversation time and time again . . ."

"That's all nonsense! Mr. Niki wouldn't look at a woman like her."

"Maybe he would, maybe he wouldn't: that's his business. What bothers me is that he's allowed her to take so many liberties that it's virtually impossible to get rid of her. She's been hanging around him for so long, and shows no sign of letting go. Another woman would have given up by now, but she carries on regardless."

Ivona frowns into the ashtray as she firmly stubs out her cigarette. Vica goes and sits closer to her.

"And I thought you actually liked her! In fact I still think that. Anyway, Mr. Niki wouldn't look at a woman like that. Don't you see how she looks, all painted like a carnival queen? No serious man would look at her."

"I don't know, Vica dear. We like to kid ourselves that men are capable of resisting, but the fact is that few do when a woman sets her cap at them. Few? I really mean none . . ."

"Well, it's nothing to do with me, but surely men aren't that stupid. And Mr. Niki's an educated man."

"Yes, but he has his moments of weakness. Don't insist, Vica dear, there are some things you don't know about, even though you've been coming to our house for so many years. It's in my nature to be discreet, but some women take advantage of it. I'm not thinking of you, of course—heaven forbid! When I say 'some women' I mean Ortansa Cristide. Do you think she'd have barged in like that if I wasn't the kind of person I am? After I've had so many phone calls warning me . . . ? Yes, about her and Niki, what else? No, I don't mean now, but some years ago. Only she still hasn't laid off, as you see. I don't know if there was ever anything between them, and whether you believe me or not it really doesn't interest me . . . I haven't talked about this with anyone before: it's only because we've known each other for so long that I'm mentioning it to you now. It's been a difficult day for me, but we've got on so well together . . . I didn't tell anyone or ask anyone any questions—she's the one who kept making allusions, deliberately offending me, but of course the whole thing is Niki's fault. Even now it gives him a thrill to bump into her, to have a little chat. I've been warned that she's a dangerous animal, but you know what Niki's like! He says all kinds of things in jest, and women take him seriously. Yes, that's it. However much I warn him, he can't keep his tongue under control when he comes across her. And as soon as she finds something out, she comes and pours some more poison in my ear. What a viper's nest! Just the kind of thing I detest!"

"Why do you get so worked up over a load of hot air? My landlady's just the same, another viper: she does her best to stir things up, snooping around, slithering backward and forward between me and Reli. She used to wind me up, to make me cry—until one day I said enough is enough. Now, if I see her in the distance, I cross the road to avoid her. And if she barges in on me, I show her the door. That's all: no good morning, no kiss my ass. I've no business with you, and you've no business with me, bye-bye. It got like I couldn't have any peace in my own home. But then I got Madam Viper off my back and made my life a hell of a lot quieter. You shouldn't act the way you do: please, do come in, make yourself at home, let me get you something. You should put a stop to all that!"

"Ah, Vica dear, how right you are! The real problem is my indecisiveness, my inability to speak my mind for fear of hurting people. But do you know what I regret the most?"

Ivona slides her pack of cigarettes closer, takes one out and lights it.

"I really regret saying what I did about Clemenţa. I don't know what came over me. I knew who I was dealing with, but I seemed to blank it out. Now I've given her plenty of fresh ammunition, and unless a miracle happens you'll soon see what it'll lead to. If Niki doesn't show up in the next quarter of an hour, there'll be no more question of going to the wedding. And then she'll blow everything up out of proportion . . . I could go alone, of course, but that's not what I'm going to do. First, because I haven't felt well all day and I'm at the end of my tether—a complete bundle of nerves. All these years I've spent cleaning up after Niki, repairing his blunders, dealing with awkward situations. And I'm tired of it—sick and tired of keeping up appearances! He, on the other hand, has no worries, no reason to get upset; he knows I'm always on duty and ready to step in if necessary. Well, today he's going to get a surprise . . . I know I'll be taking a big risk, but I'm not going to the church on my own. Honestly, if Niki had come back I'd have made the effort to go, but like this . . ."

"Hey! The telephone's ringing. Quick, Ivona, go and answer! By the time you're through, I'll be dressed and ready to go. I really must get a move on . . ."

Vica crams the empty plastic bags into her ragbag, puts on her overcoat, kerchief, beret, and scarf, then checks that she still has Ivona's hundred lei note. She goes to the kitchen, opens the fridge door, shuts it, and comes back chewing something. She bumps into Ivona: she didn't hear her coming back downstairs from the telephone.

"But what's the matter, Ivona dear? Tell me. You weren't like this before. Come on, out with it. I may be late already, but I'm not going to leave you the way you are. Come on, Ivona, tell me. Oh, dear, my legs seem to be giving way. Just a minute, I'll fish out a Carbaxin: one for you and one for me. Here, take it without water, then tell me what's up. Has something happened to Mr. Niki? An accident? Well, if he's in the hospital, at least it means he survived. He's worse than whoever was driving? Not a good omen! Who was it? A man? A woman? Not a good omen . . ."

Epilogue

Gelu

How narrow this yard is! So narrow that, if I stretch out, my right arm touches Reli's fence, as greasy as if covered with engine oil, and my left arm touches the peeling plaster on the wall. When the ground was slippery, though, it meant they could hold on to the fence or wall as they went to the toilet at the bottom. And it's slippery most of the time between November and March. A little rain is enough, or else some melting snow by the fence; water then collects between the old bricks lying crooked on the ground, and another freeze turns it into a skating rink. That's how it was on the late-winter night when Vica broke her hand; it had rained during the day, and frozen over by the time she returned home. It was like glass, like a mirror. She had to pay dearly for coming back so late. How her right hand hurt, especially as they had to set it twice to get it right! Her fingers swelled up and turned blue, so they didn't have any choice but to break it and start again. Since then she's seemed more careful to sprinkle salt and ash on the ice. The problem is that some of it got onto her soles, and from there into the house, so that what with all the clutter—stove, old oil lamp, daybed, Singer sewing machine, chairs, sideboard, sink, shoe polish and brushes, and so on—cleaning became a real headache. In the end, I sort of understand that she wanted to clear the house.

"It's all junk," she said. "Why should I keep it around to fall over?"

She gave heaps of stuff away, for just a few hundred lei. In installments! It was Oița, a younger second cousin of Delcă's, who bought it: not for herself—she had no wish to fill her place with Vica's old junk—but for her family in the country. Her husband came to pick it up in his car. The last thing he took was the television. She'd had it for thirteen years, but it was still working. Everyone said to her:

"Keep it, Vica! You can switch it on in the evening and watch a film, or find out what's going on in the world. Friends will come around to watch it and keep you company."

"If it'd been up to me, I'd never have thrown good money away on it in the first place! But one day I suddenly saw him walk in with it in his arms, and the thing drove me nuts for the next thirteen years. The old creep must have had a screw loose, I suppose; everyone has something. What he liked to do was lie in bed with the TV on, wrapped up well in winter so as not to catch cold. His idea was that friends and neighbors would come around and watch it, not laughing, not saying anything loud—just sit and goggle. Relatives too. And we'd give them a little something to eat, because no matter how poor you are you can't sit and watch TV without a nibble. Like that, the neighbors would see we had people to visit us."

Now (the neighbors say) Vica's gotten used to giving things away, but there's nothing much left. She shuffles about the house, touching one thing after another, wondering what she can get rid of next.

"How much will you give me for that?" she asks.

And they bargain until Vica lowers her price, or even says:

"Give me what you can, whenever you're able."

After Oiţa leaves, she suddenly feels bad that she's sold it for a song, so when they see each other again she says:

"You got that from me for next to nothing."

"What do you mean, Auntie?"

So they haggle again, and sometimes they settle on the price that Vica proposes. But when it comes to the next month's installment, they've more or loss forgotten what they agreed.

Anyway, that's what the neighbors whisper to me.

But what can I do about it?

I scratch my head and look at the faded or darkened patches on the walls and floor left by furniture that wasn't moved for dozens of years.

Like when someone moves house.

The wall on the left has been cracked all the way down since the earthquake, and a big chunk of plaster has fallen from the ceiling, so you can see the bricks and woodwork underneath.

Uncle Delcă never found time to repair it, and Vica hasn't done anything either. She doesn't even get around to sweeping the spiderwebs that collect in the corners.

She wakes up in the morning (so she says) and lies in bed staring at the ceiling high above. Once painted Nile green and gone over with silk powder, it has become blacker and blacker over the years, until only a few traces remain of the original color. But she remembers how the ceiling and everything else used to be (or so she claims). Still, it does her no good to lie awake in bed like that, between the green sheets. Green, she says, so she doesn't have to wash them too often. Even after Uncle Delcă's illness she didn't change them right away, but left them on for the best part of a month.

"I don't sleep a wink all night! What does old Pug Nose say? That I drop off at once? I've heard her say that too: that I take my pills and sleep like a log. But the most I ever get is two hours. I just lie there in bed, thinking and remembering, and worrying about one thing after another. That's how my mind works: it just keeps turning things round and round till day breaks. When it's light I go into the living room, wash myself and do all the things I've been doing all my life, then open the door and head off. I go to the market, make a phone call or two, buy some tomatoes . . ."

"Forgive me for asking, but why do you buy so much at once? There must be all of five kilos here . . . Five kilos, in this heat, without a fridge. Look, they've begun to go off, and there are fruit flies buzzing around. Now you're on your own, you can buy a little every day—just what you need. It will also give you some exercise."

"I've bought wholesale all my life!"

She laughs, delighted with her little joke, so that her bare gums show through her open mouth; she's given up her false teeth, which she used to put in when she was with someone. Beads of sweat glisten on her forehead and her surprisingly fleshy cheeks. It's too hot in the room, even though the blinds are drawn. Someone or other—certainly a neighbor— has cut her hair; she no longer wears a bun at the back of her neck, and instead of the curls on her temples thin, curiously straight, locks hang over her earlobes. A parting down the middle reveals the faded pink of her scalp.

"What did you do with the porcelain washbasin—the one with big red flowers and a matching pitcher that you used to keep on the stand in the living room? Did you sell even them? What for, Auntie?"

"Oh, to hell with them! They were cracked anyway. If I'd known you wanted them, I'd have given them to you. When your mother used to pass by here, I kept telling her to take them. Go on, I said, take them home for your boy and his wife. And that and that—take them and give them to the children. What's the point? she said. Young people don't like old stuff: they like everything to be new. They've bought what they wanted and are up to their necks in credit: it's up to them, I'm not going to interfere. That's what your mother told me. Splurged, up to their necks in credit, but now they have to divide their stuff up. What? Don't ask me how they plan to do it. I'm not going to interfere and say this is his, that is hers. I'm sorry it didn't work out between them, but I'm not going to get involved in dividing their things up . . . Yes, that's what your mother told me whenever I wanted to give her something for you. Do you know what she said to me in the end? That everything you bring into the house from now on will be divided up if that pest of a girl stakes a claim to it. When I heard that, I started to think. I'm not going to give my things for free to a ninny who threw everything overboard and didn't know how lucky she was to have found such a wonderful husband . . . What's the matter? What's all this growling and snorting? Why are you wriggling about like that? What I said is the truth, isn't it? I'd like to see her find another man who's half as good as you."

Silence. I spy myself in the wardrobe mirror, with a halo of dust lit up by the oppressive golden ray that has sneaked in at the edge of the cardboard blind. I look at my reflection, and I don't like it.

"That thieving Oița is supposed to bring me another eighty lei today. As soon as she gets here, I'll tell her to return the porcelain you were talking about—the basin and jug. She shouldn't think she's got her mitts on them: she can just kindly bring them back to where they came from. And what else do you want? I'll get her to bring everything. Just tell me, my boy."

"I don't want anything. Really. I liked to see your things when they were here, but they wouldn't be the same if I took them away with me. No, there's no question of it. Absolutely not. I won't take them, do you understand?"

As I vigorously shake my head, my eyes fall on a wound in the grayish-green plaster where the television scraped against the wall for thirteen years. How strange life is! I say to myself, without really knowing what I'm saying, as I look at the rags of doubtful cleanliness that serve as a doormat in the hall. How strange life is! I avoid breathing in too deeply the smell of coal, kerosene, and rotten tomatoes, and I try hard to forget that it's the all too familiar smell of the house, mixed in with stale potatoes, spare wood, and leftover food. How strange it is! And I let my eyes wander over the empty hall and Vica's questioning face, like that of a faithful dog.

"Why don't you stay and have a bite to eat? Look, here's the potato dish you always used to love. Have a little here, on the edge of the desk. Not in the shop: I know you don't like it in there anymore."

"I couldn't possibly! Don't be angry, Auntie, but I ate just before I came here."

And really I can't. I wouldn't be able to swallow one mouthful. How was I able to ten or fifteen years ago? Was the smell in the house less strong? I don't remember. But I do remember the red oilcloth slashed here and there, the logs piled up by the sideboard, the slop pail left discreetly covered in a corner.

And the shelves, the coal, the clutter.

So, was the smell less strong? Was I different?

"Come and see how nicely my flowers are coming along. And my raspberries. Afterward we can sit for a while on the bench under the tree. I spend quite a bit of time sitting there in the evening. Ah, how nice it is! What a miracle! It's like heaven on earth."

"Okay, let's go."

The yard is so narrow, but Vica has managed to grow some flowers there. Their whitish stems wind upward from among the crooked bricks. Yellow or mauvish-pink flowers, with mottled leaves, which climb like ivy to the cracked step beneath Vica's door. How proud she is of them, and of the raspberry bush she planted by the greasy brown fence! And of the tree at the bottom of the yard—a huge poplar, which in late spring, as it is now, fills the air with its fluff.

"Go and kiss Mrs. Negulescu's hand!"

Vica pushes me as she used to do when I was a child. The landlady's door is behind hers, at the bottom of the yard. She's sitting there as always, propped up on a stick, so that in profile she reminds me more than ever of a prelate, her long black vestments fluttering around her massive body. Her long white straight hair does nothing to soften her masculine features. I lean over to kiss her wrinkled hand, which she then presses against my head in a gesture of absolution, while her other hand remains glued to her stick.

"Let me kiss you too, my child. How tall and handsome you've become! And how those stray white hairs suit you! Young people's hair turns white so early these days: I've noticed that in my grandchildren. But how well it suits them! Isn't that right, darling?"

Her voice sounds schmoozy. When her bony pug face and graying mustache come close, I feel an unpleasant sensation: a kind of smarting, and a hollowness in the middle of my body where my stomach ought to be.

Through her open twin-leaf door, I can see her dining room furniture polished like new, without a speck of dust. Starched tablemats, sideboards covered with knickknacks . . . Incredible how that room smells of flowers, although no more than a partition wall separates it from Vica's. I've never actually been inside. The house looks neat and tidy—one of those you have to take your shoes off to enter. I'll probably never cross the threshold. But Pug Nose, having disappeared and returned with a little jam and water for her visitors, says her usual piece in that deep voice of hers:

"Please do come inside. Go ahead. Please . . ."

I don't take up the offer. I wriggle a little and, with a forced smile, stutter out that today of all days I must . . . But you come so rarely, she says, smiling in a way that doesn't take the edge off the reproach. I explain that I've only come for a short while, and that I must spend it with Auntie Vica. On the threshold of that dining room, the same smell as before, though more diluted, wafts through from Vica's room and mingles with the scent of peonies. Something twitches in my throat and fills my eyes with cold tears, while my whole being tenses up to fight down the nausea.

"How ugly Pug Nose was when she was young! Ugly and creepy! But she'd smooth-talk Mrs. Negulescu, buttering her up just to get to her son Mişu Negulescu. And, well, Mişu took her in the end. Since then she's always trying to stir things up between me and the old woman . . ."

"Why are you so against her, Auntie Vica? She seems a hardworking woman."

"The devil can take her as far as I'm concerned!"

If she doesn't see eye to eye with Pug Nose, at least she gets on well with Reli, the neighbor on the other side of the brown fence. The years pass and leave no mark on her: still the same peroxide blonde, still pale-faced with three wrinkles in the corner of her eyes, still glistening with creams and lotions, her eyebrows carefully groomed, her withered mouth painted red in a heart shape, her curlers coquettishly hidden under a headscarf fixed with two little knots. And still those sad eyes.

Does Reli have sad eyes because she split up with Mişu Negulescu, who went off and married Pug Nose. Their yards, which they had been planning to join into one, were then separated by a tall wooden fence, whose planks fit tightly together so that there is no crack to see what is happening on the other side.

And it's also covered with greasy engine oil . . .

"She can go to hell! She's just a cheap whore," Vica says in a low voice. "A whore and a hypocrite! She fools around with her cousin, who's never married in his life, because she says she can't do without it, and her husband hung up his saddle when he hit fifty. To hell with her and her kind! Come on, sit and rest for a bit in the garden. You remember what you used to do when . . ."

Vica hovers around me, heavy and important on the tips of her toes. Yes, I remember when we were crammed into one room at home, and I'd come and study here on a bench under the big poplar.

"Stop fussing and sit down yourself," I say to her.

The hard glistening leaves of the poplar rustle above our heads, rubbing against one other and against the edge of the wall. Opposite the bench is the same kitchen table on which I used to prop up my books and notebook—and on which I now rest my elbows. I put my head in my hands. The high white grainy wall, surrounding us on all sides, gives the merest glimpse of pale sky in one corner. The wall is freshly painted, and the yard has been swept recently. Everything is spick and span. The bottom of the yard is actually Pug Nose's domain, but Vica and I sit on the bench there together. On the other side of the wall there's an old tiled roof and a tall hen coop, and facing us are Pug Nose's woodpile and twin toilets: one for the Negulescus, one for the Delcăs, made of the same planed wood and with the same *00* written on the door. Identical bolts keep their doors shut. Old rags form a mat on the ground, and square-shaped pieces of newspaper hang from some string on the wall.

Each toilet has its own key.

We sit on the bench and relax. We strain our necks to catch a glimpse of the sky, then look down at the neatly swept yard. It is bare, without any grass. I get up first, and the gravel crunches beneath my feet. We walk back, passing the Negulescu door on the way; no one is outside now, but the door has remained wide open.

". . . she leaves it like that so she can see who's coming and going. That's Madam Pug Nose for you, spying and intriguing all the time."

She would certainly have seen them come and take Uncle Delcă away. They arrived at the agreed time, carrying a large roomy coffin with bronze fittings that sparkled in the sun. And a shiny lid. But they couldn't get the coffin through the door, whichever way they pointed it. Nor could they break the door, of course, or bend it . . .

So, ". . . a blanket . . . ," they decided.

Vica brought them one, an ordinary blanket smelling of coal, kerosene, and burned fat. They laid it out on the floor, beside the bed, and two men wrestled to pick up the corpse on its green sheet and place it in the blanket. Then, while we held it by the four corners, they pulled the sheet out from under him. It was like when Auntie Vica and Uncle Delcă used to bounce me up and down as a child, chanting:

Up he goes, down he comes,
Now I see him, now I don't.

Otherwise, why hold a blanket by the four corners and put a man on it? And how can you do it with such natural gestures, when his eyelids are already stuck moistly together like his lips . . .

"So long as the blanket holds . . . ," one of them says.

Not only I but everyone is afraid that it won't hold under that huge body as they drop it off the edge of the bed together with the sheet. A strange tightness in my chest holds my tears back. I steal a glance at Vica, to see if she is crying. The massive frame has doubled up on the blanket, gently doubled up; the impression that death has made him rigid is false. All impressions are false: everything is different from what I see (or think I see).

Simpler, more natural, of course . . .

Only I can't get used to this: only I, of everyone here, am terrified by the naturalness of it. How naturally Uncle Delcă's neck hangs loose and crooked on the blanket as the two men hunch under his weight! They pick their way carefully across the room, so as not to hit one of the wide-open doors, and despite their fears the blanket holds beneath the curled frame.

Shamefully curled (a strange voice whispers inside me); the final humiliation. Does he still feel the humiliation, deprived as he is of the rigor mortis, the gruesomely dignified rigidity of death?

They carry him over the uneven bricks, from which whitish flower stalks creep out slyly. The shiny coffin waits on the worn surface of the yard, among the mauve, yellow, and pink roses. The men now pull the blanket from under him, as they did before with the bed sheet. His head wobbles, still crooked, as they place him respectfully in the rented coffin, which they then raise onto their shoulders and carry to the draped truck that has been waiting for some time at the gate, its engine running.

"What a nerve to ask me if I know you! Tell the idiot how long we've known each other—known and loved each other. Who does he think bathed you in the tub? In the evening, I used to draw the shutters early and put you in the tub in the middle of the room: scrub a rub dub, how you used to whine! That was a long time ago all right! Ah, as long as you're healthy—that's all that counts. No need for hospitals and all that crap . . . What's the problem? Why shouldn't I grouse? He's already far away, at the last bed . . . No, that's not him. The big shot doctor has a whole gang of boys and girls who traipse after him. He's the general. Yes, sir, no sir, they go, trying to lick his ass. And don't think he comes every day! Huh, he comes when he feels like it! But that one who was here just now is on my back all day; I can't get rid of the idiot. Maybe he's got too used to screwing money out of me . . . What do you mean? I'm not shouting—you worry too much. What was I saying? Ah, yes, that one hangs around all day: How are we doing? Is everything all right? Can I get you anything? He's like my local doctor: the patient is my only concern! Oh, yeah! But seriously, I think he's got a screw loose . . . Stop squirming, for God's sake! Who do you think's listening? No one's got any time for us: they've all got visitors today, can't you hear the din? I plunked myself by the door, ready for my first visitor. I didn't think it would be you, though, 'cuz I know you're busy, that you've got a lot going on at work . . . But I did think someone would come to see me. I waited and waited, and there were plenty of visitors all right—but none for me! So I got fed up standing there like a tree trunk and went for a walk."

"You mean you went out? I told you to be careful. These wards all look the same, and it's easy to get lost."

"I thought about that. These corridors go off in every direction, and I wondered if I'd find my way back. I'd have liked to go to the kiosk to buy a cake: I know my way there and back. Only I didn't have a cent on me. There didn't seem any need: all I wanted was to be there when my first visitor arrived. But no one's showed their ass. Still, it's all to the good, 'cuz you brought me some cakes anyway! You shouldn't throw your money away like that. You don't have so much either . . . After all the stuff you

left me last time, I haven't had to spend more than two lei fifty. Anyway
you get everything here: I'm not fussy, I take what they give me, and
they're good helpings. I have to soak my bread in the sauce, though . . .
You can have as much bread as you like, and keep asking for more! I had
some nice soup again . . . Yes, just as well I didn't have any money on me,
'cuz you brought me some cakes anyway . . . When I saw I didn't have any
on me, I gave up the idea of going to the kiosk. People were rushing
around everywhere, and I thought I'd better not get lost. God forbid!
Loads of people kept coming—you should have seen how many! Some
had four or five at a time: there was no end to them. They came to everyone, but not to me . . . Then I started to worry in case anyone who came
to see me went through the wrong door. If they came in by a different
entrance, round the back, they'd go into a different ward and miss me.
Didn't you see how many doors there are—all those doors and corridors
and people . . . They might have gone into a ward, not found me there,
and gone off. Made the journey for nothing . . . What do you mean who?
I'm talking about whoever it was came to see me. I didn't know it would
be you: I didn't know you'd come, but I thought it's impossible that no
one will come. So, Madam Delcă, I said to myself, back to the hen coop!
Ha ha! I shuffled back to my bed, lay down, lay and lay . . . All of them
with visitors: some didn't even have a chair and had to sit on a bed or stay
on their feet. Only I was all on my own! . . . I lay all alone there, worrying
about one thing and another: how's your mother, I thought, why doesn't
she come and see me? And where's that goofy Niculaie? What's happened
to everyone? Then I look at the door and see you walk in. And that doctor, the big idiot, is back and wanting to chat. Do you know this young
man? he goes . . . Good thing he's cleared off, so we can talk about our
business, the things we need to talk about. So, tell me, what's new with
your mother? . . . Ah, yes, ever since I've known her, I've been telling her
not to swan around half-dressed. But does she listen? Well, never mind,
she'll get over it. But when you give her her pills, you have to stay with
her. I know her trick: she sticks them under her pillow as soon as you
turn your head and gets rid of them afterward. And what about you?
How are things at work? Come on, they're not going to fire you! How
could they? Where will they find another clever boy like you? . . . What's
the matter? Why shouldn't I say it if it's the truth? I'm not going to eat
you . . . Just tell me how everyone else is . . . You haven't seen anybody?
But you must have spoken with them, no? . . . Niculaie? His daughter

who never stops moaning? Didn't you say they were splitting up as well? No? No way? Are they going to have another child? . . . But if you didn't say it, who did? Niculaie? When would that have been? . . . Look, it must be a year since I laid eyes on Niculaie . . . It's true, I tell you. I'm not mixing things up . . . What? How long is it since my old man, your poor uncle, passed away? . . . Only eight months, you say? Eight months. Well, I never! . . . No, no, it's better here. At home I sat around, and if I didn't take something I'd have a funny turn. Then there's nothing anyone can do about it. If he was still there, to say a word to me now and again, to . . . And you going on about my pills . . . Your mother was the same, always telling me to quit taking them. But what would have become of me if I'd given them up? Anyway, it can hit you out of the blue, and there's nothing you can do about it. You're defenseless . . . At my age, you can't sit there and howl like a wolf . . . That's what I'm saying: I think I'd have caved in if I hadn't had my pills . . . I popped one or two, however many it took, and then I calmed down. I was out of it . . . I missed him so much. If only he could have still been there, to open his mouth now and again, to grumble at me, and for me to answer back. What I wouldn't have given for him to be there! But what can you do? Nothing. You're helpless . . . Tell who? And tell them what? What could I have said to you? You're young: you've got troubles of your own . . . Your mother said to me: you nagged him enough when he was alive, so why do you pine after him so much? He's off your back now, you can have some peace and quiet! Well, I didn't like that one little bit. I didn't quarrel with her, but I didn't like to hear her talk like that. Peace and quiet? What a joke, all alone in an empty house! Not to mention the thieves who climbed over the fence at night and broke in! Yes, they did! I'm telling you they did! You don't know everything, my boy! You've got it into your head that they didn't break in and I just worked myself up into a state. But it wasn't like that. You're not right about everything, you know. You should listen to what an old woman says: she's been around longer, she knows more about life than you! . . . So, even you don't believe me. I can't even talk to you about these things. Who can you trust if you're not trusted by anyone? Reli and Mrs. Negulescu are the same. Calm down, they say, get a grip on yourself; he bugged you enough when he was alive. But what do they know? Do they know that he never strayed once? How people used to look at us dancing the waltz together, in the days when I first got to know Niculaie and his woman . . . Don't be silly. I'm talking about his first one . . . Ah, what fun we had dancing! How happy we were! And when your uncle got me to dance everyone stood there gaping. He was a big man, big and strong, but he was lighter than anyone when it came to waltzing . . . Am I never going to see him again—after all those years together? Is that right? I just moped around at home, in that empty house, missing him all the time. What I wouldn't have given to have him back! . . . Luckily, though, I've always had enough willpower. So when I felt it was coming over me, I'd go and take a few pills right away. Then, whether it came over me or it didn't, I was out of it. After all, there's nothing you can do, and at my age I'm not going to sit and howl like a wolf. There's no one you can complain to, no one to open your heart to. I learned that from poor Ivona, after her husband died. No, Vica dear, she'd say, there's no one you can complain to, because no one can understand what you're going through . . . Which Ivona? Who do you think? Ivona Bonaparte? Mrs. Ioaniu's Ivona, that's who . . . It's true, you didn't know her. But she knew you. The two of us used to talk about you and her son who went to live in the West. He cleared off with his wife, a long time . . . When was it? Ten years ago? Or five? I've had other things to do than keep a running count. Anyway, we used to sit and drink coffee and chat about you and her Tudor. What a wonderful woman she was! So intelligent and so well-educated: you should have seen all the books she read in her life! And she liked and appreciated me. She was really quite attached to me. You've golden hands, Madam Delcă, she used to say— golden hands. You give me a boost when I see you, Vica, you always try to look on the bright side. I kept saying I'd bring you to see her one day, and she'd say, yes, please do, I'd like to meet your Gelu. Bring him around so I can see him: yes, that's what she'd say when we talked about you and her son . . . Her son and daughter-in-law wanted to have her to live with them in the West, but it took ages to sort out her possessions and get permission for her to leave—and by then there was nothing of her to have: she'd gone to her grave as well . . . Why did she want to take so much stuff with her? I don't know. She just couldn't bear to leave the whole house and everything in it. You should have seen all the antiques and stuff inside, and she was the kind of woman who couldn't bear to throw a safety pin out. She couldn't make her mind up, so everything was left behind with her in the end . . . But what's happened to my teeth? Where the hell are they? I bet it's the hooligans who climb over the fence at night. I tell you, it must be them who came and took them. They come at night, and if the gate's locked they jump over the fence . . . Okay, forget it! Let's talk about something else—the things we need to talk about . . . They're saying it's time for you to go, but we haven't even started. I haven't had anything like my fill of you. Just watch him come and start asking me questions . . . Eh, who do you think I mean? The idiot doctor. I was all alone, with other people's visitors all around, alone in my little corner by my bed. Not a soul come to see me. So I was getting worried. What's the matter? Why don't I have any visits? Suddenly I see you walk in, and lo and behold I've got Doc Loopy chatting to me. What's up, Loopy Lou? Leave me alone, will you? Of course, how can I call him anything else: no one with their head screwed on right would ask the kind of questions he does. Last time you were here it was the same. Who is that gentleman? he goes. How long have you known him?—that kind of bullshit. So I told him you're my nephew! Listen, I said, he's my nephew, a real clever boy, good-looking and well-behaved. Too well, in fact—'cuz if you're well-behaved you get left on the shelf. You don't have any luck. It's the pushy guys who have all the luck . . . What's the matter with you? You're too jumpy, too quick to lose your cool, as they say. You should listen to others a little, don't keep . . . Okay, forget it, let's talk about what we need to sort out . . . They'll try to throw you out in a minute. But we need to talk. I lie awake all night worrying. What's going to happen? I ask myself. Will Loopy Lou keep me here or tell me to go home?"

"Why do you lie awake worrying? Calm down. He'll let you stay here. Why shouldn't he?"

"But you did give him the envelope, didn't you? You did give it to Doc Loopy? The envelope with the money we talked about. Don't keep shushing me: I'm not talking loud. Take it from me: I know how to behave when people are around. See how softly I'm speaking! . . . But I have to ask you, 'cuz I'm worried about the envelope with the money. That's why I can't sleep, why I don't close my eyes all night. Did my Gelu give him the envelope, or didn't he?"

"Oh, for God's sake! I told you I gave it to him . . . I told you last time I was here. You've forgotten, that's all. I told you that I gave it to him and what I asked him to do, and I told you what he answered . . . What reason did you have to lie awake worrying? I gave it to him—period."

"You gave it to him, then?"

"Yes, yes, I gave it to him!"

"And?"

"And what?"

"What did he say? You gave it to him, and then what did he say? Did he say he'll keep me here?"

"Don't worry, he'll let you stay. I told you all this last time, but if you want I'll tell you again . . . Big deal if you've forgotten—it happens to me all the time . . . The main thing is for you to stop worrying. He'll let you stay here. Then we'll see . . . I've given up making plans too . . . Why? Because you can't know what will happen from one day to the next . . . So, he'll let you stay for a while, until it gets warmer and you don't have to bother about heating your place. You're not supposed to carry wood and things, exert yourself, bend down, get tired . . . Don't worry, I explained everything to him . . . I told him about your house and how you live there alone, that you don't have any wood or coal left because winter started early, that your pension is what it is . . . And he knows better than me that you're still weak . . . He knows you can't leave now . . . I told him everything. I also gave him the envelope, after watching and waiting for the right moment. There was always someone else there, but in the end I found an opportunity . . ."

"You're not bold enough, that's your problem. Others just get on and do it . . . You were pampered too much . . . Others come from the back of beyond and use their elbows to get ahead . . . But your mother and father, and me too, spoiled you too much when you were little."

"That's a nice thing to say. And you're surprised I get worked up! After I sort everything out for you, you . . . Well, if you want to know, I don't like being pushy. And I don't like pushy people. What an idea: you spoiled me too much! . . . I don't like it, that's all. And if you want me not to get worked up, don't come out with that kind of stuff again . . . I'm not talking loud at all: I'm talking normal. Anyway, it doesn't bother me who hears. I don't like it, that's all."

"Ho, ho! You're sounding like a stuck record. What's got into you, shouting like that? You like this, you don't like that—who gives a damn? Do you think life is about enjoying things? . . . So what if you don't like being pushy? You've got to live, haven't you? Don't you want to be free of worries, free of troubles? I wish I could see you settle down, like other people . . . Yes, that's why you get so worked up over nothing, why you . . . Take my advice: you've got to be a little pushier. I can see you haven't really grown up yet. You've still got the mind of a child. But you have to be a bit pushy in life, you really do!"

"How you go on! I haven't given up my time to come and hear you lecture me!"

"You should take my advice, though; it's for your own good. I've got a lifetime behind me. You may have been to college, but I've been through the school of life. Yes, life's evening classes: that's what I said to Madam Ioaniu, and how we both laughed! . . . What's so bad about you and me having a little chat? Isn't that what the Good Lord gave us tongues for? Why do you get so mad over nothing? Anyway, let's talk about what we need to discuss: they'll be throwing you out in a minute. Tell me about my pension . . . What did the postman do? Did he agree to leave it at Reli's? I can't remember if you told me last time you were here . . . So what if you tell me again? And did the demolition man come? . . . He didn't come, or you're not sure? If he didn't come now, he'll come when the thaw begins . . . Come on, stay a bit longer. The others can leave first: they got here earlier."

"Don't worry, I won't go just yet . . . Anyway, I'll be back on Thursday . . . Look, most people have left now . . . But next time I'll force myself to come earlier . . . Keep calm until then. Look after yourself, and try to sleep properly."

"Sleep! It refuses to come. I keep worrying about Niculaie, who's also getting old, and about your mother, who's ill all the time. It also worries me that you have problems—you even said that at work they're . . . you said they're trying to get rid of you."

"What? I said they got rid of some people and could just as easily get rid of me . . . Can't someone say something without you starting to worry? But what's this toilet paper doing here? Why do you keep it under your pillow? Okay, okay, but so much? . . . Let me open your drawer: I'll put the cakes in there . . . Phew, more toilet paper! Incredible!"

"Shhh! They're listening to us. Can't you see they've got their ears pricked up all the time? To find out what we're up to . . . And leave that paper there. What do you mean, why do I keep it? So I'll have enough when I need it. What if there's none left when I need it? . . . You think I'm making myself look ridiculous? Huh! What do they know? There's bread in the drawer too—yes, bread! What else? But where do you expect me to keep it? . . . What are you doing? Why are you emptying the drawer? Leave it alone, leave everything as it is! I know what I'm doing. If there's bread left over after dinner, why should I throw it out? Why on earth should I let them take it? What's the point of wasting it? . . . Cockroaches?

What are you talking about? There aren't any cockroaches here. There can't be any, 'cuz I sprinkled kerosene in all the corners where they like to nest . . . I sprinkle it at home, and I sprinkle it here, so not one of those little buggers would dare to . . . I do it at home, and I'll do it here . . . What's the big surprise? If I didn't do it myself, the whole ward would be full of them. What do you imagine? . . . Anyway, leave all my things where they are: leave the toilet paper where I can get to it, and leave the bread alone—it may always come in handy. Who knows if tomorrow . . . I'm not making either of us look ridiculous. Don't look so scared . . . Think of how lucky old Pug Nose is—you know, my landlady. All those sisters and nephews who pamper her with everything under the sun! You should have seen them arrive from their farm with grapes and wine and poultry: everything you could wish for! And they get together on holidays and sit and have a good time! . . . No, they don't steal it. What an idea! They help themselves to it at the collective farm. And that pest of a woman twists them around her little finger, snaps her fingers at every-one. I'm sure she had a word with the one who climbs over my fence at night . . . What do you mean no one comes? I tell you he did! He jumped over the fence at night, because the gate was locked—I'd locked it and put the key in my pocket—and he jumped over the fence and came and took my meat grinder . . . How did he get into the house? What a ques-tion! He broke in: he's a thief after all. They have master keys, don't they? . . . Old Pug Nose put him up to it, I'm sure. Now's the time, she said, go to Madam Delcă's and take her meat grinder! And they jumped over the fence at night, opened the door with a master key, and came in and took it . . . I tell you, that's what happened! How could it be in its usual place? How could the grinder be in its usual place? No, that's impossible. Let's drop it, then. Let's talk about the things we need to discuss. Soon they'll be coming around to throw you out . . . And I haven't had my fill of you."

Gabriela Adameșteanu is one of Romania's most acclaimed authors. Her other novels include *The Equal Way of Every Day, The Encounter,* and *Provisional.* She is also the author of collections of short stories and non-fiction. Her books have been translated into French, Spanish, German, Italian, Hungarian, Russian, Bulgarian, and other languages.

Patrick Camiller translates from Romanian, French, Spanish, Italian, and German. Among the many authors whose work he has translated are Mihail Sebastian and Norman Manea, Karl Popper and Ernesto "Che" Guevara.